AVERSION TO HONOR

Other Titles From New Falcon Publications

Cosmic Trigger: The Final Secret of the Illuminati
Prometheus Rising
  By Robert Anton Wilson
Undoing Yourself With Energized Meditation
Secrets of Western Tantra
  By Christopher S. Hyatt, Ph.D.
Eight Lectures on Yoga
The Pathworkings of Aleister Crowley
  By Aleister Crowley
Neuropolitique
The Game of Life
  By Timothy Leary, Ph.D.
Zen Without Zen Masters
  By Camden Benares
Condensed Chaos: An Introduction to Chaos Magick
  By Phil Hine
The Complete Golden Dawn System of Magic
The Golden Dawn Tapes—Series I, II, and III
  By Israel Regardie
Buddhism and Jungian Psychology
  By J. Marvin Spiegelman, Ph.D.
Astrology & Consciousness
  By Rio Olesky
Metaskills: The Spiritual Art of Therapy
  By Amy Mindell, Ph.D.
The Mysteries Revealed
  By Andrew Schneider
Beyond Duality: The Art of Transcendence
  By Laurence Galian
Soul Magic: Understanding Your Journey
  By Katherine Torres, Ph.D.
A Soul's Journey: Whispers From the Light
  By Patricia Idol
Carl Sagan & Immanuel Velikovsky
  By Charles Ginenthal

And to get your free catalog of *all* of our titles, write to:
New Falcon Publications (Catalog Dept.)
1739 East Broadway Road, Suite 1-277
Tempe, Arizona 85282 U.S.A.
And visit our website at http://www.newfalcon.com

AVERSION TO HONOR

*A Tale of Sexual Harassment
Within the Federal Government*

Thomas R. Burns, Ph.D.

NEW FALCON PUBLICATIONS
TEMPE, ARIZONA, U.S.A.

Copyright © 1997 by Thomas Burns, Ph.D.

All rights reserved. No part of this book, in part or in whole, may be reproduced, transmitted, or utilized, in any form or by any means, electronic or mechanical, including photocopying, recording, or by any information storage and retrieval system, without permission in writing from the publisher, except for brief quotations in critical articles, books and reviews.

International Standard Book Number: 1-56184-128-5
Library of Congress Catalog Card Number: 97-65809

First Edition 1997

Cover Art by Denise Cuttitta

The paper used in this publication meets the minimum requirements of the American National Standard for Permanence of Paper for Printed Library Materials Z39.48-1984

Address all inquiries to:
NEW FALCON PUBLICATIONS
1739 East Broadway Road Suite 1-277
Tempe, AZ 85282 U.S.A.
(or)
1209 South Casino Center
Las Vegas, NV 89104 U.S.A.

ACKNOWLEDGMENTS

I wish to acknowledge the invaluable assistance of Nicholas Tharcher, Vice President of New Falcon Publications whose questions and encouragement have enabled me to continue when I was in doubt about the value of telling this story.

I also wish to recognize the insights given me by those who have reviewed this work, although some do not wish to be named for fear of retribution by the system within which they currently work: the U.S. Public Health Service (PHS) and the Department of Health and Human Services. David Benedetti has been a friend and has warmly supported this venture, too.

I wish also to recognize my family: my sons Paul, Phillip and William; my daughter, Deanna; my wife, Maria, for her love and support; my father, Clarence, whose intelligence remains crystal clear at age 90; and my mother, Mildred, who at 85 is unflagging in her love and support of us all.

Finally, Mr. Charles J. Engel (Tim), Mr. Duncan Whitaker, and Ms. Deborah Conner of the law firm of Howrey and Simon in Washington, DC are gratefully acknowledged for their invaluable assistance and unwavering support in the case against Donna Shalala, Secretary of the Department of Health and Human Services, which provided the inspiration for this allegory.

Table of Contents

	Forword	9
	Preface	11
1.	Sandra Locklear	13
2.	1975 Beginnings	17
3.	Standing Bear	36
4.	The East Beckons	62
5.	Giroux	67
6.	Jane's Recriminations	112
7.	Connections	131
8.	Confrontation	145
9.	Complications	151
10.	Giroux's Plan	174
11.	Depositions	181
12.	Her Turn	194
13.	Final Things	234
	Afterword	254
	About the Author	255

Foreword

This is a book for those who wish to be informed while being entertained. I wholeheartedly recommend *Aversion To Honor* to all who are interested in the actual lives of Native Americans in contemporary North America—and to those who desire a very entertaining dose of realistic romance and intrigue.

The novel's charm resides in its strikingly realistic and vivacious characters who interact with each other in the complex, real-life perambulations of the top-level management of the Indian Health Service. Burns' lifetime of experience in these intricate matters shows through in every page and his audacious character portrayals bring to life the very human situations arising from the clash of cultures—and the clash of individuals.

Aversion To Honor displays that rare quality of being able to describe real events taking place at all levels in the Indian Health Service, with all their political, historical and cultural complexity. Moving back and forth from remote reservations to the Legislative Chambers of Washington, DC, we travel with characters who are touched with all the humor, foibles and vibrant sexuality of actual, living people—and we are thereby inevitably drawn into their personal, social and governmental intrigues.

In following the Native Americans and others involved with the Indian Health Service, this novel informs the reader about the complicated workings of Native American culture as it multifariously tries to survive within the present-day world of the United States and Canada. But, while presenting us with all this authentic information in an almost documentary style, the novel remains thoroughly dramatic and entertaining as it follows the daily lives of real men and women trying to live and enjoy their lives while contributing to the health of native peoples.

— David Benedetti, Ph.D.

Preface

On December 15, 1995, the prestigious law firm of Howrey and Simon in Washington, DC, acting *pro bono* on behalf of the plaintiff, filed a suit against Donna Shalala, Secretary of the Department of Health and Human Services. The suit alleges violations of Title VII of the Civil Rights Act of 1964 (sexual harassment) in failing to provide equal protection to a career officer of the U.S. Public Health Service (PHS).

The case upon which this suit was based was originally referred to the Washington Lawyer's Committee for Civil Rights upon failure of the plaintiff to receive satisfactory resolution of her claim of sexual harassment and hostile work environment from the Indian Health Service (IHS), Department of Health and Human Services, Office of the Surgeon General.

The facts of the case are these: The defendant, an employee of the IHS, sexually harassed the plaintiff and others for over a year, beginning in February 1992. He aggravated the circumstances by threatening the plaintiff's life. The plaintiff, an employee of the same department, filed a complaint of sexual harassment and hostile work environment and undertook an arduous legal battle with senior management officials of the IHS to be protected at the work site.

Management officials minimized the situation and ignored the request for protection; they tried to transfer the complainants and their supervisor. Though the plaintiff obtained a restraining order against the defendant—preventing him from getting with 100 yards of her—the restraining order was not honored by IHS management officials for over three years: consequently the plaintiff and other female complainants had to vacate their workplace whenever the defendant demanded to enter the work site. The plaintiff was branded, in writing, a "troublemaker" despite multiple independent investigations which documented the harassment and threats of bodily harm. One of the bodies investigating the case was the federal Office of Personnel Management (OPM) in Dallas, Texas. OPM corroborated the plaintiff's claims, recommended reforms in management practices and recommended action against the Agency officials who participated in the harassment and failed to protect the employees. The IHS management officials, and officials of the PHS ignored the OPM report and continued to ignore the complainants' pleas.

The plaintiff followed all the procedures of the PHS until administrative remedies were exhausted—without resolution. When the Acting Surgeon General stated that the plaintiff had no protection through the Department, she challenged the internal policies which denied her protection and sought legal redress.

(In deciding the case, Audrey F. Manley, M.D., M.P.H., Acting Surgeon General wrote: *"Commissioned Corps Officers do not have the right to appeal a Final Decision to the Equal Employment Opportunity Commission [EEOC] or to the U.S. District Court because they are not covered by the Civil Rights Act of 1964, as amended, or by the Executive Order 11478, as amended."* (Signed September 15, 1995, emphasis added.) The internal policy of the U.S. Public Health Service (October 1976) states that the Surgeon General is the final arbiter on cases involving EEOC complaints. Hence, there is no equal protection under the Civil Rights Act of 1964. To say the least, the policy is an anachronism.)

At this writing, the matter is before the court in the Federal District of Maryland.

Why is this book in the form of a "story" instead of a factual narrative? An answer can be found in the Afterword of this book.

I caution the reader not to be literal in the interpretation of people, places, times, and events in this story. Fact is fictionalized, and fiction appears factual. It happens that way with coincidences. People, events, times and places are not real; i.e., they do not mirror the actual case which has been allegorized in this tale.

(Interestingly, as we prepare this book for publication, the story has been subpoenaed by the Department of Justice for its defense of the Secretary of the Department for one of the cases. I am amazed at the length the government will go to protect itself and say it has done no wrong!)

Finally, it is important to remember that sexual harassment is not about sex: It is about *power!*

— Thomas R. Burns, Ph.D.
New Mexico, March 1997

CHAPTER ONE

SANDRA LOCKLEAR

Hardly a day went by that Sandra didn't dream of being a nurse like her mother. The years had come and gone like magic. Someone had waved a wand. She sat there now in a crowded commencement exercise at the University of Virginia about to receive her diploma and degree in nursing, a tear running down her cheek. She remembered her earliest fond memories of her mother, Emma, gliding down the whitewashed halls of the Indian Health Service Hospital in Schurz, Nevada from the men's ward at the west end to the women's ward at the east end of the hallway. She was an angel of mercy and looked every bit the part. Sandra longed to follow in her footsteps.

Schurz was a remote hospital in the Indian Health Service hospital system, the home of the Walker River Paiute Indian Tribe, 45 miles southwest of Fallon, Nevada and 28 miles southeast of Yerington, Nevada, a green oasis along the Walker River amidst the barren moonscape of the rocky desert between all points of the compass. As far as the eye could see, the brown sandy desert was broken up with jutting red and yellow sandstone ledges that gave way in the distance to hardscrabble rocky mountains 7,000 feet high. They brooded over Schurz. The setting of the sun brought with it the inky stillness of night that enveloped the valley in darkness.

Sandra was just a middle school child with the exuberance of most children when the Locklear family moved from the cool green pines of White River, Arizona to take up residence in the old whitewashed nursing quarters not more than 300 feet from the old hospital built in 1934. She and her two older brothers, Harley and Reston, quickly settled into the three bedroom three bath renovated nursing dormitory. Sandra's memory brought a smile to her face even as a tear poised in the corner of her eye, ready for its descent down her cheek.

Neither of the children much liked the transition from the sweet smelling pines and cool mountains of Northern Arizona to the blowing wind and sand of the desert. At the time, it was a transition they could hardly understand. But they knew not to challenge Emma's dedication to serving the needs of the sick. Nursing was her life's work, a sacred profession she wore like her skin. Emma had proudly served the White Mountain Apaches for nearly a decade even though they were not her tribe, the Cherokees of North Carolina. It was time to serve others as the Director of Nursing in her final bid for a more secure retirement. Emma was in her third decade of nursing and becoming more frail with the passage of time and encroaching illness.

Sandra smiled. She recalled the development of her budding interest in nursing, pulling at her mother's white frock to gain her attention with a thousand questions of what Emma did when she went into those wards. It was a sacred mystery she wished to divine.

Sandra dared many times to enter the wards quietly behind her mother — only to receive a stern but gentle rebuke and reminder to remain at the nurses' station in the middle of the hallway until she finished her rounds.

Emma would tell her, frowning at her little angel in mock anger, "Child, you know the patients are very, very sick people. They need lots of rest and deserve the very best care. I'm sure they would like to see your bright face and would be warmed with your beautiful smile, but we cannot let you in to see them until you are much older and can serve them, too."

"But Mommy, I won't hurt them!" Sandra protested. "I just want to help them get better, too."

"I know, sweetheart. I know. We will talk more when I am done. Go now. Wait for me at the nurses' station. I won't be long," Emma replied. Dutifully Sandra waited eagerly for her mother, her idol, and would busy herself with dusting around the station. As other nurses and physicians came into the station to write their reports she would ply them with questions, her favorite Saturday activity.

None seemed to mind. They delighted in her inquisitive mind and memory. As she graduated from the eighth grade two years later and entered high school in Hawthorne, a Navy ammunition depot some 35 miles to the south, Sandra became a candy-striper with the local American National Red Cross chapter. Sandra soon became a popular regular on the wards attending the patients alongside her mother and warming them with her winning ways. She reveled in simple patient cleanup and brief nursing procedures.

Sandra was soon entrusted with helping recovering patients become ambulatory once more after surgery was performed in Reno 100 miles to the north. Schurz was the recovery hospital for all the Indians in the western part of Nevada and northern California. It all seemed so distant a memory now, Sandra thought, collecting herself.

Sandra rose with her fellow nurses to be called to the platform. Emma would have been so proud to witness her raven-haired daughter's graduation. She had often talked about it from her final hospital bed in Cherokee, North Carolina, the victim of terminal cancer. A mist filled Emma's eyes as she knew the inevitable would prevent her from having this pleasure. This was her hospital, her last assignment before breast cancer forced her into medical retirement. Cherokee was her birthplace into the world and into the Cherokee Tribe. It would be her final resting place, too.

The graduation so long anticipated was now a year after her death. Sandra was serene. All the hospital visits made during Sandra's junior year had ended. Regrets were laid to rest with Emma. She had asked Sandra not to think of her in her final hours the way she was, skin drawn tight around protruding bones. Only the contrasting brightness and fire in her eyes reminded Sandra of her once boundless energy and selfless devotion to her Indian people. Emma hoped in her last moments Sandra would give to Indian people the same love and devotion she bore in such large measure. Sandra vowed to keep this promise and follow in her footsteps as a proud daughter of the Cherokee.

Underneath her maroon graduation gown Sandra proudly wore the uniform of an Ensign in the U.S. Public Health Service.

Earlier in the morning she was sworn into the service in a private ceremony attended by her aged father, Michael, her brothers, Harley and Reston, and five other nurses all close friends of Emma. The ceremony was presided over by Captain Andrew Giroux who was rumored to be made the next Assistant Surgeon General and Director of the Indian Health Service.

Giroux had led a distinguished career in the Public Health Service rising quickly in the ranks. A star loomed on his horizon. This week he was in Charlottesville recruiting promising young physicians and nurses for service with the Indian Health Service. He appealed to their sense of pride as medical and nurse professionals and spirit of self-sacrifice in living and working in remote facilities in the West.

Sandra had heard his speech on the needs of Indians and Alaska Natives once before. She had known those needs from the time she was a little child and young adult. Sandra didn't need a special invitation. She sent in her application as soon as she had become a junior in nursing school. She was now ready to live her dedication to providing the best care Indians would need wherever she was required to render this service. Sandra, her four other nurse companions and one physician stood erect with their right hands held high for the simple induction ceremony.

Mother would have been so pleased, she thought. As she reached for the diploma in the hand of the Dean Sandra turned about and raised it aloft to the proud war hoops of her brothers, the flash of lights, and to Michael's insistent banging of the ancestral drum.

"For you, Mom!" Sandra said in triumph knowing Emma was witnessing the event in her own way.

CHAPTER TWO

1975 BEGINNINGS

The month was April and it was ugly. It rained for a week solid. Steady and incessant. One of those eastern rains that fill the streets with the leftovers of a tropical storm that hit the Carolinas and moved inland to the Northeast. A rain that people don't like but they endure simply because they can't go anywhere else except maybe indoors to get away from it.

In this rain a loosely organized group of Indians had descended upon Washington, DC intent upon impressing their congressmen the need for health care reform. There was nothing particularly unique in their pleas. They simply wanted what had been denied them even though guaranteed to their forefathers in treaties broken for centuries. Some maintained militant postures for the sake of press coverage. Indians taking over Washington, DC looked good for the home town folks.

Others in the group were truly committed. Getting good press coverage wasn't their main goal. But it would not be discounted as irrelevant, either. Their beads, braids, and bracelets were the objects of admiring stares wherever they went — and occasional sales of the impressive art work to subsidize their trip. Still others were hardly distinguished from congressional staff in their three piece suits and carrying stylish briefcases.

One by one the visitors filed into the Senate chamber to take their seats in the rear. Seats near the front were left vacant for some expected guests. The proposed legislation to finally improve the health of American Indians and Alaska Natives was many years in the making. Hopefully, it would bring to closure the debate on the many outstanding health needs on the nation's reservations already assessed years before by Senator Kennedy and his staff.

Visitors filed into the chamber and greeted each other with smiles of recognition and occasional laughter. Alcoholism, only one of many health problems under Congressional review, was the subject of this special hearing prompted by the concerns of Indians and Natives across the nation.

Senate staffers wanted to insert language into the bill to initiate a strong alcoholism control effort in response to heavy lobbying from tribes throughout the United States. Agency staff were not keen about this grass roots effort and wanted to play down their effort to tell the Indian Health Service how to run the program. Another manifestation of the annual cat and mouse game in the budget process.

"Who would have thought five years ago us drunks would be in the Senate today, huh?" John Standing Bear asked his knot of friends in the corner looking at the deep rich mahogany paneling. "Man, this place is something else! This is my first time here. You know I could get used to this." He laughed deeply to his close friend as if to belie the truth of his feeling.

Standing Bear turned his head sharply to hear his friend, Flying Eagle remark, "Look, you haven't started to run for office and aren't elected yet. Don't get any bright ideas." Pausing for a moment, he added, "Hell! I wonder who the fool was who let you out of jail then. Remember what it was really like? And now you are thinking of taking up residence here? We're on the verge of making our own history, so don't get any funny notions, brother." Standing Bear's aquiline features were accented by his hair pulled back in a braid, a bone necklace around his throat, and large turquoise wrist band accenting his watch.

"Was that a jail? Hell, I thought that was the hospital," Standing Bear quipped to Flying Eagle. "They were one and the same to me." Each laughed in recognition of a truth that caught each one. To them it was an inside joke. Standing Bear was admitted to the Pine Ridge Indian Health Service Hospital more often than he could remember, arms outstretched, 'Here I am again warden,' he would remark to the head nurse.

"You should know. You spent enough time in each place! Hell, I remember when you got out of jail at Standing Rock, bounced into the hospital the same night, got patched up, and the cops came looking for you the next day. You were something else then. No one could keep you locked up for long." Flying Eagle slapped Standing Bear on the back. Each was aware of the personal hell he went through to become clean and sober for over a decade. Both laughed heartily and looked about the room to see who was there.

They quickly saw another knot forming close to the elevated platform where the Senators and their staff soon would be seated in their glistening leather chairs. They looked about to see if anyone listened to their conversation. Satisfied to know most visitors were becoming adjusted to their surroundings and weren't the least bit concerned about them they continued their deliberations in hushed tones.

One of the group, a boyish looking young man, began, "Look, as your attorney, I recommend that we talk about community support and control of alcoholism somewhat cautiously today. We know it is a touchy subject for the Feds but we really don't know what the Feds are actually going to say today, and, we know we can count on the support of the Senate staffers to help steer the Senate. Let's let the staffers do their work. I think you did a good job briefing them yesterday."

As they continued their discussion, a small contingent of Public Health officers and staff walked stiffly into the chambers to take their seats in the front. They were called specifically to respond to the pending legislation to insert language under Title II to require the Indian Health Service to develop detoxification programs in their hospitals. The knot of Indians exchanged knowing glances and fell silent. They had come prepared to expect opposition from Admiral Grant and his group. Their intelligence said that a coterie of officers and civil servants close to him and upon whom he relied for consultation on important issues had convinced him he would be wrong to allow tribal alcoholism programs a role in the health team. Generally, they believed their program staff were non-degreed "reformed drunks," modern day prohibitionist zealots, more politely called para-professionals by the "true" health professionals, the physicians. Physicians were kings; everyone else were considered servants, ancillary health care personnel who should understand their place in the structure. Or at least, so they frequently thought and occasionally articulated.

Certainly the idea was not new. Nationally, Senator Hughes had only recently gotten the Comprehensive Alcoholism Treatment and Prevention Act passed. It became Public Law 91-616 and enabled the Federal government to establish the National Institute on Alcohol Abuse and Alcoholism to deal with this massive national problem. Indians and Alaska Natives were noted as deserving of special treatment though the debate today would ensure that. Indians and Natives would be served beyond the grant period.

Most of the people working in the alcoholism treatment field then were drawn from the ranks of Alcoholics Anonymous and were not trained in graduate schools. Graduate training in alcoholism was only on the drawing boards of a few prestigious institutions. Training was begun at Yale and continued with the Rutgers School of Alcohol Studies, the University of Arizona and a few others and was not a coordinated national effort among other schools.

For the past two years as the Indian Health Service staffers began preparing the 1976 budget, Charlie Matheson, Budget Officer the past six years, known for his propensity to drink, led the opposition within the Health Service. He was among those with David Grant and sat to the Admiral's left.

To his right, Captain James Hurson, the Chief Pharmacist, overweight and bulging from his uniform, shifted his bulk uncomfortably. Small droplets of sweat formed under his rather large nose. He intensely disliked these show and tell functions. Short on temper and long on experience moving from hospital to hospital in the system, he was promoted rapidly to his Headquarters position, mostly as a last resort. James would never admit that the Indian Health Service did not know what to do with him. He would look upon his promotions as totally justified and his due for exemplary service.

Truthfully the organization didn't know what to do with him any more than they knew what to do with those whose daily service was equally good but less showy. They gave him many medals and two exceptional capability promotions to encourage him to tone down his opinions of reservations. It was not enough. He wanted a star.

Reverse psychology didn't work with him. He (like many others) viewed his promotions and medals as incentives to continue his tirades. He managed to alienate most tribal chairmen with whom he came in contact; but he was brilliant in managing scant resources wherever he was sent. The organization had a penchant for protecting such officers while expecting more from the nurses and aides than they provided resources for.

In the days of lean budgets this ability was god-like. James had little political savvy or sympathy and felt that Indians had no business in health management. To his viewpoint, their only valid concern was fish and wildlife management. They should be left to the plains, forests and streams except this would upset the Sierra groups who thought the outdoors was their own special province. People resources were expendable and too unpredictable for Hurson. While he had to admit the nurses and aides and community health representatives had an excellent knowledge of the people they served, he couldn't trust them like he could numbers on the written page.

Therefore, he reasoned, they were expendable as unreliable assets, pure and simple. He would have made a good tactician if he didn't abhor the military so much. He sat there tapping his pencil out of boredom. Sweat formed easily on his brow.

The fourth person to complete the group was Captain William Morrison — a physician like David Grant — spent many years in small hospitals mainly in the southwest at Schurz, Nevada, and at San Carlos and Chinle, Arizona although he did have a tour in Barrow, Alaska when he first entered the service to avoid Vietnam. Indian Health Service was a safe haven.

He sat next to Hurson. As physicians they spent hours on night and weekend duty — sometimes at the same location — sewing up the victims of domestic violence or truck accidents. Many victims, many accidents. Too many to count. But one common denominator always — alcohol. It figured preeminently in the numbers of those seen in the clinics, on the wards, and among those sent to referral hospitals for trauma care.

Both Grant and Morrison detested the enormous amount of money spent on the effects of alcoholism, the gastro-intestinal bleeds, the spouse abuse, accidents, suicides and homicides. With all the hospitalizations and other traumas they estimated the costs were in the millions — millions which could have been better spent on first class facilities. Indian Health Service desperately needed new hospitals and new housing units for their often overworked staff.

Clearly Morrison and Grant believed seventy-five percent of all their hospital expenditures were related to alcoholism even though they had no data to back them up. Their beliefs arose from emergency room service and other hospitalizations. The problem was huge. The demand for services was great, but it was like throwing money into a deep dark hole and they couldn't hear it hit bottom.

Morrison and Grant sincerely believed this deprived other "more worthy" Indians from getting the care they needed. Even though they knew the American Medical Association had called alcoholism a disease, they resented spending money on Indians who lacked the moral fiber to quit drinking. After all he and other physicians knew it was just a matter of will power. And now, these same Indians have been pressuring Congress for the Health Service to establish an alcoholism program. More diversion of resources! How shortsighted and unreasonable!

They often commented nothing good ever came from the community alcoholism programs as it was except more talk and AA programs. Their personnel were the least reliable of the lot, uneducated and unsophisticated. No one ever seemed to learn or change behavior. Morrison and Grant didn't challenge the prevailing belief that Indians were genetically incapable of drinking. Research was incomplete on the issue. Personal control was lacking. So this was a personal problem, not a medical one. Everyone knew that. Why the government was spending so much money and effort in holding this hearing was also unreasonable but so typical of the government. This expense could have been put into the Health Service's budget. Alcoholism was certainly not a community problem like tuberculosis except a lot of people who could work weren't working. Morrison especially believed they were a lazy lot. Their private views never became part of the public record.

Standing Bear and Flying Eagle took vehement exception to such attitudes. They opposed the Feds and those tribal leaders alike who didn't want the fledgling alcoholism effort to interfere with their life styles.

Morrison looked about the assemblage. A few Indian papers like the *Native Nevadan* and the *Lakota Times,* some supporters, some agitators — nothing new. He felt the Health Service wasn't really opposed to Indians making economic progress on the reservations. Where would people eat? Where were the libraries? The restaurants? The places where people could have some fun?

After all, unemployment was high no matter where the reservation was located. Morrison knew in some instances, as many as two out of three employable adults didn't work like on the San Carlos Reservation in Arizona.

Employment opportunities were confined to government jobs, like the BIA — the Bureau of Indian Affairs, or the Indian Health Service, or maybe the local school system or tribal office. Industry was not available except in minor instances. Industry had few incentives to locate on reservations.

Poverty was rife. Few made it to high school to get basic skills and fewer still graduated. Of those who went to college, only about ten percent graduated. Those that did graduate didn't want to return to the reservation to live. Like teachers and doctors — those who were most needed. Elder family members were known to counsel their young children to get an education and work off the reservation. Morrison overheard one older mother who put in a career with the Health Service advise her sons, "Become teachers and work in Reno. Don't come back here until you are ready to retire. There is no life here for you at Schurz."

Drinking was a problem in many families. Morrison felt the community alcoholism programs were employment programs just to keep drunks off the streets and he wanted no part of it. How could he support that in good conscience? As Morrison ruminated, Senate staffers came through the paneled mahogany doors behind the podium and took their seats next to the chairs of their respective Senators. They were buzzing with agreement about their approach to this problem.

Soon, Senators David LaSalle from South Dakota, Michael Hodgkins from Montana, Thomas Waller from Nevada, and Michelson from Arizona arrived. Guests took their seats immediately. A few throats cleared. The rattling of papers ceased.

Senator Stephen Michelson took a sip of water, surveyed the audience and fixed his gaze upon Admiral Grant and his rows of medals for meritorious service, outstanding unit citations, commendations, and hardship duty. 'They were colorful and made a nice bouquet,' he thought. The two had fought many budget battles in this same room. But there were no medals for this.

The territory was familiar and each understood the rules of engagement. This was the Senator's territory and he would let no one gain the high ground, especially Admiral Grant. None of his medals were for meritorious service in the budget battles. No one won in that theater of operations! Every program was a victim of the congressional scythe.

Grant returned his stare and thought Michelson was a grandstander and an enemy of the Health Service. He blocked significant increases in the Interior Department's budget for the past three years in a row and was of the singular mind that the health professionals had poorly managed the Nation's resources in improving the health of Indians and Natives alike with the lone exception of tuberculosis.

Sometimes Grant wondered if it was just plain luck that they managed to get their act together to conquer tuberculosis. But the evidence was there. The Indian Health Service was now thinking of closing their sanitarium in Tucson. Admissions were few and far between thanks to aggressive outreach and close work with state health authorities. The vision of total eradication was easily seen and expected with improved pharmacological interventions. Indians could stay at home.

Michelson grudgingly acknowledged in previous testimony the aggressive role the Health Service played in eradicating this bacilli among Indians and Alaska Natives. So he respected this accomplishment and the improvements made in water and sewage for homes but felt the Health Service was just trying to build its empire. Michelson relished this additional opportunity to meet the Admiral on his ground and to pontificate about the inability of the Health Service to manage its personnel.

"Admiral, please identify your party." Senator Michelson began.

"Thank you, Senator Michelson. My name is Dr. David Grant. I am Director of the Indian Health Service. I have with me today, Captain William Morrison, Deputy Director, Captain James Hurson, Chief Pharmacist, and Mr. Charles Matheson, Budget Officer.

"We are here today to respond to your questions and to speak on behalf of the medical needs of the American Indians and Alaska Natives we serve. Senators, we are pleased to report significant progress in a number of critical areas touching the lives of American Indians and Alaska Natives, such as in tuberculosis control, vector control, the development of water treatment plants and sewage control."

"Yes. Thank you, Admiral." Senator Michelson interrupted, his patience already tested by the ten page statement before him. "I believe the Indians present in the audience can speak far more eloquently for their own needs, I believe you will agree. Will you not?" he emphasized somewhat peevishly.

"Well, yes, of course, Senator Michelson. The Indian Health Service has no intention of speaking *for* Indians. I have not made this a habit. Yet, in the matter of overall health care needs I believe..."

"Please excuse me again, Dr. Grant, for interrupting you. But the Senate is not interested in hearing your beliefs or in learning your habits. The Indian Health Service either is, or is not, supportive of the concept of including tribally run alcoholism programs within the IHS health care delivery system as a matter for this pending legislation." Senator Michelson objected, strongly focusing on the topic.

He paused to recognize a committee member. "The Chair recognizes the esteemed Senator Waller from Nevada."

"Thank you, Senator Michelson. It is an honor once again to address the needs of Indians and Natives as part of this esteemed committee," he droned. "The United States government has a long-standing commitment to meet the health and welfare needs of its first Americans and cannot long ignore their concerns. That we have done so is a tragedy. Before we begin to address the substantive issue before us, which has caused untold devastation among Indian families, however, I would like the witnesses to be identified for the record of this 'hearing.' "

"Indeed, Senator Waller, thank you for your suggestion and your comments." Senator Michelson continued. "My interest in this issue which you correctly point out has caused disruptions in so many Indian families and has created such a negative social and economic impact on Indian society, perhaps overshadowed my interest in protocol for the moment. My apologies to all present." Looking to the Indian constituency the Senator asked the group to be identified for the record.

The Indians looked around at each other. None was willing to get up to the microphone. James Arnold, a brilliant young attorney recruited from recent service with Senator Mitchell, came to the attention of the Chairman of the Ogalala Sioux when he toured North and South Dakota in the early 70's with Senator Ted Kennedy. He gained a firsthand impression of the devastation caused by alcoholism introduced himself. The Chairman of the oversight committee liked his no nonsense approach to federal resource management as he recently learned from his staff reports of skirmishes lost to his acumen.

None of the members of his group wanted to speak first. The Indians were glad to have this white man speak for them when it was convenient. James knew his way around the system despite his youth.

Senate staffers knew his solid reputation for research and his iron will in pursuing what is right. His interest in the plight of modern day Indians was first born of youthful romanticism kindled by James Fenimore Cooper and then of modern writers like Vine Deloria who put romanticism into perspective.

He relished the opportunity to do something — whatever that was, and he was not sure how to define "something" — for Indians. Somehow to right some of the wrongs of early settlers and the government, a government that stripped Indians of their possessions and their land, their pride, dignity, heritage and language, and now which wants to be paternalistic and care for them. How ludicrous, he thought.

At least that is what he told himself. After all, isn't that why lawyers search out the law, to right inherent wrong? He had never given much thought about why he enjoyed the experience with Ted Kennedy so much in years past. Something always seemed to haunt him when he would be on his team to hear of promises made and broken. Stories repeated by tribe after tribe of land stolen, water rights denied, the rape of women and the loss of heritage affected him deeply. His discomfort had something to do with the human condition — his humanity that responded with unnamed feeling and a desire for balance.

James was by no means a loner seeking like Don Quixote to joust with windmills. There were enough windmills in the Washington area. He particularly loved jousting with the Federal windmill, the Congress and the staffers; and he loved hoisting a few with his Georgetown colleagues. Drinking beer at the "Library" at Berkeley was just part of the scene for young liberals when he was in graduate school. He carried this with him when he entered law school at Harvard. James was sociable, even affable, more than intelligent, really erudite for his years, and had a good following among the intelligentsia for his scholarly papers. James brought humor to the workplace and a quick smile which lighted his face. He always seemed to know when to use his charms to disarm his opponents.

When he toured the country with Mr. Kennedy his convictions grew that the European colonization of North America and the westward expansion beyond the frontiers of Ohio resulted in the perpetration of one of the worst crimes against humanity, the dehumanization of the Indian. Often forced to live in sub-standard housing Indians were less than second class citizens. He believed the Indian Reorganization Act of 1934 was a mockery.

All of a sudden Indians had to become organized using white men's rules with a council like a board of directors, Indian corporations living on some of the worst land in the country, after the best was taken away from them by force. Little did most people know that the Iroquois federation had a constitution which predated the U.S. Constitution by 500 years. Indians were highly organized and didn't need Robert's Rules of Order.

James's mind was like a miner's pan used by the forty-niners to grasp small specs of gold. Isolated pieces of information, sometimes seemingly irrelevant in themselves, were like specs of gold to him, highly useful in the aggregate, they often combined into a golden piece of jewelry through his mental wizardry. No fact was useless that bore on the subject of his inquiry at the moment.

James introduced himself and those with whom he consulted earlier before the meeting commenced, John Standing Bear,

Director of the Pine Ridge, SD Alcoholism Program, Billy Flying Eagle, Director of the Sheridan, WY Alcoholism Program, Charlie Small, Director of the Reno, NV Comprehensive Alcoholism Program and a few others at the table who supported their movement but who had no active role to play this day. He then deferred to the Chairman to allow representatives from Health Service to resume their statement.

Senator Michelson asked Dr. Grant to continue. "We are pleased to be here today to discuss with you our efforts to provide comprehensive health services for American Indians and Alaska Natives and to describe our concerns about alcoholism activity.

"The Indian Health Service is the Federal entity charged with administering the principal health program for American Indians and Alaska Natives. Its goal is to raise the health status of American Indians and Alaska Natives to the highest possible level.

"Its mission is threefold: 1) to provide and/or assure the availability of high quality, comprehensive, and accessible health services; 2) to provide increasing opportunities for Indians to manage and operate their own health programs; and, 3) to serve as a health advocate for Indian people."

Now that he knew he had the floor Dr. Grant used it to describe the growth of the Indian Health Service since its inception from the Bureau of Indian Affairs in 1955. The BIA relinquished its authority to provide health services. They had enough trouble managing the economic and property affairs for the Nation's tribes.

Dr. Grant pointed out significant improvements in the health of Indians due to the eradication of tuberculosis; improvements in water and sewage treatment; trachoma control; and infant mortality. He then described their living conditions as squalid.

On many of the Nation's reservations, Indians lived in substandard housing with poor sanitary conditions and unreliable water supplies. These conditions led to excessive rates of childhood diseases and mortality, pneumonia, tuberculosis, eye and ear infections. Not only were living conditions deplorable but also the economics of reservation life were not much improved from the days when the War Department, and its heir, BIA, managed their affairs.

Alcoholism control was a different matter. He acknowledged that it was a fledgling effort among IHS providers. He referred to its publication, *Alcoholism: A High Priority Health Problem,* commissioned in the late 1960's as the best source of data on the impact of alcoholism on the lives and social structure of American Indian and Alaska Native families.

Dr. Grant concluded it was regrettable IHS was precluded from dealing effectively with the problem since its experience, so well demonstrated with tuberculosis and trachoma control, would suggest superior ability. However, he suggested that the federal government in its wisdom had established the National Institute on Alcohol Abuse and Alcoholism as the focal point for all national efforts. He supported this division of labor as being within the interests of all citizens including the Indians and Alaskan Natives. To detract from this effort by including a provision in the Indian Health Care Improvement Act would result in a fragmentation of effort.

"Let's put rhetoric aside, Dr. Grant," Senator Michelson interjected. "I am hearing you say quite clearly you oppose including a section on alcoholism in the proposed legislation. Isn't that correct? Are you opposed to alcoholism treatment, Dr. Grant?"

"Senator, the Indian Health Service is not opposed to alcoholism treatment. On the contrary, it provides this treatment on a daily basis. Every time a truck loaded with people driven by a person under the influence drives off the road and sends people to one of our hospitals for surgery or other treatment, we provide alcoholism treatment.

"Our dedicated doctors and nurses spend untold hours in operating rooms repairing people broken or maimed from fights or accidents or domestic disputes. We are always hoping this will be the last time we have to see them in that condition. Often our beleaguered social workers have to make home visits to counsel family members who are left on the death of a loved one who has drunk himself to death or died in an accident. Often they are left without any resources to provide for their daily needs."

Senator Waller broke in to ask Admiral Grant, "Are you saying, Dr. Grant, you are doing such a fine job you don't need any help? That you have enough personnel to provide counseling services? That these social workers know all there is to know about alcoholism? How is it that you don't seem to be making any headway on the problem? Your own data say that the problem is a national problem, Dr. Grant. How many social workers do you have? 50? a hundred? 500?"

(Standing Bear had already given Senator Waller the number of about 70.)

Dr. Grant squirmed in his chair under this barrage of questions. He looked to Morrison who looked to Matheson who quickly shuffled papers in an attempt to find some charts bearing on this topic. Matheson was relieved to find a chart listing the growth of the social work program in hospitals as from one in 1955 transferred from the Bureau of Indian Affairs to set up the program to 70 in 20 years. He slid the note to Dr. Grant.

"The Indian Health Service social work program has shown remarkable growth, Senator. We now have about 70 social workers nation wide. These are highly trained people with masters degrees, Senator. They are very competent in dealing with the problems that arise from alcoholism," Dr. Grant sat back relaxed, assured the problem was under control.

"Let me understand this, Admiral. You believe that 70 social workers are fully competent to deal with or control a problem that your national publication says affects 95 percent of the population. Is that correct?" Senator Waller retorted.

James Arnold passed his own note to Standing Bear. It read. "Strike one. He didn't even respond to the issue. Your work is beginning to pay off." Standing Bear gave Arnold a thumbs up.

Senator Waller continued. "I may be a little naive, Dr. Grant, but it appears to me that you may be overly optimistic about the numbers of staff needed to deal with this national problem, especially when the primary responsibility of the social worker is to provide support to hospitalized patients and not the community control of alcoholism. Mr. Chairman, I yield my remaining time to my esteemed colleague from South Dakota."

"The Chair recognizes the Senator from South Dakota." Senator Michelson stated flatly.

"I thank my valued colleague from the beautiful State of Nevada for yielding his time to me on this important occasion to ask the Indian Health Service a few questions," Senator LaSalle remarked as he put aside a few notes given him by his staff assistant.

Standing Bear, his little knot of friends, and Arnold had busied themselves for the preceding three days making the rounds from one Senate office to another to prepare for this occasion in followup to a host of telephone calls. Before this, they had spent an additional two months gathering data from a variety of resources both in and out of the federal establishment to bolster their cause. They were now waiting for strikes two and three when the Feds would have to yield part of the ball game.

Senator LaSalle started. "You have testified, Dr. Grant, you oppose assuming responsibility for programs currently under the control of the National Institute; and, further, your medical staff are overwhelmed by the effects of this disease; and, curiously, your social workers are fully competent to handle the problem, and yet, that is not their primary task. Dr. Grant, just when do you suppose these workers will be able to deal with this national problem when you have testified earlier on the matter of adding new staff to your hospitals, that you believe they are overworked? What will you do if you do not get program increases as you wish?

"I don't believe you responded to my valued colleague's concern about your staff's competence in matters dealing with alcoholism. I believe you simply said that your staff would handle this overwhelming problem in stride. My staff informs me that most schools of social work provide at best, only a few clock hours on the subject of alcoholism. This is the same situation for most medical and nursing schools is it not? I submit that your staff are ill-prepared to deal with alcoholism, aren't they? Would you comment, Dr. Grant?"

Neither Dr. Grant, Matheson, Morrison nor Hurson were prepared for this direction taken by the Senate. Hurson gave a noise, shifted papers, and muttered under his breath, "Fucking bleeding hearts!" Matheson poked him in the side. Hurson grimaced and looked daggers at him.

Dr. Grant acknowledged that his training program in medical school was lacking in regard to alcoholism theory and treatment practice. Ninety-nine percent of the training dealt with medical complications of the disease. When it was discussed in the psychiatric rotation, even the psychiatrists seemed unconcerned about alcoholics. They were looked upon as the dregs of any psychiatric or psychological practice. Most social workers also preferred to look upon the alcoholic as having an underlying neurosis. Alcoholism was not a primary disease; it was an extension of a psychiatric illness.

"Dr. Grant, I must conclude that you appear to take exception to the American Medical Association's and the World Health Organization's classification of alcoholism as a disease. Regardless of your stand on this issue, Dr. Grant, it would appear that the Indian Health Service could ill-afford passing up additional resources in its fight against the common enemy, alcoholism," LaSalle emphasized.

With a handkerchief in hand, the perspiring Dr. Grant replied, "Senator, I must repeat, the Indian Health Service is committed to carrying out the wishes and requirements of Congress. That is primary. We are concerned, however, about these programs under the administration of the Institute. They are in the poorest of facilities; they have not had any technical assistance; none have been evaluated; and their staff are untrained," Dr. Grant stated. His staff nodded their heads in unanimous agreement. Dr. Grant continued, "We should also note for the record, Senator, the Indian Health Service does not have trained administrators ready to assume this additional responsibility."

"So noted," Senator Michelson responded.

Arnold gave Standing Bear another note. "Two strikes. One more and he is out, and you are in." Standing Bear agreed. They had already lobbied the Senate staff well in advance to establish an alcoholism service. Congress simply had to insert in the bill language to require the transfer of the grant programs from the Institute to the Indian Health Service. It would then have to find its own way to meet the new obligation.

Senator LaSalle yielded his remaining time to Senator Hodgkins from Montana who was recognized by the Chair. Senator Hodgkins grilled Dr. Grant on the level of his coordination with the Institute to effect a transfer of programs. Grant was unaware that the Senator had been fully informed that the Institute was more than willing to work out the details. They supported the need for the Health Service to provide this essential health service since by law they were not able to do so more than six years. Grant protested that these were not qualified health services, and for the third time he struck out.

Senator Michelson assumed control of the hearing. "It would appear, Dr. Grant, the Indian Health Service is reluctant to establish what is clearly a vitally needed community service. You have insufficient staff to commence your own efforts; you do not have facilities in which to place programs; you do not have the finances with which to offer these services to the public. Yet, the problem of alcoholism affects up to ninety-five percent of the population in one way or another. The National Institute is willing to relinquish 158 of their grant supported programs provided Congress will ensure their survival.

"Dr. Grant, Congress fully intends that this effort be successful and directs the Indian Health Service to expedite an agreement with the National Institute on Alcohol Abuse and Alcoholism which will guarantee the transfer of all programs now funded by grant.

"These programs will not be reduced in any amount to enable the IHS to develop an appropriate organization to service them.

"Further, these programs will not be evaluated for efficiency or effectiveness prior to the required transfer. Evaluation will not be an excuse for early termination of any program. And, as a final note, urban programs will not receive less support than reservation-based programs. Dr. Grant, in short, it appears you now have an alcoholism program, one that is firmly based in the Indian community."

Standing Bear would soon be enroute to Rockville, Maryland following the successful end of the Senate hearing. It was long his dream to fashion a grass roots response to alcoholism that would put the power in the tribes rather than the medical establishment to treat the alcoholic. From his long experience as a patient and a sober community activist he believed strongly in their latent ability to manage their own affairs. A little more effort and Dr. Grant would be convinced to hire him as the first director of the fledgling alcoholism control effort.

Before returning to Pine Ridge he and Flying Eagle made a series of appointments with their congressional representatives to thank them for their support and for championing their cause. Most importantly they wanted to plan their next steps.

"We know the Feds will try to drag their heals in coordinating the transfer of programs from the Institute. So your concern is ours, John," Miles Davenport from Senator LaSalle's staff said.

Standing Bear felt comfortable with his statement that he would call the IHS periodically to receive a status report and alert him of any problems that surfaced. "I just want to reiterate, Miles, that I recognize your sincerity and your commitment to Indian people. My biggest worry is not your support. Flying Eagle and I have long been in the trenches fighting the bureaucracy and have reason to be concerned for our brothers and sisters out there whose only interest and concern is to keep the drunks off the streets and food in their bellies and a roof over their heads."

Flying Eagle added. "What the brothers and sisters are telling us is that as soon as their programs are transferred out of the Institute into the IHS, they will evaluate them and close them down. I don't know, Miles, if you've ever been to see any of our programs including many of those in the cities, but they don't have fancy places. Some of them are real lucky to be able to put three meals a day out. Most of them just barely have enough money to pay the rent. None of them have gotten a pay raise under the Institute."

"We want the IHS to assure us, Miles, that none of the programs will be cut. We want the urban programs to be treated like the reservation programs. We want all the programs to get technical assistance and training. We know that many of the people aren't trained to provide intensive treatment but they really want to do a good job for their own people." Standing Bear paused to see what effect these demands were having.

Davenport listened patiently. Standing Bear looked to Flying Eagle and continued. "You see, the Indian Desk at the Institute has only had one person to deal with all the grants — I mean to do everything," he emphasized, "not just take care of the money business — the training and the technical assistance, too."

"John, you heard the Feds. They think they can do everything with the people they have."

"With all due respect to their ego's, Miles, they don't know what they are talking about. It's not just those people in the Senate room the other day. Their attitude is multiplied by the rest of the staff they have in the field hospitals. Hospitals don't want to take drunks. They have no training either in how to handle people under the influence or to treat them with counseling. They think all they have to do is give them some Valium and send them out the door and hope they don't come back.

"We have to be realistic. We have an uphill struggle with the medical people, Miles. You can see that. And did you notice, there wasn't an Indian staffperson among them? To really deal with this problem we have got to have well-trained staff in the field, medical people who aren't afraid to help, and national direction. But the attitude of those jokers won't help us get what we want." Standing Bear rested his case leaning back in his chair.

Miles looked at him and reflected on the proceedings.

"Maybe, maybe not. I think we may need to prove to them that communities know what they are doing. You said so yourself. Change happens slowly. Remember your new organization has never had an alcoholism program before. Now it has one. And you are it, my friend."

Standing Bear looked to Flying Eagle a little uncertain about the meaning of the statement. "Yes, but Grant controls the purse strings, Miles. My office isn't a regular part of the structure. It exists because we persuaded Congress to support it. But even Congress didn't give us any money to run it — they handed over just those programs the Institute didn't want or know what to do with. The leadership of the Health Service has got to change from the top down. An Indian needs to direct the agency, Miles."

Standing Bear and Flying Eagle soon left the Senate Office Building to return to their reservation. They had to make preparations for flying back to Washington as new "Feds."

They were unaware that Miles had begun the long journey to replace Grant with an Indian. Andrew Giroux's name had surfaced as a strong contender.

CHAPTER THREE

STANDING BEAR

A year had passed since Standing Bear had been installed as the new Alcoholism Program Director. The honeymoon was over and he had been called in for his first evaluation. Standing Bear returned to his office around the corner from the Director's office a little less complacent than he had been previously and a little more determined than usual to make his mark on the Indian Health Service. In a private meeting attended only by him and Dr. Morrison, Dr. Grant reviewed his first year's performance as less than stellar.

"I hope we can be candid, John," Dr. Grant began in subdued tones with Morrison sitting at his right hand. They looked somber in their uniforms. Each did not smile. Standing Bear quickly assessed the placement of chairs, their reserved appearances and concluded his evaluation would not go well. Uniforms made everything so official. It was no small wonder many of the Indians resented the Health Service. Memories of uniforms were long.

"When I first came here a year ago, Dr. Grant, I said I would do the best I could. I would work hard to establish a credible program. But I couldn't do it alone. I would be direct with you, too and expect your support."

"We know this is your first year in the system and we can't expect miracles. After all Rome wasn't built in a day, was it? " Dr. Grant tried to break the awkwardness of the moment with a lame witticism. Clearing his throat after getting no response, he continued, "We have given you a deputy and secretary and some travel funds. Quite frankly, we are a little bit surprised at the results of all your travel this year to all the Area Offices."

"What do you mean, Dr. Grant?" Standing Bear asked in surprise shifting uncomfortably in his chair. He felt as if the two officers were ready to pounce upon him. He had to be prepared to defend himself.

"Well," Morrison began, "A number of the directors have telephoned us about some of your presentations there." As if to bolster his comments with facts, Morrison unfolded a manila folder with notes from telephone calls.

He was interrupted by Standing Bear. "Such as who? What did they say?" He sat up straight in his chair, alert.

Morrison looked to Grant for confirmation that he should continue. "Well, such as Peterson in Albuquerque, and Smith in Aberdeen, and Hawkins in California. There are others. Each of them says you have been making community presentations which more or less requires them to open wards for alcoholics. Where do you get the notion we have resources for that?"

"Dr. Morrison and Dr. Grant, I thought that was what we were in business to do. To treat alcoholics and to reduce alcoholism. Surely you can understand my enthusiasm for my job. You did get me in from the field to take this job which none of your docs would take didn't you?"

While Standing Bear was smiling, Morrison and Grant were not. Grant stepped in. "John, don't misunderstand us. We appreciate your dedication and your enthusiasm. Unfortunately, you are right. Not too many doctors want to deal with alcoholism. It's a nasty business and they're not particularly well-trained to deal with drunks."

Realizing whom he was talking to, Dr. Grant cleared his throat, too. He tried to recover. "John, we mean no offense, but we have to caution you. The legislation only gives IHS the authority to transfer programs from NIAAA. It doesn't give us the resources to develop a full blown treatment and prevention program. We just can't promise people in the field we are going to develop detoxification programs in our hospitals and clinics. Do you understand? You are one of us now. You are a Fed."

This was small comfort to Standing Bear. He did not like the dressing down. But he was a street fighter and knew he had to gather his support elsewhere. Somehow he had to beat them at their own game, the game of professionalism. The new service had to become professional.

"I know this must be difficult for you, John." Grant continued bringing his chair closer to him. "Dr. Morrison and I have been talking. We think your program should remain attached to our office for the time being. Morrison will work more closely with you. And, to followup on what may be a problem in the field, we are prepared to give you one additional position. A training officer. Perhaps this kind of position can help with the hospitals in the field."

"I've been thinking too, Dr. Grant. There are some professionals in the Area Offices and in the programs. If you will give me the support necessary I believe we can make the program more professional."

Tucson is in the lower Sonoran desert. Saguaro and barrel cacti abound with mesquite. When the cacti bloom after the spring rains, the desert is a fairy land alive with color and fruit. The cacti were a staple crop for the Tohono O'Odham Indians living on the harsh desert bordering Mexico. As the fruit matured, they were often seen in family outings picking the cacti for jam, candy, and for wine used in tribal ceremonies, the most important of which occurred in the spring. "Singing down the clouds" ensured a bountiful harvest.

Mt. Lemon rises from the desert floor to dominate the landscape to the northeast of Tucson. Its winding approaches to the summit are dotted with picnic and camp grounds. When the monsoon rains come in July — and they inevitably do — thunder rumbles and roars through purple clouds to announce their coming. Those who live below its brooding visage know to avoid the arroyos and concave streets for fear of not finding safe portage.

To the west of Tucson the Kitt Peak Observatory, which houses one of the largest telescopes in the world, keeps track of celestial happenings and overlooks the movie lot of Old Tucson where wild west shows depict life on the frontier for the benefit of TV and movie audiences.

To the south lies Green Valley where wealthy retirees congregate and play on well-tended golf courses. Nogales, Mexico with its attendant poverty lies further south. Phoenix is north where swimming pools dominate the urban sprawl and where there are more boats per capita than in any other state. A strange

Aversion To Honor

phenomenon for the desert. Phoenix and Tucson encroach upon each other. Some fear the metropolis their combination will create will be worse than Los Angeles. But they are alarmists and have little to worry about at least until the next century.

For now, Tucson is more laid back than Phoenix where the pressures of daily living seem to dictate more frenetic activity. In Tucson life responds better to *mañana* and to margarita's in the shade of palo verdes under the hot summer sun. The influence of Mexico is readily felt there in art and architecture and language use. Many residents are bilingual.

Higher than Phoenix, Tucson is at least five degrees cooler in the summer — which is a relative matter given temperatures over 105 degrees — and is often visited with summer showers that make the desert green while the streets roil with turbulent waters.

The small group assembled at the Pueblo Inn hotel in downtown Tucson. One came from Seattle, another from Albuquerque, two from Phoenix, to meet with John Standing Bear from Rockville, MD. On his flight there Standing Bear had to silently acknowledge neither he nor Flying Eagle had the technical expertise to develop a new data system or of developing standards for the newly authorized alcoholism program he led. This was a new, uncharted area for the Indian Health Service. But he knew from many complaints he heard that the old National Alcohol Program Information System of NIAAA was rejected by most Indian program managers. It wasn't developed by Indians for Indians.

Standing Bear almost got into an argument with Grant over the role of the hospitals in the treatment of alcoholism; but he backed off when he saw Grant getting red in the face as he defended the hospitals for doing their best without additional resources. Standing Bear almost laughed when he thought it was to this white man's disadvantage when he began to turn colors. He knew better than to press the issue. Ever the politician, Standing Bear suddenly agreed that additional resources were needed.

Adroitly, he then pressed another issue — getting Grant to support his bringing together a team of interested staff from the field to develop a new data system and to develop standards that would professionalize the programs in the eyes of the medical and nursing professionals. Grant had little choice and reluctantly agreed to provide him the necessary money.

When the group assembled, Standing Bear explained to them that Congress had passed the Indian Health Care Improvement Act and set in motion the transfer of Indian alcoholism programs. No one knew what to expect of the recently transferred alcoholism programs or what standards should govern their activities or programs. The IHS had agreed with the National Institute on Alcohol Abuse and Alcoholism to accept their programs carte blanche — without evaluation of their performance. It was a political matter. While it meant nothing to NIAAA to agree — after all, they were losing programs that had steadfastly maintained their uniqueness among all programs nationally — their political systems (tribal councils) were not well understood.

IHS on the other hand, understood well their political structures but had no working relationship with alcoholism program activities and had no basis on which to be critical of the efforts of other federal departments. More importantly for the tribes involved, the Indian Health Care Improvement Act — thanks to Standing Bear and his friends — required IHS to accept the programs and go on from there. Standing Bear was ready to explore this for all it was worth.

The walled courtyard was lush around the swimming pool with blooming oleanders, cana lilies, and verbena. The profusion of blooms spilled onto the walkway around the swimming pool where they gathered in the mid-afternoon heat. As a group they decided the sun was too bright and hot to begin discussions without a swim first. One by one they entered the pool and began splashing each other as children much to the consternation of three hotel guests lounging in their chaise lounges. Two looked at each other in disgust, got up and left in the midst of the increasing noise.

The third guest, a lithe attractive woman in her mid-twenties alternately reading and watching, instead laughed heartily at their antics. She was arrested by their playfulness, pausing in the reading of a mystery novel to watch them. Two of the four were of no interest to her. The third appeared preoccupied and uninterested in her. She had no interest in him and he too was ignored. But the fourth, tall and athletic, enthusiastic, energetic, was more outgoing than all the others and was apparently the leader. He caught her attention as more playful that the rest.

As they played the fool, Standing Bear noticed her stare and met it with an instant recognition of a fundamental urge. He pretended to throw her a rubber ball the group found in the water. She was caught off guard but bemused. She jumped in the lounge as a spray of water splashed her. She raised her book in time to ward it from her face. Most would have been irritated at such an affront. But she didn't resist this advance of playfulness. She put her book down on the table beside her leaning over sufficiently to display her ample frame.

"Now that you're wet, come on in," John laughed admiring her striking figure. He tried to coax her into the pool. Her string bikini left nothing to his fertile imagination. It was the first thing he noticed about her.

Standing Bear reflected it had been some time since he had a white woman in his bed, This one appealed to him. She was uniformly tan all over. She obviously enjoyed nature. Sunglasses hid her eyes. Chestnut hair fell into a flip at her chin and framed delicate high cheek bones and full lips. Her laugh was rich and throaty and betrayed a fun-loving nature. It was a nature Standing Bear wanted to know more intimately. The sooner the better.

John commented softly to Jake Bronson on his right, "I think I am definitely in love. I want you to go ahead with the meeting tonight, Jake. I may join you later. What I want you to do is get some discussion going on standards. We need something that will keep people on track while they do their counseling. That sort of thing, you know what to do. I've got to check this one out."

Bronson was peeved that he would leave them in the lurch and snorted, "Is it love or lust?" a note of disapproval and maybe a little jealousy in his voice. Standing Bear never wore a ring to tip anyone off to his marital status. Bronson envied his ease in making such arrangements since his own marriage was problematic; but he lacked the courage to change it.

"What the hell difference does it make, Jake? Fucking is fucking whether you're doing it to your wife or some other woman," John added. "It happens all the time. It's all in the game. Maybe you ought to try it sometime. I'll call you later to see how the meeting went."

Standing Bear leapt out of the water confidently, walked over to the young woman who by then was smiling, lay beside her on another lounge and engaged her in light conversation. He was a master at it. From his vantage point Bronson noticed it was full of mirth, smiles and arduous glances. He turned, threw the ball to one of the others and hopped out of the pool to retire to his room. They laughed. He knew it was about him.

"An Indian?" she asked. "You don't look like an Indian," she said. "You're not very copper and everyone knows Indians are supposed to be copper. At least that is what the movies tell us, right?"

"Well, I'm not so sure the movies are always right. Perhaps I should call one of my friends up here to confirm that I'm the genuine article." John laughed pretending innocence.

"Oh, I wouldn't do that. I'll just have to take your word for it. I heard them call you, John. John what? " she asked peering over the rims of her glasses.

"Standing Bear."

"Standing Bear? Now that is original! I must admit it sounds Indian all right. Now, you aren't teasing me again, are you?" she cooed flirtatiously.

This was too much to resist for Standing Bear. John paused and said, "I admit I would like to tease you. But not here in front of my friends. Maybe after dinner tonight though." Without giving her a chance to respond he added, "What do you like to eat when you are in Tucson? Steak, chicken or Italian? I know a wonderful Italian place. Scordato's. It's about twenty or thirty minutes from here. No. I know, you're a meat-eater, and I bet you like it rare. Am I close?"

"You get any closer and it will be rare!" she said unabashedly.

A stewardess from Texas, Jean was in town for the evening on a stop over from Seattle enroute home to the Dallas Fort Worth Airport. Standing Bear didn't fit her stereotype of an Indian. He was engaging, more outgoing than she expected. Like many she persisted in the stereotype of the wooden Indian. Like most who maintain such images, her experience with Indians was confined to the movies and books. Her curiosity piqued, she invited him for a drink at the bar but was surprised at his selection of lemonade to her margarita. She liked the men she invited to her room to share a little alcohol before they make love. But this was one strange Indian. No alcohol.

"I don't need alcohol to make me feel good, Jean. I get high on love," Standing Bear mused, a twinkle in his eye.

"Or making it?" was Jean's equally quick and flirtatious reply. She wanted to confirm his interest in her and looked intently at him.

Standing Bear smiled knowingly and assured her he had considerable skill and credentials in the love making department. He acknowledged he and alcohol didn't mix, contrary to stereotypes, and drank his lemonade and waited impatiently for her to finish her margarita. She took a healthy gulp, put the empty glass down, and with one hand on his leg she insisted he accompany her to her room to wait while she changed for dinner.

Standing Bear willingly obliged knowing the ruse and feeling his own arousal accompanied her into the elevator to the third floor of the hotel. Out the door and down the hallway to her room Standing Bear followed a step behind her. Glancing downward he thought the view magnificent. Delicate waist and nicely rounded hips and muscular legs. It was obvious she was fond of exercise.

Jean took the key from her bra, unlocked her door and confidently without turning around to see Standing Bear following her into the room, unhooked her bikini bottom, letting it drop to the floor, and reached behind her back and took off her top. She turned for his fuller view and asked, "You do want a shower, don't you?"

Standing Bear admired her directness and rose to the occasion and relieved himself of his clothes almost as fast. The trail led to the shower door. Jean took one look at him naked and exclaimed, "Oh, my God! I wish mother would have told me about Indians sooner."

As the water flowed over her body in rivulets Standing Bear lapped at her intensely. Time stood still during their mutual explorations of their bodies. No desire was left hidden to chance.

Drying, they continued onto the bedroom as before, passion knowing no bounds.

After their climactic dessert, they went to Scordato's in his rental to catch up with their other by now raging appetite.

Meanwhile, when he had finished dinner downstairs with the other two consultants, Bronson convened the group for a briefing on what their tasks were. Neither he nor they were directly on Standing Bear's staff but were brought in to do his staff work. They only had interest on their side and no authority to commit the government to anything.

It was strange he thought. The government has a unique way of thinking any problem is solved when it throws enough money to the problem at hand, or it gets experts to design a solution whether it is useful or not. Clearly this was not the case of throwing money at a solution. Standing Bear had none of his own; and this was a motley group of "experts."

With his letter in hand from Admiral Grant appointing him to Chair this fledgling task force, Bronson began. "John ... uh ... had an ... appointment tonight and asked me to get us started.

"John probably told each of you separately that the Director asked me to chair this working group. Before we came here I asked John to share his request with you because frankly I am somewhat uncomfortable in assuming this responsibility given that I'm not Indian and have only been involved in treating Indians with alcohol problems from the Phoenix Area. This hardly represents a national perspective, which, as I see it, is to design standards that will be applied across the board to all tribal programs."

Each looked around to the other waiting for someone to take the lead in this effort; but while each wanted to be involved no one stepped forward. The people Standing Bear assembled were used to extra work. They thrived on it and came to his attention when programs were transferred to the Health Service the year before.

Bronson was graduate trained in social work and had completed additional advanced work in alcoholism program development at Rutgers University. Of those present he was most qualified academically to do the task. But his instructions were to involve the Indians in discussion. He held back waiting.

Before long, the group warmed to the task and to each other and all but ignored Bronson's disclaimer. A natural give-and-take occurred. Bill Spencer from the IHS research office in Tucson, and the only other white man in the group, took the lead. His discussions about systems and how the government should become involved in monitoring results of health efforts were as natural to him as eating jam on toast.

With a cup of coffee in one hand and a cigarette in the other he punctuated his discussion with droppings from each. The others moved their papers closer to themselves to avoid being splattered. Spencer noticed the retreat and put the coffee down and charted the course of his presentation in flow charts smudged with cigarette ash and coffee stains. His excitement mounted as the evening wore on.

Spencer was in his mid-forties and spoke with an upstate New York accent. He gestured wildly and smoked profusely. He was system's oriented and loved to envision the end product and hypothesize the intervening steps. His credo was reduce problems to their lowest common denominator and then design steps out of the hole. It was the simplest way to avoid anxiety. He wanted the group to think freely and creatively and not be bound by any traditional or bureaucratic thinking. Not everyone has an opportunity to develop an institution in his life time. This task brought fresh excitement into his life.

To the astonished listeners he envisioned the client as a product in the making being passed from station to station on the way to wellness. Each station had a role to play in fashioning the end product, a person whose philosophy of life, physical health status, and treatment needs had been checked, provided for and monitored as he made his way back into society, a whole person.

Bronson was the detail man, the note-taker, who translated the discussions into sensible text and arbitrated differences in approaches to the problems and tasks to arrive at possible solutions and methods of approach. His background in community organization with the American National Red Cross in the rural and sometimes remote hill counties of southwest Virginia often kept the group focused on the seemingly impossible task. He was adept at working with committees and had a knack of letting others assume the leadership role.

Ralph Lake, the quiet reserved Eskimo, brought sensitivity and a gift of humor to the sessions to relieve tensions between the whites who proposed a multitude of processes and ways of thinking and the Indians whose daily experiences were worth more than the theories about what should work in Indian country.

Jim Waters, the portly alcohol program director from the Gila River Reservation outside Phoenix, spoke with conviction from his long experience. "With all due respect, Bill, Indians don't think that way. Your way is the typical white man's way of thinking.

"We just can't draw a diagram and expect our counselors who usually don't even have a high school diploma to follow it like a road map. Your words are foreign; English is their second tongue; most program directors and counselors will have to first translate what you are saying into their own language so they can understand. Many of the tribesmen we have to deal with — and IHS will have to deal with — don't have native words to put your ideas into. Here in Phoenix area there are 43 tribes. These are just not natural concepts for them." Waters laughed at the white man's naïveté' and shook like a bowl-full of jelly in the room.

Bill Spencer responded, "Well, we will just have to design the data system in such a way that the system will be the road map that takes these counselors from their very first contact with a client all the way through the stages of diagnosis and treatment to post treatment followup even if they aren't trained to do treatment. Whatever we do, however, has to be done following a set of guidelines or standards of behavior. What do we want to tackle first?"

Spencer made it sound simple. Just design a data system from scratch that does the impossible, take an untrained counselor through the whole counseling process from intake, studying the problem, making a diagnosis, through treatment, and on to post treatment followup.

As he further described his notions the group realized how nearly overwhelming the task would be. Waters and Lake described the remoteness of many reservations and Alaska Native villages, the uniqueness of language and customs, poverty, and lack of educational opportunities among the hundreds of separate and sovereign tribes. To call it overwhelming was to put it mildly. It was a huge undertaking, truly monumental; and it had never been done before.

Bronson ordered a pot of coffee. It promised to be a long night, the start of many the group would endure together the next two years in similar meetings across the country. "It doesn't make any difference where we start. We have to have standards to guide counseling activity and we have to have data to record the efforts of all the counselors working in the tribal and urban programs," Bronson added. "The two activities have to come together. So let's start with developing some guidelines. What kind of programs do we have out there?" he asked.

Waters and Lake began to list various types of programs. There were detox programs, counseling, halfway houses, shelters, DWI programs and so on. They spent the next hour describing their differences. While they talked Spencer and Bronson were taking careful notes. Spencer began to place the various types on a continuum, a sequence based on treatment needs. While he did this, Bronson wrote basic definitions for each type based on the discussion.

The discussion wore on, a second pot of coffee was ordered, and the group continued until 2 in the morning. Exhausted they finally retreated to bed and sleep. It was agreed that Bronson would keep all the notes and translate them for all the meetings.

The morning came all too quickly. When Bronson arrived in the restaurant he found Spencer briefing Standing Bear on the meeting. He joined their discussion. Ashes were everywhere. On his toast and floating in his coffee. New diagrams were drawn on table napkins voiding some of the previous night's discussion. Standing Bear appeared interested but had trouble keeping up with Spencer's rapid fire monologue. His attention was on the previous night's conquest. He had already seen Jean to the airport and had gotten her address and phone number. Intent on seeing him again, Jean took his, too.

"Did you get that, Bronson?... Make a note of that, Bronson... When I get back to Rockville, Bronson, elaborate on these points... We need to write a paper for all the IHS Area Offices. Make it easy for them to understand," he said.

Bronson's head was swimming with the tasks that had to be done. But he was grateful to have a role in the development of the new alcoholism program in the IHS.

Standing Bear was politically active with tribal representatives of the National Congress of American Indians, the National Indian Health Board and, in particular, the National Indian Board of Alcoholism and Drug Abuse for the past year and a half. He didn't mind having insufficient staff to do the mammoth task of organizing a program to influence the bureaucracy. He would just call on Bronson or someone else to undertake some of the assignments he lacked the technical expertise to do. He was confident they would get done. Without his own staff, he knew he could get Admiral Grant to authorize travel for anyone he needed to work on his projects. With that support area directors released staff for periodic assignments. He would have the best of both worlds — staff to do his work, but no responsibility for daily supervision. Standing Bear prided himself on his ability to work out such mundane details.

However, Standing Bear was often distressed with the bureaucracy. It moved so slowly on resolving big issues like getting detoxification services in the hospitals. He also knew it was always responsive to the political system — not just the elected officials of downtown Washington, but the chairmen of the tribal councils as well. The Health Service fully expected heat from the elected officials. It was part of the turf. But it considered the tribal officials as more important. After all, it was their health interests that had to be met.

Appointed Agency officials could be replaced. All they had to do was offend enough tribal officials. They could easily be assigned to the Coast Guard to work on an ice breaker in Alaska! The beauty of it all! It had been done before. Commissioned officers were a vulnerable lot.

Standing Bear knew his strength was on the tribal level. He moved with the grace of a cat in their ranks — a large mountain cat sizing up its prey. He knew their weak points too, who was alcoholic, or who was sleeping with whom, or who abused their spouses or their children. It was nothing to call for favors — a strong letter from a tribal official to the director of the agency or a telephone call to a senator to get the agency moving on an issue. He had no compunction when it came to manipulation. This part of the bureaucracy was ready for it. He knew just what strings to pull to get his way.

The agency was foremost a bureaucracy — and like most bureaucracies, it acted when it wanted to act for reasons of its own — which were most often not apparent to the naked eye. The bureaucracy wasn't designed for the individual worker. No bureaucracy is. It has a thousand ways to maneuver and to maintain the *status quo.* Perpetuation of the bureaucracy is always its paramount goal. Change is not always best.

Standing Bear worked hard to gain support for his program. He delegated day to day functions to his small staff of a secretary and a deputy. More difficult matters were farmed out to loyalists in the field like Bronson. This gave him the time necessary to pursue his ends by telephone, periodic trips to the other IHS Areas where he would hold perfunctory meetings with staff and then do his real business with tribal officials. Who needed what? Expand a little program here. Emphasize the need for additional funds there to congressional staffers.

Without the knowledge of the agency, Standing Bear easily became a power broker through the manipulation of information. He returned from field trips with knowledge to dispense to congressional staffers who, in turn, would convey inside information about congressional plans to meet deficiencies in programs. This information was useful to trade with other IHS staffers to gain necessary support for his program.

He had yet to meet Senator Dominguez's chief staffer. He had meant to go downtown for a number of months but just had not gotten around to it until now. Trying to keep on top of budget lately had become almost a full time operation.

"Cindy, this is John Standing Bear, calling from the IHS Alcoholism Program. I'll be downtown tomorrow to meet with the Office of Minority Health, and I wondered how convenient it would be if I stopped by for a chat with you in the afternoon. Perhaps we could have coffee somewhere." John paused. "Two-thirty sounds great. Yes, at the Senator's office."

John wondered why she seemed so eager. He had never met her before. Since his program was only now getting established in the system with two more years of transfers of programs to look forward to, John had been systematically asking other staffers who could be trusted among congressional staffers. Cindy's name frequently surfaced as a straight arrow among western delegations.

He did not know her but he was also eager to meet her. John left the Parklawn building for the long drive down the Washington Parkway. He used the time to collect his thoughts and plan his first meeting with her. An hour later he found a parking spot in easy walking distance of the Senate Office Building.

Cindy Mitchell was Senator Dominguez of New Mexico's lead staff member. She was a tireless worker, soft spoken, self-assured with degrees in accounting and public administration from the University of New Mexico.

Cindy grew up at Crown Point on the Navajo Reservation. She was well-versed in the traditions and the plight of her people and had made it her point to become equally versed in the machinations of the white world to help her people achieve good health and economic stability. It was her goal. She was uncompromising in her beliefs and values but pragmatic and accommodating if it meant that her people would get something they lacked.

Alcoholism was a priority issue with her. Alcoholism caused the death of her father and two uncles on the lonely stretch of highway between Gallup, New Mexico and Window Rock, Arizona while she was away at the University. Many Navajo's lost their lives on this stretch of road. She grieved that they would not see her graduate with honors when they sacrificed so much to help her get through school.

Cindy was anxious to meet him. He represented the key to resolution of alcoholism among her people. She had heard a lot about him. And, not all of it flattering. But that, she realized, she could put aside for the moment. She had to learn all she could from this man.

While waiting for Standing Bear to arrive she researched the problem of alcoholism among American Indians and Alaska Natives and learned that there were many anecdotal reports in the literature but few scientifically based psycho-social studies. The Indian Health Service itself published little. No data to speak of. Just early references that spoke of its effect on 95 percent of the Indian population. Hard critical epidemiological data were lacking. And, no published plans to correct the problem. "How odd!" she thought for an agency that was supposed to be the prime health care resource for over a million people.

This latter observation intrigued Cindy as she walked about smudging her office with sweet grass, a custom she borrowed from her plains cousins. Corn pollen was in a pouch she wore around her neck. She wanted her office and herself to be clean and protected from any impurities so their minds and spirits could truly engage this problem.

Cindy loved the smell of the grass burning. It brought back the desert and the vistas of Monument Valley and images of endless blue sky and puffy white clouds. Sometimes images of small white crosses marking highway deaths also intruded themselves. Her father and uncles killed by a drunken Navajo trying to return to the reservation in the dark of night, his eyes transfixed with the glow of oncoming headlights beckoning him to meet them in a head-on collision. Miraculously, he lived; they didn't. She had little sympathy for the man; he took too much from her.

The smoke curled up from her feet, over her head, down her arms and back in swift motions. After smudging herself in preparation for John's visit and to clear her mind of the resentment she felt, Cindy closed her eyes and centered her vision inward to the center of her life where she felt strength and purpose. Lost within herself she had not first heard the intercom. Her secretary again repeated her call announcing Mr. Standing Bear's presence.

Cindy looked up to see a tall athletic looking man in a three piece suit. His dark hair, flashing eyes and aquiline features were all that distinguished him as Indian, although he could appear to be middle European she thought. Gone were his braid and bone necklace. No; he wasn't what she expected. Of course, she reasoned, since working in the nation's capitol she met many Indians from the east coast that challenged her ideas of what Indians should look like, particularly those from the Northeast, who, when they talked, sounded like the late President Kennedy!

Cindy rose from her chair and extended her hand in a cordial greeting. "So nice to meet you at last, Mr. Standing Bear."

"I wanted to meet you for some time, Miss Mitchell. But getting away from Rockville is more difficult than you imagine. It's my pleasure." John said in his most business like way seating himself at her gesture.

He continued. "I'm John by the way. May I call you Cindy? I hope to be speaking with you often as you work on the IHS budget and related legislation. I hope we can be less formal."

"I would have no problem with that, John, so long as you and I can agree that it must be our work that unites us." Rumors of his liaisons with others came to her as they talked.

John replied, "I would have it no other way, Cindy. You are undoubtedly aware of how significant the alcoholism problem is among our people. Actually, I don't know many Indians who aren't aware that alcoholism claims four of the top ten causes of deaths among Indians."

"Yes, I know. Personally and professionally. I've done a lot of reading about it lately. Probably what I've read about 95 percent of Indians being affected in one way or another by alcoholism is true. Maybe that's why the numbers haven't changed much."

Standing Bear interrupted. "Now could I buy you that cup of coffee?"

"Is there something we can't talk about here, John?" Cindy asked innocently smiling all the while.

"No, not really." He paused. "To be honest with you, Cindy, I don't want information getting back to the front office that I am lobbying. We Feds aren't allowed to do that, I'm sure you know."

"So, you are here to lobby?"

"Can we talk privately? What about that cup of coffee?" John countered.

"You know I can't support federal lobbying any more than you can. But I do believe in collaboration. And when it comes to this particular problem I want to collaborate as fully as I can, John. Is that clear enough? Now what about that coffee you promised me? You've kept me waiting long enough."

Standing Bear was surprised by this last remark. It held a hint of personal promise he thought he might like to explore later. They walked to the Senate dining room which had cleared of the lunch time crowd.

Cindy and Standing Bear talked for nearly two hours in the Senate dining room until distinctions blurred between lobbying and collaboration. Within that time they learned who was related to whom, who in the Indian Health Service, the Bureau of Indian Affairs, the Senate and the House committees could be worked with on delicate matters, official business only, and which matters not to bring to staffers.

Standing Bear took careful mental notes for later use. It was essential information highly useful for his future planning. "Cindy, this was a most enjoyable cup of coffee. I know you are a very busy person, but I hope that I may call on you later. I also want you to feel free to call me especially when alcoholism is talked about. Perhaps I may be of some help to you then."

Cindy agreed. They parted and returned to their respective offices. Cindy was less sure about Standing Bear's reputation with women. He was so self-assured, polished, and had made no efforts to force himself upon her. He acted very much the gentleman. She was relieved but a little disappointed and astonished he had not lived up to his reputation.

A month went by without contact. Then Standing Bear's telephone rang. "John, this is Cindy from Senator Dominguez's office. Oh, yes, I am fine. I want to take you up on your offer about talking about alcoholism. We're beginning to work on the 1983 budget and are really concerned about the programs that the Institute has transferred to you. All 158 programs will have been transferred by then. Congress has no idea whatsoever of what condition they are in; what their funding needs really are; or whether they should be canceled. Can you talk with me on this? What is the mood at IHS?"

This was the opportunity Standing Bear had waited for. A smile crept across his face as he replied, "Yes, of course I can talk with you about that. Today? Certainly. I can be downtown at about 3 PM. Your office? Great. I'll see you then."

Standing Bear was punctual; Cindy was not. She was running from office to office to meet critical deadlines. As she passed by she signaled to him to wait. She would be with him in a minute.

"I'm really sorry about this, but sometimes it takes a lot of coordination to get the language just right for these budget bills. This is especially important when tribal interests are at stake. The wording must be just right.

"Now for the reason I asked you to consult with me. On May 5th, 1978 the IHS signed a memorandum of agreement with the National Institute on Alcohol Abuse and Alcoholism. It didn't make a difference whether the transferring program was a reservation or an urban program. IHS agreed to accept them without any evaluation. This put Congress in a difficult position. Programs want increases. Congress, of course, doesn't have any data to speak of to justify increases. But it also believes increases are necessary. Enlighten me on this will you? I think we have a little bit of a dilemma."

Standing Bear was happy to oblige. With an air of self-importance, he smiled and offered his long explanation.

"I can't turn my back on my brothers and sisters in the programs, Cindy, any more than I can with the agency because of the agreement. Before the Indian Health Care Improvement Act became law I was one of the Indians who argued as loudly as anyone for no evaluation. I knew there wasn't any data to speak of. Most of the programs hated the National Alcohol Program Information System and sent anything in to the bean counters. That's why I adopted as one of my first goals to get a data system developed with Indian input. There were also no standards for the programs to be judged against.

"The IHS is doing that now. We have a set of standards that my committee developed over the last two years. We also have a data system that has been pilot tested which we are ready to put into every program in the country. Indians developed each of these with guidance from IHS staff and we are proud of the effort.

"We can't give you many numbers now, Cindy, but I will guarantee you that if Congress will allow us a year, I will get a national evaluation under way in 1983. You will have your numbers and they will be reliable." Sincerity poured from every syllable. He felt she was being swayed.

Standing Bear wondered how this gorgeous creature could only talk business. "Speaking of numbers. What is yours, Cindy?" He hastened to add, "You never can tell, I may need to call you in an emergency."

Surprised but flattered, Cindy protested. "John, we had an agreement, I believe. Nothing personal. I will help you as much as I can. But please, nothing personal." Cindy was drawn to him but knew the bounds of propriety held her fast. It was one thing to work collaboratively, but quite another to get involved. Indeed, he was charming. She felt alarmed at how easily he tapped into her feelings.

"Oh, there isn't anything personal." He smiled expansively. "I was just checking to see if you were listening. It looked like you were doodling on your note pad."

Embarrassed Cindy quickly placed her hand on her scratches, crumpled the paper and tossed it into the waste basket. Standing Bear knew his time would come. A few more passes, perhaps a dinner, another suggestion and he would get what he wanted — full cooperation in building the program tribal constituents needed on the reservations.

On his return to Rockville Standing Bear considered his meeting a grand success. He was troubled however, that getting the resources necessary to fully establish the tribal programs in the health arena was only meeting one side of the equation.

The IHS remained intransigent. It failed to provide full acceptance of their programs. The responsibility for that rested with the newly installed Director, Admiral Andrew Giroux.

He appeared to be a reasonable sort of man. Like his predecessor, Giroux was a physician who came to his position from working in the field hospitals of several states. More academically inclined however, he published many papers in internal medicine and lectured frequently from his position as adjunct professor for the University of Arizona.

There were few Indian physicians in the country. Among them he was an established leader. It was only natural for them to advocate strongly for him to assume the leadership role in providing health care to all Indians and Alaska Natives.

When Admiral Grant chose to retire the arduous process of choosing a successor was reduced considerably when hundreds of letters were received in Congress calling for Giroux's appointment. Most said it was timely for the Indian Health Service to be headed by an Indian. None had served in this capacity before. Indian nations wanted the leadership of the country to espouse their cause.

Giroux had a reputation for scholarship, dry wit and athletics. His followers in the professional circles propelled him forward eager for him to be the point man.

Standing Bear had met him before. He was comfortable with Admiral Grant whom he had finally won over to his side. Under his leadership he had gained prominence among tribes nationally and additional positions to establish his program. He wasn't sure how he would fare with Giroux.

Giroux had been openly critical of alcoholism programs before he assumed the directorship of IHS. In his experience most of the programs he referred alcoholics to for treatment failed to measure up to his sense of professionalism. Directors were often appointed by tribal councils based upon kinship rather than training and experience. Their staff lacked critical skills. Most programs were housed in debilitated structures. Hence, they were not professional treatment programs.

It was precisely these points that spurred Standing Bear on to advocate on their behalf with whomever would hear his message. In his experience, Standing Bear knew that IHS hospitals were notorious in their disregard of alcoholics. When alcoholics presented themselves to emergency rooms for treatment, they were often the last seen. And, once seen, they were most often not accepted for treatment and were referred out. Neither the doctors nor the nurses wanted to deal with them. His personal experiences confirmed that.

Standing Bear wanted to correct these deficiencies in attitudes among the IHS staff. But he knew he did not presently have the necessary support to tackle the administration directly. It was too overwhelming. Both the area offices and the field hospitals held these views and had the support of administration for no change.

Whether each reflected on these concerns or not, their lines were already drawn before Giroux became Director. Now that he had been the Alcoholism Director for many months, Standing Bear had to work on his strategy to induce change within the system.

He continued his drive out the Washington Parkway and was soon past the Central Intelligence Agency entrance at Langley, Virginia. A few more miles and he would be in Maryland.

Exiting early he drove east to Rockville Pike. He was hungry and decided on an early supper. It was five-thirty. He wasn't in the mood to go home just yet and had heard so much about O'Donnel's Restaurant in Bethesda. Their sea food and breads and prime rib were reputed to be outrageously delicious. He wanted to try it and take some time to think how he might approach Giroux.

He was seated, presented with a basket of breads, and given time to look over the menu. In the interim before the waiter arrived to take his order, Standing Bear looked about the restaurant casually to observe who was there.

Even though early in the evening, the dining room was filled with people and a group was forming in the waiting Que. He had nearly leapt from his seat when he noticed among those waiting to be seated, was Giroux with an attractive Navajo woman whom he had seen working in the director's office.

Standing Bear quickly changed his seat to avoid being seen. He hoped they would be seated elsewhere and not notice him. Luck was on his side. Giroux and the Navajo woman were seated in another aisle. Giroux's back was to Standing Bear and the Navajo woman didn't appear comfortable looking around.

The woman was not Elizabeth, Giroux's wife, whom Standing Bear had met at his installation party many months ago. Elizabeth was a Winnebago Indian woman whom he met at college. The woman with him now was a secretary in his office. "How interesting," he thought.

Since they were standing in line together talking he knew it was not by chance that they met here. That would be too much of a coincidence. Looking at his menu, Standing Bear knew a secretary would not be able to afford this place. Prices were too out of line.

Giroux had to be paying for it. 'Is he paying for anything else?' Standing Bear wondered. He laughed to himself. 'Perhaps he and I have something in common after all,' he remarked to himself as he ordered a juicy medium rare prime rib with all the trimmings. The restaurant's reputation was deserved.

Over the next few weeks Standing Bear sought to learn all he could about Giroux. From his extensive contacts in the field he learned who his relatives were, what he was like as a student, his activism on the campus, and in what high regard he was genuinely held, standard things, but nothing that would point to usable information. He held his disappointment in check for now.

Standing Bear reflected. The system had to change. He knew from personal experience that IHS staff had little regard for skid row alcoholics hospitalized in their system. How often he had heard them talking about him being a bum when he was down and out and had come to IHS clinics for care. Many doctors and nurses hated to deal with alcoholics and assumed they couldn't be hurt due to the anesthetic effects of alcohol. Usually the alcoholic would be the last to be seen in clinics often despite severe trauma.

Standing Bear wanted this to change. But without the cooperation and the real leadership of Giroux this would be impossible. Working with Admiral Grant taught him how hard it was to change a physician's ideas of reality. Physicians ruled the IHS. He expected Giroux to be a challenge but he wasn't quite sure what form it would take.

Now that he himself was entrenched in the IHS, Standing Bear fully expected to use his own brand of influence to come to bear on Giroux. 'Whatever it takes,' he thought to himself. 'This program has got to succeed.'

It was a strange telephone call. Her voice was subdued, almost tranquil, and not like he had heard it so many times before when Anna came to Phoenix on business from Colorado River.

"I have to see you, Jake. No, no, I need to see you. I want to talk to you privately. Meet me in the parking lot of the Medical Center, please." Bronson was puzzled but admittedly curious. The urgency in her voice commanded him to respond. "Give me about ten minutes, Anna. I have to finish up something then sign out from the office."

Bronson parked his car in the east parking lot near where Anna stood waiting in the hot sun. It was already too hot for mid-day in May, near 100 degrees. The palm trees were motionless against an azure blue sky as if they were conserving their energy. Dark brown skinned children ran up and down the sidewalk in front of the Phoenix Indian Medical Center under the watchful eyes of parents or other relatives waiting for their turn in one of the clinics.

Anna waited for Bronson to exit before coming to him. Her jet black hair framed her face with the ends coming in a flip from each side of her head to her full lips. Beaded earrings hung loosely from her ears. A white bone necklace with five strands from one of the Plains tribes formed a choker around her throat. A white blouse with the first button unbuttoned accentuated her dark skin. It hung outside her clinging black skirt. From a distance she almost looked oriental.

In the brilliant sun the total effect was dazzling. It was not lost on Bronson. She was stunning and wore her grace with ease. Her beauty had troubled him before. Coming around the front of his car Bronson asked, "What brings you here to Phoenix, Anna?"

She put her right hand on his arm and looked at him directly. "I have a meeting to go to at St Luke's Hospital later this afternoon that you can take me to, Jake, but first I want to make love to you." Bronson took a step back.

"What? I don't think I heard you correctly!" he exclaimed looking about him to see if anyone heard her.

Grabbing his hands and moving closer to his car, Anna laughed. She opened the passenger side smiling wickedly. "Get in. You heard me, Jake. I want to get naked with you. Take me somewhere. Hurry!" she implored reaching over across the seat to open his door.

This had never happened to Bronson before. Befuddled, he climbed in beside her. Jake had fantasized about her before but he thought he had controlled his feelings well enough that she would never know. He had often counseled her on long distance telephone calls as she was in the midst of a divorce and wanted to avoid an abusive husband.

Jake offered, "Look, Anna. You don't have to do this just because I've been able to help you with your husband, you know."

"Don't be ridiculous and so patronizing. Start the car. My motor is running. I might just want to find out what a white man is like to sleep with. This is a beautiful day." She laughed and slammed the door.

Jake drove to central Phoenix to Encanto Park, an almost tropical paradise with lagoons, lush vegetation, date palms, white swans and paddle boats. Many lovers walked arm in arm on the pathways and over white connecting bridges oblivious of all but their surroundings.

He wanted to take Anna right there. Jake had known only one woman in his life, the one he had committed to over a decade ago in marriage. He hadn't yet touched Anna. Thoughts of recrimination were now flooding his consciousness even though he and Norma had been in counseling themselves for years and were growing slowly apart with irreconcilable differences.

Amidst the battles he had never thought of abandoning Norma. He never wanted to face that prospect. Catholic teaching and tradition told him that divorce was out of the question. It was his cross to carry, he believed.

The more he thought of his situation the more he resented it. The more he resented it the more he wanted Anna. She was right there, beside him, telling him all she wanted to do was go to bed with him, to enjoy their bodies and the day.

"I've never been here before, Jake. It's really lovely. Thank you," she paused drinking in the scene.

"Would you like to go for a walk like that couple crossing the bridge?" Jake asked.

"No," she answered quickly. "Not really. Let's find a motel. I don't want to wait another minute until we can be together."

Old resolves faded in an instant. As if it was a dream. Jake soon registered in a local motel. No sooner in the door and each stripped to begin an afternoon of delight. Satiated, they lay back on the bed. Anna spoke first. "I'm sure that in the business you are in with all your travel you must have had many women before. You were wonderful! And I feel wonderful!"

Jake laughed and looked out the window. He turned and sat on the edge of the bed to tell her a secret he hadn't told anyone.

"Up to this point I have not been unfaithful to my wife, Norma. She's accused me of that so many times I've lost count. Now I guess it doesn't make a difference, does it. To tell you the truth, I hadn't had any women before marriage or since, until now with you. Not that I haven't wanted to."

"Do you mean I am the first? Really? This is hard to believe. I feel privileged to be the first Indian woman to sleep with you. We are very much in touch with Mother Nature aren't we? But if I were a drinking woman I would go out and celebrate a toast with you. Instead, you can feed me. Now, I am hungry and don't want to be late for my meeting."

Jake leaned forward to kiss her. "Enough, Jake. You've already had your share for today." Anna slid through his spread arms to alight on her feet on the other side of the bed. "I need to get a shower. Later!"

"Are you saying there may be a later?" Jake asked as Anna moved past him out of his reach. He liked her and thrilled at the notion of this being more than a one night stand. "Perhaps. But with me being in Parker and you in Phoenix separated by 180 miles of desert we will just have to see." She closed the shower door.

Months elapsed. Jake busied himself in the tasks of his committee work that grew out of his commitment to Standing Bear's need for standards and data to guide alcoholism programs in the field. His travels took him to the states of Washington, Oregon, New Mexico, Oklahoma, and finally Rockville, Maryland to meet with tribal officials and agency representatives — but no where near Parker, Arizona. It was a very dry desert, indeed. The winds had blown hot and fast.

Jake ruminated often on the encounter recalling it in vivid detail. Their second event occurred nearly a year later in Salt Lake City. While it rekindled Jake's interest and fired his imagination for a renewed relationship, by then Anna's interests lay elsewhere with another. His recriminations began in earnest.

Jake settled into his well-worn routine of visits to his tribal contractors in three states and writing endless reports until Standing Bear required his services once again. Rockville beckoned.

CHAPTER FOUR

THE EAST BECKONS

Locklear was happy to be enroute to Nashville. The past six years had gone by in a flash. There was her first assignment at Owyhee, Nevada, one of the most remote facilities operated by the Indian Health Service. There was only one road north and one road south. The northern course led to Boise, Idaho some 140 miles to the north. At the southern end Elko, Nevada rested near the Ruby Mountains where gold mining still plundered the earth, one hundred miles distant.

Owyhee is the home of the Shoshone Indians, the hunters and gatherers of northern Nevada. In the early days, they would range far and wide in search of rabbits to provide them food and fur for warmth in the harsh cold winters. In more modern times they developed trout fishing and big game hunts for elk and deer. Hunters would fly into their small unimproved airstrip and find lodging near Mountain Home, Idaho to the north or in the last remnants of a gold mining town of Mountain City, Nevada less than ten miles to the south of Owyhee along the winding road connecting the north with the south.

As a floor nurse in this remote hospital she experienced a great challenge to her dedication. The challenge of boredom. She recalled Dr. Giroux's words at her graduation calling her and the other nurses to sacrifice for the sake of others' medical and nursing needs; that it was the highest calling a person could respond to; and their effort would not go unnoticed or unrewarded. She was ill-prepared for such remoteness. Locklear craved the stimulation she could find in the East.

While living at Schurz, itself remote enough from services and things to do, she had never visited Owyhee, a ten hour drive away to the northeast across salt flats and vast sandy stretches of road. There at least, the nearest town was twenty-five miles away and one could shop or go to a show. At Owyhee the nearest town was one hundred miles distant.

Her duties as a floor nurse were rudimentary. The Owyhee Hospital was built as a special interest of Senator Canon to appease the angry farmers and ranchers of the area surrounding Owyhee who needed medical care but who had no medical practitioners within the vicinity. The Shoshone Tribe also needed a hospital to replace the outdated cobblestone hospital that served the community for generations. Their need for medical care was a natural for coordination and cooperation until the hospital was built for the emergency services to include the whites. The Shoshones did not want them using their inpatient services. Ironically, the Shoshones also did not use it for more than an outpatient facility to support community health services. Resources and staff languished and dwindled to a trickle.

Serious medical emergencies were flown out by helicopter to Mountain Home Air Force Base to the north or to Elko General Hospital to the south. The wards of the new hospital were often empty despite color television at each bed and first-class dining facilities.

For a young attractive nurse there was little stimulation beyond going north to shop or south to gamble. Locklear did not hunt or fish unless it was for a good story in the library at Elko. Physicians and teachers in the local high school were out of bounds for dating. Only married personnel were recruited. Locklear felt unchallenged except to ward off eligible bachelors and to look for other locations to serve. At last one came.

Her second assignment brought her return to the White Mountain Apache where she spent a happy childhood before being trundled off to Schurz, Nevada where the wind seemed to blow constantly bringing sand to the nostrils and hair. At least the White Mountain Apaches had the foresight to develop the Sunrise Ski Resort where she, Reston, and Harley could play to their hearts' content in the winter snow.

Whiteriver brought her professional satisfaction. The hospital was newly built and incorporated the latest in sun-powered electrical systems. An acre of voltaic cells fed the electrical needs of the hospital. A helicopter pad was near the emergency door.

Helicopters flew trauma victims to nearby hospitals throughout the year. It was an exciting hospital to work at.

Locklear advanced from a floor nurse doing general care to a supervisor of one of the wings. The "A" wing housed alcoholics who needed intervention to interrupt their cycle of abuse. Often this required her to work with their families in the community in developing discharge plans. Her love of community health services was being nurtured. It required her continual attendance at community meetings and frequent presentations to the tribal council. It was just the background she needed for her next assignment in Nashville, Tennessee as the Chief of Community Health Nursing.

Happy as a lark Sandra received her call to report to duty with a promotion to Lieutenant Commander. She packed her Volkswagen van with all her belongings, meager as they were, and had nothing to ship. She was mobile once again and looked forward to the long trip east.

1986 was to be an auspicious year for Locklear. She was proud to wear the gold leaf in this new position. She believed her interests in home health care of the elderly were finally being recognized. Through her efforts with the elderly, Locklear hoped to demonstrate its importance in mediating other significant health problems in the vast territory covered by the area Office. All the tribes from Maine to Florida and west to the Mississippi were in her domain, including Cherokee, NC where she was born and where her mother was laid to rest.

As she drove, she reflected how Harley and Reston had grown up and served proudly in the Marine Corps in Vietnam. Harley, the more quick-tempered of the two, was fierce in battle and eagerly sought occasions to go on night patrols to harass the enemy behind the lines. Reston was the quiet one whose gaze would pierce one to the core.

More skilled than Harley in ambush and stealth, he would often be sent on solo missions to gain intelligence and destroy the Viet Cong in their lairs. Each was so effective they would team up for missions others gladly refused. When the war ended, they returned to Cherokee to marry and suffer through countless nightmares and sweats.

On her drive north to Interstate 40 through Flagstaff and east through New Mexico on to Oklahoma, Locklear replayed her conversations with Harley and Reston. Each seemed disconsolate from his experience. So much so that Locklear feared for their sanity and their wives' safety. She had prayed often to the Creator in thanksgiving for their safe return. More like gentle conversations with a loved one, Locklear petitioned the Father for them to have strength of mind to withstand their torment and to acquire peace. Life following war's end was tumultuous for them.

Her distance from them was a problem for her. They were once a close-knit family. Now she envisioned opportunities to visit them at home to be the sister and comforter. Before finding an apartment in Nashville, Locklear continued on her journey to Cherokee for a short, two-day visit. She was ill-prepared for their cynicism, bitterness and hostility to her rank. The war had driven a wedge between them. It was more like a gulf that separated them, an ideology she couldn't fathom. She was seen as part of the establishment who couldn't possibly understand their pain, even though her life was dedicated to relieving pain where possible.

Locklear returned to her room at the Holiday Inn in the center of town more distressed after each day. She quickly realized there was nothing she could do on this short visit. Harley and Reston were glad she did not stay longer. They could not tolerate her good humor after their first reunion and wished her well on her continued journey.

Locklear arrived unhappy in Nashville but quickly found an apartment and settled into her work. Locklear took every opportunity to visit Cherokee on her trips south to the Miccosukee Tribe in Florida. Harley and Reston were hospitalized several times during the year at the Indian Health Service Hospital for acute intoxication. She happened to arrive during one of these episodes and convened a meeting with the community health nurse and the hospital social worker.

Many veterans suffered from flashbacks and depression from their experiences. These led to heavy drinking and sometimes drug abuse. Through her determination, Locklear helped the hospital form a veteran's group to facilitate their adjustment to the community. Harley and Reston finally accepted her determination to help them. Their healing began.

Locklear continued her crusade over the year and established a similar group in Florida and upper New York State with the St. Regis Mohawks. Harley and Reston became roving speakers for her. It was her *entrée* into many communities as she gradually learned of other problems in the communities she visited. Her reputation as a community organizer was becoming stronger. Her skills were unquestioned by both the tribes and the administrator of the Area.

CHAPTER FIVE

GIROUX

The Eastern seaboard sweltered in the hot summer sun. Even the leaves on the trees in the cemetery to the east of the Parklawn Building bent over as if they were looking for shade, too. And it was only June. More heated months to follow until fall would be ushered in with its panoply of colors and cool days to mark the end of summer. Fall painted the maples and oaks in crimson reds and golden yellows. Evergreens would be forever green but darken for the winter months. Farmers' fields would be turned over in preparation for winter's long sleep.

Giroux had just returned from one of his frequent field trips to another area office to reflect on his findings. These trips were always fact-finding missions to help him prepare for the coming showdowns with congressional staffers.

He took his responsibility to manage the health needs of the nation's Indians seriously. He could not be faulted for that. His trips were always fast paced with endless rounds of meetings with hardly little time to relax.

This time the trip was to the Nashville Area Office where he had been well-received by the staff and tribal officials. They assembled to review with him their expenditures for the last three quarters of the fiscal year and to set priorities for the coming year in keeping with IHS' priorities.

Giroux had spent many years trying to reach this position of Director. He reflected he had played his cards right, currying the favor of tribal officials across the land, and determined the proper posture so that the Republican administration would not pass him by. Luck had been with him. He had been made the Director of the Indian Health Service. He was in his prime and he felt good.

Giroux sat at his desk reminiscing about this climb to the directorship and his most recent trip. Life had been good for him.

Yes, his dream of becoming the arbiter of what is proper health for American Indians and Alaskan Natives had been finally realized. He had replaced the esteemed Dr. Grant five years back. It wasn't easy. It is never easy to walk in the shoes or the moccasins of another, he reasoned, especially one who had gained the respect and confidence of so many tribesmen. Grant was indeed a capable administrator too, Giroux had to admit with a little envy. His record of service and accomplishments was long. His support base of tribal chairmen across the nation was solid.

While this act was difficult to follow, Giroux had long ago determined he would not walk in anyone else's shadow either. He had his own mind, his own ideas, and he would carry them out with or without the help of those who remained after Grant's departure. He would make his own stamp on the organization and would gather about him those among his followers who could be trusted to carry out his wishes. Morrison and Mathieson would remain from the old administration.

They were workhorses. He knew Morrison from his association with the American Indian Physicians Association. Charlie Mathieson was another story he couldn't quite figure out as yet. Grant had said before his departure, "You may not personally like him, Andrew. But mark my words, you will find him quite indispensable when you need someone to do, shall we say, unpleasant tasks. Invariably there will be unpleasant tasks you won't want to be associated with formally."

Grant's words remained with him to perplex him on more than one evening early in his administration, at least until a need presented itself like the one he was considering.

He reflected that the IHS had long been committed to the philosophy of supporting tribal efforts at self-determination since the Indian Health Care Improvement Act was passed in the last decade. The IHS believed those tribes that were ready to take over the delivery of health care services should do so without administrative interference. At least, this was the public picture Giroux fostered; and he was the IHS.

How could he not? The law required IHS to facilitate the smooth transition of power and control over its health delivery system to those tribes that were ready and able to deliver their own health care services. Many tribes were moving in that direction over the decade, some of them too quickly, others more cautiously because they feared abandonment of its treaty obligations by the federal government.

Giroux understood this well. In all instances he publicly supported a tribe's right to self-determination even if he knew the tribe was not prepared for the total responsibility of its own manifest destiny. It was a delicate balance to maintain loyalty to the tribes that supported him and to support the goals of the administration. These were not always identical. More often they were at variance with each other.

Suddenly these thoughts gave way to fleeting images of those individuals he encountered on the trip and then inexplicably centered on the image of one person in particular, very pleasant to the eye and very distracting to his mission.

Giroux couldn't keep the image of Sandra Locklear out of his mind. It had occurred to him that he may have seen her before at other meetings. He couldn't be sure. But he swore he had never met her before until this trip.

Even then it was such a fleeting occurrence. She was required to report on the state of the health of the senior citizens in the Nashville area. The topic was rather dull, he recalled, but she approached it with such sweet enthusiasm that Giroux found it exciting just to listen to her. Her charm was evident in broad gentle smiles but not as a display as it sometimes is with southern women who wear their gentility with affectation. He realized he was captivated by the lyrical quality of her voice. It too, both soothed and charmed him. Giroux smiled at the recollection and realized her warmth as a person was exciting him.

The feeling was palpable and intoxicating. He desired to talk with her privately and imagined a relationship unlike others he had when some women wanted to be with him on his visits to reservations. Though few in number, such one night stands ran the risk of ruining his career and his image. No; this one would be different if he could only figure out how he could accomplish it without arousing suspicion.

In the weeks since his trip to Nashville and his reverie, Giroux carefully planned how he would convince Cynthia Morgan, the Director of Nurses, to fill the Deputy position on her staff. He would not do it directly. He did not want Cynthia to tie his plan to him.

Instead, he would use Morrison. Giroux knew he knew her from Talequah, Oklahoma where they went to the same high school together. He suspected Morrison continued a more than professional relationship with her even though very much married. But it was none of his business. He didn't care; it was not important at the moment. Not unless he needed to use the information.

Morrison was a four year letterman in football and had won a full scholarship to the University of Oklahoma based on his athletic and scholastic abilities. His photographic memory enabled him to breeze through high school and pre-med with honors.

Cynthia, a year behind Morrison in school, was co-captain of the cheer leading squad, slim, attractive with long flowing auburn hair (the envy of her peers), and a little above average in scholastic ability but no match for the abilities Morrison possessed in abundance. She struggled for good marks.

Instead of developing a competitive edge, her struggles to achieve resulted in a deepening sense of insecurity and incompleteness which she took out on her companions by first drawing them into her confidence and then discarding them when they served their purpose.

She wanted to be Morrison's first love. She made sure of that. While she was popular among both girls and boys of her class, she fixed her eyes upon him and would not let any other boy venture too close. She thought they were so juvenile and beneath her dignity.

Morrison on the other hand was so handsome and smart and talented. All the other girls on the squad wanted him, too. They were rivals for his attention. Kisses with other boys were warm-ups designed for greater exploration and were invited with flirtatious behavior to make him jealous. However, when a boy would venture too far Cynthia would become instantly indignant and put the culprit down with such remarks as, "How dare you? Do you honestly think I am that kind of girl?" or more directly, "Don't you dare touch me. I'm promised to someone else," she would say to her suitors to discourage them from further pursuit.

Morrison heard about these episodes in locker room chatter and resolved in his third year of high school to date this seemingly inaccessible creature. If she was promised to someone else he had to know who his competition was. His ego was at stake. This was intolerable for a football and academic star.

Over the years their relationship intensified until Morrison was invited to the University of Oklahoma on full scholarship. It seemed to seal their fate. While Cynthia remained to complete high school, Morrison fell into the routine of study and football practice dating others along the way, far from the habit of Cynthia.

Their paths diverged until some years later when Morrison refused to go to Vietnam as a young physician in the late sixties and sought refuge as a staff doctor in one of hospitals of the Indian Health Service. Assigned to the remote hospital in Owyhee, Nevada Morrison learned that Cynthia also joined the health service and was assigned to a hospital in Ada, Oklahoma. Each kept track of the other as years passed and they rose within the system as if they were running a parallel course.

Much to their delight they found each other now assigned to the IHS Headquarters operations in Rockville, Maryland and lost no time renewing their fascination with each other. Cynthia had remained true to her idealized image of Morrison as her one true love even though narrowly escaping several trips to the altar. Morrison, on the other hand, had married another and had remained faithful to his wife, Heather, at least until now.

Giroux called Morrison into his office. "Bill, come in and have a seat. I wanted to get your thoughts about our trip to Nashville last week," he said leaning back deeply into his chair as he did when he wanted to convey the utmost interest in what someone had to say on a subject. He seemed absorbed in thought.

Morrison paused, then answered as if with a prepared statement knowing what Giroux wanted to hear. It was a typical surface response designed to allow Giroux to express his own viewpoint. "In all honesty, Andrew, I think you have some good staff down there. But they seem to be so inhibited or afraid to express their opinion when the Area Director is around. I watched him closely. I don't know if you noticed, but every time you presented your viewpoint on contract care or other budgetary matters the AD would always say he would have to pass that by his tribes."

"Confidentially," he added, " I seriously wonder if Robert has a brain in his head or can think for himself. Personnel issues are another matter, particularly with grievances. My review with their personnel officer indicated they have seven unresolved grievances at the present time that are ready to go formal.

"Even though I know Carville is required to handle their personnel matters you would think his staff at Cherokee would like to resolve their EEO complaints more informally.

"I don't know why our staff has such problems getting along. They seem to go at each other like cats and dogs. I think personnel issues are a major concern for us there. It is such an expensive thing to allow complaints to go formal and then matters are more or less taken out of our hands."

Giroux responded. "I think you may be right, Bill. Robert is a difficult bird to figure out sometimes. Personally he irritates me by deferring to the tribes on every issue. But that quality is what endears him to the tribes, you see? He won't make decisions about anything without consulting them first whether the issue is substantive or not. You have to give him credit. He's loyal to them.

"Sometimes I need swift action, Bill, but I certainly can't expect it from Nashville, right? When it comes to retirement he'll have it made. He'll probably walk out our door one day and into the tribal side the next. He's smart like a fox."

Giroux got up from his desk and moved to his couch, and, as if unsure whether he should sit, walked to the window to peer out looking toward the apartments in the distance. He then sat near Morrison at the other end of the couch.

At first uncomfortable with his movements, Morrison sat back and relaxed watching him closely and waiting for the point of the meeting. He knew Giroux had more to say than one of his usual brief commentaries about the Director of the Nashville Area Office.

Finally, Giroux looked out the window to the apartment complex partially hidden by the trees and asked, "What about some of the other people there?" He paused waiting for a response.

Not getting one right away he continued knowing Morrison would be uncertain of where his interest lay.

"I wondered what you thought about encouraging that Locklear woman, Sandra, I believe her name is, to join our nursing staff. You know we have a vacancy for the Deputy Director of the Nursing Branch. She seems to me to be bright and from what I could see quite capable. Heaven knows we desperately need a little more creativity in that office. I mean no offense, Bill, but don't you think Cynthia could use some help with the community health nursing side of the house?" Giroux tried to recover from his inadvertent criticism.

Clearing his throat, Morrison reflected a moment unsure of Giroux's question. He didn't like his description of Cynthia. Yet, he knew Giroux often meant something else while stating the obvious. He asked in return, "Oh, you mean as the Director of Community Health Nursing? She does seem intelligent enough and seems to have her act together. But I'm not sure whether she is ready for such a transition."

Morrison anticipated Giroux's next thoughts. "Isn't she the same grade level? I take it you think she should be transferred here." Waiting a moment, he continued, "I guess that to have her transferred laterally would pose no problem with Personnel since she is Indian and of the same grade as the vacant position. It would probably be a good idea to head that office so long as we don't have a problem with Cynthia."

Giroux had his answer. He suggested, "Work on that for me, Bill, won't you? I heard that Cynthia may not exactly appreciate the skills that Locklear seems to have. She does get along well with the tribes, and, frankly, Cynthia's office could use a little more diplomacy and tact in that department. I'm sorry to be so blunt, Bill."

Giroux changed topics knowing his approach may be a little too sensitive for Morrison. He talked about the upcoming weekend to divert his attention. As Morrison left the office trying to figure out how he would approach Cynthia with sharing her domain, Giroux reflected on the way Sandra looked. He wanted her on his staff but wouldn't tell Morrison his ulterior motive. Giroux had no misgivings; but Morrison need not know it was personal.

Two weeks passed. Risking Cynthia's displeasure Morrison reluctantly carried out his assignment and had to acknowledge to Cynthia it wasn't his idea. Cynthia was incensed that Giroux practically ordered Morrison to transfer Locklear to her department. She immediately viewed her as a threat and at once didn't like her. Locklear always seemed so cheerful and had a good word for everyone. This made her suspicious. "Does she want my job too?" she would ask Morrison over and over.

Cynthia was fifteen years older than Locklear and had grown cynical with time and had fought long and hard to get to her position as Chief of Nursing Services. Though he remained a sometime lover since finding himself assigned to the same office, she resented the intrusion of Morrison into the workings of her branch.

Cynthia let their past relationship color her judgment. She relented when she understood the boss wanted Locklear's transfer; and, she wanted more to be in good standing with him. Even though she fumed over the accommodation being required of her. Politics was not her *forté*. Maybe this time it would lead to bigger and better things for her, she reasoned.

Sandra Locklear was more than a little surprised to receive Cynthia Morgan's call from Rockville about relocating from Nashville. In fact, she was shocked. Aware of Cynthia's dislike for her, they did not see eye to eye on a lot of issues affecting nursing services, particularly on the community side. Sandra had become a good community organizer and garnered much Tribal support.

Cynthia, on the other hand, came from the hospital side of health care delivery and reveled in being a teacher of young doctors. But she was often abrasive and almost caustic at times. She almost turned Sandra off when she said, "I didn't know you had such influence with the director's office, Sandra." The comment was biting, filled with sarcasm and innuendo and, strangely, perhaps the comment sounded as if Cynthia was a little jealous. Locklear thought that odd and without a basis in reality.

She replied coldly, "I don't, Cynthia. I only met the man when he came to Nashville for a meeting a couple of weeks ago. The only other time I've seen him was at the Nursing conference in Oklahoma City last year in addition to being sworn in by him many, many years ago. That hardly qualifies as having influence with the Director, don't you think?"

Cynthia didn't expect the rebuke and abruptly returned to the task of convincing Locklear to take the job. Sandra mulled the idea of the transfer over in her mind quickly and welcomed it for personal reasons. It would give her a much needed boost and relief from a taxing office environment and a recently failed relationship with a young aspiring actor.

She also tired of the Area Director stopping by her office in the morning looking for a fresh cup of coffee and a dash of charm. She did not want to be his cheering section but she knew she could not just dismiss him. One had to survive; she had to learn how to play politics, too. It made little difference whether the brand was federal or tribal politics or the politics of a personal relationship with a sometime actor whose ego always seemed to demand so much from her.

While Cynthia sounded as if she could be difficult to work with, Locklear knew her relationship with her would only be an eight to five requirement. She could have her own life after that. She agreed to the transfer.

Cynthia was almost hesitant to transfer Sandra. She was jealous of her good looks and wary of her known ability to get along with just about everybody. She feared her competence may become too well noticed.

Yet, after studying the matter more closely Cynthia recognized that if Sandra worked well in her office her accomplishments may just as well enhance her career, especially if she played her cards right and did nothing to offend the Director. Besides, she reasoned, it was what he wanted. Who was she to stand in his way?

The relocation was done with the Personnel Office's blessing. No one questioned the move, especially Locklear who believed naively her talents were finally recognized and would be put to good use. She welcomed the challenge.

Within a few weeks after she relocated to Rockville, Giroux invited Locklear for coffee to convey his personal welcome to Headquarters. She thought it odd for the Director to personally welcome her in this way. But then she dismissed it as routine when he assured her he wanted to discuss his views on Community Health Nursing Services. He wished it would become more proactive in meeting community needs. He assured her, "This will be a significant opportunity for you to make such a difference in the lives of so many Indians and Natives throughout the country, Sandra."

Locklear was entranced with the notion of working for him. He was so convincing and so pleasant. She listened with rapt attention to his words. He was so right; she could make a difference. Little did she know Giroux never did anything without a reason, often not apparent to anyone, even his closest advisors.

This was an inspection visit not unlike a commanding general viewing his troops. This time it was only one troop. He wanted to know what Locklear was made of and to confirm his growing interest in her. Sandra's voice was warm and soothing, her laughter, infectious and lyrical. It invited a willing ear; and, he wanted very much for it to be his ear only.

As they sipped their coffee, Sandra was alert, charming, intelligent, and instinctively reflected on the boundaries separating them in time and space. He was an admiral; she was a lower grade officer, hoping to be promoted. But lieutenant commanders did not fraternize with admirals, no matter how charming. She asked no personal questions (she dared not) even though he did. She answered without reservation as if she was obliged to be scrupulously honest. Locklear was surprised and not a little intimidated.

Giroux was delighted in his assessment. He suspected she would not cross those boundaries that were so important to him. He needed her to respect the line between them. When coffee was done he knew she would be his next conquest.

Impressed with his knowledge and charm but confused with his directness, Sandra had no idea she was being recruited for a more private service. The immediate thought of it would have been repugnant to her. She wanted — no, needed — to believe his interest in her ideas about necessary improvements in nursing services was genuine and sprang from a shared commitment to excellence.

Truly, she found him charming yet sincere, insightful but not critical, warm and magnetic. She had seen glimpses of these traits in various national speeches he had given at conferences. She had hoped one day she would work for him directly rather than in a field office out of touch with how decisions were really made. And now, she could hardly believe it. She had her chance to make a difference. He had said so. It was what she clung to.

Oddly in her sleep that night Locklear dreamed of Giroux fending off Daniel, her ex-boyfriend, an egotistical Plains Indian who sometimes got bit parts in western movies and who recently left her for another woman. It was not easy being the other woman in her waking life. She wanted Daniel for herself only. But Daniel wanted to share his bounty with whoever turned his head.

Locklear knew Daniel was unfaithful to her (how often her friends had warned her!) but at the moment she was not strong enough to be without him. She struggled to be less dependent but Daniel made her feel she could not exist without him. She knew a break would have to be made. Her transfer to Rockville was her God-sent blow for freedom and self-reliance. She knew Daniel would never follow her.

In the dream Giroux was not the Giroux of the Indian Health Service but a more accomplished actor who wooed her away from Daniel with great finesse and charm. Daniel's verbal skills were no contest for Giroux's quick wit. While what Daniel lacked in wit was more than amply compensated for in physical charms, it was not enough for Sandra who longed for joyful conversation and intelligence in a companion.

When she awoke Sandra was inexplicably pleased with herself but laughed at her private and provocative dream. The fantasy of her being romantically linked with the Director was an absurd aberration of her first meeting. She sensed his power and was at once captivated by it and repulsed at her inability to control a mere dream. As she busied herself getting dressed for work she realized the liability of breaking up with Daniel. Other men may look more attractive than they really were.

Locklear went about her business getting settled in her new apartment near the campus of the Parklawn Building. She welcomed the ease with which she could go to work; it was an easy five minute walk. No commuting charge or parking fees to worry about. Living in a high cost area would be enough to consume her meager salary leaving her precious little for fun and excursions about the country side to indulge her historical passions. But she would have to make allowances for that somehow.

It was May, and May was beautiful in Maryland. Yellow and white daffodils, purple irises, yellow forsythia, pink and white dogwood were in bloom everywhere throughout the countryside and along the freeways. Days were more often filled with high floating white clouds and bright sunshine than in the preceding months of early spring. The dark clouds of winter had surely vanished, taking the depression winter sometimes brought.

For those in federal service the budget cycle had passed. It was now June, time to deliver service before the next cycle began with its inevitable avalanche of reports to be generated, budget exercises to be completed, and estimates to be made as to the effect of budget surpluses and deficits.

The sun sparkled with special intensity in an azure cloudless sky. Leaves on the trees in the cemetery southeast of the Parklawn Building in Rockville fluttered in constant motion with the cool breeze. Scarlet red azaleas and purple rhododendrons bloomed profusely around the Village Square Apartment buildings a stone's throw away to the south where Locklear lived.

Visitors and staff poured into the monstrous building that reminded everyone, visitors and staff alike, of a giant maze in the early hours of the morning. They appeared intoxicated with the sweet aroma of spring. Unlike the dour winter months their faces were relaxed and voices upbeat and expectant. Early morning joggers returning to the lower level where the health unit was located checked their latest times and paced in small circles and stretched to wind down slowly from their morning run.

The pace of life and work in the government offices supporting life in the District was always hectic. Workers often maintained mental alertness through jogging or walking. Around the corner by the three east entrances a flight up, stragglers gathered to have a last minute smoke. Individual rituals completed, they too went to work to their respective wings of the building. Wings A and C were on opposite ends of the building with B tucked in between.

While the Indian Health Service is a small agency in comparison to other institutes of the Department of Health and Human Services, its offices were scattered on the fourth, fifth, seventh, and eighth floors of the A wing. It would have been less confusing to have programs relocated centrally. But space was at a premium and an issue among all the tenants of the Parklawn Building. Agencies vied with each other for space assignments. As a relatively new agency, the Indian Health Service had little power to request greater convenience or accommodation.

At mid-morning in the fifth floor conference room of the A wing, Admiral Giroux convened a handful of staff to brief him on the latest status of the Anti-Drug Abuse Act of 1986 and its relationship to tribal community health programs. The passage of the Act was landmark legislation and created an air of excitement and expectation among the Health Service's staff. They were not alone. Indian tribes and Alaska Native villages likewise expected the Act to resolve many problems they seemed to be powerless over. Everyone imagined whole new systems of health care would emerge, jobs would be created, people would be able to work.

Tribes expected the Act to feed the failing economies of many reservations through the development of new youth regional treatment centers and the prioritization of other aspects of the existing health care system around alcohol and drug treatment. It was designed to finally address the Health Service's number one health priority by requiring the Service to cooperate with Tribes in facilitating their preeminent role in reducing substance abuse. It had only been seventeen years since the Health Service had declared it the nation's number one priority.

Standing Bear had worked diligently behind the scenes with the Committee to insert language in the legislation to put power into the hands of the tribes rather than in the Indian Health Service.

Privately, Giroux was mostly concerned that alcoholism activities would be getting the lion's share of the additional resources Congress made available while other viable programs like community health nursing and community health representatives, the unsung heroes and main health support of many communities, nursing activities, and other social or mental health programs would be left in the cold. It was an imbalance he wanted corrected.

He like his predecessors, wished it were otherwise. But he knew Congress considered alcoholism a hot topic and he wanted the Health Service to at least appear to be responsive to their direction even if he disagreed. And he did disagree privately among his inner circle. Giroux did not want his private opinions to be aired in public.

He recognized some agitation from the field to put detoxification facilities in hospitals. Publicly he agreed with the need. Privately he instructed Charlie to rule out any references to such facilities in budget documents that would go forward to the Office of Management and Budget. Charlie dutifully obliged and relished the opportunity to oppose Standing Bear.

Control was an issue, John Standing Bear to the contrary. Giroux expected him to agitate for more resources in addition to what the new legislation would provide. That's the name of the game in Washington; garner all the resources you can, most of all, personnel. Get people on your side. Play the political game for all it's worth.

Crisply dressed in his white uniform and looking about the small group he welcomed staff and recognized how valuable their time was. Giroux leaned onto the table with his hands folded in front of him and began, "I'm pleased and gratified that Congress has finally recognized the importance of the community in the control of alcoholism." (Standing Bear smiled recognizing the immediate truth of the statement, however, thinking silently to himself, Giroux made it for his benefit only. He was amused.)

Giroux continued. "I have long held that the secret to successful intervention in this activity lies within the tribes rather than with us in the formal health care system. You all know that. But quite frankly, I am also concerned that whatever we do to help tribes become more organized in their fight against alcoholism, we should not lose sight of other significant life style problems for which we have little resources. Suicides, homicides, depression, family violence, problems with the aged are all increasing. How are we going to address these issues? Can we somehow incorporate these concerns into the alcoholism activity?"

He added for the benefit of John Standing Bear, "We need to support John and his staff in their struggles with this tremendous problem. It is not without good reason that the tribes have such a major role to play."

Privately, Giroux was convinced much like his predecessors that most community-based alcoholism treatment programs should be left alone, out of sight, out of mind. They weren't part of the medical complex and weren't all that competent. Many of their personnel were not trained. At best, their place was on the side lines as referral resources.

Yet, he wished their resources were his. He knew what to do with them. So many of his hospitals were ill-equipped. The additional resources, millions of dollars, would go a long way toward improving them. Such resources could buy much needed support from his clinical staff. He fully expected resistance from their ranks toward improvement in alcoholism services when they felt left out of that piece of the pie.

Giroux was also feeling pressure from lengthy discussions with Standing Bear that tribes would not accept anything less than equal partnership with the medical establishment. Giroux wondered how he knew what the tribes wanted.

Standing Bear seemed to talk with authority on this issue. He gave Giroux the disquieting feeling that he knew just what the tribes would do if they didn't get all that was promised. He did not fully appreciate Standing Bear's ties into the community and was getting apprehensive over his suspected high level involvement with Senate staffers on the issues.

Giroux could not prove Standing Bear had been leaking information to Senate staffers in the preparation of the legislation but it was as if they had answers even before questions were asked. He wanted to catch him in lobbying. Perhaps he could then get this thorn out of his side once and for all. Giroux promised himself he would talk with Charlie about this. He knew Charlie was loyal and Charlie was a magician who could work miracles for him.

Locklear walked into the meeting as each of the vested interests presented their cases in a heated debate over what or whether they could commit to support the effort. She apologized for her lateness and looked about for a seat.

Dr. Howard, Chief of the Mental Health Branch, engaged Standing Bear in a reasoned approach to use the additional resources for the benefit of the many. Howard expounded that over 85 percent of the problems seen by mental health personnel in Indian country were related to alcohol abuse. In his opinion, it was time for the two branches to cooperate together in a joint plan of action with a sharing of the resources.

Standing Bear retorted that this may be true but he was committed to using the resources as they were directed in the Act specifically for certain activities, none of which were described as mental health in nature.

Giroux motioned for Cynthia who sat next to him to allow Locklear to take her seat on his immediate left. The room was small. Chairs were pushed closely together. "You haven't heard the benefit of the complete discussion, Sandra, but from your own experience as a community health nurse in the field, what do you think we should do?" Giroux asked.

Adjusting herself in the chair, Locklear acknowledged only recently reading the legislation. She hadn't formed a complete opinion but tentatively allowed, "I have seen a lot of families suffering from the effects of alcoholism. You know, the usual poverty, family violence, divorce, neglect, and so on. Much of this may be avoidable through well-planned prevention and early treatment.

"I think the emphasis on youth treatment and cooperation among all parties such as the Bureau of Indian Affairs and the Indian Health Service are points well-taken." Locklear sat back after adjusting her notepad and pens in front of her. She was not aware that others had become silent. No one had dared infer the need for cooperation by the Service with the Bureau. But the point was clearly noted in the legislation.

"Well, yes, that's true, Sandra, there is a need for all parties to talk with each other," Giroux began only to be interrupted by Standing Bear.

"Ms. Locklear is correct, Dr. Giroux. Right on, Ms. Locklear! We do need to work together with the Bureau but the tribes are the ones now with the leadership role. They are the ones who must show us the way. We must take a back seat to them,"

Standing Bear added with a slight grin much to the discomfort of Giroux.

In defense, Giroux redirected the meeting to welcome Locklear to the headquarters operations and said, "You can see why we recommended her to join our staff. Such directness may encourage us to grapple with the issues more effectively. How has this affected nursing programs in the field?" He asked directing his question to Locklear once more.

Locklear was embarrassed with the attention and began haltingly to describe her field experience in home health care. She warmed to the familiar topic and became more animated with her enthusiasm for service to the elderly and families.

Giroux nodded his agreement with a little smile only too glad that Standing Bear had been stopped. As he listened he heard every word she said; but he was more captivated by the sound of her voice. It was rich and smooth and almost melodious as it came through well-formed and rounded lips. It enkindled his earlier suppressed desire for her. Giroux found himself imagining how his tongue would feel in her mouth. Soft and liquid smooth. He was aroused.

Locklear was unaware of these stirrings of interest in her. She continued her presentation unabated. But the Admiral was now only paying cursory attention to the details she presented. She smiled more easily and was comfortable with the group. Her face was animated with interest. Coolly professional and very much in control Sandra sparkled with the apparent attention of the group. Pausing momentarily as if arrested in thought, Sandra took in a deep breath. The movement was not lost. Giroux caught it quickly out of the corner of his well-trained eye. He chuckled to himself.

Under the conference room table unknown to the others, Giroux had reached over and placed his left hand on Locklear's right leg. Locklear was momentarily shocked, withdrew her leg, took in a deep breath, uncertain of the meaning of this affront. She paused to shift her position in her chair, and continued her presentation. She soon ended her presentation, unsure what to do next.

She never expected Giroux of all people to make a move on her. He was the Director, the leader of the people. She began to consider those in the room. Perhaps Standing Bear would be capable of doing such a thing. She had heard unpleasant rumors about him before she arrived in Rockville; but he was paying no attention to her.

Or Howard perhaps? Locklear thought it highly unlikely for Howard to be so forward. Was it a mistake then? That must be it, she reasoned, sighing with her own reassurance. No one would deliberately do such a thing in a staff meeting. Least of all, the Director.

Not fully letting go of her anxiety, it at once excited and troubled her. She did not dare make a sound; it would disturb the meeting. She glanced about the room. Of course, she thought, that is what "he" counted on. She was becoming angry. If it were either Standing Bear or Howard she would feel free to tell either of them to get lost when the meeting ended.

But, Giroux — she stopped herself in mid-thought — she simply couldn't imagine the Director being so brazen. He had much to lose with a scene in his office. Yet, she would not want to embarrass him. 'No, he really didn't mean it,' she thought to herself in the hope of dismissing the idea. She was all too ready to excuse his behavior.

Her mind continued to play tricks with her. Well, she would have to confront him, she thought. That kind of behavior was so adolescent it could not be tolerated. But, again she wondered how she could confront the Director. What should she do?

Locklear thought she had much to lose too if she made an outburst. She had just arrived in Rockville and had gotten settled. This was her first small meeting in Giroux's office with other more senior staff to discuss important issues. It was upsetting and unprofessional.

The idea of the Director making a pass at her astounded her. It was becoming a recurring theme, hard to dismiss. She knew he would obviously have a personal style of his own as a leader; but she never expected this personal affront.

She quietly slipped off her shoe and tentatively moved her right foot around to find his leg. She firmly kicked his leg with her searching foot. Giroux began to summarize the meeting.

Locklear abruptly withdrew her foot, readjusted herself in her chair, and criticized herself for reacting so impulsively. It was not characteristic of her either. Gaining control of her personal feelings in relationships was so important to her especially after her recent separation from Daniel.

She felt panicked and was breathing somewhat shallowly. Or was it something else? Embarrassment? Pleasure? Like sudden delight or forbidden fruit in mid-day? Her heart beat faster with confused apprehension. The meeting continued around her, a dull buzz in her ears. She remained lost in thought and apprehensive. She was completely oblivious of the remainder of the discussion. The people in the room appeared as if in a mist.

Locklear wanted to bolt from the room, worried that he would think she was available for more ... and feared the worst. She fought for control, gathered her papers and closed her book neatly.

The clock seemed to be moving so slowly with each tick feeling as if it lasted a minute. Mercifully, five minutes later Giroux glanced at his watch. He feigned an important appointment to prepare for and dismissed the group giving his appreciation for their time and suggestions.

Locklear fumbled with her papers and looked for her shoe as the others arose to leave. As they moved about her to exit, Giroux said sharply to Locklear, "Sandra, I want you to remain a moment longer."

Cynthia thought to herself, 'I hope he reads the riot act to her. She really embarrassed him with allowing Standing Bear to make his remarks.' She turned as said, "Sandra, dear, please come into my office too when you are through. Thank you." She was becoming fearful. Giroux sounded so stern. Then as most were standing and preparing to walk past, Giroux said in a more conciliatory tone, "There is a point I wish to discuss further with you, Sandra."

She gulped thinking to herself. 'Oh, my God. What do I do now?' Giroux wanted her and knew she would not leave without giving him the time he demanded. His voice was commanding and compelling. She dared not leave. As a young commissioned officer and nurse she could not refuse the Director his request.

Sandra smiled weakly, rising blood pressure making her temples pulsate strongly. She agreed to remain as he directed, more panicked now than ever before and not quite sure of the point he referred to. She hoped he merely wanted to talk about what happened at the meeting. It too would give her an opportunity to tell him more kindly that she didn't want his attention.

As the one nearest the door she stepped back closer to him to allow the others to pass. Their arms brushed against each other with electricity. His thoughts were of her warmth and how her body would feel next to his; hers were of uncertainty and insecurity. Sandra felt flush and momentarily confused. She wondered if she should excuse herself, but before she answered herself, Giroux interrupted.

"Hold my calls for a minute, Jane, while I talk with Ms. Locklear, would you please?" he asked his secretary, Jane Candelaria, over Locklear's shoulder. Dutifully she did.

As Jane returned to her work her sixth sense was already at work too recalling other incidents like this involving her friend, Janet. Jane was concerned to think of Sandra as another victim. Her sudden suspicions shocked her. Sandra was so pleasant and always had a smile for her and treated her with respect.

Jane corrected herself. She thought her suspicions sounded too much like an indictment. Perhaps she was being too hasty in condemning Giroux. After all, he may really only want to talk with her about the meeting. Feeling more relieved she convinced herself to return to work in earnest. She buried her head in her papers.

Giroux quietly closed the door behind him, panic and uncertainty arising in Locklear as he did so, turned to Sandra and embraced her without further comment. Not a word! He encircled her waist with his arms, and with parted lips kissed her. No discussion. No lead in. His move surprised her — even shocked her despite her premonition of his more than academic interest she sensed from having coffee with him before.

Locklear tried to push him away but felt caught. His gesture was designed to fulfill two purposes. Giroux wanted her to know he had authority to do what he wished and that he would use it whenever he wished; and, he wanted her to know he wanted her to be his lover.

Without an attachment now for several months, Sandra was vulnerable. "Please... No... Please, I don't want..." she uttered unsure of the meaning of this mixed signal and looking away from his intense gaze. The immediate shock of it all threw judgment aside for the moment. "I can't," she said weakly looking away trying not to look into his eyes. They were compelling.

She knew instantly what was on his mind. She felt the pressure of his insistence. He didn't have to say a word; and, he wasn't listening to anyone but himself.

At an opportune moment Sandra pulled back to telegraph her refusal but he quickly pulled her closer to him without further protest, feeling her temples pulsate with his contact, and her nipples harden with the pressure of his medals on her chest. She felt herself embracing him in return, despite her resistance, with a deep sigh as if it weren't she doing this. As if outside her body she could see herself slowly relaxing her inhibitions even though against her will. She reflected silently, "These kinds of episodes only happen in the movies. What is happening to me?"

Control and reserve were vanishing. What was control, she reflected, but an unyielding master? Locklear prided herself in knowing how to handle difficult situations. However, she had never been accosted by an employer before. Anger was displaced by growing confusion. "How can I stop him?"

As if outside herself, she watched herself let go of apprehension and inhibition for the moment despite a struggle against this impulse and melted into his embrace. 'Am I really doing this?' she asked herself. She hardly believed she was in the arms of the Director. She felt him harden against her and was embarrassed.

Perhaps if it were someone else doing this it would be different. Ever so slowly he released her until his hands cupped her breasts. He held her for an instant savoring her fullness. She looked at his offending hand as if it had a mind of its own. "Oh, my God," she said silently.

Looking into her now watery eyes he said, "I have been very aware of you, Sandra. I'm so glad you decided to be part of my team and took the assignment here. I know you could have refused. But here you are. I admire your qualities and professionalism," he said pausing to touch her breast once more as if it were now his possession. "And I know I can count on your discretion, right? I want to see you again."

Sandra's head ached. She feigned a smile but was overwhelmed and frightened of his hollow offer. The Admiral was direct and forceful; going to bed with him was a command. She couldn't deny the meaning.

Giroux had done his research into her background. Charlie had seen to that. He knew she didn't have a lover and suspected the relationship with the actor would not fulfill her needs. Sandra stood before him flush and breathing shallowly. He had made an impact upon her. Just the impact he wanted, but not the one she wished.

Locklear felt panicked by his forcing himself on her. She didn't like force. It was alien to her. She now wondered how she could have been so easy; this was not her style. She pondered; should she have slapped him? Could she have done that? She knew she couldn't. It, too, was force.

Shouldn't she have told him he was making a mistake? That she didn't really want this? The words almost formed on her lips just now but she held back. If she had said something, she reasoned, she envisioned being shipped out to cold Alaska or some other godawful place.

Locklear reflected momentarily, smiled weakly, and without further hesitation quietly protested almost as much from her hunger for companionship as it was from confusion with a small hint of courage, "I'm... I'm... I'm not just available whenever you want me, Sir. I don't want a relationship." She couldn't look directly at him fearing the worst. He was a national leader, but...

Giroux embraced her again sensing acquiescence. He stepped to the side and allowed his beginning erection to subside before he opened the door to let her out. Sandra avoided looking into his eyes. On her leaving he said, "Of course not. But thanks, Sandra, for telling me how you feel. I understand." He smiled and whispered, "Just be ready for my call anyway."

Giroux already knew how vulnerable she was and anticipated her need. He took pride in his ability to intuitively grasp a woman's vulnerability.

Locklear departed flush with his attention without saying anything to Jane as she passed her desk. Was this a game for him? Neither his demeanor nor hers betrayed the game, if it were. Each prided himself on the ability to look and act professional at all times. The situation required adherence to rules she thought.

But what rules? Whose rules? None were stated. Suddenly the impact of this meeting was felt. It was an irrelevant disguise or charade, an elaborate put-on to allow him to test his effect on her. Sandra was angry at him for this but more so at herself for so easily giving up her control as she walked out the glass doors of the suite down the hall to the restroom.

Jane peered over her reading glasses to watch Sandra walk down the hallway with her head bent to avoid looking at others. She sensed something was wrong. Janet, her friend, flashed into her mind. Yet, she didn't like herself for being suspicious; and suspicious she was.

Jane swallowed hard and listened to herself. She immediately told herself she wasn't a rescuer, and it was really none of her business if Giroux made a pass at Sandra. How lovely Locklear was and pleasant — pity. 'I can't get involved,' she said almost audibly as if to put a check on her increasing concern. Jane busied herself with her tasks to avoid further thinking.

Giroux settled to his desk, chuckled to himself, and put aside several papers arranged for his review and signature unaware of Jane's surreptitious glances. He arose again and went to his bank of windows to admire the day and his handiwork. It was more beautiful than before. He was proud of his snare. Sandra felt good in his arms. Her lips trembled with a hint of promise.

Giroux knew Locklear could have reacted violently and made a scene. She could have told him to get lost. But she didn't. She only said she was not available. Many women say that while meaning if you want me, you will have to work for it, he thought.

Pleased with Sandra's response and his manipulation Giroux began calculating how and when he would make his next move to have her fully — and to dispense with his current dalliance. It was easier than he thought it would be.

Not knowing fully that she had just been manipulated into becoming Giroux's next affair, Sandra glided down the hallway and stepped into the nearest restroom, her temples still pounding. Relieved of her tension, she stood before the mirror adjusting her makeup and straightening her blouse to her uniform. Pleased she was put back together, she paused to comb her hair and felt her stomach beginning to flip flop. She blurted out loud, "What is he doing? What is he thinking? He must be crazy! How dare he?"

She turned about suddenly, mindful that this was a public restroom. She looked to see if the stalls were empty. They were. "Thank God!" she exclaimed. Her panic returned as she found herself considering his statement, 'Just be ready for my call anyway.'

She stared moments longer into the mirror. She was flush with excitement and confusion. "Oh, my God! What is he saying? Sure he's intelligent and charming. But how dare he do this to me? I'll have to play this very carefully. I can't call him. I won't. That's what he wants. I can't. I won't give in to him."

Certain that he wanted her, Sandra questioned her immediate reaction. How could she say, 'no' or even, 'hell no.' He was the Director. Sandra returned in a daze to her office forgetting Cynthia's demand for her to see her, too. She shut her door to await his call thinking it would come at any moment. With the safety of the telephone between them she hoped she could tell him calmly and rationally that this would be a mistake for both of them.

It was true she was hungry for companionship. She had to admit her own needs. She hated Giroux's forceful approach. It reminded her of the family violence she had seen on various reservations and she hated it in all its forms. She reasoned loving someone should not require force.

Sandra hadn't had a lover in so long. Her body ached for the pleasant release of sex, but "force" was another issue. Its very thought repulsed her. Psychological pressure was force of another nature, wasn't it? Even the aphrodisiac, power, could be force. Giroux undoubtedly had a certain command presence. She observed that when people were in Giroux's presence they paid attention to his every word. She was no exception.

Locklear sat there immobilized. Cynthia knocked on her door, let herself into the office and began her monologue on proper behavior in the presence of the Director; what to say, what to avoid; her expectations for perfect support of the Director, etc. etc. etc. She let herself out satisfied that Sandra had paid utmost attention to her.

Sandra was in a fog; Cynthia's visit was a blur. The end of the day came and went. His expected call didn't materialize. Somewhat relieved, Sandra thought, 'Oh, well, he probably got tied up with something else. Thank God!'

Sandra collected herself, her purse, and her wits about her and departed down the back stairwell past the freight elevator and slower passenger elevators, glided out the back door of the Parklawn Building, skimmed across the driveway and west to the parking lot of Best Buy's Store and through the opening in the wire fence. It was an easy five minute walk from the office to her apartment. She didn't recall her feet moving across the pavement or the chill in the wind presaging a summer storm.

That evening the events of the day were replayed again and again and again with minor variations. She was participant, witness, and critic in the play. She added to the scenario the coffee in his office on her first arrival. It was obvious now it was not coffee he had on his mind, she concluded. Giroux was sizing her up.

By midnight all the variations she imagined had been replayed numerous times. But it didn't fit well. She acknowledged she was attracted to him. But how could she go to work knowing he was down the hallway and she couldn't carry on a decent human conversation with him. If he wanted a relationship, surely talking would be part of it. How could he put her in this predicament?

Did he even want one? She could not tell. She wanted desperately to straighten this mess out but she couldn't bring herself to call him. It would mean she would have to acknowledge his desire.

Giroux was the Director of the Indian Health Service and an Admiral. He could have any woman he wanted, she reasoned. Glamour attended the position. Power attracts. 'Why me though?' she asked herself as she became sleepy with all the nuances. It was becoming more troubling than it was worth. She tossed and turned throughout the nearly sleepless night.

For nearly two months their paths never crossed even so much as in the hallway. Little did she know he wanted it that way to keep her off balance. This puzzled her; but she never called Giroux's office to find out why to fulfill her promise to herself. It was strange. She knew better than to put herself or him in jeopardy. Yet, she was curious about the silence. 'Did he finally get the message?' she asked herself, relieved.

She eagerly dived into her work. Her assignments carried her north and west with welcome relief to become familiar with her new field staff in Billings, Montana, Aberdeen, South Dakota, Portland, Oregon and Anchorage, Alaska.

The work was demanding and allowed little time for herself to reflect on the episode. She loved her assignment and the respite from worry it afforded. So many programs to review and communities to visit. It would keep her mind busy and away from her current dilemma or what she feared may be in store for her. She began to worry and to be relieved at the same time. Did he change his mind? What had she done? Should she have said she was unavailable? Will she be transferred? She was tempted to call him to explain to him her feelings (he owed her that much!) or to ward him off in his pursuit. She held the telephone receiver in her hands several times only to put it down again in shame.

She wanted to call back her words to explain she had just gotten settled and that she had just ended a relationship, and it was too early to think of anyone else, and the hundreds of things that crossed her mind to tell him. But her words were out there hanging and she feared they implied there would be a time she would welcome a relationship.

Sandra was pleased that the Director was traveling to other stations. It relieved her to know she would not encounter him soon. Andrew's travels were west and south to meet his many speaking engagements. He was a gifted speaker and in demand in many places. He also had an ulterior motive to be away from Rockville.

Andrew spent the first of the two months setting in motion his plan to replace Janet with Sandra. A contracting officer, Janet was becoming annoying of late. In the beginning of his six month's fascination with her, Andrew talked about the need for discretion — no demands save the fulfillment of desire for simple pleasure when he needed it, no telephone calls or slips in conversation. Above all, he could not be compromised in his position. He felt Janet was slipping in her ability to play the game.

Janet, of course, agreed to his rules in the beginning of their affair. What woman wouldn't agree to an affair with the Admiral. They all do. Jane suspected but would never talk. She feared for her job; and Giroux was good to her.

But in the last month of their affair, Giroux felt Janet was becoming too familiar and was beginning to breach his canons of behavior in affairs. She felt close to him and a little possessive. Sure in her mind that her sex was enough to convince him to leave his wife, she began to pressure Jane to allow her to talk with him citing "problems with the Inter-tribal Council" or "inter-agency agreements" or other equally lame excuses.

Jane would never comment out of her loyalty to Andrew even though she was troubled with her suspicions of his infidelity to his wife, Elizabeth.

At first, Andrew tolerated her need to see him and to steal a kiss or touch in the office. It excited each of them. Yet, he was becoming increasingly uncomfortable and knew he had to change women and find someone who would respect his wishes.

Sensing alarm, Andrew brought Charlie Mathieson into his office and into his confidence. Charlie often did his bidding now on delicate matters. He was devious and knew how to use his power selectively.

"Charlie, close the door behind you would you please?" Andrew asked. "We have something to discuss privately." Charlie knew the signal. It wasn't the first time Giroux had signaled that his vast experience was sorely needed.

"I have something for you to use your coyote ways on for me, Charlie. It's a little delicate, and I want you to feel free to say no to me, of course. I'll understand. Would you like some coffee?"

Charlie sank into the Director's leather sofa as he had done on other occasions demanding delicate treatment. He enjoyed the sense of power it gave him to run interference for the Director. Andrew needed him and he knew it. As the Budget Director, Charlie wielded immense power and control over most departments and could scuttle any Associate Director's plans in the twinkling of an eye.

His knowledge of legislative and budgetary processes was legendary and greater than any Director's. It was even better than the legal staff's knowledge. Before they would render any legal opinion about the effect of a law they would call Charlie for his viewpoint and advice.

Charlie could facilitate or retard the growth of any program. He had no qualms about using his knowledge and skill. Charlie saved Giroux and Grant before him on several occasions from embarrassment with the Senate Select Committee on Indian Affairs. His support for the Director, though, was personal. He genuinely liked Andrew and enjoyed their "chats" together. This would be another he could get off on. Andrew immediately called into question Janet's "increasing demonstration of poor judgment," "her lack of political sophistication," and "her dependence."

Charlie easily guessed she was getting to Giroux and asked, "What is it with this woman, Andrew? I sense that something else is the problem. Although so far you haven't told me anything that couldn't be used to describe half the staff you have working for you here and probably half the field staff as well. There's more to it, isn't there?"

Giroux adjusted his position in his chair to look Charlie directly in the eye. He said laughingly, "I am a little embarrassed to tell you this, Charlie, but if it gets out of this room your ass will be in a sling along with mine. I hit on her a couple of times. Now she is making demands on me, and I need her transferred somewhere. I know you can do it without too much of a hassle. You get the picture? Will you take care of this for me, please?" Feigning embarrassment Giroux looked away.

Snickering, Charlie replied, "Well, Boss, as one coyote to another, you don't have a thing to worry about." He cackled some more. "Let me take care of the bitch for you. Consider her as good as gone. It may take a little while to set things up, but, believe me, she will be packing!"

Charlie was in good humor and laughed some more as he recognized the difficult position Giroux was in. This assignment was something he could get off on, screwing the bitch who was screwing the Boss. It was a pleasant irony, a task he felt uniquely qualified to perform.

Giroux relaxed and out of a sense of fairness said, "I know I can count on you, Charlie, but please find her a good position. Maybe a promotion, too. I don't care where it is. Confidentially, she was one helluva lay. You didn't hear me say that, of course." He too laughed at the prospect of satisfying his concern for his safety while still giving Janet something for her trouble. It was the least he could do.

"Of course not, " he assured Giroux.

In the ensuing weeks word soon reached him that various innuendoes surfaced about Janet's competence from Personnel, Budget, and Finance. He knew Charlie was working hard. The evidence was in. Exactly what the doctor ordered he thought. Repeated suggestions were made to her to consider moving to a less stressful office environment in a field location. Maybe a Chief's position with a grade increase. She would find Personnel very helpful.

Reduced frequently to tears and not knowing what was happening so suddenly with the collapse of the world around her, Janet took the advice and relocated the second month after her going away party in which Admiral Giroux praised her for her considerable skills which could be put to good use in her new assignment.

It was the most aseptic comment she ever heard about anyone coming from him. It was sterile and unfeeling and most apropos, she thought, coming from a doctor. Janet received the usual plaque, a pair of turquoise earrings, and other valuable gifts but left the office empty in heart. She later surmised correctly that he simply had no further use for her and was sending her away. Out of sight, out of mind.

As her hurt subsided, her anger mounted. "That bastard! He didn't feel anything! I wonder if he ever had any feelings for me?" she asked herself. "That creep! I'll have to do something about this. He just can't get away with it."

Not knowing what she would do or how she would get even, Janet stewed and moved to Paradise Valley in north Phoenix locating herself at the Anasazi Townhouses within walking distance of the Paradise Valley Shopping Center. She was bitter but indulgent and found solace in her sumptuous surroundings.

Satisfied he accomplished his need for safety and that Janet was safely out of the picture so he would not have to see her daily, Giroux resumed his intention of having Sandra become his mistress. One Friday afternoon early in August the telephone rang at Sandra's desk. The day was hot, but the humidity was not as oppressive as it can be in Maryland in August.

Sandra was preparing to leave for the day with her work accomplished. She felt satisfied the week had gone well and relished the coming weekend off, free from the stresses of work. She looked forward to an excursion to Annapolis, Maryland to see the ivy-covered colonial homes, the early colonial legislature, and to take a walk around the campus of the U.S. Naval Academy. She wanted to sample the seafood of the area as well. It was a weekend to experience history.

Early American history was a passion of hers. So far, despite a hectic travel schedule, Sandra managed to take weekends such as this for other excursions to Jamestown and Williamsburg, Virginia.

She was enthralled with the re-creation of the early English settlements at Jamestown, the Colonial Assembly hall and the ivy-covered William and Mary College in Williamsburg. Visiting Annapolis too would give her an added note to her growing knowledge and appreciation of early America. She wanted to know more about life then to give her some idea of what her ancestors might have seen. It was only an hour's drive away.

But it was not to be this weekend. The telephone rang insistently. Sandra was tempted not to answer it. She stared at the instrument in exasperation knowing from long experience that calls late in the day only delayed her exit.

Someone usually needed something. She wanted to be home relaxing with an ice tea or something stronger. Irritated and tired she answered it haltingly. Her service commitment sometimes made her feel guilty. Yet she knew she was not the only one who stayed late in the evenings. Many were committed to service like her. At least she thought she was in good company; and just, perhaps, she was really needed.

Giroux spoke softly, almost pleadingly. "Sandra, this is Andrew. May I talk with you a moment? It has been such a long time."

Sandra gulped, looked wildly about the office and out the window to see if anyone was watching her from another window or desk, and cupped her hand over the receiver as if to talk without anyone seeing her mouth move. She had dismissed Giroux's attention to the far reaches of her mind and had grown comfortable with herself once more. Out of sight, out of mind. The episode in his office was best forgotten. And now, he was on the phone. She hesitated for a moment then attempted to be pleasant.

"Well, this is a surprise! (I know it must be!) How are you? (Fine.) I had given up on you. I mean... I thought you must have changed your mind, that you must have agreed with me, it was a bad idea," she intoned with a sudden surge of vibrancy, then shook her head in amazement at her tone of voice. She really didn't want to be cordial. It was a matter of habit.

She sat down, crossed her right leg over her left. She watched her foot sway back and forth rhythmically in dreadful anticipation of his conversation. She put her leg down and sat erect. She thought she had worked this impossible situation out and was a little disappointed with herself at how easily she accommodated her tone to his.

As if speaking more objectively to a colleague with whom he wanted an appointment, Andrew said, "Well, I'm sure you were relieved. But that's okay. I plan to come into the office tomorrow morning to clear some paperwork from my desk. I'll finish by ten. Will you be home at ten-thirty?" he asked expectantly.

"What do you have in mind, Sir? No! I had planned to do some shopping tomorrow and then go on a trip to Annapolis. (Without letting him interrupt she continued with mounting courage.) Dr. Giroux, I'm not so sure this is a good idea. I think we really do need to talk about this, but yes, I guess I can be ready for you and plan a light lunch so we can talk about it at my place. I'm not so sure about this. I guess we can talk more privately there."

Sandra sat there shaking her head in disbelief at what she allowed. She was perplexed with a multitude of feelings flying about within her. All the feelings of confusion, anxiety, pleasure, and anger surfaced again. She only caught snatches of his further conversation.

"Certainly, if you don't mind postponing your trip to Annapolis. I think it is a good idea. I look forward to ah ... lunch," Andrew said as if he had just chosen from a menu ignoring for the time being the hint at rejection. "I'm not sure how much time I'll have for a long ah ... lunch or a long conversation for that matter. I do have another afternoon commitment and have to meet someone in the early afternoon."

Momentarily puzzled, Sandra asked testily, "Oh. Do you even know where I live?"

Giroux replied warmly, "Yes, indeed, thanks. I've watched you go home from my window several times. Don't you remember, when you first came here you invited me for an open house? It is 12510 Village Square Apartments, isn't it? Number 401?"

"Yes. Oh, how silly of me. I forgot you were here once. How thoughtless of me. Ten-thirty then?" Sandra held the telephone for a moment longer, as if in a trance, then hung up. Puzzled, she smiled and chastised herself again. "What do I do now!" she exclaimed in amazement, still surprised that he remembered where she lived and could answer without a moment's hesitation. She wondered if he had planned this for some time.

Sandra cleared her desk once more preoccupied with her inability to firmly tell Giroux that it was not a good idea and that she wanted no part in this affair, yet she could not confront him. She didn't know why not. She had other opportunities in the past to tell doctors she was not interested. It was not difficult then. Why now? She and they had only to endure brief moments of awkwardness or even anger. Each lived through them and got on with their lives.

Giroux was somehow different. So was she. A little older but wiser? Sandra was alarmed at her question. Was it wise to even agree to allow Giroux to come over to talk about his interest in her? Would he be reasonable, have lunch, and go about his business? After all he said he had another commitment.

Sandra went down the back stairwell as usual and out the back door walking briskly across the parking lot to her apartment building uncomfortably mindful of Giroux's comment, 'I've watched you go home several times from my window.' Was he watching her now? She dared not turn around to look. She felt as if his eyes were upon her seeing through her clothes as she walked.

That evening she tidied up her apartment and changed her sheets. She had a strong feeling Giroux would not let it rest. Her only company that night would be her solitude and sense of foreboding. The contrast with the specter of sudden pleasure mixed with unease was intoxicating.

Sandra showered and dropped the plastic bottle of shampoo as she reached with her eyes closed to replace it on her shower caddie. 'Clumsy!' she expressed surprise at not having a better grip on it. Was it an omen? Should she 'come clean' and confess to him she is not ready for an affair? After all, how difficult could that be?

Sandra pondered her position as an officer so much lower in rank than him several times as she lay in her bed after her shower. She also recalled Andrew's firm embrace and his wet kiss of a few months before as she did many times since. Her resolve waned. Sleepily, the more she tried to resist the more her mind turned over and over again the image of his hands touching her breasts and the feel of his growing erection against her belly. Her hands wandered where her thoughts went. As she pondered these delicious images in exhaustion Sandra drifted off to a fitful sleep in anticipation of an onerous morning.

She protested to herself she was not looking forward to the 'appointment' but, in truth, she wondered what it would be like to be the lover of a national leader. She believed he must have felt she was special. Or was he toying with her?

It was a long time since she felt special, she had to admit. She longed to be held, to be caressed, to have the arms of a man around her, consuming her with his passion. She quickly put aside her thoughts of being pressured in anticipation of being a woman once again. But would he? Do I really want him to do it?

Ugly images of being pressured welled up to disturb her sleep. She awoke. She knew deeply within her that Andrew just wanted sex and nothing more. Could she live with that? Did *she* want more? Laboriously arguing with herself if she had to submit she convinced herself that was all right with her, fretting that she had little choice in the matter. She would give him whatever he wanted just to get it over with. In the giving, she would also be getting. She consoled herself.

When they first met, Sandra considered Andrew intelligent and so caring (wasn't he really, despite the pressure?) He was a leader she admired, even though she had qualms about the way he had approached her. He didn't allow her any escape. When she thought back on the first episode in his office, he even blocked the way out the door. Yet, she had to admit she was flattered to have his attention especially since she was a lower grade officer.

Most of the men she met in IHS failed to meet her criteria for a relationship. ('Were they having one?' she asked herself.) They were either alcoholic, or poor conversationalists, or womanizers or incapable of a mature man-to-woman relationship; they represented poor risks. She so wanted a relationship with someone who was safe. ('Was he safe? He couldn't be a womanizer, could he?' she wondered.)

She desperately needed to feel safe but felt pressured to give in to Giroux. He could have approached her differently, elsewhere perhaps, and not that way in his office. She resented his display of power.

But indeed he was not to be resisted. Giroux could make or break anyone's career. This thought sent shivers up her spine. She didn't want to think of him as ruthless or vindictive. He didn't present this first impression. He couldn't be if he wanted her. Sandra then relegated those uncomfortable thoughts to the far reaches of her mind in an attempt to give herself some peace.

If he insisted on having an affair she determined she would make no demands on him. She was professional and discriminating at work and in her personal life. Sandra's mind kept up its incessant barrage jumping to conclusions.

She certainly did not want or need a husband or marriage — just a sex partner she could have fun with if it came down to that. And that was a big *if*. Sandra concluded such an affair would be a bargain for each of them — as easily ended as begun. If he tired of her or she tired of him he could walk away as easily as she, after all, he was the one who started this. With that argument ended she finally dropped off to sleep, unconsoled.

The remainder of the night passed all too quickly. She didn't feel entirely rested. Having finished her morning shower, drying her hair, and applying light makeup, Sandra fixed her shoulder length hair in a neat flip the ends of which curled outward to her perfectly formed lips framing her delicate and blemish free face.

She applied a light red lipstick to her generous lips and splashed Wind Song perfume behind her ears, at the nape of her neck, between her firm well-matched breasts, wrists and behind her knees. Not neglecting her pubic region she said to herself, 'Let's get it over with.'

If she had no choice, she thought, she would make the best of it. Chances are it would be a one time thing. The Wind Song fragrance filled the morning air coming through the open dining room window. Her white cotton blouse, the last two buttons unbuttoned, revealed no brassier. She needed none. Running made her fit. Over her hips she threw a comfortable cotton print skirt. Nothing elaborate to enhance the moment. Underneath Sandra wore no panties to encumber her.

She wondered how it would go. What would he do first? Would he say anything? Bring flowers? Or a gift? Should she say anything? Sandra felt awkward and panicked, almost as if she wanted to run but couldn't. Her feet seemed glued to the floor. She looked at them strangely and took in a deep breath.

It was an odd feeling ... to be attracted and repulsed at the same time, a sure sign of danger. Suddenly she told herself, 'Get a hold of yourself, woman. You can't go through with this! What if word gets out? What would people think? What would Mom and Pop say if they found out? She went to her dresser drawer to retrieve some panties saying to herself, 'I'm not going to give him anything.'

Her reflections ceased with the sound of his greeting someone at the entrance. 'Oh, my God! He's here!' she exclaimed to herself. At ten-twenty-five Sandra heard his footsteps ascending the stairwell and coming down the hallway. He walked lightly but with purpose. She sat nervously in the kitchen. The doorbell rang precisely at ten-thirty. Giroux prided himself on his punctuality.

Shaking nervously she opened the door to her flat and smiled. Smiling in return, Giroux said nothing but closed the door behind him quickly so as not to linger or allow anyone else a further glimpse of her visitor.

He was equally casually dressed and looked handsome and more rugged than in the office environment with his pullover shirt unbuttoned to give a peak at his chest hairs. He wore khaki Dockers with an elastic waistband and sandals on his feet and a small gold herringbone necklace. How odd she thought. He looked so different out of uniform especially with his shirt unbuttoned. One would never have thought he would look so ... so human. Not unattractive.

She began to greet him, but, as on the first time in the office, Giroux did not allow her to talk but embraced Sandra firmly and pulled her into him, and tentatively explored her parted and astonished lips with his eager tongue.

Sandra reacted impulsively, her determination to talk this thing out vanished. Putting aside her uncertainty she pulled his face into hers reaching behind his neck with both hands. Her insertion of her tongue was not so tentative as his. She explored his mouth and neck sending ripples of pleasure down his spine.

He returned the favor and explored more fully her lips, cheeks and neck and spied her open cleavage and bedroom door with downturned linen almost simultaneously. Without a word he guided her to the side of the bed breathing more heavily. The excitement of the conquest consumed him.

Giroux unbuttoned the rest of her blouse parting it with his head now to her heaving chest. The blouse fell to the floor in a heap revealing her hardened nipples. He admired the symmetry of her conical upturned breasts, gently fondled them, and removed her skirt bringing his left hand to mingle with her pubic hair. Sandra sighed and inhaled deeply with the rush of instant pleasure at his massage.

Reaching up she pulled his shirt over his head and arms letting it fall in a heap with hers. Her hands explored his chest from nipple to nipple and her nostrils flared with his scent of musk. Sandra moved her right hand lightly down the center of his chest to his belly reveling in the feel of his hair moving through her gentle fingers.

She then lowered his pants and admired the fullness hidden by his briefs. She pulled them down too with one stroke and he was free. Sitting on the edge of the bed Sandra continued to move her hand and fingers now through his pubic hair to cup his balls in her left hand while raising his penis with her right. He began to respond to her. Sandra put aside for the moment Giroux was the Director. Now he was a man just like any other, subject to his own naked truth.

"Ooh! How impressive!" she lied, feeling as if she had to compliment him. He would have expected it. Now reclining on

Aversion To Honor

her bed she moved to the center beckoning him to join her. "Come lay down beside me." She patted the bed.

Giroux smiled, leaned over to lay on his back beside her. He was impressed with her directness. She moved closer with her right arm over his chest so her breasts touched his. Her left hand soothed his head. She moved her hips in closer so her belly touched his thigh with small rhythmic movements. Her right leg crossed his.

But something was wrong. Sandra couldn't quite divine the nature of it. His sudden lack of enthusiasm worried her. Was he being coy? Perhaps she was too aggressive. He turned to face her. She stopped and rested on her left arm slightly raised above him to allow her to look at him attentively.

Giroux loved center stage. He said finally, "I'm sorry, but I need to set some ground rules, Sandra. Please allow me. In my work I have a lot of pressures on me, many not of my choosing." He cleared his throat for effect. She knew to listen.

"People are always making demands on me — staff, agency people, congressmen, their staffs, tribal folk. My time is not my own. I have to get away from it some times to refocus my energy to be the leader people expect of me. I'm sure you understand." He looked away from her for a moment awaiting her comment.

His prepared speech at an end, Giroux paused to see her reaction. There was none. She knew he was saying this for her benefit. Flustered, he cleared his throat once more and continued not immediately sure of the meaning of her silence. "I value our relationship, Sandra. I want it to last. But if there is anything that will destroy it, it is demand. You can't demand anything of me. I don't know if you can understand and accept this, but I have to know now I can count on you being there for me whenever I have to get away. Our relationship must be as simple as that. No complications, no fanfare. None. Just sex. Agreed?"

Sandra could hardly believe what she had just heard ("our relationship"), a man who wanted a relationship but who set limits to it before it even began. She rested her head on his chest once again trying to control her growing exasperation and looked into his eyes. She squeezed him and said softly, "I know, Andrew, believe me. May I call you Andrew? I understand fully what you intend. You don't have to say anything. I think I knew the first time you kissed me that way in the office."

She laughed haughtily and then added for her benefit, "Remember, you started this affair. We can stop now before any harm is done. And perhaps we should. But since you have a rule it is only fair I should tell you mine. I can walk as well as you." She paused waiting for his acknowledgment. She felt she was lectured and wanted to put the affair into perspective. It was an affair initiated by fiat. She knew she had little choice in the matter and wanted to protect herself.

Caught by surprise Giroux thought for a moment. "You're right. I apologize. I guess I was just reacting to something in the office. It was not fair of me, I suppose."

"Let's talk about it, Andrew. You won't be able to enjoy me whenever we get together until we clarify where we are. You know that as well as I do. One must be free to enjoy sex," Sandra added. "If you are hung up then you won't enjoy me or yourself. I suspect that is why you started this." She emphasized her remark to let him know she knew her place in the union. It was his turn to be lectured. Moments passed in silence.

Giroux and she understood their relationship would be sexual and wholly subject to his call. Although she didn't like it. No feelings other than respect for this most elemental of all contracts could enter into the picture. If feelings entered into the picture the picture itself would have to change. Sandra knew it instinctively. Her observations of the night before were confirmed. She would be for him only as his need arose for contact. It was no relationship at all.

Giroux then began to detail his week and the mounting pressure he felt from the many meetings he had attended. She knew he was trying to relieve the tension between them. The Office of Management and Budget in particular weighed on him. OMB always presented him with difficulties. He would come prepared with presentation graphics and narratives to explain the need for flexibility in dealing with the health issues of the Indian people. Yet, OMB staff would always come down to how much would their dollars purchase, as if they were dealing with widgets in a factory somewhere. He resented it.

Giroux found it a pain until he had to acknowledge that no matter how excellent his presentation nor how well-integrated his ideas, OMB would only understand the widget concept. He might never be able to change their viewpoint on health care among Indians and Alaska Natives. On this score they were very much like the Office of Inspector General — accountants who had no sympathy for people.

They lay embraced and motionless for a time. Tensions relieved. Giroux then stirred and touched Sandra's breast and that was all she needed to know he was ready. With her right hand moving over his chest in waves she moved her hand lightly down the middle of his stomach, sure of the reaction she would get.

She was not disappointed. His penis began to raise as she reached his length and began stroking his muscle ever so slowly caressing his skin to the corona. Giroux's penis was wide and filled her hand, its tip extending well beyond her light grasp. She moved her hand to the base and cupped his balls at the same time as she raised and lowered her thumb along his shaft.

Giroux's breathing was more labored. Sandra moved her head directly over his penis and soon had felt the hardness in her mouth expertly moving her tongue around the underside and up to the top repeatedly. Giroux's hips rose and fell with her movement grasping it with her soft lips. He imagined how delicious the rest of her would soon be.

She, too, undulated with his movements. Quickly his right hand moved between her legs. As she parted them he massaged her deepest parts as she moved her head up and down on his member. She delighted in his pleasure and her own. She was on automatic pilot.

He quickly turned her over and mounted her in his excitement. Giroux pulled and pushed her into him with his hands on her buttocks and then rolled onto the bed exhausted. At the height of their experience they came together with a mutual cry of ecstasy and embarrassed laughter. She fell into his arms and rested snugly beside him, guilt mounting in her for not resisting her passion. Her expectation was out of proportion to the reality of his sex. It was over so fast, too fast for her. It left her a little cold. She reached for the sheet to cover her nakedness.

Giroux was speechless for the moment. He had not expected Sandra to be this good. He thought of others he had dominated over the years. Clearly, she was a skilled lover and they were good at copulating, a fact he reflected upon as more indicative of his own superior judgment in women. But this woman was artistic in her movements. This both alarmed and excited him. He wanted more but realized he would have to be careful with her. He was attracted to her unbridled enthusiasm during sex. Her performance was more what he wanted to be able to do but couldn't.

Sandra, too, wondered what Giroux thought of this first time together. She almost asked but hesitated thinking that if he didn't like it he wouldn't be back for more. She hoped it would be the last. And that, frankly, would be fine with her. He was powerful as a person but not overpowering as a lover. He apologized for his brevity.

As passion subsided and sanity returned, Sandra almost felt it was a command performance anyhow. She still resented his forcing himself upon her in the office. Now, she would just wait and see. Sandra was not interested in more. She did what he wanted and now she wanted to go about her business as if nothing happened. She was ready to dismiss the potential for more.

After showering together and dressing they ate the light lunch she prepared to maintain the pretext of a relationship. Conversation was also light, almost banal, certainly shallow. Mainly about the convenience of her apartment to work, where she shopped, restaurants she was especially fond of, etc. etc. He talked of where he lived, schools he attended, books read recently — nothing she found of any consequence on this first coupling that would let her know the man behind the demand. He looked at his watch and said he had to go to pick up his wife from where he left her shopping.

"Wife?" Sandra asked in surprise. "Oh, yes, how stupid of me." Sandra turned aside to look out the kitchen window for a brief moment. Then she returned his gaze icily. It had not occurred to her that he was probably married. She instantly recognized the limitation she placed herself under. She had never had an affair with a married man before.

Suddenly it was a threesome. Another woman was present. She wondered what she looked like. How did her voice sound? Was she tall or short? Fat or thin? Or...

"Why, yes. Didn't you know I was married?"

"How could I? You didn't tell me, Andrew. What is her name, your wife?" Sandra asked flatly, still flush with their tryst but becoming equally flush with the confirmation of his loyalty to her in his tone of voice. His, "Didn't you know?" rang in her ears and sounded vaguely like, 'Yes, Stupid, don't expect any changes. You may be a girlfriend but she is my devoted wife.' His tone of voice was accusatory.

"Elizabeth. Her name is Elizabeth. I'll call you, Sandra," he said matter-of-factly as he rose to leave. "And, please, let's keep this between the two of us. All right?"

"Believe me, I won't tell anyone, Andrew, and, rest assured, I won't call you. I know you are busy. I made up my mind some time ago I wouldn't. So you have nothing to fear from me. And, incidentally, neither does she." Though bothered by his running off to see Elizabeth so quickly, Sandra took off her shoes and raised her feet to his chair reflecting on their beginning as he shut the door behind him.

The affair was over for now. Not bad for a first time, but not auspicious either, she thought. Although she felt a sudden twinge of guilt on his mentioning his wife. Automatically that word, wife, the other woman, came to mind. He had acted as if he had none; but she knew instinctively even though wanting to deny it. Sandra poured herself a glass of wine partially reveling in the aftershocks to divert her attention from this source of new anxiety. A more complete woman than moments before. How well did she measure up to this, Elizabeth, she wondered.

She realized she was committed for now at least. No backward looks. Just one day at a time. Her first affair with a married man held a dim sense of foreboding or dread. That term, married man, resonated. Maybe that's what made it feel good. He did not have to make any commitment to her. He owed her nothing. She considered how powerful Giroux was — the head of the agency, the person who made the final decisions in health matters that affected a million natives everywhere, the one who so many looked to for support for their cause or their pet projects.

The wine was having its effect. It was suddenly comforting, flattering really, to be the one whom he would look to for his own personal support. Sandra wondered if she was giving him something he lacked at home — youth and enthusiasm perhaps, or, a shoulder to lean on, or, the filling of a void in his personal life, or, whether she was deceiving herself into believing she held greater importance than a roll in the hay.

To be considered an object displeased her. She quickly put these thoughts out of her mind as being too frivolous. Yet, she also felt violated. She desperately needed perspective. Her physical need sated for the moment, Sandra tidied up her apartment and set in motion her earlier plan for the day — a quick trip to the market and then on the road to Annapolis to tour the old homes and legislature on the historical register. That evening the tears came. A flood that would reinforce her vulnerability as his object.

Giroux carried on the affair over the weeks and months as it began, furtively in her apartment without a hint to tomorrow, physical excitement and acceptance deepening with each visit, yet always the caution expressed, 'Don't say anything to anyone, Sandra. Not even your closest friends.'

Sandra made no demands and respected his privacy and wondered how she could allow herself to continue to be used. Her only consolation, she was also using him to satisfy her needs. Giroux became secure in his belief that no one noticed him coming to the apartment. It made little difference anyhow. He felt secure as well in Sandra's discretion. She was a good nurse. She didn't call for favors for herself or for her program or to surreptitiously visit on pretexts like, what was her name? Oh, yes, Janet.

Giroux liked this in her and began to plan where they could meet on official business trips. Speaking engagements and conferences would be most likely he thought. He had spied her in his audiences in years past. Perhaps that was where his first desire was enkindled. It would not be difficult — a direct plan with her, an indirect hint to Cynthia for supportive costs to allow her to attend.

His visits were as frequent as their schedules allowed. Their conversations were rarely personal. She always had time to listen and to empathize with Giroux. More and more he confided in her his concerns about relationships with Congress, difficult employees, other Native affairs — and, for his level, they were affairs of state since Native governments were really independent nations within a nation. He relished the notion of himself as an ambassador to heads of state.

Giroux was beginning to feel a differently about this conquest; it was not like others he had. There were several in the intervening years since he had become Director. One night stands and longer alliances as this one would become. He wasn't sure why he felt differently about Sandra than the others. But there was something he just couldn't describe.

His relationship to his wife, Elizabeth, had little or nothing to do with his inclinations he told himself. Andrew had simply grown to like variety. No two apples tasted or looked the same. No flowers of the same species ever appeared the same either. Some apples were good for pies; others were meant to be eaten; and still others were beautiful to behold and to turn around in the hand to fondle. While a rose is a rose, no two roses come out of the same mold. Each is distinct in texture, scent, and visual pattern.

Having born him three children in the past twenty years Elizabeth nevertheless maintained her weight and vigor through regular exercise and moderation in eating. He reasoned Elizabeth was good for making pies; Sandra was meant to be tasted; at least until Andrew wanted a different flavor. Giroux had grown to like variety and was not content with one.

Elizabeth was no fanatic about her weight but insisted on well-balanced nutritious meals, an attractive home, and regular vacations away from business. She thought it good for their relationship. Regular, relaxing vacations would make life interesting and she feared boredom. Many of her friends even suggested that she join a spa to get regular massages, to be pampered, to free her mind and tone her body so she could be her loveliest. Geraldine, the charming wife of their attorney friend, Robert Harris, even hinted she should do this to 'prevent' Andrew from straying.

Intelligent, well-mannered, and friendly, Elizabeth liked to entertain. As befit the wife of an important executive in the

Washington area, she did this frequently with great skill. She entertained his friends and her volunteer associates with aplomb. Many envied the ease with which she managed dinner time conversation. Guests left their home well-satisfied in mind and stomach.

She lacked neither skill nor interest in the bedroom. Her only flaw was that she was familiar to Giroux like a well-worn garment. She was no longer a challenge to him. While he protested he loved Elizabeth in the speculative sense for all her fine qualities, Giroux developed a roving eye, a taste for variety and consummate skill in manipulation. He perfected his natural charm to an art. His bedside manner with patients extended to many bedsides over the years.

Sandra's bed was not the least among them. It was comfortable and inviting and available just five minutes from the office. This was most important to Giroux. He had to be able to steal away without raising suspicions and return quickly. Sandra was accommodating.

Giroux felt comfortable no one knew of his liaisons with the exception of Charlie. He had done his best to be discreet. But Charlie was valuable; he was useful on more than one occasion. He could keep a secret; but more importantly, he could intervene for the Director on many issues. He could take the heat, but he could also turn it on when needed to extract information or require a service.

Sandra intrigued Giroux. Unlike Janet who regarded herself as a professional too — and, perhaps she was in her own way, Giroux thought Sandra the more professional of the two. Sandra delighted him with her conversational skills and her insights into the politics and the problems of the office. He fancied her as an Indian Geisha knowledgeable in relieving stress and making him feel important. She was a jewel, to be kept.

She could easily become a confidant. Her listening and observational skills were acute drawn from years of practice as a nurse in a clinic. He reasoned he had to watch what he would say to her. It was too easy to let down his guard with her, and oh, so attractive, not unlike an Indian Heather Locklear, he thought.

This type of thinking was dangerous for a man in his capacity. Sandra made him feel at ease at once, as if he were the single most important person in the world even though she knew he was exploiting her. It was comforting, and oh, so soothing to be stroked in her capable hands. But he had to be on guard. It was not his intention of becoming involved beyond the bedroom and recreational sex. Indeed, he liked this form of recreation! So much better than baseball which he excelled at in college.

Giroux would not expect to formally date her — no shows or dances or restaurants — unless the meals were part of a business trip. Nothing public. People would know or speculate immediately and the word would be around Rockville like a wild fire. No, trips would be the safest. It is not unusual to be seen with the Director at dinner during a conference. That of course would give him time alone with her. 'Yes,' he said to himself, 'I must learn her travel schedule as soon as I can.'

CHAPTER SIX

JANE'S RECRIMINATIONS

Jane was unsure what to do. She knew she had to do something. Her Christian conscience was making a nuisance of itself. Her attempts at suppressing her anxiety were becoming futile. She had never before been faced with the possibility of betraying an employer. That was how she was looking at the mounting evidence. Yet, for the past three or four months she became more uncertain of what she thought of herself as a human being.

She needed to feel good about herself. But she didn't. This was crucial to her. She went to church regularly and heard sermon upon sermon about being morally right; that it was her Christian duty to stand against evil; that she should help the less fortunate; but she had likewise not been faced with the moral question of how long she could remain quiet about what she suspected of the Director despite her loyalty.

Pastor Johnson of the United Presbyterian Church, her friend and confidant for the past ten years, heard her concerns and clarified that they were legitimate and not petty or twisted imaginings.

He discussed how difficult the sexual appetite was to control especially for men in power or the public eye. They were often tempted to exploit those who were vulnerable. However, she should not do anything without prayerful consideration.

Jane thought this was a real test of her Christianity. Sermons were no longer an academic exercise. Her introspection gnawed at her stomach and became a source of pain for her. If she didn't say or do something others may get hurt; and if she did, she could get hurt, too. She could be fired and that would be intolerable. She confessed she liked working in the Director's office. Jane felt confused and divided in her loyalties.

For nearly a decade Jane had been a loyal and trusted secretary to Admiral Giroux. He commanded respect and she gave it unstintingly. She started working in his office soon after Admiral Grant's retirement in 1980 and had witnessed the boundless energy and devotion and all-consuming passion with which he attacked the enormous problem of improving the health of American Indians and Alaska Natives. Was his passion too much, even for him?

A Chippewa from Minnesota, Andrew Giroux was an outstanding athlete, leader, and scholar at the University. He excelled in the sciences, debate, and sports. A four-letterman in varsity baseball as a second baseman and role model to Indians on campus, Giroux applied his leadership skills in diplomacy to win the support of administration in housing issues and prejudice faced by fellow students in the community — both Indians and non-Indians. Giroux walked well in the white world while holding onto his Indian values.

Charm, tact and diplomacy were his stock tools; concessions were his results with acceptance in the community. His idealism and morals were unquestioned — at least until now. Jane felt she was a traitor in questioning him.

Jane regarded herself as a loyal employee, one who would do whatever was asked of her. But, she thought, if he was involved with other women, and really taking advantage of them, this was so upsetting. Jane resented her conscience. It was a nuisance, argumentative, and insolent. Her peaceful days were waning.

Through this decade she had often seen Giroux use his charm, tact and diplomacy to gain the support of an often divergent group of administrators under his control as well as congressional staff aides without whose support resources would not be forthcoming for the Indian people.

Jane questioned whether the job or the life in Washington somehow corrupted Giroux, made him devious. Or, maybe her devotion to him had clouded her eyes for years. She worried that maybe he cheated on his wife for all those years.

She worried incessantly. Did Elizabeth know? Or did she tolerate his behavior with other women as happens with other women she knew? Jane reasoned Elizabeth must not know. How could she? Poor woman! Elizabeth would have no reason to stay with such a man if she knew. She was competent in her own right and probably could get any man she chose if she set her mind to it.

In the silence of her heart, Jane concluded, 'Whatever happened to him is still not reason enough to hurt other women or to betray his wife.' Jane felt strongly that leaders were supposed to lead, to be an example of moral strength to those who looked up to them for guidance, to somehow be above whatever failings dragged others down. She finally made her mind up that his use of women was sexual abuse and she could not be quiet any longer. Jane felt she had to tell someone.

Jane knew Janet would be in Rockville for a training conference in one week. She liked Janet and was upset that her friend had been transferred so quickly when those ugly and untrue rumors were circulated of Janet's increasing incompetence.

Jane decided purposefully to take a day off and have lunch with her before Janet returned to Phoenix. She would tell her concerns about her transfer and how she was treated. Perhaps she would then be direct and find out what really happened. Jane resumed her typing, more content that at least she had a plan. Until then, each day would pass as any other.

Janet made a reservation at the Crown Plaza in Rockville and was eager to have lunch with Jane when she called with the arrangements. She was Janet's *entrée* to Giroux, at least in the beginning of their relationship. She longed for her friendship even though her caring for Giroux had vanished. Janet still felt betrayed, yet longed to be with him. She knew Jane was loyal to him and that perplexed her. But now, that no longer mattered. She only wanted to tell her what she thought of her boss.

Meeting her at the Holiday Inn Crown Plaza at the corner of Bouic Avenue and Rockville Pike next Thursday would be delightful and yet, would give her an excuse to unload on Jane. Janet really hadn't confided in anyone about her affair with the Director or her suspicions of her betrayal.

Until Thursday morning Jane's resolve waxed and waned. She wanted to be truthful with Janet but found difficulty eating throughout the week. She questioned whether she had the stomach for truth. Being a Christian was hard. Sleep the night before was fitful. She was not rested but wanted to have her wits about her. Her mounting anxiety took over and she vomited her sparse breakfast.

When she arrived at the Crown Plaza lobby, Jane was pale and not very hungry. Janet was already there waiting in an overstuffed chair and reached out for Jane to greet her warmly. Jane was friendly but stiff. Her preoccupation with the lines she rehearsed inhibited her from being spontaneous. She hated her stomach for being tied into knots.

"Jane, have you been ill lately?" Janet asked innocently. "You look dreadful. Is your family well? Are you still working in the front office, or have they transferred you too?"

The questions unnerved Jane. She began to twitch around the mouth and avoided a direct glance at Janet. Jane fought for composure.

"Janet noticed. "Come on! I thought you and I were friends, Jane. You're acting so strangely. Surely you can tell me what's wrong. Are you and Philip having troubles? Is he drinking again? Has he been abusing you?" she asked halfway feeling that might be the case. Philip, Jane's husband of fifteen years, had a history of drinking and abusive behavior. Janet already knew how bad the problem was. She had become Jane's confidant.

When Janet worked in the Parklawn Building she would have lunch with Jane periodically in the third floor cafeteria. Everything happening inside and outside the office, including home life, was usually on the menu and shared equal billing with the dessert. Gossip was always delicious. However, she had not seen Jane this visibly upset for a long time.

"Let's go downstairs to the Hideaway, Jane," Janet said. "This is one of my favorite places when I lived here. I liked to have cocktails here. I love the sound of the waterfall. It is so restful."

They were seated in the muted pink and white room on the north wall of the Atrium. The view of the Atrium was also pleasant. Jane understood why Janet frequented the restaurant. Water descending from the two story lava rocks to the pool below muted their conversation. While the waiter delivered their fruit plates, Janet waited for a response. Jane gained some composure, took a deep breath, and threw out a straw to see if Janet would grasp it.

"No. Philip is not the issue. I have been having some horrible thoughts about Dr. Giroux, Janet. And I don't know what to do about them. I've thought about seeing a counselor but I'm sure he would just tell me to mind my own business. I've wanted to talk with someone, but there isn't anyone I really trust here now that you have left. And I know it isn't really fair of me to bring up my ugly suspicions to you."

"Go on, Jane." Janet was the model of patience and drooled on the words, 'ugly suspicions.' She knew some gossip was about to be shared and settled into her chair.

"You weren't in headquarters when I finally became the Director's Secretary in 1983. Our budget was just getting restored after Congress made us take a cut in 1981. Staff were excited about being able to do something with the tribes. We all felt good. I'm sure you remember.

"I didn't think I had a chance for a job there but when Margaret left so quickly as Dr. Giroux's Secretary I applied for it and got it much to my surprise. I was so excited to be his secretary. He had such a fine reputation as a scholar and director. But the strangest thing happened to me shortly after that.

"One day I received a telephone call from Margaret. She sounded drunk. You know, slurring words like she had had too much to drink. I felt she had sour grapes or something but she said, 'He's a louse, Jane. He can't be trusted with feelings. Don't get involved.' It is strange but that remark stayed with me all these years even though I dismissed Margaret's comment as due to the alcohol. But you know, I don't even know if she drinks! I may have jumped to conclusions."

By then Janet was intrigued. She asked, "What happened then?" as she dabbled with the fruit on her plate mixing the strawberries with the plain yogurt. She didn't like plain yogurt and the mixed variety had too much sugar in it. Jane began eating hers and found her appetite once more.

Janet finished her first glass of Chablis and signaled the waiter for a second. She thought wine always enhanced the taste of good fruit and a good story.

Jane continued. "For the longest time I wasn't sure what she meant. I've wanted to call her and ask her to explain. But I didn't have the nerve. Then when I was promoted to be Dr. Giroux's Secretary there was so much to learn that the time escaped me."

Jane shifted uncomfortably in her chair as she continued to pick at her lunch. She now began to drink her Chablis to keep up with Janet. Then, she too ordered a second. As a tear came to her eye, she acknowledged, "Dr. Giroux made me uncomfortable once. It was early in my work with him. One of the congressional hearings was scheduled and he asked me — no, really, he told me to stay late with him. We had to go over his speech. I thought it odd then, because it seemed so polished. He did his own editing, you know. He is such a good writer.

"Anyway, I stayed against my better judgment. You know how you get funny feelings sometimes. Well, I dismissed my concerns despite my nagging conscience. He asked me to join him in his office and to close the door behind me so we wouldn't be disturbed.

"It was late and most everyone had gone by then. Dr. Giroux beckoned me to sit next to him on the leather couch. It is such a comfortable thing. We started to review his speech. Then he stopped for a moment and said, "I don't think that sounds right, do you?" It sounded perfect to me. His words are always so measured that you can't mistake his intent.

"He came closer to me to show me the text — right up next to me for heaven's sake — I could feel the warmth of his body against mine. He put his hand on my leg. Of course, I reacted immediately. I gasped. I don't let any man put his hand on my leg, you know," she added defensively, almost expecting immediate reproach from Janet.

"He just looked over his glasses at me and apologized saying something about his not intending to be offensive. He was just trying to emphasize his point in his speech and was only seeking confirmation." Jane looked to Janet for validation. She smiled in recognition of Giroux's real intent but said nothing immediately.

Finally, Janet remarked, "I didn't realize he came onto you back then, Jane. You never said anything to me about it before. I'm truly sorry. But it seems that when you reacted he knew he had better not go any further with you. Don't you think?"

Jane took another drink of her Chablis. Janet was debating about having another glass but deferred for the moment. Jane continued. "Go any further? Perhaps you are right. I didn't want to believe he was capable of doing such a thing. Recently, though, I have been thinking more about that very thing."

"Are you saying you want him to go further with you, Jane?" Janet asked in disbelief recalling her own failed relationship with Giroux.

Jane gulped trying to hide her fascination with this prospect. "No, of course not. He's married. Elizabeth is such a lovely woman. I wouldn't dream of hurting her or their children with such silliness. And, believe it or not, I wouldn't trade my marriage such as it is. Philip has finally learned to be a good provider even if we did have problems. And we certainly did! Well, you know all about that, so I don't need to tell you things are now better."

The waiter stood by on the sidelines and prepared another serving of Chablis. Jane asked pointedly, "But I do wonder how involved with other women Dr. Giroux is, don't you?"

"Involved? Like with whom?" Janet was on guard and getting prepared to tell her about her and Giroux's affair. She hadn't told anyone despite what he did to her. She held her tongue. She wanted to know what Jane knew about their relationship.

"Well, Margaret, for instance. Even though she sounded drunk she clearly meant for me to watch my step with him. That could only mean one thing to me, Janet. She was probably involved. Or, Sandra Locklear for another."

"Sandra Locklear? You must be kidding. You don't seriously think she is having an affair with Dr. Giroux? Do you really?" Janet asked incredulously, her voice raised in mock jealousy. "I must admit she is attractive — but oh, so professional. Well, you know what I mean. How could he be interested in her? Or do you think her professionalism is what attracts her to him?"

Janet elaborated about Sandra's incredible way of keeping her opinion out of any personal matter she is asked to deal with. She seemed to put her feelings aside in public and it seemed further she was very selective in her friends. Indeed, there were few Sandra felt comfortable with whom she would disclose any personal information. She once said word gets around too fast in the Indian community. Janet explained such a thing as having an affair with the Director would be hard to explain or deny.

Suddenly her situation dawned on her. Janet continued to comment with her impression of Sandra and how unlikely such an affair would be. When she finished her narration with obvious increasing tones of jealousy, Jane interjected, "Or, perhaps even you."

With that retort, Janet ordered the waiter to deposit a second bottle of Chablis in the ice bucket. The two ladies were becoming so engrossed they hardly noticed the waiter had anticipated their desire. "I'll have another," Jane said suddenly with a little more life. "Me too," Janet added.

"How did you know, Jane?" Janet asked.

"It was none of my business really, Janet, but I suspected Dr. Giroux had designs on you when he called you into his office so frequently early in your relationship, presumably to discuss contracting issues. But nothing seemed to come to me for completion. Then you would practically demand to see him. However, that isn't the point of my wanting to talk with you today before you return to Phoenix.

"I've been having real problems wrestling with my own thoughts and feelings on this whole business even to the point of my getting sick over it. I know I really shouldn't get involved like I am. But I guess I can't help it now. I should think you would want to do something about this, too. I mean if he did it, you know.

"Naturally I can't be part of anything since he really didn't impress himself upon me. But, you and Margaret and Sandra, if she is involved, should at least talk about it together. Don't you think? Perhaps I can help in a small way," Jane allowed.

More subdued by the wine, Janet said, "Jane, I must confess I came here fully intending to give you a piece of my mind about your boss but you really have caught me by surprise. Not that you could do anything, mind you. I just wanted to unload. My transfer happened so fast I couldn't think. One day I was in Rockville happily doing my work; the next day I was in Phoenix where I hardly know a soul. It really hurt me to be dismissed."

She paused. "I'm ashamed to admit it, Jane, but I did fall for the man in a big way. My head was swimming. I thought I must be special or something for him to want me. I've never told this to anyone before. I guess there is no time like the present." She shrugged her shoulders, smiled weakly, and took in a deep breath as if she needed all the reserves she could muster to tell her about the affair.

"Dr. Giroux called me at my office one day. Out of the blue, the Director was on the other end of the telephone! He was always so impressive in his uniform! I almost felt I had to stand up and salute when I heard his voice! You know, it is so resonant and commanding. He said he wanted to take a break and thought he would go to the cafeteria on the third floor and wondered if I would like to join him for a cup of coffee or some juice.

"You should know how it is. You don't refuse the Director anything. I was so flattered and curious. So I said certainly and would meet him at 3:30 just before their closing. When I got there, not too many people were there, just a few scattered in all directions. Everyone was preoccupied with his thoughts or looking at the television in the middle of the cafeteria. No one could hear what we were talking about, I'm sure.

"He began with small talk and flattered me for some work I did on a particularly difficult contract. He seemed so sincere, but I was confident he didn't really know anything about it. Was I surprised! In the next minute he recited all the main details to my utter amazement.

"I was impressed with his knowledge of what I was doing and his understanding of the contracting process. And pretty soon he just looked at me in the eyes — I couldn't look away — and he remarked how well he liked the dress I was wearing.

"I remember feeling so strange. He shifted gears so quickly. I was caught off-guard. It was the first time I had worn it to the office. He said he hadn't seen it on me before and said it enhanced my figure and made me desirable. I'm sure I blushed. I was flattered and flustered. Actually, I was speechless. You know, most men never notice a thing like that." Janet paused to take another drink, looked about to see if anyone overheard her tale, and continued in hushed tones.

"Then he was on the chase and I knew it. He asked me if there was anyone special in my life. I said no, there wasn't and laughed out of nervousness and embarrassment. He put my hand in his. Without batting an eye he said I should have a lover. I laughed some more.

"Can you believe that? 'I should have a lover.' I couldn't believe what I was hearing. I didn't have the presence of mind to tell him it wasn't any of his business or even to ask him why he wondered. But needless to say, my mind was racing. I knew the answer to the question. I was actually getting panicked. I could feel my heart rate increase and my breathing deepen. My legs seemed like rubber; and I couldn't get up to leave.

"Suddenly, almost apologetically, he leaned closer so as to guarantee that what he was about to say would not be overheard. He then asked me if he could fuck me! He said I was such a charming and welcome addition to his office and so very attractive. He wanted to be able to touch my hair and caress me. I almost knocked over my cup of tea. Surely, I thought, everyone in the room heard my heart pounding. My eyes teared.

"When I looked around the cashiers were closing down their registers and the manager was locking the cafeteria doors. Some of the lights were being dimmed. The patrons were all eager to leave trying to get out the last unlocked door. They weren't paying any attention to us. He counted on that, I'm sure.

"By then, we were the only ones left in the room. He just simply said, 'You look surprised,' and then he laughed. Surprised wasn't the word for what I felt. I was shocked, really shocked. My heart was pounding furiously. The prospect was tantalizing and forbidding.

"I didn't know what to say. I was lost for words. He responded to my silence by asking if it meant no, or was I considering it? Or should he have not asked, or if it was against my principles to fuck him. You know, if someone else had said that to me I would have slapped him in the face to be sure. But he was the Director! My God!"

The waiter raised an eyebrow, smiled and gave up his vigil after partially clearing the table and providing two bottles of Chablis. He knew to leave the women to their discussion.

Another half-hour passed. Jane paid the bill and gave a generous tip to the waiter for his patience. They repaired to a tiny alcove near the white baby grand piano to continue the tale by the gazebo.

Janet obliged. "I said I would. But I could hardly believe my own ears. We set up a date right then and there and met at my apartment across the way at the Village Square Apartments after work that evening. "Oh, it was so wonderful." Janet blushed as she recalled their first assignation. "I had just gotten refreshed when he rang the door bell. That was the first time in my life a man whisked me off to the bedroom just like that. It was such a rush; my head was swimming delightfully from some wine I drank before he arrived."

Janet leaned forward to speak confidentially in hushed tones and continued. "When Andrew mounted me I came almost immediately. I was ready for it and felt like I was in seventh heaven." Janet couldn't contain herself and narrated the sequence of events until she remembered her anger. Then she was consumed by a different passion. Her face became contorted for a moment. She sighed.

"It was like that for the first few months. He would always call me and didn't want me to call him to come to the office for anything. He didn't want any suspicions aroused. In the beginning, of course, I did what he asked. But I began to need him. There really wasn't anyone else in my life, only him. I refused several dates from others and he seemed to want me. And," with a tear in her eye, she continued, "I wanted him. I know now I made a huge mistake. I thought — or, really, read into our affair — that he was ready to leave his wife or was probably anxious to. Well, you remember. It was one of those times I came to you and practically demanded to see him. Remember?"

Jane looked at her watch and realized the afternoon was nearly gone. She was far from bored with Janet's narration of her affair, but her conscience, partially dulled with the Chablis, began to assert itself. She found herself taking pleasure in the tale and scolded herself for it.

"Oh, my goodness. It's almost 6:15," she said. "I'm going to have to run." The gazebo was beginning to fill up with the early evening crowd of executives and businessmen with dates. Part of her didn't want to prolong Janet's recitation of the events. The other part wanted to know more of the intimate details. Janet was so miffed she couldn't continue.

"Janet, I remember so well the times you came to see Andrew. On a few occasions I remember seeing your reflection in the glass door of the bookcase in front of me and your readjusting your dress. That isn't a common sight in the office. And, although you did it hurriedly so I wouldn't see anything, I knew, but still didn't want to believe you were enjoying more than a polite conversation with the Director. I had blinders on then about his behavior, too. I was so willing to excuse him.

"I also remember the last time you came and demanded to see him. When you left, you were drying your eyes and sped past me without a word. I knew that something dreadful must have happened to you in his office."

Jane paused, noting a tearful eye. "Janet, you know I am so sorry for you. Have you ever thought of doing something about it? Really? You know, reporting it to someone? From what you told me he not only came onto you but you were vulnerable then. I think he picks out his prey very carefully. He should be stopped," Jane said hoping Janet would volunteer.

Janet reflected dejectedly. "Jane, yes, I thought about it, believe me. But what would I say? I had an affair with the Director of the Indian Health Service? Even if I could prove he made sexual advances to me in the beginning and took advantage of me because of his position, wouldn't people say this is just consensual sex among adults? It happens all the time, right, especially here? Surely you heard stories about others here. This wouldn't be any different now would it?"

Jane conceded it could look that way to many people, maybe even most people. She reasoned though if there were a pattern to his behavior a good lawyer may just be able to prove sexual harassment or abuse of some kind.

"Janet, this really bothers me. We women have to stick together. No one else is going to look out for us. The Anita Hill affair proved that. Men in power will continue to abuse so long as they know they can get away with it and get supported by the establishment or their cronies. I know a lot of Indian men who would probably applaud him; but this sickens me. How many others has he taken advantage of on his travels? And, you know, I type all his travel requests!" Jane sobbed a little with guilt for her involvement.

She thought she had resolved these issues and had come to accept her involvement, minimal though it was. Jane felt she may have facilitated his abuse even though it wasn't true. Jane looked disheartened and dismissed herself. "Well, I've truly got to go, Janet. Do take care of yourself and call me. I want to help. Really, I need to do it for my own sake, if nothing else."

Janet remained behind and watched Jane ascend the stairs past the alcove seating area on the lobby floor. From below they looked like ribbed lifeboats protruding over the atrium floor. She felt calm listening to the water flowing over the two story lava rocks to the pool below. Palms, ferns, indoor ficus trees and other flora marked the meandering brown paving brick trails around the gazebo leading to the exits. She watched the twin elevators crowned with strings of lights alternately rise and fall. They reminded her of space capsules lifting from a landing platform.

The more Janet thought about the situation the more she disliked being a pawn moved about at will by the Director only because he had no use for her in bed. She thought about her experience night and day for many months. It festered like a sore.

Her anger had not abated. It was enkindled by this meeting with Jane. Objectively, she knew Giroux made the advances, and, yes, she consented to a relationship. But he was no ordinary man in her view. Andrew was the Director, the person who held power in the palm of his hand. That kind of person ought to have a different level of responsibility to those he directs. In her view, he was not unlike Judge Thomas to Anita Hill or teachers taking advantage of students or clergy with their charges.

The more she thought about it tonight the more resolute she became in her growing disdain for Andrew Giroux and decided she would do something about him.

Her failure in sex with Giroux was her problem. Obviously she didn't please him in some way. Maybe she didn't move just right for him or something equally stupid she thought. Although she admitted she never experienced such blatant disregard for her feelings from any other lover. He was callous and used her for his own pleasure and summarily dismissed her all the while flattering her to get what he wanted. It suddenly dawned on her this was not about sex. This was about power.

Having sex with Giroux was never a two way street. An affair with a married man rarely is, Janet thought. She could understand failures in relationships. They happen. But usually lovers will allow some time, however brief, to acknowledge their responsibility to each other and to let each other go when it doesn't work out. Words failed her to describe her feelings.

While she acknowledged the Chablis had something to do with her current resolve, her growing interest in talking with someone else — a professional, perhaps a lawyer, with some experience in sexual harassment was enkindled by Jane. Janet knew she had to convince such a person she was indeed used, and probably abused. At least she felt abused. But how to prove it. She now knew she was probably not alone. She had to talk with Margaret or Sandra if she could find either one while she was here for training.

Night had fallen and Janet ascended the space capsule to her room on the Concierge level. It was fortuitous she was given this suite due to a mix-up at the front desk in reservations. Somehow she felt vindicated with the special treatment. It was her due.

As she rose above the atrium she glanced to the floor below and reflected bitterly how little some men were. The alcohol she drank seemed to have little effect on her now as she considered calling Margaret. Her mind was racing, the adrenaline masking the effects of the alcohol.

Janet unlocked her door and entered the room eagerly searching for the telephone directory. She resolved to give it a try. She found the telephone book in the dresser drawer and flipped the pages open to the P's. 'Back up, Janet,' she told herself.

To her surprise, Margaret Mitchell wasn't listed. 'Damn,' she said, but she noticed there was an M. Mitchell. 'It's probably not her, she reflected. As she closed the book she briefly noticed the address. 'Ah, ha!' she exclaimed. Apt B16, 16585 Twinbrook Parkway. 'Maybe.' She hurriedly opened the book again, dialed the number and received no answer. 'Double damn!' she exclaimed in frustration.

Janet kicked off her shoes and sat in the overstuffed chair in front of the television. She wasn't hungry just yet. She turned on the television, changed channels repeatedly, looked at her watch.

'Too early to go to bed,' she said. She threw the television remote onto the bed in frustration.

She grabbed her car keys and made it to the parking lot, started her rental a little too quickly peeling her tires and startling a nearby pedestrian, sped around the corner past the entrance to the Metro, and south to Twinbrook. In five minutes she drove past the House of Chinese Chicken where many of the federal employees eat their lunch and was cruising slowly by the apartment complex she assumed Margaret lived in.

It was not difficult to find the building listed in the telephone book. She parked the car in the visitors spot and found the apartment easily. Janet pressed the door bell and waited. She pressed it again and again but no one came even though lights were clearly visible through the drawn drapes.

Greatly disappointed she turned to leave and heard footsteps coming in the portico. Janet was in luck. She couldn't believe her good fortune. Margaret was just returning from a nightly walk deep in thought. "Margaret?"

"Janet? What brings you here? I haven't seen you since you left for Phoenix. How are you?"

"I've been in for some training for my new job and just had to see you, Margaret. I know I am here rather late and hadn't called you in advance, but may we talk for a while? It's rather important, at least for me. I'll try to be brief," she said hopefully.

"I would love to, Janet, but can we do it tomorrow? I'm really tired." Margaret looked worn out from her brisk walk. The walk failed to lift the weight of her thoughts and she was not ready to entertain any guests.

"I know it may sound rude, Margaret. Tomorrow may be too late. I'm returning to Phoenix on the early morning TWA. I really need to talk with you, Margaret, please. Even if it is only for a little while." She looked desperate.

Margaret fumbled for her keys in her pocket to let Janet in the apartment. As soon as she opened the door, the aroma of sweet grass and sage filled the entrance. The apartment was small, clean and sparsely decorated. Margaret couldn't afford lavish furniture on her small salary as a secretary.

Montgomery County was considered one of the most expensive places to live in the country. Margaret could ill afford the trappings of luxury, designer drapes, crystal, and china. Out of her meager salary she would always send a small amount of money home to her parents out of respect for them and their needs. Margaret lived from pay check to pay check. She didn't want to take in another staff member to defray expenses like many other secretaries do in the Washington metropolitan area out of mere survival. She desired her privacy more.

Yet, the apartment was lovely in its simplicity. It reflected Margaret's beautiful unadorned soul. While she lived in Flagstaff, Arizona she managed to acquire several Apache burden baskets, Hopi Kachinas, and a Two Gray Hills rug which she considered a prize possession. The baskets and Kachinas adorned a simple re-stained Goodwill bookcase. The Two Gray Hills rug lay in front of her couch. Anyone having such a prized possession would have it displayed as a wall hanging. But it served Margaret utilitarian value and kept her floor warm near her couch.

Margaret made Janet comfortable despite her tiredness, offered her ice tea which she declined in favor of ice water. "What do you wish to see me about, Janet?"

In a manner totally uncharacteristic for Indians, Janet said, "I hope you will forgive my bluntness, Margaret, but I want to, no, I must ask you perhaps the most blunt question I could ask anyone. I will understand if you tell me to leave immediately, and, of course, I will without a further word." She looked away out of respect and not a little embarrassment.

"This does not make me feel easy, Janet. But just what is your question?"

"Did you have an affair with Dr. Giroux?"

Margaret's coal black eyes burned with special intensity. Looking at Janet with what seemed an eternity, Janet thought the look would consume her. She felt badly for asking and rose to leave. Margaret held out her hand to halt her progress and motioned for her to sit. Margaret glanced to the side, a tear falling down her left cheek onto her now folded hands. Another eternity and she asked, "How did you know?"

Janet felt relieved that Margaret talked. Anything she said would have relieved the tension. "I didn't know for sure. Just call it a hunch. But let me tell you my story about the man."

An hour later Janet finished her recitation. Margaret was fully composed by then, enough so that she volunteered her story to Janet. She was the first and only person to know exactly what happened.

Though fearful at first, Margaret was relieved that someone else could help her carry her burden. She had actually admired Janet from a distance and wished she could have been as articulate as she and so competent in handling important matters as contracting. And now she found herself entrusting her secret to her. She thought Janet must have trusted her greatly to impart this story to her.

"Janet, I'll keep your secret. No one will hear it from me."

"Oh, I know you will. But I want to be honest with you, Margaret. I am no longer going to keep it a secret. I won't burden you with the responsibility of silence. I made up my mind tonight to talk with Jane Candelaria about it. Before I transferred, she was a friend to me. She and I shared a lot of confidences. I hadn't told anyone either about this before. I guess there had to be a first person somewhere."

Margaret was perplexed. "I don't really understand, Janet. I thought you needed someone to talk to about it."

"I don't blame you, Margaret, for not understanding just yet. Actually, I didn't know why I had to see you and ask such a terrible question. But I do now. I want to make him pay for what he did to me and to you and to God knows how many others like us who have been used and abused by this man." Her vehemence returned.

Margaret's voice rose. "Oh, and you think I should help you, is that it?" Margaret asked. "I don't think so." Margaret relaxed and began to describe her upbringing. "Before I married, I was taught little about sex. It was not a subject mother felt comfortable with. She told me to observe the world about me. I guessed how men and women would do it from watching the animals. The sheep we tended as little children were good teachers.

"But as I grew older I didn't want to have anything to do with the boys I went to school with. They acted so gross. When I overheard them talking about it, the boys made it seem so dirty. I guess I had the same urges as everyone else but I managed to make school and learning more important until I fell in love in college.

"He was from another tribe. He was not accepted by my parents just as I was not accepted by his. It was not a good match. Too much drinking. And fighting. And other women. With the last beating, I left, got divorced, and in my shame I left the reservation and came here. Too many memories there to hold me captive.

"Dr. Giroux sort of took me in. Maybe I wasn't strong enough." Margaret shrugged her slender shoulders in self-blame. She paused to collect her thoughts. "I don't want to tell you everything because I really don't know you well enough yet. Maybe some time I will trust you with the whole truth. But you ask a lot if you are asking me to help you take him to court. I may not like the man for what he did to me; but he is the Director."

Margaret got up from the couch to get another glass of water. Janet reflected on what she said. Margaret was hiding something that may be important to her cause Janet thought. Something that would help make the case, but she couldn't press it, not just yet. "Well, it's late, Margaret, and I've got an early flight back to Phoenix. I apologize for intruding on you like this. You are right. My problem is not yours. Nevertheless, I just hope you will think about this some more. I also hope you will keep the door open to me. I believe I want to call you again to chat. At the least I can tell you what I am doing, right?"

Janet smiled weakly but felt little remorse and left Margaret to her disquieting thoughts. It was late at night. She had counted on enlisting Margaret's help in her new crusade. But she now knew it would take more time and effort.

Even though wounded by this man, perhaps more seriously than the others, Margaret held him in high regard as her leader. Culture forbade her from talking against him. Private thoughts were another matter that would fester like a sore.

In her private world Margaret was terribly wronged and she had wronged her baby. A baby she would never cuddle. A baby that would never see the light of day whose own dreams would never be fulfilled. Tonight the pain was rekindled.

It was a fundamental injustice but Giroux was a father figure for her and the real father of a child he would never see. Her child. Yet, how could a father ever do what he did? she asked. She felt dirty and betrayed and incapable of giving voice to the disquieting rage she felt.

As a leader, Giroux counted on misguided loyalty. He was seldom disappointed. Actually it was deeper than that. He knew there was a cadre of people working for the IHS who were dedicated in their own right. Loyalists who, regardless of the leadership, creatively managed to deliver high quality health care services despite small budgets and few personnel resources to meet the demand. Their dedication to principle and anonymity could be counted upon to counteract negative influences and stories that often circulate to call into question the leadership. Such people were often attracted to the IHS where idealism could have a practical outlet in the removal of pain and discomfort.

Giroux counted upon their naiveté to disbelieve in flawed character. He knew he was safe. The Margarets of the service would not talk.

CHAPTER SEVEN

CONNECTIONS

Both Janet and Margaret disconnected from their pre-arranged telephone call to reflect on their recent meeting at Margaret's apartment. Each agreed — Janet basking in balmy 90 degree weather in Phoenix, and Margaret basking in 90 percent humidity in Rockville — to take the morning off for their call. Each would be fresh (perhaps, Margaret less so); and as each agreed on their recent visit together in Rockville, they would talk more. They had to be sure, first, of themselves, and secondly of their need for vindication. Giroux had to be stopped. But they weren't sure how they would do it.

With knots in their stomachs each confessed to the other having had an affair with the Director; each learned he had boldly made the advance; each protested she would not have dreamed about it on her own; and each had felt taken in, used, and discarded as soon as his purpose had ended. In their minds that was abuse. Power and omnipotence gone mad.

It was especially agonizing for Margaret to come to this recognition. But there was no mistake about it now. Only misgivings about what to do. Margaret was so unsure of herself. A more traditional Indian than Janet, Margaret felt so shamed. Then, in a moment of courage, a final resolve. She knew she could not keep her story quiet. To do so would be to allow Giroux to misuse more women. Nevertheless, Margaret had her misgivings. Her previous marriage had torn down her image of herself. She had not fully recovered from the trauma of her broken marriage and was vulnerable. Giroux had sensed this vulnerability like an eagle after its prey.

As she toyed with the telephone wire making loops of it around her finger, Margaret almost whispered she would do her part in bringing to light how she believed Giroux took advantage of her. She was hesitant; but, she felt support for the first time.

Someone else experienced what she experienced; as if not only her body had been misused, but also her spirit had been raped.

Tearfully, she related the whole story to Janet in painful detail, *especially* not omitting her vulnerability. As she fixed blame on herself for not being in control of herself that evening she sounded as if she excused Giroux for consoling her and filling a void.

Janet interrupted her. "Excuse me, Margaret. I mean no offense, but, please, you have no reason to protect him. He took advantage of you when you were down! No real man does that sort of thing." Anger was mounting in Janet. More than for herself, she saw how open and child-like Margaret was. It was in her nature to trust and not condemn. She realized Margaret needed her to be there for her.

"Margaret, it is almost as if you can't allow yourself some measure of peace and dignity. Forgive me for saying this, but the bastard took that away from you!" As the words tumbled out Margaret, smiling a little, felt a wave of relief flood her with calm. She wished she had the courage to be so bold like Janet.

Listening intently, Janet immediately became more concerned and alarmed about her as she heard the rest of Margaret's story. She realized it could have happened to her. She was not even remotely prepared on this telephone call for Margaret's further disclosure about the impact of the affair. The more she thought about their plight, the decision to contact an attorney was more easily arrived at. It was a simple conclusion. Each needed affirmation that it was right for them to do; and their feelings told them that. Janet just needed to know she was not alone.

Yet, neither could make the move alone, especially Margaret. She was traumatized by her relationship with Giroux, more severely than Janet or, they proposed, nameless others. Each knew she was not strong enough alone and depended upon the other for affirmation and resolve.

But where to start the action. Margaret remained at work in Rockville, and, of course, that was where the agency *(and he)* was located. Janet was located in Phoenix, Arizona, far removed from the stress of encountering him, even by chance. While her resentment about the immediacy of the transfer to Phoenix still smoldered within her, Janet thanked God she did not have to see Giroux daily.

She suggested she would gladly cooperate with any attorney and pay her share of the complaint but Margaret said she could never start such a thing. She had neither the assets nor the strength to confront him alone in court. Not even for her baby or its memory that haunted her by day and night.

Baby! Janet felt sorry for Margaret. She learned she had been caught with unprotected sex. She was alone, far from family, and without many friends in a foreign city. Her emotional investment was heavy, her denial of events more complete, until therapy unlocked the awful door. This only enhanced her inability to confront the Director alone. Navajo women don't confront their men in public. What they want done is left for private discussions in their hogan.

But in this case, even that was impossible. Giroux wasn't her man. His visits to her were for sex only. And he made it perfectly clear he would tell her where and when it would be. Margaret was no different than Sandra in that regard. Giroux was not very giving. His charm masked his need to dominate.

Margaret was especially vulnerable. And Giroux would never know why. She hadn't the courage to tell him she was pregnant for fear she would be put on the streets; and that would be another problem she would have to hide. Alone in a strange city, it was too much.

It was obvious to Janet that Margaret was an intelligent woman, college-educated and functioning well below her capacity. She trained as a teacher and taught fifth grade at the Chinle, Arizona Rough Rock elementary grade school for two years after graduating with honors from Northern Arizona University in Flagstaff, Arizona. She was happy with her first assignment and fell in love with her young eager students who sensed her unbounded willingness to give.

Tall by Navajo standards with jet black hair Margaret resisted the advances of her class mates until the junior year. She fell in love with an Apache man two years her junior from Whiteriver, Arizona. Gordon was not well-liked or accepted by her family but was intelligent, athletic, fiercely proud and a good lover. They married in her senior year much out of graces with each other's family. Much in love, their romance was fiery until Gordon demonstrated a jealous streak and became overly possessive in their second year together.

Gordon liked to fight and to drink. It was not uncommon for him to combine the two over a woman he met in a bar. Margaret collected him so many times from jail. Then they would argue. The less control over alcohol he showed, the more deeply enmeshed they became. All the more he projected his infidelity onto her, and the more he would beat her for even looking at a man, however innocent the occasion.

Margaret recalled how shaken she was. It was not easy to forgive, let alone forget, such abuse. She did not want to visit her family back on the reservation during these times and would go to lengths to avoid being home when her mother said she would be coming to town. She felt intense shame at not being able to please her man and make her marriage work. "It's all my fault," she would say. Gordon would then beat her for these admissions careful not to touch her lovely face until one day.

In the third year of marriage, Margaret's mother came unannounced and found her at home. Reduced to tears, she ached for her daughter. Margaret was in bed with bruises on her face and arms and chest. She claimed she fell; but mother knew. "Those kind of bruises do not come from a fall," she said simply.

Margaret could not lie well. Her mother had instilled love and honesty in her daughter. Gordon was wonderful when he didn't drink; he was a devil when he did and spared no punishment. He degraded her and made her beg for forgiveness for her imagined faults. When done with his verbal and physical abuse he would drag her off to bed and continue his physical degradation protesting how much he loved and needed her and worshipped her.

Without hesitation Margaret's mother quickly packed her up in caring silence and took her home to Chinle. In a rage at Gordon's abuse of his daughter, her father put out the word that if Gordon showed up to claim his daughter, he would never leave the reservation and would never be found. Gordon got the message and a few months later Margaret applied for a divorce and a job teaching at the elementary school.

Margaret had many friends of both sexes but did not believe in playing the field as a young lady even though she could have had any young man she wanted. She was beautiful by any standard. While growing up young men would trip over their own feet trying to gain her attention and favors. But she wanted to save herself for the one who would bear her children. She explained, Gordon swept her off her feet and into his bed. He was the first man to have done so. No others had touched her. But they did not conceive a child. This was a blessing and to her benefit because she could be mobile.

Despite being purified in the Navajo way, Margaret couldn't shake her feelings of shame. She loved teaching; but her heart wasn't in it. She loved the children and their eager minds and talented souls. She looked to her mountains to invoke their spirits to give her strength and to help her decide what to do. But it was not enough.

Mother and father protested her beliefs had been compromised by leaving the reservation and going off to college. They entreated her to remain on the Navajo. In her desperation to solve her problems Margaret applied for a job with the Headquarters office of the Indian Health Service as a secretary in the Director's Office just to get away and find herself. She was becoming restless and wanted to leave her parents in peace and dignity. She needed to heal on her own. To her utter amazement she was hired.

Margaret moved to Rockville and located an apartment on the Twinbrook Pike in easy walking distance to the Parklawn Building. Across the street from her apartment complex was a little park where she liked to take picnic lunches on her days off. Behind the buildings was an even larger undeveloped area for strolls. There she walked and jogged and communed with nature. She was beginning to heal. Images of Gordon began to fade.

Giroux occasionally jogged the same trail behind the Parklawn Building in the early morning hours before work began. By chance one day Margaret jogged on the return leg to her apartment and passed Giroux on the trail going in the opposite direction. She smiled as he passed and waved to him in recognition.

Giroux was immediately taken with her striking beauty. Even though she was not hired to be his personal secretary Margaret worked nearby in the same office as the secretary for the Deputy Director. She dealt with others with quiet dignity and authority.

Andrew liked this in her and couldn't help but notice how effortlessly she walked. Like a fleecy white cloud walking the sky. He began to take notice of her.

Margaret delved into her work oblivious to his interest and was fascinated with the opportunity to meet national leaders — both tribal and federal — whose names before were only so many letters on a written page. Here, they were flesh and blood, fat and thin, traditional and acculturated, and much different than her imagination had first allowed.

Because of her competence the Deputy Director increasingly brought her into meetings to take notes. When asked to refresh the memories of attendees at these meetings, Margaret would first summarize content of discussions and then supply miscellaneous supportive data from her recall of information that passed by her daily, much like in a thesis. Her mind was organized.

Giroux noticed her ability and seized an opportunity one day to question her about wasting her time as a secretary. She obviously had skills that exceeded most of the secretaries in the agency. Innocently, Margaret explained at this time in her life she needed to be away from the reservation, from her memories of a painful marriage, to learn who she is and to gather some strength as a woman.

Giroux allowed her time to express herself without comment. Without knowing it, Margaret lowered her defenses over time and began to view him as a father figure. He could do no wrong.

Over the next six months these sessions increased after staff had gone for the day. At a particularly vulnerable moment during one of their discussions, Margaret began to cry, appearing very much alone and needing comfort. Her tears became a flood as she fought for control. Giroux moved in quickly and put his arms around her to comfort her.

Margaret sobbed uncontrollably. Giroux held her and stroked her hair which cascaded beyond her shoulders to the mid point of her back. He kissed her on the top of her forehead.

Margaret looked up to him with tears rolling down her soft cheeks. The furrows they made glistened with reflected lights. He took her face in his hands, smoothed away the tears and kissed her on the eyelids. Margaret stopped sobbing and looked at him for a moment puzzled, alarmed, yet somehow, grateful. Giroux dared to kiss her on the lips as she was about to protest.

When Margaret related this account to her, Janet saw the pattern emerging once again. Margaret was caught in a vulnerable moment and Giroux swooped in unchallenged. Not unlike herself, she thought. She was caught off guard, too. 'Was Sandra?' she wondered.

Before Margaret could fully recover from this assault, Giroux lowered her to his couch touching her gently on the neck, then more insistently on her breasts. Startled she tried to push him away but again his mouth was upon hers.

Margaret wanted and needed some passion in her life to take away her thoughts of her failure with Gordon. But most of the men who wanted to date her she learned were either married or had problems with alcohol. Margaret wanted a relationship with someone who would not complicate her life once more.

She had spent her solitude in Rockville building up a reserve of control. She had thought she was effective in gaining some mastery over her life. But control was no where to be found. It was as if Giroux took away her ability to reason. Her life had been barren for over a year and the feel of a man's hands caressing her felt exquisite but intrusive.

For the next six months their affair continued at his urging. It began to lessen inexplicably and finally dissolve when he seemed to lose interest. Margaret was confused. She couldn't understand what had displeased him.

Generally he had always been in a rush. His greetings at the door of her apartment became as perfunctory as his kisses. Five minutes would be spent in pleasantries and ten minutes in bed. Shortly after, he would be gone. And, Margaret would wonder. At that point, Giroux had fastened his interest on Janet, unbeknownst to Margaret.

Margaret became worried the last two months of the affair. She had not been feeling well particularly in the morning. Her period seemed to be late, too. One fateful morning she decided to see her physician to find out why she just couldn't keep food down well in the morning.

Dr. Sylvia Hansen said, "Oh, Margaret, you should be really happy. It's the oldest reason known to women! Many women have morning sickness when they are first pregnant." Margaret was devastated with this news, although she couldn't tell the doctor why she burst into tears. She pretended that her husband was out of town. Not being pregnant before, she didn't know her symptoms were morning sickness. Margaret just thought she had some weird influenza or virus. She ruled out pregnancy as highly unlikely. Now she felt overwhelmed and fretted over how — or, if — she should tell Giroux. He was so clear he just wanted sex from her and no complications. And, she agreed. She wasn't sure how it even happened. There were only one or two times he didn't wear a condom and one of those times she had her period soon after.

Margaret became sleepless at night and was beginning to have difficulties at work due to her preoccupation with her growing condition. Work was done with less than perfection. It was so unlike her. Too, her mood was less controlled; she seemed more nervous. Finally, she saw another physician who put her on medication to allow her to rest at night. But this, she reasoned, was not good for her baby; and, having a baby would not be good for her at this time in her life. She would not be able to explain anything to her mother. She couldn't come home; and she couldn't afford to have her mother come all the way to Maryland.

In her second month Margaret became convinced she couldn't keep the baby. While the Elavil she had been prescribed helped her with her mood, in her mounting confusion Margaret decided to terminate her pregnancy. At the same time, Giroux abruptly ended their relationship, not knowing anything about her condition. This was a double dose of bitter medicine and one for which she was ill-prepared. Without any support, Margaret began to use her medicine with greater frequency. The third dose of the bitters was being asked by the Deputy Director for her to consider a transfer to another department. Finance had a need for a good secretary, and, quite frankly, "Your work seems to be less than what it was," he said.

Margaret transferred to the Finance Department a month after her abortion at the Montgomery County Planned Parenthood almost adjacent to the Parklawn Building. She worried that the child's soul would be wandering for all eternity in search of its rightful home on the Navajo Reservation. Margaret performed her own simple ceremony asking the child for forgiveness and for understanding one day at her favorite park.

She sought a remote picnic area out of view of the roadway and casual visitors. Margaret wore an unadorned white cotton blouse with a red velveteen broom skirt. As she entered into the secluded area she wrapped herself in her shawl. Out of the bundle she carried she carefully unwrapped a deer skin hide and placed it before her kneeling to the east.

Margaret rested back on her heels and further unwrapped a small clay dish. She placed three eagle feathers above the clay dish, a strand of knotted sage brush to the left and a small pouch of tobacco to the right with some matches.

She broke a small portion of sage from the strand and put a match to it. With a gentle breeze blowing it caught fire readily. For a moment she let it burn to make embers. A small curl of smoke rose from the embers.

Margaret lifted the clay dish in her hands and with the eagle feathers she rose in place and turned north and to the four directions offering the fire to the Father. With the eagle feathers she fanned the fire until the sage gave more smoke. She fanned the smoke over her from head to foot and arm to arm and behind her head. Kneeling, she offered some cornmeal from another beaded pouch to the Father.

Margaret arose and faced the east. She said humbly, "O Great Spirit, whose voice I hear in the winds and whose breath gives life to all the world, hear me, I am small and weak. I need your strength and wisdom.

"Let me walk in beauty and make my eyes ever behold the red and purple sunset. Make my hands respect the things you have made and my ears sharp to hear your voice.

"Make me wise so that I may understand the things you have taught my people. Let me learn the lessons you have hidden in every leaf and rock.

"I seek strength, not to be greater than my brother, but to fight my greatest enemy — myself.

"Make me always ready to come to you with clean hands and straight eyes. So, when life fades as the fading sunset, my spirit may come to you without shame."

Cleansed, she knelt once more to mix water with the ashes to carry them home to bless the four corners of the apartment building and the small bundle she made to represent her baby she would bury in this secluded place.

She could say nothing to anyone else about it and endured the knife-like pain in her silence.

She returned to work the next day and welcomed the change in assignments proposed to her just so she didn't have to encounter Giroux on a daily basis, much to his delight and safety. Janet was recruited to take her place soon after.

Janet truly felt sorry for Margaret who was such a sweet person and wouldn't hurt a fly.

Sandra presented a unique problem of her own. She was still living and working there in Rockville. Very much available to Andrew but, strangely, not seeing that much of him lately. She wasn't sure what that meant. She had made it a rule not to call him for anything. And, she didn't want to ask for any favors. Sandra finally justified their relationship more or less as a pleasant business arrangement designed to relieve physical needs and nothing more. Her relationship could never be called a lover's relationship, she reasoned. Usually lovers mean something to one another. In this case it only meant a pleasant diversion once or twice a month. It was becoming so bothersome for her to think of the whole episode.

In the first encounter in his office her first reaction was to push away from him. Those first few seconds of his embrace made her recoil. 'Did he notice? What kind of woman did he think I was?' Yet, his strong muscular arms held her fast. 'I really didn't want him to hold me that way,' she said to herself, 'But it felt so good.'

Sandra dismissed this lightly as a guilt offering and went about her business as if their affair really didn't matter. Janet's call to see her on this field trip, though, brought it all back — the mid-day couplings in her apartment as a respite from the pressures of the work day, the field trips and conferences in distant cities, the little talks about office politics, and the many hours wondering where and how it would end. She knew it would end. It had to; he would never give his wife up for her. It was not part of the script. She knew she would have to be content to be in the shadows while he played on the stage with his wife for all others to see. It wasn't fair. Sandra wondered if an affair with a married man ever was.

The affair was over. She knew it and understood she would have to move on to another some day. Yes, there was a wound festering. Old recurring thoughts of being used. The relationship really wasn't freely entered; he was a superior officer. But how do you tell an admiral to get lost? She never could answer this question for herself. She struggled with it nightly for a time and it always nagged. Yet it was always put away too, in the far recesses of her mind.

Andrew didn't treat her that badly she reasoned. He just used her for sex. Sandra had to admit she finally did too, acquiescing to his demand. And now he was done. So was she. Thanks, but no thanks. 'Why did Janet have to bring all this up again? I had it resolved.' she thought to herself as she prepared to meet her.

Janet loved the Crown Plaza. This time when Sandra arrived she greeted her and walked her around to the top floor of the gazebo for a change of scenery. Little did she know it was familiar territory to Sandra.

From her description to Janet on the recent visit, Janet concluded Sandra might still be involved. She wouldn't commit herself to any action, at least not on the telephone, but Sandra also would not discount the possibility of joining Margaret and her in a suit. The thought compelled her to find out where the women were coming from.

"Janet, I don't know how you can even think we would be able to win a suit against the Director, that is, if I even admitted to myself that he forced himself upon me and I didn't have a choice. This is such a sore wound that I really resent you for trying to bring me into your problems. I've put my experience with the man in the past.

"You may not know but I was in such a bad way when I moved here from Nashville. A relationship I was in had ended. But all the abuse I had endured I carried with me. It was always with me, night and day at work and when I was home in the apartment. I was intensely lonely and didn't know anyone here. I don't know if you can truly appreciate that." Sandra paused to look around the gazebo. In a momentary panic, having coffee here with Giroux flashed before her.

"What do you really expect of me, Janet? As a commissioned officer I have learned I am bound by different rules than you are. The only thing I can do is file a grievance or something and allege it was always forced. But I began to like having a steady lover, you know? My guess is that would take something from the sting of the allegation. Don't you think?" Sandra paused in irritation.

"No, I think I want to let it drop. I haven't seen him for about a month. I guess he probably has someone else on his string now. Good riddance." Sandra sounded firm in her belief but looked dejected. She didn't want to look directly at Janet for a moment.

The waiter came and took their order for white zinfandel. Janet continued. "If that is true, Sandra, I would watch yourself. He may transfer you just like he did me. One day I was in the office and the next I was enroute to Phoenix. No choice in the matter. I think he can be ruthless if he wants to."

Sandra laughed. "That's probably how I got here in the first place." Janet didn't think her humor too funny. She immediately thought of herself.

"When did you arrive in Rockville?"

"April."

"Yes, it figures. I was out of there in February. He had to have some lead time to arrange your transfer. Not that it matters, if you don't mind my asking, how soon after you got there did he make a move on you?" Janet asked renewing her old hurt.

"One month. May. He invited me for coffee I guess to size me up. Then, we were having a meeting on the Anti-Drug Abuse Act in his conference room with a few others, the Mental Health Director, the Alcoholism Director and some others. He put his hand on my leg, and after the meeting called me into his office. He kissed me without warning."

"Put his hand on your leg in the meeting?" Janet asked in disbelief. She toyed with her glass of wine. "And kissed you! At least with me he asked me up front if I would make love to him. Actually, he used the f... word. With you he came right out and started to play with you. I think he has a lot of nerve, Sandra. I'm sorry, I suspect you are loyal to him, but that man has no loyalty to anyone but himself. I'm convinced of that.

"Did you know he got someone pregnant? I promised I wouldn't tell who. But yes he did! He didn't even watch himself and protect the young lady." Janet was allowing her anger to get the best of her. She stopped short of cussing him.

Sandra was caught short with this last revelation. In her own relationship there were times Giroux didn't bother with protection. She began to purchase condoms for her own protection after the first time, hoping he would get the message. Instead he would use hers.

Strange! The director of a major health service unconcerned about the health of a lover. This was the first time that thought occurred to her. It was disquieting. It made her feel as if she were an object, something to be played with.

Sandra felt uncomfortable. Janet followed someone and she followed Janet into his bed. Already there were three lovers she could count without having to dig further. She was one of the players in his little parade. Definitely an object.

"What are you thinking of, Sandra?" Janet asked noticing she had grown silent and appeared preoccupied.

"If what you are saying is true, Janet, perhaps I have been living a lie. It took some doing, but I convinced myself early I may be somewhat special in his life. He told me he was married. I even met his wife once. It didn't occur to me then that I wasn't the only one on his string. He almost had me believing he cared for me. He was so smooth. Reluctantly, I gave him all I had. Now since I haven't seen him for a month he is probably making plans for someone else. At least, I wouldn't be surprised."

Sandra looked into her glass of Zinfandel as if it were a mirror catching images of her and Giroux. "In this month I have actually been thinking quite a bit about that affair. After I got over my anger with his pressure, I believed it was wonderful to be wanted and truly exhilarating to be his girl friend, if that is what I could call myself. You know what I mean. But I really wonder about the way he went about it, how he came onto me in the meeting, and the kiss in his office later.

"I put all these thoughts out of my head when it happened. I shouldn't have. Being a single woman in the DC area without much rank I actually thought the only way I could get ahead in this man's world was not to resist. Truthfully, I really didn't want to do it. I wasn't looking for an affair with him. Who would believe me if I said the Director came onto me, especially since I gave in the first time?"

"So you just quit thinking about it, right? And went along with his plan to use you, right?" Janet reflected. "Sandra, the man has been counting on us to keep silent. So far he has been right. He can expect us to be afraid of his power and influence. After all, who are we in the scheme of things? He probably has markers out that he can call in any time and get us moved out of his way without so much as causing a wrinkle on his handsome brow. I firmly believe that is what happened to me. I believe I have nothing to lose by going after him.

"I have to admit, though, I am frightened to take him to court. But I don't have to be sexually harassed either." Janet paused. "Dear, I hope you will really think more about this. I think you have been had just like I have been and Margaret has been."

"What is that?" Sandra immediately caught the third person's name.

"Oh, I'm sorry. I can't tell you. I know I can trust you, Sandra, to keep a secret, but I promised Margaret I wouldn't tell anyone what she told me Andrew did to her," she paused holding onto her temptation. "This much I can tell you. Whatever it was, made her get professional help."

"Professional help?"

"Yes, she's even on medication and the poor woman can hardly make ends meet! You know how expensive it is living here."

"Was she the one whom he got pregnant?" Sandra paused, concerned about Margaret but relieved it wasn't her. She thanked God it hadn't happened to her. "And I bet he doesn't even know or care!" Each of the ladies finished their wine and left filled with their own thoughts. Janet felt foolish with her slips of the tongue. She was amazed how quickly Sandra surmised the pregnancy.

CHAPTER EIGHT

CONFRONTATION

Cox, Lanahan, and Pierce, Ltd., an all woman law firm, occupied a modest old red brick converted home in the older part of Rockville. As it turned out their office was not far from Admiral Giroux's residence. Just three streets away. What was once the side lawn was paved over for a parking lot. Several cars were there portending an active firm. The office had an air of solidity about it. A neat yew hedge ringed the outer walk. Arborvitae on the corners of the house were neatly trimmed. Red azalea flanked the arborvitae. Purple rhododendrons bloomed profusely in the corners near the street. Red tulips and yellow daffodils were at their feet. The trellis forming an archway over the walkway into the side door was festooned in blue wisteria.

Jane, Janet, and Margaret were there for the initial interview. Jane wanted to go to support them since this was really her idea even though she couldn't agree that she felt abused by Andrew. She just felt guilty. Guilt can move mountains — or, dig tunnels! As it turned out, Sandra went on an extended assignment to New Mexico and couldn't make the interview. She was actually relieved but offered her verbal support to the other ladies in their quest for justice. She preferred to be in her own tunnel for the moment.

Jane was most insistent and set the interview time and date. Phyllis Cox, the principal partner of the firm, understood that Janet had to return to Phoenix on Saturday morning. Nevertheless, she said she could only spare about half an hour Friday at 4:30. Could they come in then? Jane worked feverishly to convince Margaret and Janet to be there. By now, more removed from their intimate discussion, each was beginning to be fearful about the prospect of bringing their boss to court. This was their chance, and, yes, she would go with them. This was the least she could do.

The trio entered the office and were ushered into the anteroom to wait for Phyllis Cox. The room was comfortably appointed in early American furniture. Rock maple bookshelves and occasional tables were laced. Historical novels adorned the bookshelves. Magazines were on the tables: *Cosmopolitan, Time, US News* and *National Geographic*. Sprays of forsythia blossomed from vases placed in the middle of the top of each bookshelf. Floor lamps were at the ends of the wing back couch and overstuffed chair. The room was a mixture of warm browns, yellows, and pale blue.

After a ten minute wait, Phyllis charged into the room and introduced herself with a handshake to each. Business to the core. Upright, tall, almost imposing, with a severe hairdo, brown hair pulled back into a bun, steel rim glasses. "Hello, I'm Phyllis Cox, the senior partner of the firm. Please come with me to my office." Her angular features were the match for her angular voice. The words spilled out, sharp, clear and distinct, no syllable missed.

The trio trailed off after her, looked at each other, immediately intimidated and questioning themselves whether this was such a good idea. They quickly learned how good an idea it was. As they talked, her voice mellowed, became more modulated, and warmed with the understanding of the relevance of the matter.

"Who would like to begin?" Phyllis looked from one to the other who were also looking at each other. Each wanted to escape the clutches of her gaze.

Margaret gave Jane a nudge. "I'm Jane Candelaria. I made the appointment with you. Believe me I'm really happy that you could give us your time on such short notice. I really don't mind talking, but I'm quite sure I don't want to do anything about it."

"Well, you painted a very interesting picture on the telephone, enough to make me want to see more. What is it you don't want to do anything about, Jane?" Phyllis asked.

"About the Director." Jane stopped and saw that Phyllis looked puzzled. She continued. "I... I am the secretary to the Director of the Federal Indian Health Service. I... I am in a good position to see and hear a lot of things. Sometimes there are things I hear or see that I don't approve of that upset me greatly."

She changed position in her chair, trying to become more comfortable. It didn't work. She continued, changing positions again.

"Actually, I haven't been getting much good sleep lately thinking about what has been happening to these ladies and possibly others. It is all so distressing."

"What has been happening to them, Jane?" Phyllis asked softly, preparing a legal pad for notes. "Before you continue, I need your names and addresses. Sorry, please continue," she added as she began her notes.

Jane gave her details and observations and suspicions. Soon the 30 minutes were up. Phyllis called her secretary to cancel her dinner engagement. "Janet, tell me what happened to you."

Janet summarized her relationship with Andrew, all the while blaming herself for feeling she was victimized. She painted a picture of Andrew as greater than life size, a man unique among men, a man for whom the rules don't apply equally. In short, Janet was afraid; and, Phyllis picked up her concern.

"Look, Janet, I'm sorry, but you sound like you want to protect this man. What you have told me so far is that the man came onto you using his position of power to influence you to have sex with him. And, he continued throughout that relationship to control you, calling all the shots and, ending the relationship by having you transferred to a place not of your choosing. Is that about right?" Phyllis waited for a response.

None was forthcoming at the moment. "All right. I get the picture from you, Janet. You are still intimidated by the Admiral for the moment." Turning to Margaret, Phyllis asked, "Tell me what happened to you, Margaret."

Margaret found difficulty looking at her. Looking a little past her Margaret began to tell Phyllis about her background and strong traditional upbringing, and how important to her these ways were to guide her in her life away from the reservation. City life was foreign to her, and its ways were not hers.

Margaret was more simple in her description but eloquent in her narration of the destruction the affair brought to her. She now felt she was living in an elaborate waste land, dependent upon medication to get her through the day, and totally unable to reconcile her spirit which was adrift. She described how she looked to Andrew as a father figure who could do no wrong but that somehow she felt wronged. Her life was a shambles and she had great shame to bear. Her heart was heavy for her lost child.

Jane was caught unaware. Her right hand covered her mouth in shock. She had no knowledge or suspicion that Margaret was ever pregnant. She broke down in tears and enveloped Margaret in her arms as if she was a small child, soothing her and stroking her hair. "I'm so sorry, Margaret, I didn't know. When you called me to watch out for Andrew you couldn't tell me why." She exclaimed furiously, "That S.O.B. ought to be jailed!"

This was so uncharacteristic of Jane. She gasped at what she said. She made a conscientious effort to avoid using foul language. Her Christian training always seemed to put a bridle on her tongue.

Phyllis smiled and said, "Let's not get too carried away. So far we only have the word of two women against the Director of the Indian Health Service. From the appearance of things it would seem that he establishes a relationship that appears to be professional at the start; the relationship quickly degenerates to a sexual relationship through the abuse of his position, particularly to the point where you feel controlled; and at the failure of the relationship you believe his power was used to move you physically some place else.

"Believe me ladies. This man has feet of clay like most men. He is not a god. He may have no conscience. While there are similarities in your stories we really need corroboration from as many others as possible who may have been sexually harassed like you." The ladies looked at each other and expressed relief for Phyllis giving a name to what they experienced. "Are there others to your knowledge?" she softened.

Jane volunteered and glanced at the others. They took a keen interest in what she had to say. "I think I know of a third lady who was recruited to be the Deputy Director of the Nursing Branch. Sandra Locklear. Unlike these ladies Sandra is a commissioned officer."

Phyllis looked puzzled. "What do you mean she is not like these ladies? I don't understand."

"I don't really know if it makes any difference but Sandra Locklear is an officer like a Navy officer. She wears a uniform and is paid differently than these women who are civil servants. They get orders to go here or there just like the military. You see, the Indian Health Service uses two personnel systems to fill vacancies here and in the field. If you talk with her, I'm sure you can find out what difference it makes if any."

Jane described her uncomfortable feelings on the meeting in the Director's office. But she had no hard evidence like she had with Janet. "I know it all sounds like I am suspicious. I've never talked with Sandra about it like I have with Janet. Sandra has kept her distance from the front office and I've never seen the two of them together elsewhere. I feel a little awkward even mentioning her name in this meeting as being involved."

"Well, it sounds as if I may need to talk with her, at least to clear the air. If I do, and if she is involved, she may choose to do nothing. Actually, I think we are — or, I am getting a little ahead of myself in this. I need to ask you some questions."

For the next half-hour, Cox grilled the ladies on their understanding of sexual harassment. Finally, each understood it did not have to involve actual intercourse. Words, gestures, cartoons and innuendoes were sufficient to create an atmosphere of harassment. It was management's duty to eliminate that from the workplace. And, very importantly, Cox learned that management didn't carry out its responsibility to train staff in the meaning of the law. Each of the ladies was hired at different times and neither had received so much as an hour training.

Cox realized she had a challenging case and relished the opportunity to champion their cause. The federal establishment set the standards for everyone else in the country; and here an agency of the federal government was plainly flaunting itself in everyone's face. If the director was getting away with sexual harassment, then chances were high that others were involved. Cox agreed to take their case and outlined a plan of action.

Phyllis was disappointed that Janet had to return to Phoenix without getting her deposition. But she understood and arranged for further telephone calls to set it up via long distance. She would make arrangements with a court reporter firm in Phoenix to take a teleconference deposition. It would be expensive at first, but she explained that this case would either go to trial with obvious negative publicity for the Indian Health Service, or it would be settled out of court. In either case they would recover all expenses and a sufficient sum for punitive damages.

Margaret was relieved but frightened at the prospect of taking the Director to court. Intellectually she understood she was victimized by him. Emotionally she felt she was about to betray her father. She thought she had worked through this in therapy. But the prospect of having the whole affair revealed in an open court sickened her, especially the part about her pregnancy. Word would get back to her mother and father and she would be shamed.

"I understand how hard it must be for you, believe me," Cox said.

"No, I am sorry, but you don't. You are white. I am Navajo. I killed my baby. I was too shamed to call for help. I didn't keep my child. Indians don't do this. I haven't been purified. My baby has no home." Margaret cried profusely with the vision of her child lost somewhere in the void.

Cox touched her hand gently. "I don't know what to say, Margaret. You are right. I don't know what to say, except the anguish you feel here ought to be compensated for by that man. I won't rest until we do that. And maybe, just maybe, we can teach the agency you work for something in the process."

CHAPTER NINE

COMPLICATIONS

"Come in, Sam. I want you to look at this and give me your best advice on a very delicate matter. We may have a problem in the Indian Health Service," the Surgeon General said as he handed a packet to his Chief of Staff. Dr. Joseph emptied copies of the documents from the packet which included letters from an attorney and two women, lay them neatly before Dr. Price, and glanced at his subordinate. He looked somber and somewhat perplexed. Usually the Surgeon General didn't approach sensitive discussions in this manner with him. They had known each other for years and had no need to be secretive. Yet he offered Dr. Price no explanation. Most curious!

Dr. Price looked at the materials, disbelief growing with each document he perused. "My God!" he exclaimed. "Andrew Giroux! Do you think this is true, Dr. Joseph? His record has been unblemished. How could he put himself in such a compromising position? Three million dollars is one helluva tag."

The Surgeon General didn't respond immediately. Turning in his leather chair to view the Capitol from his vantage point in the Hubert Humphrey Building, Dr. Joseph assumed a contemplative pose and reflected.

This allegation was the most serious he had heard about any of his Agency directors. He concluded it undermined the fabric of the Corps, would bring discredit to the Indian Health Service, and call into question the morals of other men in leadership positions. If true, Admiral Giroux would have to bear this burden alone. The Corps couldn't help. And, if untrue, he would have to support the man legally but not financially.

He turned to Dr. Price. "Sam, find out what you can about this and give me a status report in two days. When you talk with Dr. Giroux, meet him some place other than his office or yours. This could get ugly, and I don't want reporters digging around in our closets."

Andrew placed the telephone receiver back on its hook and told Jane he had to leave the office for an urgent appointment. He would not be returning the rest of the day. She should cancel his appointments.

"A matter of utmost importance," Sam had said. "Cancel appointments ... career interests ... concerns for Indian Health Service; take the Metro."

Andrew felt alarm at these comments. His ride on the Metro to Union Station was filled with anxiety and mounting concern. The darkness of the tunnels added to his fears. He didn't like Sam's tone of voice, clipped phrases and concern for privacy. If he wanted privacy, why the lower level eatery in Union Station? It would be filled with people. "Mandatory that I meet with you," Sam had emphasized, much to Andrew's dislike for his peremptory use of the authority of the Surgeon General's office. Andrew thought he was being a bit dramatic; yet, he couldn't afford to ignore the unusual request. Even though Sam had no direct authority over him, Andrew knew his influence with the Surgeon General could make or break a career officer. Giroux didn't plan on retirement just yet.

Giroux speculated on what this meeting could possibly be about — maybe his differences with the boss about policy issues, or his stubborn adherence to creating a sense of awareness of Indian issues in the Surgeon General's office and the need of the government to be responsive to Indian concerns over treaty rights. Indians were entitled to complete health care by the government. This was as fundamental as the Bill of Rights in his opinion. This really couldn't be it, he reasoned. The SG would have to acknowledge Giroux's unwavering loyalty and commitment to the Indians he served so well over the years.

Perhaps Giroux's criticism of the ASG's interminable delay in signing his approval to the new health care proposal had reached the SG's ears. While he respected Sam's credentials, Giroux believed Sam lacked 'people skills'. No, that couldn't be it ... too routine. It must be something else. But what?

Aversion To Honor

Giroux figured he would just have to wait. All his speculations were inconclusive and he was getting more irritated by the minute. As the driver announced "MetroCenter, transfer point for the Blue and the Orange lines," Giroux knew his ride to the Union Station would not be long now. He would exit on the lower level and look for Sam in the crowded eatery under the stairwell descending from the top floor of the station.

The train glided to its appointed stop. Andrew looked around for Sam and easily found him. He couldn't miss him. His commanding figure stood out in his uniform enhanced by his stern demeanor. Sam had an overwhelming sense of self-importance that intruded into almost every contact whether business or social. Yet, Sam greeted Giroux warmly as if the greatest of friends. "How is Elizabeth? And the children? Are they getting along well in college?" Sam asked.

"They are fine." Andrew paused. "With all due respect, Sam, I'm sure you didn't call me to what appears to be a secret meeting to discuss my family, now did you? What is it that is so earth shattering we couldn't discuss either in your office or mine? If it was my comment I made at the oversight meeting, I'll gladly apologize, Sam."

Sam shifted in his chair, losing his congenial tone. "All right, Andrew. I'll come to the point. You and I may not be the best of friends, but, you know, working with the health service is very much like being in a small family. We're such a small group that what affects one of us affects us all. Do you know what I mean? Yes, I'm sure you do."

Andrew just looked at Sam. He was perplexed and didn't much like the ASG's round about approach. Andrew did not have to be reminded he lived in a fish bowl and that his actions were monitored by nearly everyone in and out of the service. That was one of the drawbacks to public life he least enjoyed. He was not a private citizen and frequently longed for the day he could find another position elsewhere.

Sam continued. "We each have our moments. Some of them good, and some of them bad. We are happy when our officers receive promotions or get recognized for their exemplary service; as are we saddened when life's mishaps befall anyone in our "little family." You know what I mean."

"No, I don't. Not really. What are you trying to tell me, Sam? That I'm going to be the next Surgeon General or that I'm getting drummed out of the corps? It's not like you to beat around the bush, Sam. What do you have on your mind?"

Sam leaned forward in his chair and said, "Some of us conduct our private affairs a little more privately, Andrew. You know what I mean. The Corps doesn't like dirty linen much less having that linen thrown into its face in a public way. Allegations of sexual misconduct are particularly disturbing to the Corps. I think you will agree."

Sam paused to note the effect his choice of words were having. Andrew blanched. "What are you talking about?" he demanded, lowering his voice to control his sudden anxiety.

Sam replied, "The SG received this letter yesterday." Sam handed him the letter with a flourish. He was eager to watch Andrew's response. He was not disappointed.

The cover letter read:

COX, LANAHAN, AND PIERCE, PC
3576 Rockville Pike
Rockville, Maryland 20857
Attorneys At Law
(301) 526-2930

Office of the Surgeon General
Parklawn Building
5600 Fishers Lane
Rockville, Maryland 20857

Dear Dr. Joseph:

Our clients, Ms. Margaret Bloomquist and Ms. Janet Hastings, are providing you advance notice of intent to file a suit in Federal Court charging RADM Andrew S. Giroux, Director, Indian Health Service, U.S. Public Health Service, with sexual harassment. In addition to these charges, our clients want indemnification in the amount of $1.5 million each as punitive and compensatory damages.

On numerous occasions in the depositions, copies of which are enclosed, these current employees have stipulated that RADM Giroux had abused the power and influence of his office to solicit sexual favors from his subordinates. Further, once he had ended his affairs, the Plaintiffs will stipulate that RADM Giroux had influenced other subordinates to transfer each named employee to other positions within the Indian Health Service without consultation with the employee. These transfers are viewed as retaliatory actions.

Whereas, these serious charges will result in litigation against your employee, we, the Attorneys for the Plaintiffs, believe you may wish to take other actions as provided for in your personnel policies on professional conduct.

Very truly yours,

Phyllis L. Cox
Attorney at Law
Cox, Lanahan and Pierce, PC

Andrew read every word of the letter from the attorney and the letters from the women, his color increasing as he did so. He struggled with control. It was not easily coming.

Finished with his reading, he fumed, "Sam, this is preposterous. These women have been known in our agency to be disgruntled about their lack of promotions. They're troublemakers that's all. It's plain to see they're out to destroy my career with these trumped-up charges. You know my dedication to PHS as well as the improvements I've made in service delivery in IHS. Before I came here, the so-called support of public health concepts was a mockery. Our system is the premier example of a health maintenance organization. It's really a star in your constellation of programs."

He collected his thoughts. "You can bet I'll get to the bottom of this and handle it. Tell the SG not to worry. This is totally ridiculous. I'll have my attorney look into it and clear this up right away." Andrew looked Sam in the eye in his most sincere way while his stomach churned. "I've got to get back, Sam. Thanks for your concern and for lunch." Sam looked at him cautiously and said finally, "You better look into whether or not they followed procedure, Andrew. Just a word of caution."

Andrew left immediately fuming to himself. The ride on the Metro to the Rockville station was worrisome. He realized his quip about being drummed out of the Corps may be more real than he had imagined. He had visions of being called into the SG's office where his shoulder boards would be ripped from his shirt. Word would get out on the moccasin telegraph and before morning fingers would be pointed at him. He stared at his reflected image in the window as the train roared through the vast tunnels of the Metrosystem.

This, of course, was not realistic either, he reasoned. No one really knew what truth there was to the matter, not even the SG, despite the letter. He would have to be cool and keep things under wraps until he could work something out. The only one he could trust with very delicate matters was Charlie. He helped him out before, maybe he will do it again.

Andrew went directly home. He descended the stairs at the Rockville station, crossed the Pike via the overhead walkway, passed the Montgomery County Procurement Operations office remarking cynically to himself 'how apropos.' He descended the stairwell by the United Artists Theater and walked the remaining five blocks to his house in a fog.

Elizabeth greeted him with surprise. "What brings you home this early, dear?"

"Oh, I just thought I would get away from the office today, 'Liz. Why don't we go out to dinner and to a movie? We haven't done that for awhile, have we? The walk to the theater would do us some good." Andrew said this unconvincingly as he looked through today's mail casting bills aside.

He spied a certified letter from Cox, Lanahan and Pierce. His heart jumped.

"What is that about?" Elizabeth asked innocently noticing Andrew staring at the letter. He didn't have the courage to tell the whole truth as he felt the pit of his stomach suddenly give way. He thought he would say just enough to make the matter sound legitimate, but not so much as to create alarm.

"We were notified today that some disgruntled employees were going to sue Administration about some personal dissatisfaction, and you know that means me." He couldn't lie about this. He had to maintain composure. It was not a lie; Elizabeth must not know the whole truth.

"So you came home to see if your precious letter arrived," Elizabeth stated caustically, aware that once again, work preempted her life. Andrew didn't need to look at her to know how disappointed she was that his motives were not entirely genuine. But past experience taught her not to make anything of it. She buried her feelings as she had done so often when work seemed to interfere with her evenings alone with Andrew. Again she took it on face value. What choice did she have? She wondered. Elizabeth was usually non-judgmental and gave everyone the benefit of the doubt.

Putting aside her disappointment, Elizabeth gave in. "Oh, well, why don't you go into the library where you can have privacy and read your mail without interruption, Andrew. I'll put on a fresh pot of coffee, you can make some notes, and if you want to go out later, we can." Elizabeth was gracious, as always, he thought. So giving. Poor dear!

He knew not to make anything of it either. It was all right for his mind to tell him that. But his feelings were getting in the way. His mind began to work. No use alarming her. He did not want to be found out. He especially did not want to tip her off as to what some of his "work" was that was pressuring him today.

He really did care for her; at least he did not want to hurt her. He told himself that time and again after he had sex with someone else. After all she did bear him three lovely children. But he always excused himself that his work was so pressured that he had to have a release. Sex with someone else seemed to give him that edge, just as some people jog or walk or play tennis to relieve tension.

"Well, perhaps you are right, 'Liz. I do need to collect my thoughts for a moment. I'm sorry." Andrew turned and went to the library off the entrance hall, slid the old oak door open into its pocket. As it closed behind him with a thud, he felt reassured, the problem contained at least for a while.

The library opposite to Elizabeth's sun room on the eastern side of the house in the old home built in the 1900's was well-appointed. Dark red mahogany paneling circled the room. Old floral designed wall paper adorned the walls. Western art denoting expansionist topics that presaged the demise of Indian culture, were interspersed among shelves holding Indian artifacts, bowls, baskets, peace pipes, and eagle feathers. It was his attempt to keep that culture from complete collapse. He often wondered if it had not happened already, as if he were caretaker in a living museum.

The old oak desk held his modern Macintosh computer and Hewlett Packard printer. A rich red leather sofa was complemented by an antique brocaded chair. Over the windows hung velveteen drapes and lace sheers. Leather bound books competed for space with volumes of history — both modern and ancient, art, and literature all nestled on cherry bookcases.

This was Andrew's inner sanctum, the *sanctum sanctorum*, his refuge from the assaults of his public life. It was a place where he restored his lost balance and could look issues squarely in the eye and resolve most problems. He took great pride in being knowledgeable in things western and in being Indian. Tonight, however, he was preoccupied by his dilemma, and the position he was in as an Indian, a man, and a national leader. He stared at his plaques and mementos and at length picked up a beaded eagle feather given to him by a Sioux medicine man.

If it could talk, he wondered what it would say to him as he turned it about in the lengthening shadows of his sanctuary. What advice would he hear as he fanned himself with the sacred feather? Would it tell him to acknowledge his fault before men? Or save himself by resigning his position? Or would it say nothing and let him reflect on what he did or failed to do?

Of the many eagle feathers he had received over the years this one was a source of great pride and comfort to him. When he was first assigned to the Pine Ridge Reservation, the medicine man told him not to be tempted to disregard the old ways of his ancestors in favor of western medicine. While Andrew was not from Pine Ridge, Harry Old Soldier took him under his wing and made him privy to his medicine ways. To be effective in healing he must always be true to these ways, to be clean in thought and one with the eagle spirit.

He recalled while Andrew was on duty one evening at the Reservation hospital, a distraught mother brought her 14 year old daughter in for an examination. Both mother and daughter were on the verge of hysteria. She suddenly lost her sight. Mother did not know what to do and wanted Dr. Giroux to heal her and restore her vision immediately.

Andrew examined her thoroughly and concluded to himself there was nothing structurally wrong with her eyes. He surmised that she did not want to "see" a reality she was capable of seeing. The young lady recalled to him the events of the day with flattened affect but had inadvertently blocked out of her recall two hours in the early evening — a time when she was home alone with her father.

Andrew suspected something dreadful happened to her in those two hours which had profoundly affected her. He did not want to refer her to a staff mental health specialist at this time. In his wisdom Andrew did not tell mother what he suspected occurred, but, instead, convinced her he needed immediate consultation with Harry Old Soldier before he would conduct some tests.

Harry soon arrived at the hospital, examined the young girl himself and conferred with Andrew. Angelina was out of harmony with her father and the spirits were protecting her from seeing an evil spirit trying to enter their family. He would stay with her tonight in the hospital and would confer with her mother and father in the morning. There was no need for sedatives; Angelina would rest well and would soon recover her sight fully. Angelina was placed in a private room, mother at her side sobbing. Harry dismissed staff with the exception of Andrew, closed the door, and began singing his healing song while taking out from his bundle the most beautiful eagle feather Andrew saw.

Andrew recalled how unsure he was then. He was just a young doctor but his instinct said to allow Harry to minister to Angelina and the family in the hospital. He knew that to have him remain in the room was a privilege not accorded to many. Harry was moved to allow this exception as a way of teaching this young Indian doctor that there is more to doctoring than the University of Minnesota could ever teach. They remained at Angelina's bedside throughout the night.

Harry's song filled the room and spilled out into the corridors of the hospital and stilled the angry spirits of the sick. Peace entered the rooms that night and walked the hallways quieting all fears. Harry's voice was soothing, like a cool cloth on a feverish brow.

Andrew reflected in the growing dark of his library with the spent day. He looked at the feather and could almost envision Harry Old Soldier looking at him through the distance of time.

This was the feather that cured Angelina and brought harmony to her family, the feather that was given to Harry by his Medicine Chief, and was a powerful symbol in all tribes. It was in his hands to cure others. Could he cure himself?

Andrew was disquieted and dropped the feather in his lap. He could not bear to look the image of Harry in the eye. In the dying sunset of the day he swore he saw an eagle flying away. He had no answer. Can a physician heal himself?

Just then the telephone rang startling Giroux from his reverie. "Hello, Andrew. This is Charles. More bad news I'm afraid. I've heard from the grapevine about your letter. Sorry, boss. But to make matters worse, you had an EEO action filed against you today when you were downtown."

"A what?" Giroux asked. "What for?"

"Sex harassment, boss," Mathieson replied, pausing. "Sandra Locklear. She's charging you with unwanted sexual advances over the course of more than a year." He paused trying to cover up his snicker. "Gee, boss, I didn't know you were banging her! It's a helluva thing having your private life coming out all over for the world to see, huh? Jeez!"

"How did you learn of it?"

"I've got a friend — well, you know what I mean — in the EEO office. Anyhow, she sort of let it slip to me a week ago that someone was going to try to stick you with a sex harassment complaint."

"Why the hell didn't you tell me that then?" Giroux interrupted angrily. "I thought we had an understanding. Maybe it's time I find a place for you, Charlie. Don't play coyote with me."

"Wait a minute, boss? You're out of line! Remember who you are talking to. First, she told it to me when we were in the sack. Quite honestly, the way Sarah told me sounded like sour grapes or something, and I wasn't sure you weren't laying her, too. If I believed you were making it with my woman you and I would be having problems. Second, you are in no position to be ordering me around, boss. Remember, I've saved your ass on many occasions, not just this one. Do you want me to give you the litany of times and places? Do I really need to?" Charlie asked testily.

Charlie shrugged his shoulders and waited for his response. It wasn't long in coming. Giroux quickly sensed that Charlie was fuming and just warming up to the task. He backed off his own charge. "No, no, Charlie. I have no interest in Sarah. I guess I just panicked for a minute. I apologize. Come over and we'll have a glass of wine. I really need your help on this one."

Giroux settled back in his favorite chair to wait for Charlie. Elizabeth effortlessly slid the study door open and wheeled a rock maple serving cart in loaded with an 1803 Rogers Brothers tea set and a sliced date and nut roll. Absentmindedly, Giroux said "Thanks, Dear," not looking up from his musings on paper.

Elizabeth could not help but notice his bold underlined phrase, 'not you too, Sandra'. She paused for a moment curious to know why her name was so heavily written. She asked innocently, "Is she the problem, Andrew?"

"Huh? Oh, well, yes, one of several." Giroux paused, furious with himself for not covering the scribble. "Not to worry though. Charlie's coming over soon. We need to talk about how to deal with the situation. We won't be long."

"Oh. She must be important to have *that* man over." Elizabeth smiled as she prepared to leave the room. "What's that, Dear?" Giroux called to her. "Oh, nothing, Andrew. Nothing, really. I'll see Charlie in when he arrives." "Yes, uh, thanks Liz." Giroux returned to his note taking without looking up.

His wait was not long. Charlie arrived shortly after. In his usual curt manner he told Elizabeth, "The boss asked me over. I need to see him."

"I know. I'll take you to him right away. He's in his study waiting." Elizabeth started to walk toward the study. Charlie interrupted. "I know where it's at. I will let myself in, thank you." Elizabeth paused lifting her eyebrows at his affront. "To be sure. Why don't you just let yourself in, Mr. Mathieson." She turned about sharply and went upstairs to her bedroom irritated with his total lack of manners.

Elizabeth could not understand what Andrew saw in this man. He was always curt and rude in her presence and used foul language the few times she had seen him here. She wished Andrew did not have to associate with him. In her estimation Charlie would do nothing but bring him harm. She couldn't envision how the likes of him could actually be a resource that Andrew couldn't do without. She closed the bedroom door behind her, glad she did not have to see or hear him more than on the rare occasions when he came at night to confer with Andrew. Those occasions weren't rare enough, and Elizabeth was only too glad to put him out of her mind tonight.

To divert her from the closed-door meeting below, Elizabeth turned her attention to Robert Ludlum's farce, *The Road to Omaha,* about how this white general got himself appointed the Chief of a tribe of Indians in Nebraska to hold the Strategic Air Command at Offutt Air Force Base in Omaha, hostage to achieve his hidden objectives. The novel's zany general relieved her tensions with his antics for the moment.

Giroux welcomed Charlie into his inner sanctum where he felt most comfortable with the memorabilia of his career moves. When he looked at his collection of pottery, plaques, baskets, Pendleton blankets, and Kachina dolls he drew strength from the recognition awarded him over the years.

Somehow this strength was misguided, though, in his personal life. He did not want to recognize that it had gone awry with his increasing appetite for women. Giroux had almost thought of it as a perk of office. His strength had become transformed into shrewdness in his ability to avoid detection — until now, that is.

Janet, Margaret, and now Sandra — these women were becoming meddlesome. They were out to destroy him. He wondered how this could have happened to him. But he had to deal with them; and Charlie was the best. He had helped him before. This time though he would have to give Charlie something. Whatever he asked. These women could not be allowed to stop his career.

"Charlie, make yourself comfortable. Elizabeth brought me some tea and cake a little while ago. Help yourself. Or do you want something stronger?" Charlie replied without hesitation,

"The Christian Brothers Brandy would be nice. Do you mind if I have one of my Cleopatras, too?"

"Elizabeth doesn't like smoking in the house. But go ahead. I'll just open this window a little to clear the aroma. Tell me what happened." Giroux brought out the decanter of brandy and two snifters and poured two fingers for each of them. Tonight he wasn't in the mood for tea either. The occasion called for a stiffer drink. He settled back in his own chair waiting for Charlie to swirl the brandy in his glass under his nose to get the aroma. Charlie was enjoying the build up to his story.

Charlie recounted his night with Sarah from Giroux's red leather sofa how he had pleased her and afterwards how they would talk about the agency over a few beers. (Giroux wasn't particularly interested in this part and listened out of feigned duty.) As the tale unfolded he finally said Sarah really had a juicy one to tell him 'about the Director' but she really shouldn't because it was supposed to be confidential.

"What did she tell you, Charlie, about Locklear?" Giroux asked anxiously pacing about the room alarmed that others might know about his affair.

"Charlie," she said, "What if I told you someone was going to put in a sex harassment complaint against your boss?" (He laughed; Giroux winced.)

I said, "I think you better tell me real quick, sweetie. You don't want to keep anything like that from me if you know what's good for you." She said, "You give me some more of what's good for me and I'll tell you!"

"Well, after we did it again she told me that one of her counselors was counseling Sandra Locklear about requirements for putting in a grievance against you for sex harassment.

"She hadn't done it yet, but was thinking of doing it, you know."

"Son-of a-bitch!" Giroux roared. Charlie frowned and said, "Well, since you put me in as acting when you were gone downtown the formal grievance came across your desk. I had to read it and call you when you didn't come back to the office. So here I am. What's next?"

"Why didn't you tell me in the first place, Charlie? I really don't understand this." Giroux's anger at what he thought was betrayal put an edge to his voice.

"Look. I told you on the phone. No need to go into that again. People often change their minds about doing stuff like that. They get cold feet and you don't hear from them again. How was I to know Locklear would actually go through with the complaint.

"It's not the end of the world, you know. Locklear can be dealt with. You can always transfer her some place else like you did Janet to Phoenix. You haven't heard from her, now have you?" Charlie sat smugly on the sofa, shoes off and feet raised, content that he had manipulated the system so well.

"Why do you think I asked you to come over, Charlie? Don't tell me you haven't heard about my letter and my trip to the Surgeon General. I'm in deep shit!"

"All I heard was you got a certified letter. It must be still sitting in your office. I swear no one opened it. Are you telling me Janet raised a stink too?" Charlie took a deep drag on his Cleopatra and blew a cloud of blue smoke that seemed to fill the room. "How deep is the shit you're in, boss?" Charlie asked, Giroux's face becoming a blur with his intake of alcohol and the bloom of blue smoke from his cigar.

Giroux rose from the deep red leather chair and walked to the window to get a deep breath of fresh air, inhaling he turned about, and said, "So deep the SG may have to ask me to resign, Charlie. But we can't let that happen, can we my friend?"

"We? What is this 'we' stuff? You're the one who did the dallying in someone else's pants, Andrew, not me. On second thought I have too, but I haven't been caught." Charlie laughed relenting as he asked, "Well, what is the situation, boss?"

It was Giroux's turn to tell him about the letter and the meeting with the Surgeon General's Chief of Staff. When he finished he replenished the brandy in their snifters.

Discomfited he implored Charlie, "Can you help me, Charlie? If you do, I'll make it worth your while. I know you've been wanting to get back to the Aberdeen Area." Charlie grinned. "Tell me more, boss. You have my attention."

Charlie put out his cigar and leaned over to look Giroux in the eye as he settled once more deeply into his chair. "You can't let me know what you do. No details whatsoever, you understand. But I want you to stop these women in their tracks. This matter must not come to the light of the public's day. I especially don't want it to interfere with my career. I want to keep these two stars and retire in comfort with Elizabeth."

Giroux rested looking at his master of manipulation. A weighty silence filled the air. Charlie's face contorted as he thought of various plans. He announced, "I think I can work it out. Just leave it to me. Those bitches won't be able to touch you, boss. And you won't have to give up your commission either. The SG may have to give you a slap on the wrist. But it won't be much."

Giroux rose from his chair relieved and delighted that he could once more trust Charlie with his career. He showed him to the door and retreated to his study again satisfied with the events of this evening. He felt like celebrating and poured himself a smaller brandy as Charlie bounded out of the house.

It felt smooth and hot going down his throat. He remembered Elizabeth preceded him to their bedroom. Making love to her would be smooth and hot, too. It was only nine-thirty. He would make up for his indifference earlier in the evening. He was confident she would have him.

Giroux locked the house and turned out the lights on his way upstairs to the bedroom. Elizabeth heard him ascend. She had long suspected Andrew may be having an affair and she wanted to confront him on this. But not tonight; she hadn't the energy for a confrontation. She was happy to retreat into a novel. It had become her way of dealing with an often unpleasant reality.

Andrew opened the door and found Elizabeth reading. She put the novel down onto her lap slowly watching him. As she did so, Giroux could not help but notice her Prussian blue silk robe was opened to her waist revealing her exquisite breasts. He reveled in their firmness and silhouette stretching the silk. Her reading light bathed them in lights and shadows, hills and valleys.

Giroux stood in front of her bedside night stand bending over to put the light on low. Neither said a word. He slipped off his shirt letting it slide out of his hand to the floor. He smiled knowingly. She could see his excitement grow as he unbuckled his trousers, and, too, let them fall to his feet.

Elizabeth wanted him out of her hunger and excitement. He fulfilled her needs so well. She knew her vulnerability. The old passion she felt for him earlier in their courtship gripped her unmercifully. She slipped his underwear past his hips stopping their descent just enough to allow her to kiss and tantalize his member before continuing, and, at the sight of his penis rising to greet her put aside all thoughts of another woman. Right now at this moment, she was the only woman alive. She convinced herself no one else mattered. It was a story she repeated several times in the past until she came to believe it herself, a trick of memory.

Across town Charlie knocked on Sarah's door. It was late and she didn't want visitors. She stood in the doorway blocking his entrance. "Charlie, go home, please. I just want to get some sleep tonight. I'm not in the mood for any romance. Leave me alone, please." She proceeded to close the door only to be jarred abruptly by Charlie's hand halting it.

Her entreaty fell on deaf ears. Charlie easily pushed her aside and shut the door behind him. "Charlie, get out of here!" she screamed alarmed at his intrusion and trying unsuccessfully to push him back to the door.

He grabbed her by the wrist and smacked her across the mouth with an open hand. "Don't tell me what to do, bitch. I want your ass tonight. I have needs and you can satisfy them."

Sarah protested to no avail. "You've been drinking. I don't like it when you're drinking. You're too rough!" she screamed. "Do you want it here on the floor? Or, do you want to be nice to me in your bed?" he yelled back raising his hand once more to hit her.

Sarah reeled from the blow. "Oh, God! I don't need this." Her cheek swelled and turned red from the sting. Charlie knew enough not to blacken her eyes. Holding her tightly he led her to the bedroom. Others knew of their relationship and he didn't want them to think he was capable of doing real harm to his lover. It was not his purpose tonight.

Sarah shook her hand loose from his grip, turned about, and walked to her bedroom with her head low. Charlie grinned and walking behind her knew she was intimidated. She would do what he wanted. On reaching her bed Sarah flopped down on it face first. She knew what position Charlie liked. "Put a little life into it, woman!" he demanded. Sarah complied holding onto the pillows with both hands clutched moaning to please him while holding back her sobs.

When he climaxed Charlie fell down beside her. In a self-congratulatory mood he said, "That was great. You have the greatest ass in town!

"I just came from Giroux's. I told him about our little *tête-à-tête* last week. He knows you spilled the beans about Locklear's grievance." Sarah sobbed. "Hey. Don't cry. He's not going to do anything to you, sweetheart."

Sarah sat up unsure what to do. Charlie continued. "He won't do anything to you, Sarah, believe me; but I sure as hell will if you don't do as I say. Do you understand me?"

She wheeled about, her right arm coming swiftly toward his face. Charlie intercepted it in mid air. "Don't ever try that again, babe," he said defiantly as he pulled her down to the bed and looking into her eyes, said, "I want you to delay Locklear's grievance. You don't have to do anything illegal. Just delay it. Scrutinize it from every angle. Where you can ask for re-writes, ask for them. Where you can put in a time delay, do it. Just drag it out. And, if it gets to the formal stage, do the same damn thing."

"Charlie, you're a shit, you know?"

"Just do it, babe. And one of these days, I just may take you with me to my next assignment in Aberdeen."

Charlie dressed and let himself out of the apartment satisfied that Sarah would comply with his wishes. He knew she was weak and wouldn't defy him. It would cost her too much. Sarah knew she owed him for being made the Chief of the Equal Employment Opportunity Office. It was her one big break in her career. But she began to wonder if letting him have his way was worth the price. As she arose from the bed she looked in the full length mirror of her closet door and saw how red and swollen her face was with his slaps. What hurt her more though, was the damage to her pride. Surveying her face more closely, she went by into her shower to wash away her silent rage.

Andrew and Elizabeth were sated from their unusually prolonged lovemaking. He kissed her good night, turned over and fell fast asleep. Elizabeth turned the light off but lay awake on her side looking away from Andrew into the night. The night brought disquieting images.

As her eyes adjusted to the darkness and the dim glow of the street light beyond their house, her mind grew alive with phantasms of other women sleeping with Andrew. She had no idea how many there were, or what cities they lived in, or whether she even knew them, or had met them at his work, or, perhaps worst of all, whether they had entertained them in their home during one of their frequent parties.

Elizabeth once adored Andrew and completely gave him her heart. For the longest time she, as others, believed he could do no wrong. He was a model for his staff. They were intensely loyal to him and worked hard to carry out his wishes. He commanded respect even from those outside the agency.

But then for the past two years he had been coming home late consistently. His explanations were plausible; she couldn't assail his logic. There were major initiatives in alcoholism and drug abuse prompted by the Office of the Secretary. They required high level meetings with agency officials. Or, meetings with Congressional staff and program heads to coordinate budget presentations and to get Senator Dominguez's support. Or, the development of special graphics to accompany his presentations to the Senate Select Committee of Indian Affairs. Though on a few occasions Elizabeth thought she could detect the odor of a perfume she didn't wear. She dismissed those occasions as just her imagination. She believed her suspicions were uncalled-for and she willingly suspended her disbelief.

As she lay awake now she couldn't recall why she dismissed them; but now there was a name attached. Sandra's name kept creeping into her stream of consciousness, sometimes covered over by a mist, sometimes as if it were emblazoned in neon. And Andrew's cryptic message written near her name, 'Not you too, Sandra!' It puzzled and gnawed at her for what seemed to be hours.

In a fit of guilt and shame and sleeplessness she chastised herself for her sense of betrayal to Andrew. She accused herself for believing him guilty without even knowing he was. After all he was working so hard for the people; he even said so; she should accept his explanation of disgruntled employees. She knew working for the government created so many dissatisfactions. The Washington Post was always filled with articles attesting to government mismanagement and whistleblowers.

Elizabeth tossed and turned with mixed images of Andrew with sleeves rolled up wading through mounds of paper to reveal occasional women offering themselves to him to replenish his worn spirit. These would give her a start. Finally, she fell into a deep sleep muttering, 'Not you too, Sandra'.

Giroux awoke the next morning thoroughly rested. He slipped out of bed, showered, shaved, and dressed without waking Elizabeth or causing her to stir. He walked to the MetroRail in his usual manner and exited at the Twinbrook station unusually optimistic about his day. Instead of walking immediately the quarter of a mile to the office, he decided to treat himself to a breakfast at the Crown Plaza.

It was early. He was not delayed by a conversation with Elizabeth so he had time for a leisurely breakfast. Ruminating to himself, he said, 'I must have really worn her out last night. So sleepy. Poor dear. She was wonderful. I have to admit it was almost as good as in the beginning of our marriage.'

Giroux perused the Post he started to read on the Metro and was served his breakfast of soft boiled eggs and sausage, wheat toast, juice and coffee. He looked forward to an uneventful day at the office. As he turned the page he casually glanced up from the newspaper to notice Robert Harris, his friend and sometime lawyer, looking down at him from the mezzanine. Robert grinned and gestured to see if he could sit with him. Giroux nodded his agreement and motioned for him to join him.

"What brings you here this morning, Robert?" Giroux asked innocently as the waiter arrived to see if Harris wanted breakfast. "I've got to meet a client here shortly, Andrew. While I'm waiting I might as well have a cup of coffee. Actually, I find it a little easier to talk with some clients in a casual atmosphere like this. The water fall you know, seems to make one relax. It's easier to talk."

Giroux hadn't thought about how pleasant his conversations with Locklear were in this very room for quite some time until Harris mentioned how relaxed an atmosphere the water fall created. The image of the two of them flashed through his mind enjoying the coffee and the ambiance as Harris related the nature of the case. He was a good lawyer, a specialist in domestic relations disputes, with a flair for the dramatic.

Harris loved the court room and the hunt for the truth. He was passionate in his pursuit of the rights of children in divorce cases. He would just as easily sacrifice both parents in a failing relationship if it meant that they would not receive proper protection by remaining with either. He often placed himself in an adversarial position with the courts to plead their rights and was a master at bargaining.

Harris spied his client looking for him and excused himself. "Well, I see Peterson on the landing looking for me. I've got to go, Andrew. Give me a call sometime." As he was about to take leave, Giroux said politely but almost inadvertently, "Well, I'm glad you actually came in here today, Robert, for me to see you. It is a coincidence. But there may be a matter I need to talk over with you sometime. I'll give you a call. Have a good day."

Giroux finished his breakfast, folded his paper neatly under his arm and left the Crown Plaza through the rear exit. He walked briskly through the Twinbrook parking lot under the MetroRail overpass and dodged traffic to Fishers Lane saluting lower grade officers acknowledging his rank along the way.

He was soon in the A-wing of the huge Parklawn Building a few minutes later than he anticipated and immersed in a discussion with Jane about the day's agenda. "Call Charlie and make room for him at ten-thirty, Jane. Ask him to rearrange his day for that time, will you please? It's important."

Sandra was already at work habitually early. She was ready for her nine o'clock appointment to represent the nursing department in a meeting with tribal representatives from the Navajo Nation. They wanted her viewpoint on the development of a new community health nursing component within their health authority and were preparing to testify to the need with their congressional leaders. They wanted special talking points.

Cynthia was unexpectedly in the office. "Sandra," she said hurrying into the office, "I will meet with the Navajo representatives myself today. There are some other things I wish to discuss with them privately. There is no need for the two of us in the same meeting."

"But the reason they came all the way from Window Rock, Cynthia, was to meet with me on the merits of their proposal to expand community health service delivery on the Navajo."

Cynthia was unusually curt. "So it is, Sandra. Be that as it may, I will meet with them instead. You have other tasks to do. Some of your field visit reports are late. I want you to get them done as soon as you can."

Reluctantly Sandra agreed. She was offended by Cynthia's tone of voice and curt directions given loudly enough to be overheard by Louise, their secretary. Sandra looked to her questioningly but Louise quickly averted looking at her.

Sandra sequestered herself in her office to complete the overdue reports working furiously throughout the day. She avoided contact with both Cynthia and Louise. They worked together for several years and were friends long before Sandra joined their staff. Her arrival on staff upset their balance.

Toward the end of the day the thought finally occurred to Sandra that her grievance against Dr. Giroux must be the issue between them. "That had to be it," she said to herself. Louise typed the grievance; and, Cynthia, as her supervisor, had to forward it on to the Director. That was the chain of command. It was a matter totally beyond Cynthia's control — a grievance against the Director for sexual harassment. It was a matter she couldn't fix.

It was unheard of! And in her office!

Locklear thought a woman supervisor would understand. How could she have misjudged! She now realized how foolish she was to dare think that she could rely upon her staff to empathize with her. How alone she felt. As she took in her late reports she now wondered how many others knew of her situation. The moccasin telegraph was no respecter of persons.

"Come in, Charlie, and have a seat. Jane, will you get us two coffees please? Thanks." The words came out as if it were business as usual. Charlie took his seat in his favorite corner of Giroux's leather couch. Giroux sat diagonally opposite him in his favorite chair, a coffee table between them that Jane set two cups upon with a pot of coffee in the event the conversation would be prolonged. It was to be surprisingly short.

"Again, Charlie, I don't want to know the details in case I really have a problem with this Locklear woman. But I have to know, are we on track? Are we going to be able to contain this mess?" Giroux asked showing an unusual amount of concern and absentmindedly placing two sugars in his coffee instead of the usual one.

In a buoyant mood from his evening with Sarah, Charlie dismissed Giroux's concern. "Believe me, boss, the matter is under control. I won't tell you any of the details as you asked, but for now, I will only tell you that EEO won't be a problem. We will get the informal grievance delayed and we can wear the bitch down. Eventually, I predict Locklear will go formal with it. That is to be expected as a matter of form.

"Even then, I think we can prolong the whole process until she gets tired or runs out of money with that attorney of hers," Charlie added smugly. "She won't get very far with this. We can go months internally before someone looks into it."

"Looks into it?"

"Sure. You've already been to the SG, haven't you?" Giroux nodded to Charlie in agreement. "Well, you can expect him to be checking the matter out. If he isn't already, he will when the matter comes to him for resolution. It's got to go to him sometime, you know." Charlie was sure of his information and what he had to do to protect Giroux.

Charlie pulled a cigar out of his shirt pocket and was about to light it. "Don't Charlie," Giroux said. "I don't want to look that far down the road. Do your damndest to get her off my back. See what she wants or will take to drop it. That's all. Just let me know what I have to do next."

Giroux's early good mood was turning foul. He especially didn't want to hear that despite Charlie's good efforts and the support he could expect to receive from EEO, Locklear could take the matter to the formal stage. He knew the involvement of the Office of the Secretary of Health and the Surgeon General's

Office carried the risk of greater exposure. Regardless of the outcome there, his career would be on the line. The SG would be obligated to contain him in some way.

Giroux didn't like the prospect of losing his stars. He was already blaming Locklear for their loss. But yet he didn't want to jump to any conclusions even though he knew he had forced himself on Locklear. He rose from his chair and went to his bank of windows lost in thought.

Automatically he looked over toward Locklear's apartment wishing his affair was not a matter of history. He relished the mid-afternoon breaks he had with her, imagining their couplings in her apartment so visible from his office, her rather sparse decorations, the bed, the feel of their skin together.

Jane interrupted his reverie with several attempts to gain his attention when he failed to respond to the intercom. Advancing farther into his office she announced he had a call waiting from the Surgeon General's Office. It was Dr. Price. "He has been waiting for several minutes, Dr. Giroux, and he doesn't sound happy." Giroux knew it was trouble.

CHAPTER TEN

GIROUX'S PLAN

Several months had passed. Locklear had received her response from Giroux. He completely denied any sexual harassment. That was to be expected in cases like this. Charlie had encouraged Sarah to meet with her off the record to find out what it would take for her to drop her grievance. Locklear was offended and responded by rejecting Giroux's statement and offer to dismiss the grievance.

Cox advised her to go formal. Giroux responded with the appearance of cooperation that he would order an investigation by naming EEO officers from several Area Offices to an investigative panel. Interviews would be established and a report made to Dr. Giroux. Word of the effort leaked out to the Surgeon General.

Over the next several weeks, Dr. Price was informed of the efforts of the team through an anonymous telephone call. The caller's voice sounded familiar but he couldn't quite place it. The gruff sounding voice suggested he next schedule a meeting with Dr. Joseph to give him a progress report. The investigative team had not found fault with Giroux about harassment. The team however, would report confidentially that Giroux's behavior bordered on sexual misconduct. He was a married man and was not in a position to establish a relationship with Locklear. All information would be sealed and not kept in the EEO files.

Leaving his residence in Bethesda early in the morning, Dr. Price eagerly looked forward to his meeting with the Surgeon General. Price was an arrogant man who relished whatever opportunities came his way to prove his abilities to Dr. Joseph. He knew this was a hot item and he was sure Dr. Giroux would surely be removed from office.

He raced out of his driveway in his BMW and headed for Wisconsin Avenue overlooking the evil stares he received for cutting in and out of traffic. Dr. Price was so pleased with his cunning foresight to make 'friends' with key staff of the agencies of the Public Health Service. He congratulated himself that he 'knew' the chiefs of staff and deputies on a first name basis. He would call periodically 'to chat' with each and 'to share' what was happening in the Surgeon General's office, all in the name of 'good communication'.

Sam Price was a medical 'con' man interested in guaranteeing himself one thing, a place in the agency structure in the event that his boss, whoever he might be at the time, would be out of favor with the administration and would be replaced. To protect his retirement was his prime pursuit in life. Most bureaucrats played the same game while playing their other favorite game, one-upsmanship. Their eyes were set upon the next level up.

Dr. Price would not deny his interest in being the next Surgeon General. However, Sam knew he did not possess the political acumen or the skill with Congressional representatives that Dr. Joseph possessed so abundantly. In that regard, he was realistic about his own limitations.

Lacking these skills, Sam long ago decided his talent for getting the goods on subordinates could facilitate his upwardly mobile pursuits perhaps just as well.

Passing through Chevy Chase he drove as if Wisconsin Avenue were the autobahn in Germany. Within minutes he connected with Pennsylvania Avenue on over to Connecticut and found his parking slot where the attendants saluted him daily. Sam savored the daily occurrence. Oh, how he wished the Public Health Service were more military!

If only he were the SG he would have his officers assemble in the morning wherever they were stationed to raise the flag in formation. He would require them to get haircuts and shave off their ridiculous beards. He would demand they get in shape and look the part of officers. It would be wonderful to observe protocols — as if this were the only thing their military counterparts did!

Dr. Price was ushered into Dr. Joseph's office without special ceremony. He seated himself opposite the SG. "This is what I've learned through my contacts with the Indian Health Service."

"Bob, this is Andrew. Oh, yes, I'm fine." Giroux paused. "Actually, no, I'm not fine. I need to see you about a private matter. No, I don't want to talk about it on the phone. I've been asked by the Surgeon General to meet him in his office tomorrow at 1:30. Can you go with me? I believe I may need your legal help. No. I can tell you everything on the way there. It's about a formal grievance against me of sexual harassment.

"Yes, I said sexual harassment. That's about all I can tell you here. Good! I'll meet you at your office about 12. We can have a short lunch and I'll let you know some of the details then. Thanks, Bob."

Giroux dismissed his driver for the ride downtown. He didn't want Willie privy to his private conversation with Robert even though Willie had driven him for years and could be trusted for most things. Today would be an exception. It merited discretion and privacy.

Giroux didn't know how Harris would react to his indiscretions. Harris was a good family man and strongly believed in the sanctity of marriage. When Giroux had met with him on occasion at his home to set up trust funds for his children he witnessed how effervescent Harris' children were and how loving Geraldine, his wife of 22 years was with him. He could only guess how happy they must be.

Yet, Giroux knew Harris was a bear in his family law practice. He opposed divorce as an attack on the institution of marriage; but he was also the strongest advocate a woman could have and relished the opportunity to go to trial. This both exhilarated and scared Giroux.

A worthy advocate and a worthy opponent! Giroux had not thought much about Harris as both sides of the same coin. They had been friends for several years. Their wives, Geraldine and Elizabeth, had served on the same committees in the Montgomery County School District and often went to tea at each other's house. The enormity of this complication had just dawned on Giroux as he pulled into Harris' office driveway. Too late to reconsider attorneys now.

Giroux was shown into Harris' office immediately. "I took the liberty of ordering in some sandwiches for us, Andrew. I hope you don't mind roast beef, medium rare, with a little coleslaw.

The deli does a good job for us in a pinch." Harris was almost nonchalant in his approach to lunch. He wanted to minimize Giroux's apparent urgency in meeting over the matter of sexual harassment. How could his friend, Giroux, ever be involved in such controversy? Harris knew him for years to be beyond reproach. So much for impressions!

"Now, just what is this business about sexual harassment? It seems so out of character for you, Andrew. I've never thought of you as a sexist." Harris laughed unknowingly. He took a bite of his sandwich. "Have you been caught doing naughty things?" laughing more at the ridiculous prospect of his friend before him actually saying or doing things to offend his female staff members. It just couldn't happen!

Giroux didn't know what to say at first. He fumbled momentarily with his sandwich and looked past Harris momentarily making light of Harris' good humor. Laughing with him Giroux wondered how many others' trust he had broken as he did his friend.

As an awkward silence ensued, Harris glanced over his bifocal glasses hanging precariously on the end of his nose to his friend. He observed Giroux was no longer eating his sandwich and appeared worried. He put it down in front of him. "Andrew! Tell me it isn't so. You didn't by chance get involved with a woman did you? What about Elizabeth? My God!"

Giroux was speechless for the moment. "How could you?" Harris asked in disbelief. "What happened?"

Giroux matter-of-factly dropped his pretense that his situation wasn't serious. "I really need your help, Bob. Let me start by giving you these copies of documents I've gathered and have received from the Equal Employment Opportunity Office and the woman's lawyer, Phyllis Cox. We have a few minutes before we have to get started downtown to the Surgeon General's office. Take a look at them and we'll talk about the situation as we drive."

"What do you expect me to do for you, Andrew?" Harris at once became professional and more cool toward him in his shock over the allegations of sexual harassment noting quickly the documents included a preliminary EEO file, a letter to the Surgeon General from the lawyer, and other notes. "It looks like the matter has already gotten out of hand. You're coming to me rather late in the game, I suspect."

"I didn't think you needed to ask what I expect, Bob. I want you to represent me, of course. Will you do it?" Giroux asked defensively. He was perturbed at Harris' reluctance.

Harris agreed stiffly annoyed with Giroux as he was with many of his clients who expected last minute miracles to be pulled out of the hat. He never thought of himself as a miracle worker, but he always put forth extra effort and was often rewarded with successful decisions. Nevertheless, Harris didn't like the position he was placed in; and, this time, his friend was doing it. They abandoned their lunch.

Gathering their papers they left in Giroux's car via Montrose Boulevard passing swiftly by the Jewish Community Center and the Catholic Church and a series of colonial style homes to the entrance of the freeway.

Giroux began his version of the truth. He was even somewhat surprised to hear his own recitation of events, confessing to his friend he was subject to 'the awful pressures of public office' that made him frequently vulnerable to the advances of women such as Sandra Locklear. It occurred with such regularity that he found himself being so worn down that resistance on the occasion of these complaints was next to impossible. He confessed in truth that it had nothing to do with Elizabeth. She was a jewel and had no knowledge of his recent failings. Harris listened incredulously, spellbound by the tale that unfolded. It was as if he had never known the man.

At that time elsewhere in Rockville, Sandra prepared to leave her apartment to return to work from lunch when the phone rang. It was Phyllis Cox. "Sandra, we need to talk. Can you come to my office later today, say, about 4:30 or 5 o'clock? We've got to plan out our strategy a little more. One of the lawyers from the Indian Health Services just gave me a call with some information."

"Yes. I can be there about 5 o'clock. There are some things I need to get done before I leave today. Can you give me a hint? No? Fine. Until then. Bye."

Cox explained, "Paul Sinclair, that arrogant little weasel from the IHS I told you about who has been avoiding me for such a long time, finally called today. He said, 'I want to help you help your client, Ms. Locklear, avoid embarrassment should she persist in her beliefs she can win against the Director, Dr. Giroux. And, I guess, it would be good information for you too, Ms. Cox in the event you are ever asked to assist in cases such as this.'

"He went on to say, 'I know you want to be of the greatest assistance to her. For that reason, you should counsel your client as a commissioned officer, she doesn't have any rights whatsoever under Title VII of the Civil Rights Act of 1964. By policy, appeal rights end with the Surgeon General of the United States, Ms. Cox. So, to help you help her I am going to fax you a copy of the policy dealing with grievances that is applicable in this situation. It is plainly written that the Surgeon General is the deciding official.'

"The pompous ass sent me this policy, Sandra. Have you seen it before? It's from 1976. It's ancient! All of the material you gave me before to help you prepare your grievance against Giroux never included this. I'm amazed! It's almost as if they wanted to intentionally mislead us by holding back this information. I don't understand their lack of professionalism."

Locklear took a sip of the coffee Cox's secretary prepared for her and looked at the sections highlighted for her in yellow. The document clearly stated that the deciding official was the Surgeon General. According to the policy, she had no other recourse. In hiring an attorney to represent her she could not expect the organization to pay attorney's fees even if she prevailed against it.

Cox put the document down and said, "As an officer of the U.S. Public Health Service, you are a non-person. Did you know that you had no rights under the Civil Rights Act? They deny you the rights of any common citizen. Even the lowliest janitor has more rights than you do. I'm simply amazed they have been able to get away with this for so long. I think this is blatant discrimination."

Cox's experience with other federal agencies had not prepared her for this. Civil servants elsewhere had equal protection under the law. But, she reflected, 'Locklear is not a civil servant. She is an officer.'

Chapter Eleven

Depositions

Phyllis Cox was stern and uncompromising as she preceded Locklear into the room where she was to be deposed at Tyrone and Miller, Court Reporters, Inc. She, too, was angry at the legal system for not taking care of commissioned officers but chided herself for this childish response. The legal system was not to blame for this oversight. It was a personnel matter and the attorneys for the Public Health Service long ago reviewed the documents she now had in her possession. They saw to it that the system would handle its own affairs without serious challenge from anyone so foolhardy. At least until now.

Tyrone and Miller spared no expense in furnishings or decorations. Their offices in the new ten floor office building near the Rockville Metro Station were plush. They believed they were the best in the business. Judging by sight, they had no lack of business.

Window drapes closed under an infra red system to keep the morning glare of the sun from disturbing anyone's concentration. As they closed, indirect lighting filled the room to a pre-arranged intensity. High backed velour seats were arranged around the ten foot mahogany conference table. A video-phone system was plugged into a sixty inch screen for special consultations. Closed circuit TV and tape recorders were used to augment the taking of dictation.

The court stenographer, a petite young woman in her twenties, placed mini-cassettes in the tape recorder and readied her dictation equipment with a box of paper tape. In appearance, she could easily have been a younger version of Connie Stevens and exhibited the same vivacious quality. Her simple task completed, she took on the role of hostess, introduced herself as Patricia DuPree, and inquired who wanted coffee, or sodas, or water while they waited for Mr. Harris and Admiral Giroux. With requests taken, she dismissed herself to obtain the refreshments.

Locklear was visibly nervous and apprehensive about the proceeding. She had reason to be nervous. She did not want her involvement to become a public matter. No sooner had she been seated than she arose from her chair to peruse magazines on an occasional table. She flung her selection down precipitously.

Earlier, Phyllis Cox assured her she would protect her from any illegalities; her only job would be to tell the truth to the best of her ability. Should she feel uncomfortable at any time she had the right to request a ten minute recess to collect herself. When Ms. Dupree repeated the same admonition, Locklear, not surprisingly, remained uncomforted. She was ill-prepared for the real discomfort she would feel in the session about to start.

Even though the circumstances were different from a court room, the burden of honesty required confrontation with Admiral Giroux, who through his attorney continued to protest his innocence as expected. Harris had arranged for this deposition to be taken and had served notice on Locklear.

That in itself alarmed her and caused excruciating mental suffering for the past two weeks. Locklear had never been involved in court matters before. Even television lawyers made her nervous. Since then she had spent hours going over her story with Cox until the thought of having to repeat it in detail in the presence of Giroux nauseated her. Repetition did not make her feel at ease. It repeated the abuse and resurrected the feeling of his power over her destiny.

Intellectually, Locklear knew she would one day soon have the privilege of confronting him with her own set of questions and interpretations of reality. Cox was more than capable of leading the charge. But today was not her day. She had to suppress her fears which were assuming major proportions. She excused herself to go to the restroom.

Ten minutes elapsed. Cox went to retrieve her. Locklear was trembling before the restroom mirror. Harris and Giroux had arrived and pressed her to begin at once. On entering the conference room each arose for the introduction, civility and urbanity exuding from Harris and Giroux; wariness and apprehension from Cox and Locklear.

Harris had never met Locklear until this moment. He was struck with her fresh, unadorned beauty and physical charms. She radiated innocence. Alarmed, he understood Giroux's sexual interest in her. If he were not happily married, even he might be tempted. Putting this inappropriate thought aside he breathed deeply and re-seated himself. He sighed, thinking to himself, 'What a pity it will be to destroy her today.'

Giroux rose and extended his hand to Locklear. "So pleasant to see you again Sandra," his baritone words dripped with honey, a smile on his face. Locklear automatically extended but quickly withdrew her hand curiously aware he still had power to mesmerize her and to command her attention. She shook her head at her almost automatic reaction. Giroux withdrew his hand quickly, noting her discomfort with his gesture and seated himself, unperturbed.

She flushed but quickly averted looking into his eyes and sat down embarrassed that she almost accorded him the recognition he wanted. Locklear reflected this whole proceeding was going to be obnoxious to her. She looked to Cox for support and wondered how she could have put herself into this situation. Cox pressed her hand lightly. She understood her reluctance.

Ms. Dupree began. "Ladies and gentlemen, I want to establish for the record that this deposition has been requested by Mr. Robert Harris, Attorney for Admiral Andrew Giroux, Director of the Indian Health Service, in the matter of a pending federal grievance initiated by Ms. Sandra Locklear, an officer of the U.S. Public Health Service. Is that correct?" Each assented and names were introduced into the record. "Mr. Harris, you may begin whenever you are ready."

Harris looked at everyone to make sure he had their undivided attention, took a sip of water, and cleared his throat. He was now on center stage, the position he loved at trials.

H: "Ms. Locklear, state for the record your full name, title, and occupation, please." Harris intoned. Locklear thought they must have a special course in law schools on how to use the voice to instill fear. Her heart skipped a fast beat.

L: "I am Sandra Evelyn Locklear, Director of the Community Health Nursing Service for the Indian Health Services." Locklear heard herself speak. Her self-imposed shell was cracked. A small crack that would soon open into a fissure. She thought the voice she heard did not sound like hers.

H: "When did you first assume that position?"

L: "I was promoted into that position March 1, 1991." She said earnestly but timidly, her voice quavered lacking authority. Locklear wondered why she could not speak louder.

H: "Promoted?" Harris attacked the first minor point. His voice sounded like a canon shot. "I understand you were reassigned from a previous position into that capacity. That is called a lateral transfer, is it not? That would hardly qualify as a promotion, Ms. Locklear, now would it?" Harris accused, the words came like more explosions rocking her to her core. It was the most innocuous point Harris could seize.

C: "I object on the grounds of relevancy, Mr. Harris. The editorial comment is unnecessary. What direct question do you want to ask my client, Counselor? If you have any direct questions please ask them, and let's get on with it." Cox's voice raised in irritation. Even she was surprised at Harris' immediate thrust for blood.

H: "Relevancy? (Laughing) It is quite important to my client and his future as a career officer of the Public Health Service that his exemplary record remain unblemished, Counselor. I'm sure you can understand that. However, Ms. Cox, if you insist on one question at a time then, Ms. Locklear, were you promoted into your capacity of a Director of Community Health Services?"

L: "No. I mean I was reassigned, as you said, on a lateral transfer. I just felt it was a promotion to be out of the Nashville Area Office." Timidity reasserted itself. Under the brief volley of words flying from one lawyer to another, Locklear sank back into her seat. Unused to such sharp exchanges her temples pulsated with fear for the unknown. She envisioned herself slowly being tortured or vivisected.

C: "I would like to confer with my client for a moment, Mr. Harris," Cox interjected noting Locklear's discomfort.

H: "So soon? We are barely getting started, Ms. Cox. But if you insist you need to confer with your client, by all means do so." Harris said smugly smelling triumph on the wind.

Cox and Locklear retreated into the anteroom. Cox poured her some ice water. "Sandra, remember I said Harris will try anything to get you rattled and for you not to give him anything but a direct answer?"

Still rattled by his explosiveness Sandra took a drink. "Yes, but I thought I needed to explain what I meant." Her eyes pleaded with Cox.

"No, Sandra," she said conciliatory. "You do not need to explain anything to Mr. Harris unless I want to allow it. You are just here to answer his questions. No more, no less. If the short answer will suffice, give him a short answer. If you feel you need 'to explain' something, request a recess to confer with me or lean over and whisper to me what your concerns are or write me a brief note. I'll tell you whether or not to give him more.

"By the way, believe me, I know how difficult this is, Sandra, if you are not used to it. Trust me. I won't let you down. Take a few minutes to relax a bit. I have the feeling Harris will want to drag this out today. He seems to be enjoying himself. But so long as his client is paying for this, let's take our time and come back when you are ready." Cox was confident and ready for battle. She returned to the conference room to await Sandra's return. Sandra thought to herself, 'Do you really know how hard this is, Phyllis? Do you really know how hard it is to admit you were used?'

Locklear soon returned to the palpable silence of the conference room, the smell of the verbal volley still lingering as the odor of gunshot. Ms. Dupree noted the time of the recess for the record. Noting her return, Harris jumped to the attack once more.

H: "Ah. We begin again. I'm glad you could join us, Ms. Locklear. Do you consider yourself a good nurse?"

C: "Objection. Argumentative. I'm going to instruct my client not to respond to any such questions asking for opinions, Mr. Harris. If you have a direct question, ask it. Otherwise we will be here all day. Sandra, consider yourself instructed not to respond to such questions." Cox smelled another personal attack on the wind.

H: "All right, then, is it true that you have both a bachelor's and master's degree in nursing from the University of Virginia, Ms. Locklear?"

L: "Yes."

H: "Is it true that following graduation you have served with exemplary performance at the Indian health clinics of the Miccosukee Tribe in Florida, the Cherokee Tribe at Cherokee, North Carolina, the..."

C: "We will stipulate for the record that Ms. Locklear is a fully qualified nurse and has an outstanding record wherever she has served the Indian Health Service. We submit for the record copies of her evaluations for all positions held and commendations received." She stated this knowing fully that Harris indeed had a point and wanted to attack her credibility.

H: "I am simply establishing that Ms. Locklear should not be ashamed to admit she is a good nurse, Ms. Cox. Surely you cannot object to her fine record of accomplishments. Even I am impressed. Are you married, Ms. Locklear?" Harris abruptly changed direction.

L: "No." Locklear was puzzled responding automatically but weakly to Harris. A tear was beginning to form in the corners of her exquisite almond shaped eyes. They seemed to rest on her high cheek bones, ready to fall precipitously.

H: "Such a fine looking woman and you're not married. It is a pity. Just making an observation, Ms. Cox." Harris raised his hands in feigned protest. "Don't bother to object, please. Ms. Locklear, how did you come to know Doctor Giroux? That is, in what circumstances did you first meet him?"

Giroux moved forward from his recumbent position in his chair, leaned against the table with his arms folded before him, and fixed a hawk-like gaze upon Locklear.

She trembled inside unable to speak for the moment and looked away. When she did she could not face him and asked for a recess. Her tears were becoming full and she did not want to give him the satisfaction of seeing her reduced to tears. Cox asked for a short recess.

Harris turned to Giroux and exclaimed rhetorically looking about the room in exasperation, "Didn't we just have one?" By then both Cox and Locklear exited to the anteroom unconcerned about his feelings. Locklear's was about to explode.

Fighting for control she said to Cox, "Phyllis, can't you make him be civil? With him staring me in the face how am I supposed to answer Harris' questions? Can't you make him sit back? Does he have to be present for this?" Locklear's mouth quivered, her stomach equally shaky, her control nearly vanished.

Cox answered slowly. "Sandra, this is exactly what they want. They want to unnerve you. They are hoping and trusting in your vulnerability. They want you to break down and lose control. If you do, they win. It is as simple as that. They can go on and crucify you. But you do have a case, Sandra. Their best defense is an offense to attack your credibility. You don't want to give them an inch do you? They'll take a mile."

Locklear wiped away the tears forming in her eyes. Staring into a void she said in subdued tones, "No. But his being there frightens me so. I'm still afraid of what he can do to me after this is over."

Cox said, "I know this is of little comfort to you now, but we haven't arrived at that point, have we? We have to take this one step at a time. Today is their day. We will give them that. But we will have ours, too. Besides, he can't retaliate against you. It's against the rules."

The ladies drank a cup of water slowly not speaking. Locklear thought to herself, 'They have ways of getting around them, too.' Cox looked at her watch aware of the passing time and asked out of curiosity, "Is there anything I need to know, Sandra, that you haven't told me yet?"

"No. I don't believe so." Her mind was blank. She dreaded seeing Giroux since their last scene together in her apartment. It unnerved her. She regretted afterward calling him a bastard. Now, he was plainly in her face. She looked past him and to Harris on his left.

H: "Ms. Locklear, you are claiming that Admiral Giroux sexually harassed you. Is that true?"

L: "Yes."

H: "How did this happen? What were the circumstances?"

L: "We were at a meeting May 18th, 1993 in his office. I was presenting some information — observations, really — about the effects of alcoholism in the communities I once served. You know, things I've seen and heard. During the discussion, I was startled for a moment when I felt a hand touch my right leg. It didn't stop there but moved up and down my leg repeatedly then disappeared. It was his hand.

"I was startled. The meeting continued and when I stopped my presentation, I sat back in my chair to reflect on what happened. I listened absentmindedly to someone else talking but I couldn't concentrate.

"I didn't want him doing this to me. When I realized what was happening, I felt sick.

"When the meeting ended, Admiral Giroux commanded me to stay to discuss a point, he said, he need clarified. The others had left, and he closed the door behind him. Without saying anything to me he suddenly grabbed me and put his arms around me and kissed me.

"I tried to push away from him and told him I didn't want this. But he kissed me all the more deeply and prevented me from saying anything. I felt humiliated."

H: "Humiliated? Not harassed? Come now, Ms. Locklear. At the time of this incident, didn't you in fact, kiss him as ardently, if not more so, and cause him an erection? And, didn't you in fact, move your body around in such a way that you virtually put your right breast into his hand? And, didn't you in fact, then tell him you were available?

"In what other way could my client react at your suggestive body language but to acknowledge that you desired to make love to him! What else was he to do but to tell you he would call you? I am not sure who harassed whom! I submit you plainly telegraphed to him you were more than willing and able. Well, Ms. Locklear? Weren't you?" Harris' volley of shots were finding their mark.

C: "Objection, objection, objection! Counselor. We are not in a court of law at this point. You are badgering my client. Your behavior is uncalled-for. I demand a fifteen minute recess. You know the rules of procedure. This is supposed to be a fact-finding session, Mr. Harris."

Without waiting for an acknowledgment Cox pushed her chair back suddenly and took Locklear, bathed in tears, to the anteroom. Ms. Dupree breathed a sigh of relief and poured two cups of water, took them into the room for them to drink, and left them in silence. She felt sorry for Locklear.

Cox had her arm around Locklear whose body shook with the onslaught of Harris' abuse. "I promise you he'll get his, Sandra,"

Cox vowed, yet knowing that her style differed radically from Harris'.

She had never heard of Harris before and had never had a case with him as opposing counsel. She had grudging respect for him as a tactician. Cox only hoped there would not be any more bomb shells dropped when they returned to the battle.

For nearly the first half of the recess Locklear was almost inconsolable. Then her feelings subsided and were replaced with deeper breathing and mounting anger. "God, how awful!" Locklear finally said. "Is this what is going to happen when we get into court? How many times do I have to go through this? The man is a brutal bastard! Didn't you see how much enjoyment Giroux was getting out of this? Phyllis, I can't go back in there. He's twisting things all around. Can't you see that? I didn't come onto him; he came onto me!"

"Sandra, I believe you. Harris is building a case for consensual sex hoping to get harassment dismissed. We must let him play out his hand. Then it will be our turn."

Cox and Locklear used the remaining minutes to recompose themselves deliberately taking the remainder of time before walking back into the fray. She had convinced Locklear to respond as briefly as possible.

Harris and Giroux were in a huddle when they returned. Harris sat back in his chair with a smile on his face and a glint in his eye. Giroux relaxed, looked at Locklear to see what damage had been done. Satisfied that Harris had made an impact upon her he began to clean his nails expecting Harris to similarly clean up the matter.

C: "My client stipulates that the following events occurred. Your client inappropriately touched mine; my client returned your client's kiss under duress; and that episode ultimately led to non-consensual sexual intercourse."

H: "Can't your client speak for herself? I want to hear her version, Counselor."

Locklear looked to Cox and put her hand on hers and told her she would answer these questions and any others Harris may have. "I was overwhelmed by Doctor Giroux forcing his attentions on me; and I was confused. I didn't know what to do but I knew he wanted me to give in to him. I thought if I said that I was available he would release me and that would be the end of the matter. I made a poor choice in how I was going to get away from him.

"I then thought I was safe when more than a month passed before he called me and told me he would meet me at my apartment. That was July the 7th. He came as he said he would and immediately had sex with me."

H: "I see. You expect me to believe you were a passive participant, Ms. Locklear. That is hardly the truth about your first assignation with Admiral Giroux, isn't that true? Isn't it true that you had your bed linen drawn down ready for him? Isn't it true that you greeted him wearing an unbuttoned blouse? Isn't it true that when you made love to him, you assumed the superior position on top of him? I would submit, Ms. Locklear, that your behavior does not give one the impression of passivity, of being victimized by this poor man now does it?"

L: "Yes. But you see, I had no choice. He expected me to have sex with him. He always called or told me where or when. I never knew when to expect him. It was the way he wanted the situation." Locklear was embarrassed that these details were coming out in this way.

H: "How many times had you, if I may quote you, 'no choice', Ms. Locklear? I really mean how many times had you had sex with him? Two or three?" Harris asked with eyebrows raised.

L: "A few times." Locklear was more deeply embarrassed and looked down at the table when she responded. She realized she had not told Cox everything, especially this detail.

H: "Oh, come, Ms. Locklear, don't be so modest. Wasn't it more like two dozen, or three dozen or perhaps even more over a two year period? I submit that hardly constitutes 'no choice' and that you liked being available to his call."

C: "Objection! Counselor, my client will stipulate for the record that a prolonged sexual relationship occurred. But we will stoutly maintain that it was not consensual. It was initiated by your client, Admiral Andrew Giroux, and continued under the implied threat that dire consequences would befall Ms. Locklear should she talk to anyone about their relationship. I wish to ask my client a few questions on redirect.

C: "Sandra Evelyn Locklear did you initiate sex with Admiral Giroux?"

L: "No. I was always at his beck and call. I did not call Dr. Giroux for sex at any time during the two years of the affair. He controlled the whole process. He set the times and places. I believed then, as I do now, that if I did not cooperate with him my whole career would be at an end."

C: "Why did you continue with him under these circumstances? Why didn't you just tell him that you couldn't? Why didn't you refuse him this privilege?"

L: "I just told you! I was afraid of him. I heard too many stories of people, mostly doctors, who got on his bad side and were transferred to places like Alaska. And then, I, I just got used to him. Besides he always reminded me not to tell anyone."

C: "What did you understand by his reminders?"

L: "I felt that if I didn't do as he demanded I would be sent some place else like so many others I heard about, and that I may not get any promotions. You see, Dr. Giroux approves the list of those nominated for promotions. He could easily take my name off the list if he wanted."

Harris interrupted to defuse the situation.

H: "Let us not get too carried away with this speculation Ms. Locklear. Isn't it also possible that Dr. Giroux felt that you and he enjoyed such a special and wonderful relationship that he simply wanted to guard its privacy by repeating out of his concern for you too that he wished no one else to know about it?"

L: "I don't know what motivates him. He would never tell me how he felt about our relationship. All I know is, it stopped almost as fast as it started. There was no explanation, no closure. I couldn't call him to find out if there were anything wrong. He didn't permit that. I began to be afraid something else would happen to me."

When Locklear paused, Harris looked to Giroux who shrugged his shoulders and folded his hands in his lap. "Just a few more questions at this time Ms. Locklear."

H: "Were you aware, Ms. Locklear, that Dr. Giroux was a happily married man before you began this affair?"

C: "Objection. It hasn't been established that Ms. Locklear began this affair, Mr. Harris."

H: "Well, Ms. Locklear?"

L: "Before the affair began, I did not know Dr. Giroux was married. He told me when he left the apartment the first time he had to go and pick up his wife, Elizabeth, from shopping."

H: "Yet, knowing this — that he had a wife, Elizabeth — you persisted in your illicit relationship for two years. Is that true, Ms. Locklear?"

L: "I had no way of knowing whether this was only going to be a one time thing. Dr. Giroux left me alone for nearly a month after the first time. I thought it was over with when he saw my reaction to his comment."

C: "Off the record, Mr. Harris. It seems like you are beating a dead horse. Your client insists he is innocent and was the object of Ms. Locklear's misguided affection. My client insists your client forced himself upon her and imprisoned her..."

H: "Imprisoned her? She trapped him with her body movements, Counselor! I'm astounded at your interpretation of the events! But you do have a point. It is her word against his. We are willing to suspend further questions at this time but reserve the right to recall this witness. I am sure my client will be ultimately vindicated when this matter comes to court."

Harris ended the session and Cox began to place her notes in her briefcase. She turned to the stenographer and said, "As soon as this deposition is typed and approved, Ms. Dupree, may I request a copy? Here is my card."

She turned to Mr. Harris and Admiral Giroux and said, "Expect to be scheduled for a deposition, Admiral. I believe there is nothing more my client can add at this time. It's abundantly clear Admiral Giroux forced himself upon my client and persisted for two years to coerce her into sexual relations. Good day." Harris stifled a laugh.

Cox peremptorily dismissed herself and Locklear, gathered her brief case and notes and stormed out of the office. On the way down the elevator Cox admitted a shortcoming.

"Sandra, I was under the initial impression you as a commissioned officer were just like any other civil servant, and that the only thing different about you was your uniform. I am just beginning to understand your fear of the man.

"He not only has psychological power over you he has actual power and control. You weren't kidding when you said others who crossed him found themselves transferred, were you?"

"No, Phyllis, I wasn't just making something up. He did transfer people out whom he didn't like. It's common knowledge. And I didn't put my breast into his hands. God, how awful that man, Harris!"

The elevator came to a halt momentarily. On the way to her car, Cox said, "I think I am going to have to do some deeper research into your personnel system. You can help me a great deal, Sandra."

"How?"

"Find out if you can what kind of regulations there are about grievances in your personnel system. I have to throw out what I know about the civil service system, I think. The two of them may just be as different as night and day. Then get me your sexual harassment policy for starters."

Cox and Locklear were silent for the remainder of the short ride back to her office. Each was lost in thought about the continuing brutality of the deposition.

Chapter Twelve

Her Turn

Locklear arrived at Cox's office early for the ride to Tyrone and Miller's. She was anxious to talk with Phyllis before their trip. For the past two months she had been writing voluminous notes about her ordeal with Giroux. Any piece of information that came to mind, no matter how irrelevant it seemed. She was instructed particularly to note the early contacts with him and the atmosphere of those contacts and her feelings at the moment.

Dutifully, Locklear remembered shortly after arriving in Rockville on the transfer throwing a party at her apartment to break the ice. Among the invited guests were Dr. Howard, the Mental Health Program Director, Cynthia Morgan, the Nursing Program Director, John Standing Bear, the Alcoholism Program Director, Dr. William Reilly, the Director of Health Programs and a few others for variety.

On a whim, Dr. Giroux was extended an invitation when she had heard that he had taken a special interest in her transfer. Locklear thought it odd at the time, but she was flattered and curious to know more. She did not expect him to accept and was surprised when he rang the door bell. Locklear welcomed him and he mingled easily in the crowded flat. She got him a glass of Perrier with a slice of lime, a favorite of his when he was fulfilling a business function. When his presence was made known others gravitated toward him as if he were a magnet.

A good hostess, Locklear engaged everyone in conversation at one time or another during the evening. It wore on and some guests were beginning to take their leave. Giroux remained a little longer than some but left before others. As he was about to go he took Locklear aside, placed a hand on her arm and said warmly in hushed tones how glad he was she had not refused the offer of the transfer.

Those around hardly noticed. It seemed such an innocuous statement, a comment often made by supervisory personnel to make small talk. Locklear recalled her response, "How could I ignore your offer. After all, as a commissioned officer I have to go where I can do the most good." She intended it as a light, non-committal remark without particular meaning, said partly in jest and partly to recognize his authority.

Giroux, on the other hand, looking intently said, "Well, I'm happy to hear that. I do know where you can do the most good, believe me. We will talk about it some day. But for now, I must leave. Thank you for your gracious invitation." Whereupon he took her hand in both of his and pressed it to say good night. His hands were warm and smooth much like his voice. It almost seemed an intimate gesture she was only too willing to dismiss.

Cox asked her, "But, Sandra, how did you feel about this and your comment?"

"I didn't give it much thought at first; except that later that evening I had a peculiar feeling when I thought about the way he said, 'I know where you can do the most good, believe me'. He pressed me on the arm with one hand, and my hand with his other hand. He said it as if he knew a secret known only to him."

"How did you mean, peculiar? In what way was it funny?"

"I don't mean in a humorous way because there wasn't any humor in his remark, even though I'm sure he tried to make it light. Just odd or strange and pointed like it was filled with expectation. I remember too, getting flush for the moment. This was very strange for me at the time. I felt confused by his remark. Anyhow, I fantasized that night I must have made some impact on him with the party. But I soon dismissed it because I wasn't comfortable with my feelings then."

Cox looked at her for a moment and then said, "We may just be able to use that information when we take his deposition today. It may show he had some intent for a while or some design on you all along. A man in his position is used to getting what he wants, perhaps not unlike Clarence Thomas. How do you feel about him as a superior officer?"

Locklear was uncomfortable with her question. "I've never really thought much about him being a superior officer. Believe me, after the affair was over I've come to the conclusion that there wasn't anything superior about him at all. But I know that's not what you are driving at. What do you really mean?"

Cox smiled. "What do you think about the differences in rank between you? Don't you have to follow orders like soldiers or sailors in the uniformed military services? Observe protocol? Take orders? That sort of thing? You actually hinted at it before."

Locklear laughed. "Follow orders? And observe protocol?" She threw her head back and laughed some more. "This organization is one of the worst you can imagine for following orders or observing protocol. The only orders anyone follows appear to be what each person directs himself to do.

"I would imagine anyone with a military background would probably see the hypocrisy in the Public Health Service in general, and the Indian Health Service in particular. Yet, I will admit the Surgeon General's office would like to see their officers show better courtesy and look better in uniform. Every now and then we get little memoranda reminding us of *esprit de corps.*

"In the field, lots of officers hardly wear their uniforms. I'm told some even act abrasively to other military people on bases, or even go on bases improperly dressed. It is ragtag all the way. It is a wonder some don't get kicked off the bases.

"But so far as Giroux is concerned I no longer feel I owe him any respect. He doesn't deserve it. He hasn't earned it from me." Locklear pondered her diatribe a moment and felt she had betrayed her uniform.

"No longer? What do you mean? In the beginning didn't you have different feelings about the differences in rank?" Cox persisted in knowing more about their differences. From a naval officer friend of hers she had dated, Phyllis learned that the Navy looked dimly upon "fraternization," which she defined as dating someone at least two ranks lower than you. Article 134 of the Uniform Code of Military Justice prohibited such behavior. Oddly, there was no similar protection for Public Health Service Officers.

"I guess I have to admit that I was in awe of him. You see, when he would come into a room many people would actually stand up until he was seated. Like many people in that kind of position there were some rumors that you don't want to get on his bad side. I've heard there were some doctors who disagreed with him who found themselves transferred to serve on Coast Guard cutters in Alaska. Now that really did scare me." She imagined herself out at sea off the coast of Alaska.

"I thought they were joking, but these people I heard that from weren't lying. Even though I didn't know them or learned what it was that alienated him, they had no reason to make up a story like that. I know in our relationship that first night Giroux made a strong point of my not coming to him or calling or asking him for anything, like a favor. I was especially not to call him.

"It was as if he wanted it clearly understood that there was a line between us," Locklear concluded, "The relationship was not man-to-woman. I didn't like the line he drew. I knew I was on the other side of it. And I surely didn't like him forcing a kiss on me in his office. I was not an equal. Do you know what I mean?"

"Like you were beneath him? I mean not on his level, even in bed?" Cox asked deliberately trying to get Locklear to focus on her subordinate position. It was crucial that she reflect on their differences.

"Exactly. I picked that up right away. He set up boundaries. And I guess I respected that. I don't know how wise that was, but I didn't raise any objections. I honestly felt it wouldn't do any good."

"Boundaries? You mean he set up some controls, don't you? That is hardly evidence of an equal relationship I would say, wouldn't you? Boundaries and controls are two different things, Sandra. I need to know more about the controls he set up."

Locklear thought for a moment trying to relax. "When the affair first started, I guess I expected it to be that way. I didn't believe I could or should ask for anything. I didn't want any. I don't think anyone goes into an affair with the intention of doing more than just trying it out. After all, he was the Director. You don't refuse him ... anything."

"And you, what were you? Was it really just an affair? Is that how you really regarded it? Did you go into it with your eyes fully open?"

"Phyllis, I am a nobody. Just a nurse trying to do a job. Never in my whole life was I in a position like that, not even when I was studying to be a nurse. Sure, doctors would make passes at you in training but I've never been grabbed or forced by any man to kiss him, much less have sex with him. I don't like force. It wasn't necessary." Locklear grimaced and shivered.

"When I look back on it, I don't think he ever wanted an equal relationship. I'm really sorry I needed someone at that time in my life. Despite the way it began, I mistakenly thought I could trust him. His business with his wife was his business. I truly didn't want to mess that up for him, but when he came onto me, I felt caught. Then, when it continued, I pushed all caution aside. I adjusted to the relationship and his conditions. I accepted them, I guess."

"Illicit relationships do have their moments of attraction, Sandra. There is the excitement of the secretiveness. Hoping no one will know, yet fearing someone will find out. And pretending to everyone your relationship is just business. Just business. But if we are to press this issue legally you cannot afford to act or speak as if you forgive him. You must really believe you were victimized. I'm not sure you are there, Sandra."

"Believe me now I don't feel good about him, Phyllis. I feel used especially when I look back on that first moment in the office." Cox and Locklear had arrived and walked into the Tyrone and Miller building and ascended the elevator to their suite in silence. Locklear dreaded seeing Dr. Giroux and Mr. Harris again wondering what foul mood Mr. Harris would be in. But she had no choice. Her stomach was not up to it and was churning. But she took consolation in knowing that Giroux would be on the hot seat this time.

Ms. Dupree greeted them warmly. "So nice to see you again, Ms. Cox and Ms. Locklear. Could I get you something to drink perhaps, before the others arrive? Mr. Harris and Dr. Giroux called and said they would be just a few minutes late. Something about having to stop at Mr. Harris' office on the way over. He hoped you would understand."

While she didn't like Harris' obvious attempt to put them off balance, Ms. Cox took advantage of the additional time to arrange her papers before her and to jot down some notes about her earlier conversation with Locklear.

She was particularly struck with Locklear's impression that Giroux knew something. She would take advantage of that later.

She wrote, 'What could he know?' But she was also disquieted with her acquiescence to her vulnerability and feared Locklear might reject the notion that Giroux really harassed her in the technical meaning of the term.

It was one thing to start a grievance but quite another to see it through. Cox was unsure of Locklear's final resolve.

Locklear stared out the conference room window, lost in her thoughts. Her experience with men had not exactly hardened her. But she felt vulnerable and hoped one time, at least, she would find someone she could trust. No. More than trust. She wanted someone she could build a life with, not be a mere appendage or an ornament on someone's arm or a plaything in bed.

Harris and Giroux were ushered into the conference room. Locklear purposely remained with her back toward them for a few moments while they adjusted themselves into their chairs opposite her and Cox.

Ms. Dupree returned to the room with a decanter of water, adjusted herself to her dictation equipment and made certain there was enough paper. She called roll for the record. "I believe we are ready," she announced. "Ms. Cox, you may begin."

Phyllis Cox tapped her pencil rhythmically and looked at Locklear momentarily then to Giroux still puzzled. She dictated for the record the purpose of the deposition and the names of the parties present. Mr. Harris agreed.

C: "State for the record, Dr. Giroux, your full name and position."

G: "As you know, I am Andrew Harding Giroux, Director of the Indian Health Service located at 5600 Fishers Lane, Rockville, Maryland, the Parklawn Building, as it is commonly referred to."

C: "As the Director of the Indian Health Service can you describe briefly what it is that you do?"

G: "Briefly, I ensure that the health care needs of Indians and Alaska Natives are met by securing enough funding from Congress to run our hospitals, clinics, health centers and tribal and urban health programs. It is a complex and demanding task, Ms. Cox."

C: "I'm sure it is, Dr. Giroux. What type of functions do you oversee to ensure that Indians and Natives receive the health care they need?" Cox was the model of objectivity.

G: "I'm responsible for everything, the budgeting, finance, contracting, procurement, the personnel, strategy with the communities, all of it. But I'm sure you already know that."

C: "No, Doctor, I don't know that. When I had first seen you, you were wearing a Navy uniform with the rank of Rear Admiral, and today, you are not. Why is that?"

G: "That is a common mistake, Ms. Cox. It was not a Navy uniform you saw. The Public Health Service uniform is often mistaken for one. And yes, you are correct. I am a Rear Admiral of the Upper Half to be precise."

C: "So, you are an officer with the United States Public Health Service. I also noticed then you had a number of medals. What were they for?"

H: "What relevance is there to your line of questioning, Ms. Cox?" Harris was a little perturbed; but he had an idea of where Cox was leading Giroux and wanted to deflect her.

C: "Does your client have something to hide about his service career, Mr. Harris? Certainly you shouldn't object to his acknowledgment of his own strengths, if he doesn't mind telling us what his medals were for. Do you mind, Dr. Giroux?"

G: "It's all right, Robert. I don't mind stating ... well, really, I am quite proud that I have had an exceptional career with the Indian Health Service. For your information, Ms. Cox, the medals include various commendations, outstanding service, meritorious service medals and group awards."

C: "Outstanding, Dr. Giroux! You are certainly to be commended for such a distinguished career. Undoubtedly, then, you are a fine leader, one to whom many Indians and Alaska Natives look as a role model, wouldn't you say?"

G: "Well, uh, yes, of course."

C: "Indeed, of course. A person in your position must have a commanding presence, wouldn't you say? Let me clarify that before you object, Mr. Harris. By a commanding presence I really mean considerable authority must come with the position, too, doesn't it?"

Aversion To Honor 201

G: "I believe I already stated I am responsible for all phases of this health care delivery system, didn't I?"

C: "Indeed, but please answer yes or no. Dr. Giroux you already stated how responsible you were, and we are grateful for that. But that is not the question, is it? The question was, your authority is commensurate with your responsibility, isn't it?"

Harris moved uncomfortably in his chair.

H: "I would like to confer with my client, Ms. Cox."

Harris and Giroux pushed away from the conference table for a ten minute break in a smaller adjacent conference room. They quickly shut the door behind them. Cox and Locklear went to the restroom and met in the anteroom afterward.

It was beginning to be gloomy outside. Clouds were rolling in from the west and developing into thunderheads. While Tyrone and Miller's afforded them a view of the Pike leading into Gaithersburg and the MetroRail leading to Shady Grove to the northeast, the office also seemed a lot closer to the gathering clouds and the clatter of thunder overhead and the periodic flash of lightning bolts.

Locklear was beginning to relax from the tension she built up before as the automatic lights grew in intensity with the gathering dark. She picked up a Time magazine from the oak credenza and absentmindedly turned the pages waiting for Cox to signal the time to return. She was distracted and wished the session were over. She did not have too long to wait.

Cox led the way back to the conference room. While Locklear welcomed the silence she couldn't help but wonder about it. She was afraid to ask her if everything was all right, as if her very asking would make the effort all wrong. She was beginning to be anxious again as she approached the room.

At first, it seemed like such a wonderful idea to try to bring Giroux to his knees. Locklear was angry with him for the humiliation of the first encounter here. Retribution seemed sweet to her. Locklear was so sure of it then when she first met with Cox at the urging of Margaret and Janet. She was convinced Giroux used her and forced his intentions upon her. However, it was so hard to admit it. As a commissioned officer, she knew she had to go through the administrative procedures to bring her complaint before Giroux if she wanted to follow through. That meant a grievance. But lately, she felt squeamish about possibly being the one to discredit him. Now all she wanted to do was run out the door and not look back.

She almost wanted to cancel this deposition and fade into the woodwork, grateful to slip into anonymity. But here she was, again, in the same room. Locklear had to admit there was once some delight in seeing Giroux; now, there was enmity between them. Too bad. She didn't like the taste of enmity. She was not brought up to exact a toll from anyone.

Giroux sat opposite her prepared to answer Cox's questions briefly as possible. Harris spent the interim instructing his client not to give Cox an inch. He was wary of her reputation as a worthy adversary. Harris bothered to research her training and interest in administrative law. It was not a field of his interest. He reveled in trying cases and didn't much care for bureaucracies. It was just a matter of being supportive for his friend, Giroux, that he took his case.

Harris wondered what kind of woman would want to practice in such an arena when the courtroom was such a vibrant place. He dearly loved the battle of wits and would match his to anyone's. Giroux's situation was a little different, though. While he had no personal compunction to take his case to the limits, Harris felt in deference to his friend that he didn't need the publicity that a trial might generate.

Avoid it at all costs. Giroux might not be a Judge Thomas. But he was a high enough officer in the Public Health Service. Prudence had to be exercised here.

Cox began again. "We were asking you before you conferred with your attorney, Dr. Giroux, about authority. Do you regard your authority as being commensurate with your responsibility?"

G: "Yes, of course."

C: "Is that all you have to say about it, Dr. Giroux?" She paused to take stock of his brevity. "Well then, I see. Let me rephrase my question. Are you familiar with the concept of the chain of command in the military?"

G: "Yes, of course. I did serve in the Army, briefly."

C: "How strongly does that concept apply within the Indian Health Service? That is, how strongly do you implement the concept within your service?"

Giroux glanced to Harris as if to ask permission to answer the question more fully than his previous instructions in the art of brevity would seem to permit.

Cox interjected, "Come now doctor. You have already acknowledged your familiarity with the chain of command concept. How well does it apply to the organization for which you have also already acknowledged you possess absolute authority and responsibility?"

G: (Exasperated) "I've already told you, Ms. Cox, I believe our organization — the one I head — must be responsive to the people we serve. It takes dedication and it takes discipline and it takes a willingness to put aside one's own preconceptions on how to meet needs, in order to meet them as they really exist. The Indians and Natives we serve deserve the best and that means workers who are team players!"

C: "Indeed, team players, ones that adhere to the party line, I suppose. Under what circumstances were you first aware of my client, Sandra Locklear?"

Giroux was taken aback with the immediate juxtaposition of 'team players' with Sandra's name. He was almost caught off guard. "Uh, well. Let me think. I believe I first met Ms. Locklear in a meeting in my office."

Sandra handed Cox a note hastily written while Giroux was hunting for words. Cox looked at the note acknowledging its contents.

G: "We were having a meeting on the subject of alcoholism in the community. Ms. Locklear, among others, presented some interesting information. And toward the end of it, I felt Ms. Locklear's leg brush against mine and remain there. I put my hand on her leg to push it back. I didn't want to make a scene, so I found a convenient time to end the meeting. I told Locklear to stay so I could caution her about her behavior."

C: "That's all very interesting, Dr. Giroux. But in fact didn't you attend a party at Ms. Locklear's apartment shortly after she arrived? Wasn't that the first opportunity you had on a social level to size her up and to get some idea of the layout of her apartment so you could seduce her?"

H: "Objection, Counselor. Argumentative. Speculative."

Cox smiled. "Indeed! I'll rephrase the question."

C: "Did you or did you not attend a social gathering at Ms. Locklear's apartment shortly after she arrived in Rockville, doctor?"

G: "Yes; but on her invitation. I didn't crash her party." Giroux was beginning to be edgy.

C: "At that party did you or did you not hold her arms and pat her hands when you were leaving and say to her you knew exactly where she could do the most good? Or words to that effect?"

G: "I don't remember what I said as I was leaving, Ms. Cox. Those words don't mean a thing, if indeed I said them."

C: "I submit, doctor, those words could mean much more than you want to let us know. When Ms. Locklear first arrived on station didn't you also invite her for coffee?"

G: "Coffee? What does drinking a cup of coffee have to do with all this? I invited her for a cup of coffee much as I do with many staff members just to get some idea of how they will go about their new assignment. It also gives me the opportunity to tell them my expectations. I see no harm in that, Ms. Cox."

C: "Perhaps not, doctor, but do you see the harm in this scenario? When you told Ms. Locklear to remain after the meeting, didn't you immediately shut your office door, turn around, and abruptly pull her into you, and then kiss her without warning so she could not escape you? Well, doctor?"

Both Harris and Giroux looked to each other. Neither expected Cox to pick up the lance and charge forward in attack. Administrative types abhor conflict.

H: "I request a recess to confer with Dr. Giroux for a moment, Ms. Cox. Shall we say ten minutes?" Both pushed their chairs away from the table and prepared to leave the room.

"Of course, Mr. Harris. I'm sure the good doctor may need to regroup." Cox was pleased with her efforts so far. She believed she had begun to make a dent in his armor. It would only be a matter of time in which that armor with its multiple dents would cause Giroux some anguish. And she hoped the pain would make him relent and acknowledge his harassment. She said as much to Locklear who was not so sure.

Locklear was uncomfortable with Cox's attack on her former lover. She once felt secure in his arms. Now she felt alone and not at peace with her decision to force the truth upon him. She wondered why she felt compelled to vindicate herself. The affair was over and each had gone their separate ways. Perhaps it would have been better not to give in to the other ladies. Then, again, he did force her to kiss him; and, it was he who called to arrange their first tryst.

Soon, Harris and Giroux returned appearing to be satisfied with their discussion and resolve to turn this event to their favor. Cox was ready for them and eager to draw blood.

C: "Let me repeat the question, Dr. Giroux."

G: "That won't be necessary, Ms. Cox. I remember well enough. I believe Ms. Locklear might not have portrayed the event as accurately to you as you may believe.

"First, she touched and stroked my leg repeatedly. I felt I had to caution her about her behavior. Second, I preferred to deal with her privately and asked her to wait in my office which was adjacent to the conference room. And, as I turned around from closing my office door I began to raise my hand to gesture to her to be seated.

"However, she was so close, almost on top of me as it were, and my hand brushed across her breast, quite accidentally I might add. Before I could say a word I was astonished that she put her arms around me and kissed me. She must have assumed I wanted an affair.

"Unfortunately, I was hardly prepared for such an encounter, and I didn't want to make a scene. So, I simply dismissed her. It was months before I saw her again."

C: "Let me see if I understand this, doctor. You expect me to believe you were the victim of an unwanted sexual advance by Ms. Locklear? And that you had nothing to do with the events that took place both in your conference room and your office?"

G: "I am not responsible for what you believe, Ms. Cox. I have simply responded to your question with what happened during the event you questioned. I did not lead her on."

C: "You had no compunction to invite her for a private coffee; no qualms about pressing her flesh, so to speak, and tell her in unusually hushed tones that you knew where she could do the most good. Now you state again without compunction, that you ordered her into your office; you shut the door; and she led you on? I don't quite understand this, doctor Giroux.

"I submit you knew perfectly well what you were doing and that it was your intention from the start to seduce her. You had to see how she would react to your authority — which, by the way, you said you possessed fully — so you, not she, initiated the affair with the intense kiss in your office.

"Tell me, doctor, who made the date that led to intercourse, you or Ms. Locklear."

G: (Sweating) "Well, I simply called her to speak with her one day. But..."

C: "Was that during business hours or off-duty hours?"

G: "I don't remember right now."

C: "Come, doctor. Think!"

G: "All right, it was on a Saturday. I was working in the office and wondered if she would like to go for coffee or something."

C: "No, doctor. Didn't Ms. Locklear tell you she had other plans and that she was going to go to Annapolis for the weekend to visit some historical sights? And when you arrived at her apartment didn't you immediately fold her into your arms and lead her off to the bedroom? That hardly constitutes going for coffee does it?"

Cox hammered on for another hour to build her case that Giroux orchestrated all the circumstances of additional nights and days together. Locklear was instructed not to call him; she was to be at his beckoning. It became clear — even to Mr. Harris — that Giroux intended having an affair with Locklear from the beginning, and that he would use his influence and position to command silence from her. This was not only harassment, but also intimidation.

Several weeks passed. The deposition was expensive for Locklear. But Cox said it was worth its weight in gold. Without a doubt she said it would convince any judge that harassment took place. Locklear had to follow through with her formal grievance if not for herself, then for the other ladies who looked upon her as their heroine.

Locklear returned to her office certain she didn't want to be a heroine for anyone and buried herself in her work. She didn't have the stomach for it and didn't want to speak with Cox or anyone else connected with her grievance. She hoped that visits to the field would somehow provide the respite she longed for.

She set up and made several field visits. Her visits to Sacramento and Phoenix were a blur. If someone were to ask her whom she spoke to about community health nursing issues in either area she swore she would have to plead ignorance.

The trip gave Locklear what she needed, sights and sounds different from Rockville. She could not even associate names with faces which was to her liking. She didn't care whether she would remember any details of her visits although she knew they were stored within her memory for use later.

Locklear set up a final stopover at Albuquerque, New Mexico during the last week of her hiatus. She had no working knowledge of Indian Pueblos and had always wanted to see Sky City, the village of Acoma, which was supposed to be the oldest continuously inhabited city in North America. It would be a treat she would allow herself.

Locklear reflected on her childhood growing up in Cherokee, North Carolina. Her formal knowledge of her own Indianness was scant. She always thought of herself as one of the townsfolk, maybe a little darker than some, but one of them nonetheless. She went to grade school and high school like everyone else. As she went to college for her nursing degree she felt no differences from the other students, except, perhaps her speech which had a little twang to it.

Mom and Dad, brothers and sisters grew up among the hills of Cherokee in tune with nature, themselves and the rest of the folk. There was hardly any discussion about being "Indian". She knew she had a "card" and was full-blood Cherokee and that she got her medical care from the local Indian Health Service hospital on the hill. Beyond that her Indianness was only associated with tales her mother and father would repeat about ancestors. The special quality of the relationship had yet to gather specific meaning.

When she arrived in Albuquerque she made it a point to go to the Indian Pueblo Cultural Center on 12th Street. Browsing through the book shelves she scooped up several books on the connection of the current Pueblos with the extinct Anasazi Indians and could easily imagine their communal life. How rich in spirit they must have been. It was astonishing to learn they had built and abandoned apartments five and six stories in height at Chaco Canyon and other places long before western Europeans would ever get around to building apartments.

She remained to watch the series of dancers in the plaza at the Center and was enchanted by the romance of the open blue sky and puffy clouds rolling over the Sandia and Manzano Mountains, and the vast expanse of the desert, while sitting there watching the traditional dancers of the Jemez and Isleta Pueblos in their multi-colored costumes.

Her breakfast burrito with green chili at the Center before her trip to Acoma was her first taste of local cuisine. She was transfixed by the blend of tastes, the egg and cheese and bacon and green chili wrapped in a grand tortilla. She vowed that New Mexico would forever be high on her priority list for return visits.

The following day, Locklear crammed one last pleasure into her busy return schedule. At the Cultural Center she picked up a brochure describing breathtaking views on a tram ride to the top of Sandia Peak. She finished eating another burrito and looking to a table to her right she noticed a man staring at her.

"Pardon me," he said. "While it's a rather trite and perhaps overworked way to begin a conversation, haven't I seen you someplace before?"

"I rather doubt it," Locklear remarked. "I'm not from New Mexico. Just visiting, and if I don't get started soon I am going to be missing out on a nice adventure."

"New Mexico is full of nice adventures. Now, take that tram ride you were just reading about. It promises to be spectacular today. I predict it just for you. It's a twenty minute ascent over a two mile vertical climb to the ten thousand foot level. You'll get out at the top with the wind blowing through your hair. You'll see the valley spread beneath your feet like a kingdom stretching far and wide.

"It will be your kingdom, at least for the day. You know, I do think I have seen you before though. Back east. Oh, well, I guess it doesn't matter since you said you were leaving." Jake Bronson remarked taken with her beauty.

As he was gathering his bill too, she said, "Wait a minute. Would you care to join me in another cup of coffee? I didn't mean to be rude."

He joined her at her booth and signaled for the waitress. "Mary, I think I would like another cup of coffee, please."

"Right away, Jake."

"So that is your name, Jake. It seems they know you here. Are you a regular?"

"I'm about as irregular as they come."

"I don't follow you."

Jake looked at her and smiled. "Oh, I just meant I come here when I can, which is not so often as I would like. The breakfast burritos are terrific aren't they? I love them. You're Indian aren't you?"

Locklear looked at him and thought to herself how easy it is to talk to him. She was beginning to want to delay her trip further. "Yes to both questions. Why do you think you have seen me before?"

"You're Indian. You're out here on a visit apparently cramming in the visit between business meetings. You look like you are rushed. You're eating alone. And, if I can tell a little from the inflection in your voice I would say you come from a tribe in the East, but obviously not the Northeast. How am I doing so far?" Bronson was pleased with his guess work.

"I'm not so sure if I like you, Jake. So far you have been mostly right on all counts. Yes, I guess I am putting too much into this trip. And yes, I am from back east. Actually from North Carolina; but I am working in Maryland now."

"Say no more. I know. You're a fed, and you work for either the Indian Health Service or the Bureau of Indian Affairs. Actually, I'm one, too. But that's as far as I will go in talking about work today. I promise.

"Look. Today is Saturday. You and I both have the day off. I would love to escort you on your trip up the mountain. The air is so fresh and beautiful up there. I haven't been up there for a long while. I'm sure it will help you sort out things. It helps me out to just go there and sit on a rock and look at the valley below."

Locklear looked at him again. "What makes you so sure I have things to sort out?"

"Mystery lady, you already said you are sandwiching this trip between business meetings. People try to divert their attention when, whatever is commanding their attention so much demands a change. That's okay. Even though you may be preoccupied with other things I think you can still have fun today. What do you say? I promise you no complications to what may already be a complicated life."

Locklear listened to him and weighed the sincerity with which he spoke. For some strange reason she trusted him yet was fearful of an entanglement when she was trying to get out of another web. Her pause seemed like an eternity. Finally she said, "If I am going to accompany you, I guess you should at least know my name. I am Sandra..."

Bronson interrupted her.

"Ah, ah, ah... No last names, please. If you are going to be my mystery lady for a whirlwind trip up the mountain I want your fantasy to be as open as it can be to allow you to imagine yourself on an European holiday in the Alps, of course, though, with the appropriate geographical nuances changed. There isn't any snow up there this time of year but you may need a sweater. The mountains aren't as rocky or precipitous as the Alps. But the trails are fun to walk. Where are you staying so you can get a change of shoes and grab a sweater?"

She smiled. "The Four Seasons. Do you know where that is? I suppose you do since you live here. Silly me."

"That's great! Not far from my apartment on Carlisle. But I will spare you that trauma."

Sandra laughed at his good humor and thought him refreshing. She didn't know him but felt attracted to him nonetheless. "Meet me in the lobby at the Four Seasons in an hour. I'll be there. I promise."

"I'll hold you to it, Sandra. One hour then." Bronson extended his hand to her and felt the warmth of a lifetime in her. He almost regretted saying he wanted no last names to be said. But he needed the mystery as much as she and kept his word. They each departed for a change in clothes. Within the hour they were on their way to Sandia Peak.

The tram departed from the dock and moved effortlessly up the incline. Sandra looked out the south side of the tram. As they approached the second tower Jake pointed out the beginning changes in vegetation that were becoming more pronounced as they ascended.

Passing the descending tram and pausing for a moment they moved to the rear of the cabin to get a better view of the Rio Grande River meandering below. Jake said, "In the distance on the horizon you can see Mt. Taylor jutting up. In the winter you can ski cross-country up there. Just as an isolated tidbit for your compendium of miscellaneous facts, Mt. Taylor is a sacred mountain for the Navajos. It marks their eastern boundary."

Sandra looked at him gratefully as they were ascending. "I'm so glad I didn't rush out of the restaurant this morning. This is beautiful. I had no idea Albuquerque was so striking!"

Jake smiled. "Wait until you get to the top. From there you'll see the whole valley stretch out before you. Your problems will seem so insignificant. If you stand on the platform and look long enough you'll swear you can see them fade into the distance riding on a white cloud. And, I promise you more surely, if you let me buy you dinner they'll vanish with the dying sun." Locklear was non-committal. Bronson glanced away. He knew she was thinking about his offer. but he did not want to press the issue.

The tram moved slowly into the docking station at the top. A brisk wind was blowing and rocking it slightly. As the door of the cabin opened, she breathed deeply. The freshness of the pine filled air filled Sandra's lungs. She shut her eyes momentarily shielding them from the bright sun, held her breath and savored the aroma.

She and Jake moved to the platform immediately with the crowd. "Welcome to the Land of Enchantment, Mystery Lady," Jake said, moving to her right. "Your kingdom lies before you!" He bowed with a sweeping gesture.

Locklear looked to the south so as to shield from his view a tear forming in her eyes. She was inexplicably glad to be sharing this moment with this stranger with whom she felt an affinity. She turned to say, "Jake, I..."

"I know..." he interrupted once more, "It's one of the more beautiful sights in the southwest, Sandra. But come inside and learn a little more. I want you to expand your mind about

Albuquerque, the Sandias, and this little part of heaven. When you are finished we'll ride the chair lift to the ski lodge, get some hot chocolate, and talk some more."

A romantic at heart, Sandra was beginning to feel the cliché, the Land of Enchantment, was holding special meaning for her. She envisioned some of her concerns riding those white clouds to the horizon. They were getting smaller, one by one as he said. She began to think, 'God must be up here somewhere smiling down at me. Such a wonderful day!'

The afternoon and the conversation sped by all too swiftly. Soon they were on their way via the chair lift to the top of the mountain again. Jake coaxed Locklear into a walk along the rim through the heavily forested area to the lookout on the edge. "I want you to work up a good appetite, Sandra. We'll eat at High Finance by the tram before we return to Albuquerque. Then we'll watch the sun set as we descend. Sound like fun?"

Sandra was surprised that Bronson had not made any move toward her. She halfway expected it; but she was grateful for the peace and respect he gave her. Many times on the walk to the lookout Bronson would simply walk in silence, occasionally calling her attention to brief descriptions of various forms of vegetation appearing by the way side, or to special views found in clearings.

On arrival there Locklear found the view of the valley below equally spectacular yet different from the one afforded her at the tram platform. And here she was on a mountain top with a perfect stranger, feeling safe and not alone, in a place where anything could happen but fearing nothing. It was the most wonderful exhilarating feeling of utter contentment and peace — the same kind of peace she often felt in church. She felt midway between heaven and earth, her thoughts suspended.

Bronson was lost in his own thoughts. He was recovering from a failed long distance romance and felt the need to grow independently. He was challenged by the need, the desire to know Sandra. He wanted to be close to her. His resolve to avoid the same pitfall was foremost in his thoughts. He was cautious.

Looking at her intently drinking in the landscape before her, his eyes caught hers as she turned. Without saying a word her gaze fastened on his. Each was saying thanks simply for being there. The intensity of the moment was not lost on either.

She extended her right hand to him.

Neither Jake nor Sandra wanted to lose the moment; yet, neither wanted to make more of it than the magic would allow. As the shadows of the pine trees were lengthening, Jake said, "I think, fair lady, I should feed you. I'm afraid my own appetite can get out of control too easily here."

Sandra laughed aware that he was not talking about food as the appetite that was raging and responded, "Food would be nice, too."

Their return walk to High Finance was slower this time. They wanted to drink in the fantastic lights and shadows brought on by the descending sun and deliberately took their time. Jake had already made a reservation and they were quickly seated on arrival.

The walk had stimulated their appetites. Supper was no sooner ordered than it seemed to disappear before their very eyes. Small talk dominated their conversation until Jake noticed the sun dipping beyond the horizon.

"I'm afraid, Sandra, the moment has come. We have to leave. I want you to see the sun set from the tram."

Standing on the platform they could see the Prussian blue of the eastern night sky above them giving way to a purple crimson of the western horizon. During the descent in the tram the western-most horizon was mingled with clouds painted crimson and orange and white.

Sandra said nothing but was consumed with the beauty. Jake stood by the railing. As they lowered from the mountain top the city lights sparkled on a blanket of black velvet. He said, "This is what I want you to see and remember." Sandra moved closer and Bronson folded his arms about her carefully, without consuming her. Her heart quickened.

They docked momentarily and Jake returned her to the Pinnacle Hotel Four Seasons and to her room. On leaving he said, "I'll find you."

Sandra's return flight to Washington National Airport was filled with mixed emotions. Her thoughts were of Jake. Nothing had happened between them, yet, everything had. She knew nothing of him, who he really was; yet she didn't want to know anything more because she knew everything she had to know. He treated her with dignity, imagination, and respect, allowing her to have her own thoughts without intrusion into her life. Within him she sensed intense passion, something she longed for and had never experienced with Giroux or anyone else.

On arrival she managed somehow to retrieve her bags, board the MetroRail to the Twinbrook station, get a cab for the short ride to her apartment and get unpacked all the while thinking of him. Jake was on her mind. 'He's insufferable. He didn't even give me his last name. He even insisted that we not know either one's last names or where we work. How could he do this? How could I let him do it? How could I go along with his fantasy? How is he supposed to find me like he promised? Do I really want to be found? 'Yes, yes, yes!'

She surveyed her apartment and found nothing out of order. Mail stacked up on her kitchen counter top threatened to fall on the floor in heaps. Sandra scooped it all up throwing all but the latest paper into the trash and retreated to the living room sofa with the remainder of envelopes and periodicals.

Curling her feet under her she divided the stack into three smaller piles of junk mail to be thrown out immediately, of magazines or periodicals for later more leisurely reading, and of bills or other interesting pieces that looked like they may need action of some type.

While doing so, she punched on the telephone recorder button. Seventeen messages were recorded. There were several outside sales calls, some calls from chatty friends at the office with late breaking news, three from Cox who strongly urged her to call her if she gets in at a reasonable hour, and one from Giroux, quite unexpectedly. Since she arrived after ten-thirty PM she told herself she would call Cox in the morning.

As for Giroux, Giroux's message was quite disturbing as it was simple; "I think we need to talk, Sandra." To which she replied, "The creep!" The very thought of his wanting to talk with her sent a chill up her spine and aggravated her composure. She wished for but didn't have Jake near her to calm her.

Funny how he came to mind in the midst of her new panic. She smiled at his image standing beside her on the tram, closed her eyes, and wished for him to come walking into the apartment with a bouquet behind his back to make the specter of Giroux vanish.

"Devoutly to be wished," she thought as she opened a number of the envelopes hoping to take her mind off her problems by forcing more pleasant musings.

Then she snapped, reached for the telephone and broke Giroux's cardinal rule, 'Don't ever call me,' and dialed his number. Elizabeth answered. Then she heard another click on the other end and knew Giroux was listening.

Very matter-of-factly Locklear said, "Elizabeth, I am sorry to disturb you. This is Sandra Locklear. Please tell your husband not to leave any messages on my answering machine. Thank you. Good bye." She didn't bother to wait for her reply. She reasoned that if Giroux had confided in Elizabeth this would convince her he was not to be trusted, and, if not, then Giroux would have some explaining to do for leaving messages on strange women's telephones. Proud of herself, she chuckled and decided to get a hot bath and sleep.

Early the next morning Locklear walked to work as usual but more pleased with herself. She no longer had anything to hide and was beginning to feel that life held other promise for her. She decided to delay her call to Cox until lunch time. She could call from the privacy of her home.

The office didn't lend itself well to very private discussions with anyone. Only the chiefs of services had private offices in which you could close a door, and, technically while she was chief of the community health nursing program, she should have a private office, Locklear was not so lucky. The space for her program was small and Cynthia wanted her out of the office as much as she could stand the travel, as she said, 'For the support of the tribes, you understand.'

Locklear knew fully well Cynthia didn't want to see her face around the office. The day she came there with her grievance in hand was a black day for Nursing Services. Regulations required that the initial informal grievance be submitted to one's supervisor for a response before it could go any higher.

Cynthia's mouth dropped open as she read and re-read the document in total disbelief and denial. While she understood the document was not really meant for her, Cynthia could barely come to grips with its content. Her anger got the best of her and she blurted out, "How could you do this? How could you bring such dishonor to the Nursing Branch, Sandra? How could you put yourself in such a situation?" Then she caught herself for what she said to Locklear and apologized profusely. By then the damage had been done.

Locklear remembered, too, how shocked she was for not receiving the support of her sister nurse. She expected Cynthia to understand that Giroux came onto her. He initiated the affair and she was fearful he would deny her promotions. Instead, Cynthia blamed her totally for the affair, and worse, that she really deserved whatever would happen to her for bringing dishonor to the Branch and the Commissioned Corps.

In tears and disbelief, Locklear remembered giving her the regulations running out of the office to take the remainder of the day to recover some composure. The following day Locklear returned to her office to be told that Cynthia had responded that she had no power or authority to grant the relief she sought — that she be protected from Giroux's sexual harassment.

Instead, as the regulations provided, Cynthia forwarded her grievance to the next higher authority, Dr. Reilly, the Chief of the Office of Health Programs. Dr. Reilly held onto the document for days while he conferred with his Equal Employment Opportunity officer. The complaint was a "hot potato."

Sandra ruminated on these events while she made her expected reports for the field trips, she answered the month's accumulation of correspondence and memoranda littering her desk. Glad the morning had finally ended she left the office, went down the back stairwell, walked across the driveway through the parking lot of Best Buys and into her apartment.

She prepared a lunch of cold cuts and dialed Cox who was in ill-humor. "Sandra, do you recall when you received your reply to your informal grievance how upset you were when the Indian Health Service denied your accusation and your relief? And when you finally agreed with me that we will have to make this a formal grievance? Well, I'm afraid all of our effort and your pain has gone for naught. They have denied your claim again saying that both your deposition and his simply amount to your word against his." Cox paused listening to Sandra's heavy breathing.

"Say something to me, Sandra. Those little shits don't have the balls to do what's right! I've talked with their attorneys until I'm blue in the face. Now they won't even answer my calls.

"We've exhausted their protocols. The only thing that's left before we can sue Giroux in a *Bivens* action is getting their statement that we have complied with administrative requirements. And, off the record the last little shit I talked to said the Indian Health Service won't give us that until we appeal. And that will keep us busy for a long time. Talk to me, Sandra. Tell me what you want to do."

Sandra paused for the longest time. It was getting on Cox's nerves. She was doing her own heavy breathing. Finally Locklear said, "Give up. That's what they want us to do. Just forget that it happened."

"What?" Cox interrupted. "You can't be serious! Give them what they want? Not on your life, Sandra. This is a matter of principle to me now. My filing an appeal is not going to cost you a dime believe me. This one is on me. They expect us to give in without a fight. But we are going to surprise them. We are going to fight! Our line of appeal is to the Office of the Surgeon General and to the Office of the Secretary of Health, and, believe me, we are going to turn this thing around."

Locklear was tired of the whole episode but told Cox to do what she thought was best. Locklear didn't know what good it would do but would trust her judgment. Cox filed the appeal and within a week heard from the Public Health Service attorneys in a terse letter confirming receipt of the documents. "The matter of Locklear vs. Giroux will be taken under advisement," it said. "An independent investigation may be commissioned to make a determination in this matter," it concluded.

Cox was delighted that, at least, the Public Health Service had the sense to call on people from outside to investigate the matter. Locklear suggested she shouldn't count on anything. Cox admitted that so far, the Indian Health Service and the Public Health Service attorneys have been less than cooperative.

"I have never encountered such wimps before in my life. But right now my only worry is that they may think that their delay will allow the statute of limitations to run out on the *Bivens* action. We're already at the half way mark on that."

Locklear asked, "What about the other ladies? I haven't spoken with them in a long time. Where do they stand?"

"They still haven't heard anything about their formal grievances. The IHS attorneys have been stalling on theirs, too. The last time I talked with them they were trying to get Margaret and Janet to have their grievances joined with yours."

Cox was candid about their prospects for success. "I'm avoiding that since the IHS has effectively dismissed yours and allowed us to appeal. To be honest with you, their dismissal of your case doesn't make their cases look good for the ladies. I'll probably have to appeal their cases, too. Since it's too early to tell, I haven't told the ladies anything yet."

"I'll be sure not to tell them." Locklear felt dejected after her telephone conference with Cox. She finished her cold cuts and returned to the office dreading each minute there under Cynthia's watchful glare. How she wished she could be back in Albuquerque. But then she had to dismiss her fantasy as unrealistic. She buried herself in her work much like an ostrich with its head in the sand.

In the second month since her return from Albuquerque, the EEO office had notified Locklear that field personnel from the New York Regional Office of Personnel Management were assigned to investigate her case.

Cox was immediately notified at the same time. Locklear mounted an anxiety attack under the threat of having to disclose her relationship with Giroux. Yet, with Cox's urging and support, she knew this may be the one chance she needed to vindicate herself. Armed with a prescription for Elavil Sandra and Cox met with the three field staff assigned by the Department of Health and Human Services.

Hannah Cochran, Peter Douglas, and Michael Wilson were ensconced in an office provided for them by the EEO. Hannah, a nurse for many years, was designated as their lead person, the one who had the final responsibility for the report. Peter held an advanced degree in personnel administration and had served successfully in large corporations before he joined the federal work force. Michael was their Equal Employment Opportunity specialist.

Hannah explained. "Let me tell you our roles and responsibilities. As a team we have been designated to conduct our own impartial investigation into your claim of sexual harassment, Ms. Locklear. Each of us has read and re-read the file several times including the informal grievance, the formal grievance, the proposed dismissal of your claim by the IHS, all the correspondence, and the depositions. We have developed a set of questions that we will be asking everyone concerned.

"You may add names to this list. After we interview everyone our team will make independent reports which I will have the responsibility to develop and consolidate into one report with a recommendation to the Department of Health and Human Services and to the Indian Health Service." She paused for breath.

Cox was concerned and asked. "Pardon me, but who interviews whom; and what weight does your report have? Is your report and accompanying recommendations binding on the Indian Health Service?"

The trio looked at each other and Locklear looked at the trio. "The Public Health Service is paying for this investigation. We hope the recommendations we make are perceived as binding."

"Excuse me. You *hope* the recommendations are perceived as binding. You don't *know*? You are telling me and my abused client that the IHS, if you will pardon my French, can read your report and do what it damn well pleases! Correct me if I am wrong, Ms. Cochran, *but you have no authority whatsoever.*"

Peter and Michael winced. Hannah turned red. Cox and Locklear looked at each other and shook their heads then laughed. The trio was stunned.

"Look, what's so funny?" Hannah asked nonplused about their behavior.

Cox answered for the two of them. "We actually believed for a moment there would be some justice in the system. But you are just going through the motions, aren't you? Please tell me that you are not, Ms. Cochran. Please tell me, Mr. Douglas, Mr. Wilson." Cox held up her hands with open palms waiting for a response from the trio.

Each started to talk almost at once to defend their integrity. Ms. Cochran silenced them. "Look, Ms. Cox and Ms. Locklear. I understand your anger. Off the record. Peter, Michael and I are really in tune with what happened. We have seen and heard and investigated so many cases of sexual harassment over the years in so many agencies and programs we know what to look for. And we will find it."

Cox interrupted, "But with this agency?"

"Let me level with you. No. Not the Indian Health Service. But these are federal people. They have a trust to uphold. A responsibility to the people. I'm confident they will do what is right." Ms. Cochran then outlined her plan. Cox and Locklear each took a deep breath.

Cochran would interview Locklear with her attorney and anyone else they recommended. Mr. Douglas would interview those in the Director's office closest to him. Mr. Wilson would be responsible for interviewing Sarah and anyone else who was involved in the EEO office. Files were to be made available and copies of reports made for their official file. The process would take about two weeks. A final report with recommendations would then be made to their agency head and forwarded to the IHS for a response.

Cox said, "Your process sounds very thorough. I expect that you will forward us a copy of your report of findings and recommendations." Cox shifted her position.

Hannah responded, "Well, not quite. The report is the agency's report. It will have to go through the clearance process before we can release it."

"I see. You mean I will have to request it of you through the Freedom of Information Act. Right?"

"Ms. Cox, we will be cooperative with you to the extent we are permitted. I can assure you, before we return to New York I will have a close out with you to tell you in general terms what we have found. Meanwhile, we have to get started." Staff were dismissed to their tasks. Cox and Locklear remained with her the next two hours for her testimony.

Cox and Locklear were impressed with their good-faith effort. The trio, and Hannah in particular, seemed genuinely interested in her case and concerned about her well-being. They concluded they would have to wait for their close-out to get a sense of where they stood.

Glad her interview was over and anxious for the result of the whole inquiry, Locklear returned to her daily tasks. The weekend came and went without incident. Her feelings were beginning to return to normal. At least as normal as her anxiety would allow.

In mid-week, as she was leaving her office with several community nursing staff who were in from the field for a conference, Locklear walked up the hallway engrossed in conversation. It was lunch time. She heard a familiar voice behind her calling out her name, "Sandra, may I have a word with you?"

She wheeled about sharply disbelieving her ears and eyes. Jake came up behind her with a wide grin on his face. "Do you have time for lunch with me?" he asked.

Locklear tried to maintain calm but the others with her noticed her excitement. Looking to themselves they smiled at her and excused themselves, giggling up the hallway and talking in hushed tones.

She could hardly contain herself and reached for him with both arms. Unconcerned about impressions they hugged tightly in the hallway and exited down the nearest stairwell to go to lunch at the House of Chinese Chicken a few blocks from the building.

"I never thought I would see you again. How did you find me?" Locklear's heart was racing as she walked holding onto his arm tightly. "Are you going to be here very long? Where are you staying? What are you doing here anyway?"

"Whoa, mystery lady. One question at a time! I don't think a day has gone by that I haven't thought of you and remembered what a wonderful time I had being with you in Albuquerque. I really didn't expect to see you again, even though I wanted to so very much.

"I began to ask around the different offices of the Bureau of Indian Affairs who you might be. Everyone I knew there thought I was weird. They didn't know who I was describing. So I asked around our offices, too, and got the same result. One loco white guy!" They laughed.

"The truth of the matter is, I gave up until I was called by John Standing Bear to come in for a couple of weeks to help out with making some charts and graphs for Dr. Giroux to use in his report to the Senate Select Committee next week. I've been here a few days. Thank goodness we happened to come out of our pigeon holes at about the same time isn't it? If we hadn't I might still be searching."

Sandra wondered, "Standing Bear? What do you have to do with him?"

"This isn't the first time I've bailed him out. He always calls me to do his heavy work. I've been here a few times before but I guess I've never seen you. I would have remembered. You're pretty hard to forget.

"Anyhow, this time he wanted me to develop his data into graphs so Giroux can tell the Senate all the wonderful things IHS is doing to combat alcoholism and drug abuse. So I did some number crunching and made some fancy graphs and contracted to have them developed on poster size boards. Giroux asked me to go to the Senate with him as he presents his case. I get to turn the charts as he talks about the information. Pretty neat, huh?"

Locklear smiled as they arrived at the restaurant thinking to herself. 'Why does my life have to be so complicated? I've slept with the man and can't stand to see him, and now the person I wouldn't mind sleeping with thinks he is pretty neat! How am I going to deal with Jake?' She began to feel guilty and wondered if their budding relationship would be destined for failure.

Jake sat her at the table oblivious of her consternation. He was in a world of his own. His hopes for a relationship were flowering with every gaze. She ordered shrimp with lobster sauce and he ordered lemon chicken. Each shared with the other.

"Tell me about you, Sandra, what has been happening in your life?" Jake asked earnestly.

Sandra looked away. "Say, do you know I don't even know your last name? The last time I saw you, you said you want this to be a mystery. And now, you have an unfair advantage. You know my name and I don't know yours. That is not very gentlemanly. Do I call you mystery man too?" she asked pretending to be hurt reaching out a hand to be held, her dark eyes burning with an inner flame.

Jake's lips thinned out in an expansive smile. "So there is no mystery between us, Bronson is my last name. I would still prefer to keep you my mystery lady."

The waiter came with the bill and said to pay the cashier. "Well, it looks like they are trying to get rid of us. Every time I've been here, this place has been crowded. Today doesn't seem to be an exception. This has been a wonderful lunch, Sandra, but I guess we had better get back to the dungeon before they send a search party for us."

On their return to the Parklawn Building, Sandra confided, "Jake, there are a lot of things I would like to share with you, (she reflected on the matter with Giroux) perhaps in due time. This is all very strange for me. I hardly know you but I feel very close to you. It's the damndest thing! And, I think I want to get to know you even more. I don't understand it."

"Sounds like confession time. Then I guess I have one, too. When I let you go in Albuquerque I was panicked. I kicked myself in the butt — figuratively, of course — and thought what a dumbbell I was not to give you my name or telephone number or where I worked. I figured I really blew it. It's fantastic what little miracles there are in life!

"But, of course, this calls for a celebration, Sandra, like eating out with me tonight."

Sandra grimaced. "Ugh! Don't talk to me about food. I'm so stuffed!"

"Ah, I have just the right thing. Tennis then?" Jake offered.

"Oh, no! I'm not in shape for that. It sounds like so much exercise. How about something sedentary? A movie? I hear *Sleeping With The Enemy* is pretty good!"

"Ideal! Then we can eat a bite afterwards."

"You win. When we get back to the office I'll write down my address for you. It's just around the corner from where we work. Actually I don't think I need to write it down for you, do I? I'm sure you can remember."

The rest of the afternoon flew by. Each anticipated the evening and was unconcerned about the details of work. When four-thirty came Jake walked briskly down the stairwell to the fifth floor east exit, skipped across the street to the parking lot, and drove the few short blocks to the Crown Plaza.

Locklear was in a fast walk to the rear stairwell, down to the third floor and out of the building in a flash. She arrived at her apartment oblivious of the intervening steps, unlocked the door, and glided straight into her bedroom to undress. She drew a hot bath and put in extra bubbles. As they rose to the surface they seemed to reflect her mood, light hearted and gay, the events of the past few months very much absent.

Jake, too, was the happiest he had been for months, perhaps even the past few years if he were honest with himself. Most of the women he had dated seemed shallow and more concerned about themselves than people with whom they came into contact. He wanted someone with whom he felt close; if they didn't want to talk that would be okay; the silences would be full of closeness, and, if they did talk, their communication would be enriched with the possibility of deeper understanding.

Sandra was different. He knew it, he felt it, and he wanted her to be his special friend. It was his purpose tonight to explore this relationship without alienating her. If more than friendship were to evolve Bronson would welcome it knowing that he was free. He resolved he would never force himself upon her.

Locklear emerged from her bath renewed in spirit and anxious to begin a new phase in her life. Somehow she felt a sense of promise in Bronson even though their contact was so limited. She welcomed that too, not wanting to rush into a physical relationship and reasoning that if it were meant to be, it would become a loving and trusting relationship.

As she selected her clothes for the evening she noticed the insistent blinking of her answering machine. There was one message. Giroux spoke, "Please, Sandra, don't turn off the machine and hear me out. I apologize for calling you before. While I didn't expect it or like it I have to admire you for calling my home and telling Elizabeth to ask me to cease calling you. It took nerve.

"I guess I am violating your space once more... Forgive me for doing so, please. I wish you and I could have a decent conversation again. I miss ours... I really have hoped we could get by this impasse, that we could get together again. You're the most fantastic lover a person could ever have... I need you... I want to be with you. Please call me so we can sort this out in the office. Thanks."

Locklear sat back on her bed in a heap. Her heart was pounding with new anxiety. She could feel her blood pressure rising. She was tempted to erase the message. She turned to sit at her dresser to look into the mirror. She talked to herself while she brushed her long flowing hair into a sheen. Her face was beginning to be contorted with her imagination. It saw Giroux looming over her with inordinate power. She decided. 'I better keep it. I may just come in handy.'

Locklear thought of all nights for him to leave a message. 'I wish he would just let it go. I can't even go out and enjoy myself without being badgered by him. If I go into his office I just know he will tie me in knots! No. I can't do that! That's exactly what he wants. Then, again, maybe if I face him I can get this over with quicker. I've got to tell him I don't want a relationship.' The pendulum of her mind swung back and forth.

Locklear realized how fast the time was going. Jake would be here soon and she wouldn't be ready. 'Oh, Jake! Should I tell him about the affair with Giroux? What if he finds out from someone else? What will he think of me? What if he already knows? Oh, God! What if he does know? How can I ever be serious with him? Could he love me for who I am? Or will I always be Giroux's woman? How horrible! Wait I'm getting ahead of myself. This is just a date with Jake. Calm down, Sandra. He just may get bored with you real quickly.'

As she slipped a casual cotton blouse over her head and began to tuck it into her waist, the doorbell rang. Oh, my God. He's here. She yelled out "Just a minute!" Locklear ran about the bedroom, picked up her clothes and tossed them into the hamper, adjusted the towels in the bathroom, and quickly surveyed the living room to see that it was in order, then casually opened the door.

Trying to appear nonchalant she said, "Hi, Jake. Would you like to come in for a minute. I just have to get my coat. Sometimes the evenings here are a little cool."

"Of course. We have plenty of time for the late show. No hurry. Take your time." Locklear walked into her bedroom to pick up a wrap. Jake stood there by the door. When she returned, he said, "You have some lovely things. Your collection of baskets and pottery are outstanding. I've always wanted to do something like that but I've never gotten around to it."

"What has stopped you?"

"Oh, I don't know. I really do love beautiful things — you know — paintings, baskets, pottery and the like." He wrapped her coat around her shoulders and continued as they walked out the door and down the steps from her apartment. "Even though I've been all around the country in my work I've never taken the time to really see it and enjoy it."

Sandra looked at him to ask, "What a pity! Do you plan to take any time on this trip just to enjoy yourself?"

Jake seated her in his rental Chevrolet. "No. I guess not. Funny, the thought didn't occur to me that I *should enjoy* myself on these trips. A real stick in the mud, huh?"

"What would you think if I said I want you to enjoy yourself and that you should spend some time on this very trip doing it?" They exited the Village Square Apartments into the ever fast moving traffic leading to the White Flint Shopping Center on Rockville Pike. She smiled elusively.

"Well, maybe until now I haven't had a reason to consider it." Jake smiled in return. "If I did, would you be able to show me around, Sandra, if you don't have any other commitments, that is?" He shrugged his shoulders expecting a rebuff.

"I thought you would never ask. I would like that. Saturday we could take the Metro to the Mall downtown and exhaust ourselves climbing the Washington Monument or walk around to see the other monuments, or visit the Smithsonian. There are lots of places to see and things to do in Washington. It's also a lot of fun walking around Georgetown to see the old houses." Locklear's enthusiasm was mounting.

"I think this is going to be the best trip I've ever made to DC thanks to you. I guess I have just been all business. This is going to be the first time I break my own rule."

"Which is?" Sandra asked.

"The organization is paying me to work. That's what I have to do. I have never taken a delay in returning home. I guess I have missed out in a lot of pleasure. I know a lot of people who take side trips when they go on business somewhere. But, I guess I just thought I wasn't supposed to or something." Jake thought he had to explain he had a high sense of duty. Sandra seemed to understand but didn't respond.

"Well, here we are at the Flint. There is a wonderful sidewalk cafe I want to take you to that serves gourmet coffee and delicious cookies I discovered on one of my trips here. But I suppose you have been there dozens of times before." Jake offered, "If you like, we can window shop before the movie begins."

"Oh, of course, I've been there just hundreds of times!" Locklear laughed. "But never with you." She was amused with the look of chagrin on Jake's face as she teased and pressed her hand on his.

The warmth of her hand went through Jake and made his heart skip a beat. As they shut the car doors to walk into the Mall he took her hand in his. She offered no resistance and moved closer to him comfortable with her feelings. Jake hoped their closeness would last forever.

While Jake and Sandra were watching *Sleeping With The Enemy* with rapt attention and not a little fear, Giroux ushered Charlie into his study intent upon a very private conversation. "What have you got for me, Charlie?" Giroux asked in hushed tones.

Charlie sat expansively in the leather chair by the fireplace content with himself that he had pulled off another coup for Giroux. He held a thick manila envelope by his side relishing in advance the victory he knew would surely be Giroux's in the coming months.

"Well, boss, I managed to get a copy of the report those pricks who investigated Locklear's allegations sent forward through their boss in New York to the Secretary. Here it is."

Giroux grabbed the report out of his hands not saying a word. He leafed through it hurriedly to the section on findings and recommendations. Charlie lighted a Cleopatra cigar, blew a perfect ring of blue smoke, got up from the chair, and poured himself a glass of dry sherry. "Help yourself," Giroux mumbled.

He looked at Charlie quizzically, dumbfounded at his joviality. "What are you so happy about? This condemns me — not only me but the whole organization! I don't understand. I told you before, if I go down you do, too."

Charlie blew another perfect ring and made another pull on his sherry. "This is excellent sherry, doctor. I really enjoy it. Let me tell you why you shouldn't worry about this report." Warming up to his analysis, he was enjoying this moment. He knew if he planned it just right his future would be secure in IHS.

Charlie rose to get another sherry. "Do you mind? First, this is just a draft report. You'll notice there are no signatures attached so it doesn't have any weight. It can be changed. We can put a lid on this so tight it won't see the light of day.

"Second, their finding that you did indeed, use your position of authority and your power to influence and control the relationship with Locklear is so loosely worded that even our half-ass over-paid lawyers would be able to rip it to shreds. Your lawyer certainly would be able to do it in his sleep.

"Third, your lawyer should be able to reduce their finding to nothing but uncorroborated hearsay. There are no witnesses so it is just your word against hers even though they pieced things together pretty well.

"I figure we can work internally with the Department to either get it watered down or we can invoke some kind of agency privilege to have much of this stuff deleted. You'll be left without a scratch on your good name. Locklear's attorney, that Cox woman, won't be able to get a complete report. Her case will just die on the vine, boss." Charlie finished his second glass of sherry, very pleased with himself.

The possibility of being protected from further embarrassment delighted Giroux. "Why don't you have another sherry, Charlie, and pour one for me, too. This demands a toast to your good work."

As they toasted each other Giroux reflected. "What about their finding of the lack of a training program on harassment among our managers?"

"I figure we can give them this one," Charlie said. "We can't be completely clean. The Department will expect us to clean up our act. They won't know whether the allegations are true or not by the time we get a more sanitized report, but they will be suspicious. So, I think we will have to give them something, boss."

"And, what about the other ladies who filed complaints, Charlie? Those Department people must have talked with them. And your EEO friends. What about them?" Giroux got up from his leather couch and paced to the fireplace.

"We have to assume they talked to the women. But again, their complaints aren't in the formal stage. Each one came in at different times. I'm sure I can get EEO to propose dismissal of their allegations, too. Besides, how would it look to them when Locklear doesn't get to first base with the Department? I think they can be convinced they don't have a leg to stand on.

"As far as EEO is concerned, the Department will have to work with them to deal with the training stuff. We'll get their reports to jive, trust me." Charlie was confident.

He had every reason to believe the finalized report would be a sanitized version of reality not personally condemning of Giroux but supportive of training of supervisors. The IHS would have to admit it had not undertaken to train any of its front line managers in how to deal with sexual harassment, a small price to pay for concealment and protection.

"One thing more, Charlie, before you leave. Find a place for Locklear in Albuquerque, or California, or Portland. I don't care where, okay?" Giroux dismissed him assured that it would be done somehow.

That weekend with Sandra cavorting on the Mall, visiting the Smithsonian, and savoring their time together in downtown Washington filled Jake with the promise of deep conviction that Sandra and he were meant for each other. When she saw him off to Albuquerque at the National Airport, Sandra didn't hesitate to kiss him passionately. She wanted him to know he mattered in her life.

Jake relished her loving embrace and reciprocated with his own. She mattered to him. On departure he said, "I don't know how I'll do it just yet, but I want to see you again ... soon. I want to be with you, Sandra."

She feared telling him about Giroux but believed she may have to one day. She had to know if their relationship would survive such information. Locklear simply responded with a tear gathering in her eye as she waved goodbye, "I know. I do, too."

Locklear remained to watch the TransWorld Airlines flight 123 leave the gate for the long flight to St. Louis and then Albuquerque. She was already lonely for Jake even though he had only left a few minutes before. She wished they had made love for she knew it would have been love, and not the transient satisfaction she had with Giroux. The thought of it put a smile on her face and a sense of loathing for Giroux.

Out of the blue Cox received a telephone call from Paul Sinclair, one of the IHS attorneys who was scrupulously avoiding returning her telephone calls. He said flatly, "I'll be brief, Ms. Cox. We have received the report and findings of the special assessment team looking into the allegations of your client, Ms. Locklear, of sexual harassment by the Director of the Indian Health Service.

"Based on the Department's report there is little evidence that Dr. Giroux is significantly involved in sexual harassment. On the other hand, there is evidence that he does not have an acceptable policy or training program dealing with this topic. Accordingly, the agency will be required to institute a firm policy and training program for its managers."

"I can't believe this, Mr. Sinclair." Cox interjected angrily. "You're whitewashing and condoning this man's abuse. You, sir, are allowing this man to perpetuate his tyranny over women and…"

"Ms. Cox, I do not have to accept this abuse from you either." Sinclair interrupted. "I will cut short this conversation and hang up if you persist," he said stridently.

"All right, all right. I get the message, Mr. Sinclair. I want a copy of that report sent to me as soon as possible."

Three weeks, five telephone calls, and a certified Freedom of Information Act request later, Cox opened the package addressed to her from the Department of Health and Human Services. The long awaited report had arrived she had requested through the Freedom of Information Act.

Indeed, it was astounding to Cox. The report had been sanitized. Almost every page of the twenty page report had spaces blackened out corresponding to complete sentences and even paragraphs. Several pages were also missing in their entirety.

The report made little sense without the missing data and information. The meat of it was gutted leaving nothing but a skeleton. It was obvious PHS didn't want the truth to get out. The agency claimed the original report was protected and therefore it could not release it in its entirety.

In her fury, Cox immediately called Hannah in New York City to cry foul and to ask her what she knew about the report. She reminded Hannah she had promised to render a fair and impartial report that would faithfully document the harassment.

She then said, "I can't believe what I have in my hands, Hannah. This report is completely useless. I can't believe this represents your best work. How did they get to you?"

Hannah was silent for a moment then reflected. "I completed the report *as I was required to do,* Ms. Cox. Do you understand what I am saying to you?"

"No, Hannah, I do not. You are going to have to spell it out for me. I am dense. I do not understand how a woman, and how a team with your experience, could allow such a report to be emasculated when you know fully well how important it is to stand up for women's rights! Didn't you learn anything from the Clarence Thomas/Anita Hill affair in 1991? Giroux is another just like him." Cox was livid. "Talk to me, Hannah!"

"May I have your telephone number, please? I may need to return your call, Ms. Cox."

"Of course. I hear some static on the line. It's 301-996-5988." Cox understood her signal. Hannah wanted to tell her more. "I'll wait until I hear from you. Goodbye and thanks."

In the hour interim Cox read protectionism throughout the report. She concluded Giroux was a company man and the company protects its own. If he were a lesser placed staff it would not be so important. Lesser employees are expendable. Giroux was insulated.

As promised Hannah returned her call from the privacy of her car phone. "I am dreadfully sorry, Phyllis. I made a complete report, and believe me, I included everything. Nothing was left out. As soon as I got the first draft done my supervisor stayed behind closed doors for a whole day.

"When he finally came out he threw it on my desk and had written all over it. On the top of it he wrote, 'This is trash! Your report is completely unacceptable. You'd better revise it. Don't make this kind of mistake again.' He has never done that to me before. I don't understand it. I revised it three more times until he was satisfied." Hannah was ashamed but knew her report was objective.

Cox was perturbed, but understood. "Hannah, this report leaves out whole sentences, paragraphs, and pages. As it stands now it won't help us much. Is there any way we can get a clean copy — one that doesn't have anything deleted other than through the discovery process?"

"I don't know, Phyllis. In the years I've worked here I've seen some nasty cases. Most of the agencies involved, however, wanted to be cooperative and to clean up their messes. I can only guess that, in this case, the Public Health Service doesn't want to let anything get out to the public. So they'll take care of their own." Hannah paused unsure of where she stood with Cox.

"Cover up. That's what it is. Well, I know you didn't need to tell me this, Hannah. It puts you out on a limb to risk word getting back so, I appreciate your candor. I'll keep this conversation in confidence. The way the PHS and IHS attorneys avoid me I could have guessed they would stonewall our case. Thanks again. Goodbye."

Cox put the receiver down. She had to acknowledge Locklear's case did not look good to her. It was not Locklear's fault so much as the agency. Someone had built a wall around Giroux. But she had to share the report with Locklear.

"This is the way it looks to me, Sandra. The report the representatives made to the Department has been gutted. You've read it. There is very little meat on these bones. It's a whitewash. Giroux only gets his hands slapped for not having implemented a sexual harassment policy and for having no training in place for managers. It says nothing about his personal responsibility in reference to you.

"The process will go something like this. The Department will forward the report to the Surgeon General of the Public Health Service through the Assistant Secretary of Health. They will write another report to the Indian Health Service instructing them to remedy those two areas. And, they will say something like this that the whole case is your word against his.

"What makes this so appalling is that while we want them to say we have exhausted all administrative remedies so we can take Giroux to court in a *Bivens* action, the court will hold it against us that we have not succeeded in either the informal or formal grievance process. What is worse is that our appeal has not been vindicated in this special study.

"PHS knew what it was doing when it didn't revise its 1976 policy. It relegated its commissioned officers to the status of non-persons! You won't even be able to get attorney's fees out of them. Their policy is even clear on *that* point."

Locklear was tired. Her effort had taken two years of her life. It had exhausted her savings and had left her an outcast in her department. She was under medical care and becoming increasingly bitter. It was hard to understand how the Department would not take care of one of their own. Wasn't she one of theirs?

She was a commissioned officer, too, and should be protected. Why didn't the Department take care of her? Cox explained to her later the Public Health Service would never revise its 1976 policies despite the pressure she had attempted to bring upon those in authority. To do so, she explained, the PHS would have to acknowledge the existence of sexual harassment and that some of its officers were guilty of such conduct and behavior. It would open itself up to lawsuits and a world of negative publicity that it so eagerly desired to avoid.

At all costs it had to suppress the effort of any officer of any gender who would challenge the system. Their interpretation of the public good demanded they protect themselves.

CHAPTER THIRTEEN

FINAL THINGS

Phyllis Cox was stunned. The administrative law judge Byers had just ruled. His stentorian voice still echoed in her ears, each syllable reverberating with the next. Giroux won. Harris was ecstatic that his client was vindicated. He gloated on the victory and wanted to savor it to the fullest. Cox was morose. "Well, the least I can do, Counselor, is buy you a cup of coffee or a drink, perhaps. You look like you may need a pick-me-up."

"Go to hell, Harris. It's obvious the system has no spine." Cox was aggravated Locklear lost. It wasn't just that she lost; she represented countless others that may not have had the courage Locklear had in challenging the system that protected their own so well.

The legal system in which Cox had placed such great faith and trust and which she had served so well for so many clients over the years had somehow also failed her this one crucial time. She didn't want to believe it. No one could impeach the honesty of Locklear she thought. How could the judge not see the trail of events, the imposition of Giroux's will, his requirement for her silence, his establishing the times and dates for their encounters. It was beyond her belief.

Locklear's affidavit, Hannah's testimony, and Giroux's statement couldn't have spelled out a clearer picture of sexual harassment. Giroux had clearly wanted her for his own sexual gratification. He had assessed whether Locklear would be compliant. He had her moved near him so she would be accessible; he made the first move; and, he carried out his plan warning her each time not to talk to anyone about their affair. What more could Judge Byers have wanted? Giroux used his position and power to influence Locklear to have sex with him. It was incontrovertible.

Yet, Judge Byers ruled that Giroux's and Locklear's statements canceled each other out in the absence of other supporting evidence. There were no witnesses, no corroborating testimony.

Hannah's findings, on the other hand, weakened as they were, simply affirmed that a sexual relationship existed between lovers. The relationship appeared to be consensual. At the failure of the relationship Judge Byers concluded every appearance was given that bitterness simply motivated Locklear to seek redress through the grievance process. Statements by Janet and Margaret were not allowed since they were not a party to Locklear's grievance. They had no direct knowledge to contribute. Cox made every effort to have them included in the testimony to show a pattern engaged in by Giroux. But the PHS attorneys were successful in keeping their actions separate. It was a set back she had not anticipated and a terrible blow to her strategy. The testimony boiled down simply to Locklear's statement against Giroux's denial of harassment.

The agency would not affirm that harassment took place. Judge Byers said that Locklear would be informed through the Office of the Surgeon General that Giroux did not sexually harass her and that there would be no redress for this. The 1976 policy would be affirmed. Locklear could not appeal to any higher authority. Giroux would be free of the taint of sexual harassment.

Byers concluded officially that Giroux could only be faulted for not having a clear and unambiguous sexual harassment policy in place with clear safeguards against such conduct. This was affirmed through Hannah's report. He was therefore ordered to develop the policy and institute a training program for his managers. A small but necessary concession. A slight tap on the hand. Giroux's pain would be negligible.

It was the only concession Byers would make on the record. Off the record and beyond the earshot of Harris Judge Byers said, "Had your client grieved against Giroux for sexual misconduct I would have had to conclude differently. So, in essence for what it's worth, I believe the merits of her case were misdirected. Perhaps, then I could have allowed the entry of your other witnesses to the record. Think about it, Ms. Cox. I believe this should end the matter. The Agency has its policy and they believe it is sufficient for all officers."

Judge Byers turned and walked away toward his driver secure in the belief the agency would remain protected. As Cox walked dejected out of the Hubert Humphrey Building into an unusually clear September day, she thought the proceeding was a farce, and the farce bordered on travesty. She couldn't help but remember Locklear's words to her last year, 'The Public Health Service will protect its own. You won't be able to do anything about it. So don't get your hopes up high on my account. I don't matter to the system, Phyllis.' Cox thought she seemed too resigned to defeat. But, now, she had to wonder about Locklear's foresight.

Her faith in the checks and balances of the system convinced her that Locklear overestimated the power of the system to protect its own. She firmly believed that the Anita Hill/Clarence Thomas affair was sufficient warning to Federal agencies to clean up their act. At first, she was amazed the IHS hadn't bothered to apply the case to itself. At last, she understood the Agency could do what it wanted. Until now, no one had been so foolhardy to challenge the system.

In that she was naive and now realized, too, she failed Locklear. Her last hope would be to try the case in federal court on a *Bivens* action, a personal action against Giroux. She had taken all the administrative avenues available to her. This personal action was the last resort. But she needed to think. She must not give up hope that Locklear would be vindicated somehow.

Cox retrieved her maroon Thunderbird from the parking garage two blocks west of the HHS Building. Maneuvering quickly through the early afternoon traffic she entered the Beltway around Washington and headed for Maryland. The drive would give her the time she needed to appeal to Locklear to press on in the *Bivens* action. But she needed to think.

Neither Locklear nor Giroux was present for the hearing. Only the attorneys were there to represent their clients. Cox was anxious to call Locklear in Albuquerque and sped the distance to the Montrose exit. A short fifteen minutes later she parked her car in her place at the office and, shutting the door of her office behind her, dialed the number Locklear had given her on her departure.

Over the past several months Locklear had found new reasons to visit Albuquerque. She convinced the Nursing Director of the Albuquerque Area of the Indian Health Service that an audit was needed on their nursing activity. Site visits were scheduled to outlying service unit hospitals at Laguna, New Mexico, Santa Fe, and the Albuquerque Indian Hospital, as well as smaller clinics at points in between. To the surprise of no one she found desperate needs for clinical training in pediatrics and care for the elderly; interest in community health nursing was on the decline; front line nurses received little continuing education. This endangered their licenses; yet, the clinical directors of the hospitals were only concerned about their own continuing education.

Locklear developed a plan with the Department of Health Services of the State of New Mexico and the University Hospital to conduct training on site at several locations to reduce loss of time from the local hospitals and expenses. It enabled the state staffs to become more intimately acquainted with local health needs and to develop partnerships among health care providers.

Her aggressive efforts resulted in ongoing training seminars that met many of the educational needs and personal goals of the nurses by fostering stronger university ties. Local community leaders expressed strong support for her efforts on behalf of the elderly. Some even lobbied for her transfer.

Unknown to Locklear tribal leaders independently called Cynthia Morgan with increased frequency to seek her transfer. For the first time in many years they explained that they felt the Indian Health Service was truly concerned about them. Locklear appealed to them. She was enthusiastic and did not dictate to them how they should manage their own health affairs. She took their concerns to heart and found ways to make health care come alive. Confidence increased in their hospital staff and in the quality of medicine they practiced.

Cynthia envied her ability but she was in no mood to argue with the self-evident. There was no room for a star on her staff in Rockville. Conveniently her old lover, Morrison, and Charlie Mathieson had both been pressuring her to develop another placement for Locklear. She easily saw through their efforts as representing Giroux's interest. She thought they would be her pathway to the front office suite.

Giroux needed her out of Rockville. Sandra was an embarrassment for him as well as her. More importantly, Sandra was an impediment to her own suppressed wishes to move forward in the chain of command. To move her from Rockville was worth the effort. After all, Charlie had hinted that Giroux might indeed be very grateful for her consideration.

Without hesitation she telephoned Linda Maxwell in Albuquerque to explore the feasibility of a transfer. "No, Cynthia. Sandra is doing a marvelous job for us in Albuquerque Area. Since she has begun to focus on our Area there has been a real turn around in the delivery of services here. The Director is so pleased he even stopped in our office the other day and said he wished she worked for us permanently."

"Well, Linda, that is the reason for my call. I don't know if you are aware, but we have received a number of calls from several of your tribal chairmen requesting us to consider finding a place for her there. This is to say nothing against your program, but you do lack a community health nurse.

"We would hate to lose her, but, in all honesty I think her heart may be in field service. As you may know before she came here a few years ago she worked for the Nashville Area and also did an outstanding job for them working closely with the tribes.

"No, we haven't had any problems with her, Linda. She has received a promotion here and several commendations. But our philosophy has changed. We have been asked to identify outstanding people, give them new experience, and then return them to the field with a greater vision.

"If you have a position, I am prepared to fund it for one year to continue the outstanding work Sandra is doing for you. Does that sound agreeable?" Cynthia asked as Charlie stared at her in amazement.

When she hung the phone on its hook, Charlie said, "I didn't know your budget allowed for that, Cynthia."

"It doesn't, Charlie. You should know that. You control the budget. I expect you to find me the money." Cynthia smiled in triumph at her attempted manipulation of the system.

"What?" Charlie looked at her intently, incredulously wondering how Cynthia could think she was in a position to demand anything of him.

With mounting bravado, Cynthia continued. "I expect you to find me the money, Charlie. You are the one who came to me to find a place for Sandra. Remember? I am doing you a big favor and you know it. I also suspect I am doing your boss an even greater one. I don't think you can refuse me now, can you, Charlie?" She oozed triumphantly as Charlie sat back in his chair studying her in amazement. He smiled knowing Cynthia was a rank amateur at intimidation. He decided to give her this one and marched out of her office in a pretend huff.

Robert Harris left the administrative judge's chambers after Phyllis Cox. He had no reason to be hasty in his departure. He had just vindicated his old friend, Giroux, and protected him from certain embarrassment. His only price to pay would be the development of policy and procedure. Not much considering the damage that could have been done if the matter had come to trial.

Frankly, he saw no future in Cox's threat to bring the matter to trial in a *Bivens* action. All the administrative levels of the Indian Health and the Public Health Service had found no harassment in Giroux's relationship with Locklear. The depositions, reports, and administrative law decision were now a matter of record.

Sinclair and all the attorneys of IHS and PHS had cautioned her against such a costly move. Commissioned officers had no standing in the courts. PHS policy had seen to that in 1976. They had given their lives to the health service and it would take care of their needs. As officers and gentlemen they simply had to be reasonable.

Harris knew other tests of the system remained with the suit that Margaret and Janet were pressing. So far each formal grievance was rejected by the Indian Health Service and the appeals they had lodged with the Public Health Service remained to be answered. He worried a little about them and wanted them to be handled as separate matters not joined together; but he was running into trouble with the PHS attorneys on this issue.

Sinclair and his staff just hated the paperwork involved with the grievance process and the usual appeals. But they knew for a fact most officers and civil servants who undertook the process got discouraged early. If anyone persisted beyond the informal stage of the grievance they usually found out the system has little tolerance for those who would upset its balance. PHS was a master of delays.

Of course, all managers would swear that they would uphold the letter of the law and not retaliate. Heaven forbid if they would break the law! Heaven would forgive managers who would studiously inquire into their own rights and responsibilities and allowances under the law. Managers would subject grievances and appeals to rigid adherence to time lines. In fairness to all concerned parties, managers would handle objections and requests for more information, and make appeals to the grieving party for permission to change the time lines. Whatever works to the advantage of administration in wearing plaintiffs down is appropriate management.

It is a question of tactics, persistence, and energy. Most lawyers have that. They are the protectors of the *status quo*. Individuals filing grievances are mostly embarrassed that "things" may not be going right for them at work. When they file a grievance they just want the "bad things" to disappear and the balance in their environment restored. They don't know that grievances can work against them; that unwritten black marks can appear on their record; they can be branded as trouble makers; and this bit of intelligence makes its ugly way through administrative ranks to affect promotions.

Administrators deny it. But managers usually stick together when the subject comes to who is a team player and who is not.

Harris understood Sinclair's discourse but he was uneasy in allowing Margaret and Janet to be joined together. He feared the old adage of safety in numbers. As with Locklear he expected to wear each one of them down separately and have their allegations dismissed at each level of the grievance and appeal process. Neither one of the ladies would have enough money to see it through to the end. Divide and conquer.

Sinclair did not object to his tactics. He admired them. But the paper work! He figured he could pair Janet and Margaret's grievances and appeals into one and simply get the unit dismissed. But he had to acknowledge Cox was a pain in the ass and she might try to make any potential suit a class action for the named and unnamed victims of Giroux's alleged harassment. He believed but didn't tell Harris that Cox would file a *Bivens* action against Giroux just on principle. If she did, he suspected she would attempt to get that action included in Janet and Margaret's action. Yes, Cox was a pain in the ass. But she was Harris' problem not his.

When Harris returned home from the hearing, Geraldine was preparing supper in the kitchen. She had planned a special meal for her and Robert of broiled salmon, mini-carrots cooked in butter, Chinese snow peas, and new potatoes. She had already baked a fresh loaf of bread. Its aroma filled the house and evoked images of many such pleasant dinners. Wine had already been chilled. Two glasses sat by the plates, ready for their golden contents.

Geraldine had often gone to special lengths at mealtime. For Robert, the old cliché, that the way to a man's heart is through his stomach, was especially true. He enjoyed good food, better wine, classical music and an occasional cigar. The last was a vice Geraldine only tolerated because of its infrequency. Robert may have been fierce in the courtroom, but at home he was the proverbial lamb. Geraldine understood the differences and catered to Robert almost as much as he did to her. His love was deeper than his profound knowledge of the law. Geraldine knew this and counted upon it.

Robert opened the door of the house and was immediately soothed from his long commute by the aroma of the fresh bread, salmon, and steaming vegetables. This evening, as with many other evenings, during the commute home he reflected how agitated the traffic on Rockville Pike made him feel as commuters dodged in and out of traffic, seemingly unconcerned for their safety or that of anyone else. He knew he could only let down his guard once he entered his driveway, parked his car, and opened the door to the safety of his home. There, his frayed nerves found their rest. The commute to his office in Bethesda was his price to pay for living in the suburbs. It was an early concession to Geraldine.

When she heard him park the car, Geraldine prepared to meet him in the foyer to their home in Gaithersburg. This was a habit she developed early in their marriage. It had now become a custom he treasured. They kissed. She brought him the newspaper while she put the finishing touches on the meal.

It was consumed with relish after his toast to their continuing love and fidelity. It was the most poignant toast he could make given the day, his new reflections on the state of his old friend, Andrew's probable marriage, and Geraldine's concern for Elizabeth.

She began her most serious conversations quietly. His own apprehensions made him sense where she was going in her comment. "Darling, we have had many good times together with the Giroux's, haven't we? It is such a pity but Elizabeth confided to me the most terrible news today. I have been wondering why she hasn't gotten in touch with me lately. She said that Andrew has been cheating on her. She has no choice but to divorce him. Did you know anything about that?"

Momentarily, Robert paused while lifting a portion of a crepe that Geraldine had prepared for dessert. The crepe continued on its journey to his open mouth while Robert studied his response. For a moment he considered being candid, then said, "I can't tell you what is involved, Geraldine, but, sad to say, Andrew is, indeed, my client."

He sipped his Chardonnay and saw the deep hurt in Geraldine's eyes. She had grown fond of Elizabeth over the years, deepening independently of the business relationship Robert had with Andrew. Andrew's betrayal was almost felt personally. Robert sensed the relationship would have to change.

"I really regret I must think what this may mean about our relationship. I don't want to make a hasty decision, but I am concerned about it. So much, in fact, I may not want to continue socially. You can, of course, dear. I don't think I can, though."

Harris refused to return Giroux's telephone calls.

"Who's that cute Navajo lady you've been balling?" Charlie asked. Standing Bear sat stunned in disbelief at Charlie's question. He rose to shut his office door and retorted, "I don't know what you are talking about, Charlie? There are a lot of Navajos around here."

"Don't give me that shit, John. You've been seeing Dominguez's staffer for the past year at least. And chances are you've been giving her a lot more beside. We know, believe me. But what we don't know is just how much you've been telling the Senate about our business."

"Fuck off, Charlie. You're just guessing. You're just jealous that my program is the only one that's growing and you can't do anything to stop it. You ought to know I don't make the rules; Congress does that. When they ask for consultation, you know the drill. You answer their questions. That's all I've done." Standing Bear sat back smugly in his chair.

Charlie pulled out a small well-worn notebook from his shirt pocket and began to leaf through the pages making clucking noises as he read. "Let me tell you the times and the dates you were on the Hill last year, my fucking friend. Three times in January, twice in February, and four times in March according to my notes. Do you want me to go on? Do you want me to spell out for you the actual dates and the times you met with little Miss Indian America of the Navajo variety?"

"You bastard. You're trying to shake me down! What the hell are you trying to prove. You got me wired or something?" Standing Bear stood menacingly. "Get the hell out of my office. You want to play games? You've got it."

Charlie retreated quickly before Standing Bear had a chance to throw him out. Reaching for the door knob he said, "A word of advice, John. Stay home. Stay away from the Senate and mind your own business. The boss doesn't like it."

"Fuck you and the boss! And shut the door on your way out." Standing Bear sat down, swiveled the desk chair, and looked out his window lost in thought.

He was beyond being angry with Charlie. He knew he was capable of hurting careers, but he suspected he was acting on orders. He had never had problems with him before. His behavior was more than obnoxious. Just a little too theatrical for

Charlie. Giroux had put him up to it. He just knew it. Giroux wanted him quiet but didn't have the balls to face him himself.

Maybe it was time for him to do his own dirty work. He knew just exactly what to do. Using his own black book he reviewed some notes about Giroux, some questionable earmarked contracts for tribes in his home state, difficulties with congressional staffers, rumors of sweethearts in locations visited during speeches, and of course, observation of him and Margaret at O'Donnel's and Janet coming out of his office on Saturdays.

"Mrs. Giroux?"

"Yes, who is this?"

"Mrs. Giroux, I regret not being able to give you my name. But I am in a position to know a lot about your husband I think you should know."

Elizabeth sighed and paused for a long while uncertain if she wanted to hear what the unidentified caller had to say or whether she should hang up immediately. His voice sounded muffled. Finally, reconciled within herself, she said, "Ordinarily, I wouldn't bother giving people like you the time of day. But I guess, right now I'm particularly interested. Should I sit down? Is it about a woman?"

"Well, I'm not sure if it's about a woman or several women really. Maybe I shouldn't have called you," he said in mock agitation.

"Oh, come now, whoever you are. The cat is out of the bag. Don't be so modest. Just tell me all the devastating news you are dying to tell me. You don't have to watch me fall apart. I won't give you that satisfaction. Do I know you? Have we met somewhere, perhaps at one of the office functions? Your voice sounds familiar."

It was her anonymous caller's time to be silent for a moment. He felt caught. He had met her at a Christmas party and had briefly talked with her at an awards banquet. But, of course, there were so many present. It was unlikely she would put a face to the voice. But he wasn't sure whether she was really trying to recollect or whether she was trying to trip him up. He cleared his throat and doubled his handkerchief over the receiver to disguise his voice further. Then continued.

"Yes," he admitted, "You may have met me before. But I won't give you my name. Just know that what I have to tell you is firsthand information."

The caller related what he had seen and guessed at and heard from his friends in different cities. Elizabeth listened no longer concerned who the caller might be. She had hoped Giroux would have straightened up after her warning about his infidelity. She now had more information than she wanted or dreamed was possible.

"I'm not grateful to you for this. I've known for some time Andrew was not faithful to me. But I thought it was under control. I believed him when he told me he had quit with this Sandra woman. I didn't want to believe there could be more."

She paused to collect herself fighting back the first signs of her emotional upheaval. "I really don't like you for what you are doing to me. As a matter of fact, I hate you for it. I don't know what motivates people like you but I think you should crawl back into the hole you came out of. Good bye."

Standing Bear looked at the phone in his hand and smiled. He didn't have to deal directly with Giroux. He knew Elizabeth would be far more effective. Giroux would not know what hit him.

Giroux was pleased with himself for the speech he delivered at the Inter-Tribal Health Symposium at Denver's Brown Palace downtown. For the past year he had worked hard crisscrossing the country drumming up support for new health initiatives. He wanted and needed the time away from Elizabeth. He was beginning to be bored with the sameness of his life once more and he was growing restless.

Giroux knew his own behavior. First there was the resentment of having to agree that he had strayed from Elizabeth's side, unstated, of course. This became a festering sore, small at first, but growing and destined for rupture. Second, the growing apprehension that he was losing his touch with women due to living as he agreed made him feel uncomfortable with his 'goodness.' Third, was the growing thirst for someone new or at least someone he could trust.

Elizabeth had been getting on his nerves. He did not put in too many extra hours at work but neither had he neglected his work. He came home much sooner than he had for some time past and had appeared solicitous to give her comfort. For nearly a year it had been like this. A year of famine.

Giroux had admitted he had offended her. He regretted that but was more pained that his affair with Sandra had come to light. It had been a while since he had another woman. He was far from home and began to reason as he had so often in the past Elizabeth would not know if he just gave his old friend, Sally Powers, a tribal council member from the Cherokee Tribe in Oklahoma, a telephone call. There is no harm in talking on the telephone he reasoned. She might not even be home. But if she were, it would only be for a few minutes and he could go about his business reassured.

A few short rings later Sally answered the telephone. "I've been expecting your call, Andrew. I heard you would be in town."

A smile creased his lips as he began to salivate at the sound of her sultry voice. In the nearly three years since his last night with her the effect of her voice had not been lost on Giroux. The minutes passed quickly. Sally offered to continue the conversation in person, not unexpectedly. A half-hour later she was in his room disrobing in his dimly lighted suite to soft mellow music.

The following day Giroux returned to Washington National Airport, picked up his car, and drove leisurely home to Rockville happy with himself. Parking the car in his garage Giroux took his time retrieving his baggage from the trunk and walked to the side door.

He found the door locked. Inserting his key he found the lock wouldn't yield. Puzzled, he walked briskly to the front door only to find his favorite Pendleton blanket folded neatly in a bundle by the front door with a note pinned to the top. It read, "Andrew, Darling. Word of your midnight caller at the Brown Palace arrived by noon. Don't bother trying the locks. They have all been replaced. Don't bother trying my heart either. While it is broken now, it will mend with time. Take your blanket somewhere else. You know what I mean. Yours truly, Elizabeth."

Giroux cursed to himself. 'Damn, she did it. I never thought she would.' He descended the front steps unsure what to do next. Panic set in. He walked around all sides of the house to see if there were some signs of Elizabeth. As he walked to the car he quickly looked up to their bedroom window. He could have sworn he saw the curtains quickly come together. Now they appeared motionless.

He knew Elizabeth was watching him. 'Well, Andrew, what next? Better get a room for the night while you think this through.' Giroux located a room to spend the night at the Ramada Inn in Gaithersburg. It was not far from restaurants and a bus line connecting with the MetroRail two stops away from the Twinbrook exit and the usual short walk to the Parklawn Building. Most people would not think a change had occurred in his life. He would appear in the office as usual.

As he negotiated with Elizabeth's attorney through Harris in an attempt at reconciliation required by the court, Giroux received word that Janet and Margaret's case was dismissed by the Department of Health and Human Services as expected. He was disappointed that this brief note of progress on his behalf only cleared a final hurdle for their suit against him. Cox vowed she would pursue him with a vengeance.

Engulfed in this morass Giroux was called by the Surgeon General who was well-apprised of the details. "Andrew, please come to my office tomorrow at ten. There are some matters we need to discuss privately. There is no need for Mr. Harris to accompany you since this does not concern him."

Giroux reluctantly assented. Although he didn't want to admit it he was beginning to be worried. Elizabeth had left him. Janet and Margaret were going forward with their suit. Sandra, of whom he was fond and with whom he had the longest and sweetest relationship, abhorred him and turned him in to his wife. Now the Surgeon General was calling him for a private meeting. 'What else could go wrong?' he wondered.

It could only mean one thing; his head was soon to be on the chopping block. Where could he go? What could he do? How was he going to exist if he couldn't work something out with Elizabeth? Surely she owed him this much for all his years of support. He couldn't stay in a hotel for much longer. The expenses were getting too great and legal fees were eating him alive.

The remainder of the day was shot. Too many thoughts crowded into his consciousness to allow him to concentrate on business. He knew his position was a political appointment. Too many uncertainties with that. No protection like in the civil service.

If he were a civil servant they would have to prove him guilty of harassment. But all the reports had turned out in support of him, and that included even the Department's report. His attorney would vindicate him like he did before.

Would the Surgeon General allow him to remain at least until the new administration took office? Or would he insist he immediately turn in his shoulder boards? Would he allow him time to get situated somewhere else? Vexatious questions.

He counseled himself. 'Wait, Giroux. You haven't even met with him. You don't know what is going to happen. Hold on. At least tomorrow you will know.' The day was beginning to drag painfully slowly. Giroux settled into some routine tasks sufficient to impose external order. Inside him it was chaos.

The dreaded hour came. Giroux was early for his ten o'clock appointment. As Sam went into Dr. Joseph's office Giroux could have sworn he had a smile on his face. He knew Sam didn't like him but now it made no difference. He expected to be sacked. The best he could hope for was enough time to make necessary preparations for a successor at the Indian Health Service. Surely they would grant him that.

Giroux's heart skipped a beat when the secretary announced he could go into the Surgeon General's office. "All right. Thank you," he said. She rose to open the door for him but he had already leapt to the task himself.

"Andrew, please sit down. Would you like some coffee or water? " Without waiting for a reply he motioned the secretary to bring in both. She set them on the credenza before them and left the room shutting the door behind her. Giroux maintained his composure. He would not speak unless he was spoken to.

Dr. Joseph began. "I have been studying the case of the three women who had grieved against you, Andrew. It is a very perplexing matter to me.

"I've read everything I could on this case, Andrew — the depositions, the investigative reports, and the EEO files. Frankly, I'm convinced of the truth of what these ladies allege against you despite the administrative judge's opinion. I believe you did harass them. The sad fact is that none of the official reports back up their allegations so there is little or nothing we can do to support them.

"That means there is little or nothing I can do to you. I don't know how you accomplished this or what you did to manipulate the circumstances. But you did manipulate them. How do I know this? I've learned recently that your wife has put you out of your home over another woman. Women don't do these things unless there is some truth in the matter."

Giroux began to rise to leave the Surgeon General's office in disgust. He expected a more business-like approach to his dismissal and did not want a tongue lashing. Dr. Joseph motioned him to remain seated.

"I didn't dismiss you, Andrew. I expect you to take what is your due. So please sit down. Up to this point there hasn't been a blemish on your record, Andrew. And because of the lack of corroboration from the investigation in this case, there won't be. But make no mistake about it, Andrew, I believe these women.

"I had great faith in you as a leader for your people. You survived all the background checks and had demonstrated originality in your thinking and creativity in your approach to managing limited resources. You have begun to establish a good track record. But no one could have imagined this propensity of yours to dalliances. Your behavior is reprehensible, Andrew.

"You are a public figure, a representative of what is supposed to be right and correct in America; and, you are a representative of this office and this administration. I expect better behavior from my officers.

"I want you to think about these things. I want you to think about professional conduct and about putting the interests of your people and the nation before selfish personal interests, Andrew."

The Surgeon General was finished. Dr. Giroux sat silently awaiting his request for his resignation. He did not make a move to leave.

Dr. Joseph rose and dismissed him with a final comment and a wave of the hand. "Andrew, I'm considering a change of leadership in the Indian Health Service. You may be interested in a position in the National Institutes of Health in Bethesda. The Assistant Director of an epidemiology project!"

Puzzled, Dr. Giroux looked at him unsure of what to say. Finally he said, "Be assured, I will give serious thought to these things, Dr. Joseph. Thank you." He turned about and left, amused at his fortune.

Descending the elevator he chuckled to himself, relieved, and remarked how lucky he was to have Charlie Mathieson on his side. How he managed to engineer the agency reports to his favor was a marvel he did not want to unravel. Charlie saved his career and he owed him another debt. That was the only thing that mattered. The Surgeon General would not have his resignation. Charlie could have what he wanted most, an Area Director's position when the next vacancy occurred.

The doorbell rang insistently. Charlie rose from his chair. He was put off that he couldn't see the tagteam complete their outlandish domination of their opponents at this moment. He felt ready to pounce upon whoever interrupted his leisure.

Opening the door, he almost yelled, 'What do you want?' to the police officer. His face turned red as he acknowledged the officer. "Are you Mr. Charles Mathieson?"

"Yes."

"This is a warrant for your arrest on rape charges filed by Miss Sarah..."

Charlie blew his top. "Sarah! That bitch filed charges against me?" As he was turned around and handcuffed, Charlie swore he would get even with his lover. It was not to be.

Hannah curled up on her living room couch in Baltimore, smarting from being fired. This was the first time she had the nerve to take such a vehement stand against the decision of her supervisor on behalf of a case. She held the deep conviction that Locklear had been sexually harassed. Hannah believed it was totally unethical for Max to order her to sanitize her file.

Max wanted the file purged so it would appear that the record was "inadvertently erased" in routine file maintenance. Behind closed doors they argued back and forth. Their voices raised and tempers flared. Max hurled accusations of tampering with evidence. Neither would relent. Finally, a furious Max fired her.

In astonishment, Hannah retreated to her office, packed up her belongings and secreted a copy of the original report on a second disk among her goods. Max feared this might happen and raced to her office, too late to catch her leaving the office. Rummaging through her desk, he discovered the original labeled disk and put it into the computer, satisfied she had left without it. With composure restored, he erased the file and smiled in triumph. It would soon be short-lived.

Hannah sat back upon her couch in gleeful anticipation of a return call from Phyllis Cox. When it came, the call actually startled her from her reverie. "Phyllis, I am so glad you returned my call. I have some news for you." She related easily, and without embarrassment, her story of the firing and her delight in mailing a copy of the disk to her.

Phyllis was shocked at the unexpurgated report of the three investigators. It was easily the most thorough report of its kind she had ever read. The redacted copy she had read was damaging enough. This copy was gold. Phyllis could not use it in court, though, because of the way she received it outside of official channels. She quickly conceived a plan that would take on a life of its own.

Inexplicably, weeks later, reporters from the Washington Post investigative division called upon the Surgeon General. An inquiry was being launched into sexual harassment among the officers of the Public Health Service. Curiously, they were well-informed of the actions of a certain officer, Dr. Andrew Giroux of the Indian Health Service. They wanted to know more about other officers in the Public Health Service. Their requests for information about this case under the Freedom of Information

Act were not well-received. Simultaneously, requests for copies of the files of the Equal Employment Opportunity Office for all cases alleging sexual harassment were received by the Indian Health Service and the Surgeon General. Panic filled their ranks.

Giroux had not yet been transferred to the National Institutes of Health. When word circulated among the officer corps of the efforts of the Washington Post, the Surgeon General called him into his office. His glee in escaping responsibility for his actions was quashed. "Andrew, your reprehensible behavior in the Locklear case has caused me no end in embarrassment. I can no longer excuse it. I can no longer tolerate it. You will sign this immediate resignation. Consider yourself fortunate that you are to retire immediately with your pension intact. The Indian Health Service which you have dishonored is not so fortunate. It will be years before it will be able to recover from your tarnished record."

Giroux left without a rebuttal in mind.

Margaret gathered with her family in the hogan and knelt before the medicine man. She was to be ritually purified this day of the evil spirits she had brought upon herself when she aborted her baby in Rockville. His spirit would also be cleansed so it could join his ancestors.

The medicine man began his chant as he leaned over to pick up the colored sand to paint the images of her own mind that burdened her until her return to the Di Neh Reservation.

At last she would be relieved of the burden that weighed so heavily upon her. Giroux would be forever out of her life. Her child would be safe and she would be at peace.

Bronson changed flights in Chicago. He was troubled and turned over in his mind the names of women he had heard were transferred to different positions in the IHS who might have been involved with Giroux. The stories he heard on this trip from Standing Bear were remarkable, tantalizing, and troublesome.

Some of the women were his friends. But he knew to leave well enough alone whether the stories were true or not. Bronson acknowledged Standing Bear had an ax or two to grind with Giroux so, he reasoned, the stories could have been embellished. No use in repeating them.

Yet, if it were true that Giroux had hit upon some of his friends, it would make working with him on any project difficult at the least and possibly a major barrier not easily overcome. His friends were important to him — much more important than trying to gain points for his own career.

His flight lifted from O'Hare's crowded runway. At last he was enroute home to the arms of his lover, Sandra. He had made up his mind on this trip that he would ask her to marry him. It was as if they were soul mates from the day he first met her in the restaurant at the Indian Pueblo Cultural Center. She was never far from his mind.

He smiled knowing that she would meet him at the airport wearing his favorite perfume, White Diamonds, her long denim skirt with nothing underneath but desire. Before they make love he would ask her to marry him. Nothing else mattered.

"It doesn't matter, darling. I believe in you." Jake looked deeply into Sandra's dark eyes. She had tearfully completed her story of Giroux, his use of her, and her own inability to get out of the relationship for fear of retribution. Now, she feared it would ruin her life with Jake.

Jake continued, "I trust you, and I trust our love for each other. Your relationship with Giroux is over. He doesn't matter. Whatever happens with Phyllis' new desire to take the Agency to court, I am with you for the long haul. I love you."

Afterword

Perhaps the instant case which inspired this tale is exerting its own moral authority. In Volume XI, No. 1 (January 1997) of the *Commissioned Corps Bulletin*, (USPHS) the following paragraph can be found:

> We will continue to advance a number of legislative proposals that are designed to improve administration of the Corps, such as an amendment to the PHS Act that would place Corps officers under the same equal employment opportunity laws and regulations as Armed Forces members. Enactment of this proposal would clarify the current confusion in Federal courts about whether Corps officers are civilian employees with respect to the provisions of Title VII of the Civil Rights Act of 1964.

In the Preface I asked: "Why is this book in the form of a 'story' instead of a factual narrative?" The answer is: "Because it will take the Public Health Service and the Indian Health Service a long time to remedy its wrongs legislatively." In this instance it lacks the moral authority and power to voluntarily do what it knows should be done to right inherent wrongs. At this writing, the Agency continues to protect offending officers and employees. Indeed, in the case of some, promotions and high-level awards, (such as Meritorious Service Medals) have even been conferred.

About The Author

THOMAS R. BURNS, PH.D., is a retired Captain of the U.S. Public Health Service. He currently lives in Rio Rancho, NM with his wife Maria. During his 25 years of experience in the Indian Health Service, he served as Chief of Social Work Service at the Indian Health Service Hospital at Schurz, NV. He then become Alcoholism Consultant with the Phoenix Area Office, IHS; Social Work Administrator and Director, Substance Abuse Mental Health Program, Phoenix Indian High School; and lastly, as Special Initiatives Officer at the IHS Headquarters Offices in Rockville, MD and Albuquerque, NM. He retired in May, 1994.

Tom has published articles on alcoholism and substance abuse in the *Public Health Reports*; the *White Cloud Journal of American Indian and Alaska Native Mental Health*; the *Journal of the National Center for American Indian and Alaska Native Mental Health Research*; and the *Indian Health Service Provider*.

He has advanced degrees in social work (Case Western Reserve University), alcohol studies (University of Arizona), and health care administration (Columbia Pacific University). He has been a Field Instructor for graduate students in the School of Public Health of the University of California, Berkeley; the University of Hawaii; and the Arizona State University School of Social Work. He has also taught many courses in the alcohol studies program at Rio Salada Community College, Phoenix, AZ where he has received an outstanding faculty award.

In addition, Tom is the recipient of a number of U.S. Public Health Service awards. Included are citations and plaques, the commendation medal, unit citations, and the Administrator's Award for Outstanding Group Performance from the Health Resources Services Administration for his many contributions to American Indian and Alaska Native health.